light in the head
brian langan

POOLBEG

Published 1999 by
Poolbeg Press Ltd
123 Baldoyle Industrial Estate
Dublin 13, Ireland

The Arts Council
An Chomhairle Ealaíon

A catalogue record for this book is available from the British Library.

ISBN 1 85371 905 6

Cover photography by Tony Stone
Cover design by Artmark
Set by Poolbeg Group Services Ltd in Goudy 11/14
Printed by The Guernsey Press Ltd,
Vale, Guernsey, Channel Islands.

About the Author

Brian Langan graduated from UCD in 1993 with a Master's Degree in Film Studies. He is an editor with Oak Tree Press. He is 29 years old, is married to Marie, and has a baby son, Christopher. He lives in Dublin. *Light in the Head* is his first novel.

Acknowledgements

While writing a novel is a solitary vice, many people have contributed in their own way to *Light in the Head*.

In particular, Kate Cruise O'Brien was a great source of inspiration and encouragement. Her belief in and enthusiasm for this novel were vital to its shaping, at a time when I was unsure of its direction. Her untimely death in March 1998 came as a terrible shock. Many young Irish writers have lost their champion. I hope you like how it turned out, Kate.

I would also like to thank Mary Maher for her important role in bringing the early chapters to Kate's attention, for her ongoing advice, and for not letting me get away with anything.

Gaye Shortland did a wonderful editorial job in the latter stages of the novel's gestation. I am very grateful to her, and to all at Poolbeg Press, for all their help during the last year.

To my mother and father, I owe an eternal debt of gratitude for everything you have done for me, for all your support and love, for being there when it matters. Thanks also to my sisters for spoiling me rotten. And thanks to my friends and colleagues for listening to my ideas and not laughing.

Finally, to Marie: Thank you.

To Marie, for your warm love and generous spirit
And to baby Christopher,
who has made us both light in the head

Chapter One

At the exact moment of Luke's conception, his mother Avril saw stars. Not the fireworks of orgasm, because the actual moment of conception occurred a good two hours after she and Fran had made love. Not that she *hadn't* reached orgasm; they had, in fact, both reached a shuddering climax, which had been more of a shock than anything else. They had stared at each other in amazement. How long had it been? Too long. It was as though they had been saving up their year of marriage for that one moment, and now their disbelief had struck them dumb.

They had held each other, wordless, for a long time, Avril's small dark frame resting on Fran's long, awkward body. Finally, aching muscles won over and she slid off him tenderly. They lay side by side, holding hands. Eventually, Fran's breathing told her he had fallen asleep. Avril watched him for a while. Marriage had shifted his features subtly, from skinny, gangly and unfit to the slightly flabby side of comfortable. In sleep, the awkward angularity of his body vanished. She smiled to herself at the small noises from his throat.

Avril wanted to sleep too, to feel the sensual drift of time abandoning her loved body. But something kept her wide awake, an acute awareness of something of importance preparing itself. For two hours she lay unmoving, afraid that her body would jolt whatever precious promise had whispered inside her. For two hours she lay, aware of every pulse of movement inside her, every nerve ending awaiting ignition, every muscle tensed, expectant.

Gradually, a feeling of complete and utter serenity crept over her body, and she relaxed into it: not sleep, but an acceptance. An openness, an opening. As this supreme readiness reached some sort of plateau, Luke chose his moment; or rather, the two halves of Luke's potential were suddenly drawn together. One of Fran's sperm reached Avril's hovering ovum and, without so much as a by-your-leave, blundered into it with a blinding crash. Full, head-on collision. If they had been people, they could not have survived. Instead, life was sparked.

Avril sat bolt upright. Her body clenched. The stars came out.

Millions upon millions of shimmering stars, their white light refracted into a rainbow burst. Light as she had never seen it before, colours she had never imagined. A life flashing before her eyes, or somewhere behind her eyes, but not her life. The life just begun? No, surely not? For a few milliseconds, she saw time and space compressed into light in a way that would have made Einstein gape. And then, just as quickly, it stopped.

Avril sat in the bed, hyperventilating, sweat escaping from her long black hair, running in rivulets down the notches of her spine. She looked down at her body in amazement. She knew exactly what had just happened. Her body had reached a state of extreme awareness, ready for the crash. Like an empty road at Christmas. Impossible, she thought. How could it be so obvious, so heralded? But somehow, she knew it to be so.

Quickly, she reached over and shook Fran's shoulder gently. He stirred, mouthing sleepily: "Hmm? What . . . what time is it?" He turned around to look at her dark shape in the nightlight. Seeing her sitting up, sensing her tensed confusion, he sat up quickly himself, switching on the bedside lamp. They both blinked at the sudden invasion of light. He looked at her with concern. Her small breasts and stomach shivered feverishly, and her breathing worried him. "What is it? What happened?" For a moment, it seemed as though she was pulsing, moving between a solid, vibrant vitality, and a wraithy, ghostlike transparency, as if her body was uncertain if it should stay or go. Trick of the light. His eyes soon settled, and his rising panic abated. He asked her again, reaching out, "Are you OK, love? What's the matter?"

She smiled, and her whole face changed. All signs of confusion and fear disappeared. She looked ten years younger, as she had when he met her first in college. The hard lines of her cheekbones grew soft. The light, he thought, appeared to gather in her. "Fran," she said, "I'm pregnant."

For a moment longer, thrown off balance, he looked at her. Then he threw his arms around her and hugged her close. "Oh, my love, that's wonderful . . ." His elation was . . . a thought struck. Without intending to, a cog turned in his brain, his subconscious doing some quick arithmetic. It had been so long . . . he froze, and gently pulled away, until he could see into her eyes. "When? I mean . . . how long? When did you find out?"

She glanced at her bedside clock, and laughed at the redundancy of the gesture. "About two minutes ago," she answered.

3

He frowned; his turn for confusion. "You . . . you found out about two minutes ago?" He didn't want to sound sceptical, but he was afraid it must surely have come out like that.

Avril was unfazed. "No," she contradicted him, "I got pregnant two minutes ago."

His temporary relief that she was not having an affair, and that the baby was his, was quickly swamped by more confusion. "You're . . . you're joking, right?" She shook her head.

"But how could you possibly know that?"

It was her turn to frown. "I don't know. It just . . . it just happened, and I knew exactly what happened. I saw stars."

"Stars?" he asked cynically, not even trying to disguise his scepticism this time.

"Don't make fun. I'm serious. I saw this bright light, and I just felt it happening inside me, like a spark, like a life." She paused, hardly able to believe it herself now. It sounded so ridiculous. "I'm going to call him Luke," she stated.

"What? You already know that it's a boy?"

"I . . . I don't know why I said that. I . . ." Suddenly, doubt filled her soul, and she hugged herself. She began to cry, softly. "I don't know what to think."

All his incredulity melted, and he folded her in his arms. They held each other until she squeezed a tear from his eye. He kissed her tenderly on the head and stroked her cheek. "I'm sorry, love. I believe you. Look, we'll get a kit, and test you, just to be sure."

"I love you," she whispered into his shoulder.

They clung to each other, until he realised she had fallen asleep. He carefully extricated himself and leaned on his elbow, looking down at her soft slumber. As he watched her, he knew that every word she said was true. Not simply because she had said them and he trusted her with his life. He remembered now, his dream coming back to him. Just before she woke him, in his dreamtime, he had felt that same spark, that same explosion of light. And in his dream, he too knew exactly what it was.

Three weeks later, science confirmed for Avril and Fran Laverty what they already knew to be the truth. The little patch of blue litmus from the pregnancy test was more an anticlimax than the supreme portent of joy it could have been. All that remained to do was to tell parents and friends, and prepare the way.

Safe and nurtured inside Avril's womb, Luke contemplated his future. This wasn't such a bad life, such a bad world. Amniotic bliss. Nothing to threaten him, nothing to hurt, Luke grew in the knowledge of comfort, the comfort of consciousness. He never questioned that same consciousness – why should he? He settled in, fed and slept, and thought. Only one thing worried him. He was growing, ever more rapidly, and, though the walls around him seemed to grow with him, he felt as though he was outpacing them. What would happen if he got too big for his home?

Meanwhile, outside the womb . . .

Other than the initial shock of feeling, with such intensity, the exact moment of conception, Avril noticed little out of the ordinary in her pregnancy. With the exception of a couple of incidents, it was a textbook pregnancy. Textbook, in the sense that it followed the patterns described in the various baby books which she gathered around her. She consumed them with such avarice that Fran, who had very quickly caught the baby bug, soon became an expert on breathing techniques, breast-feeding and contractions, and something of an amateur gynaecologist. He grew to love the evenings of testing his wife with multiple-choice questions on the advantages of waterbirth. He fretted over the fact that his own body was incapable of sharing the experience, the pains and the pleasures (mostly the pains, strangely enough). Early on, he even insisted on watching her bouts of morning sickness, when all Avril wanted to do was to sit alone on the floor of the shower and douse herself in icy water. Finally, after Fran had strapped a small sack of potatoes to his belly for a full day, and raided her bottles of vitamin supplements, Avril called a halt. Sympathy was fine; empathy was pushing it.

The two putative grandmothers weighed in with their ha'penny's worth of advice. As multiple mothers, they both felt that it was their duty to train in the greenhorn. Which was fine by Avril, who was happy to let others take some of the burden, if only metaphorically. The only thing she had to be careful about was to keep the two women apart, as their expert advice and opinions were completely contradictory.

But for the two unsettling incidents, Avril would probably not have had any inkling that her baby would be any different to all the other small bundles which she began to notice so much. So far as she could tell, the morning sickness, the mood swings, the cravings, and eventually, the fatigue, the heaviness and the aching bones – all were as they should be. The first kick was spot-on. She sang to her baby, she cried for him, she feared for him, she rocked him gently in the rocking-chair which Fran had bought for her. (He'd seen it in some film, a happy mother-to-be gently rocking, contented hands cupping baby. Luckily, it worked. Avril loved it.)

But for those two incidents.

The first would have seemed unimportant except that it linked in her mind with that moment of conception, that dazzling light. Five months pregnant, she was walking down the street, distracting herself, somnolent, humming a soft tune to Luke. Without thinking, she turned to cross the road. It wasn't the blaring car horn which caught her breath, though; it was the sensation of being physically pulled back from the verge. A life flashed before her eyes. A life . . . Once again, not her life, but somehow, the life to be, laid out before her eyes. Unable once again to see details, she nonetheless picked out faces. Some were familiar, her own, Fran's, but others she didn't recognise. Then it was gone, and she realised she was standing unsteadily at the kerb. She turned to thank her quick-thinking saviour, but there was nobody there. Without fear, scarcely realising what she was doing, she reached down and caressed her swelling belly, and muttered a soft "thank you".

Later that night, lying next to Fran, she thought again of the faces she had seen. They were very definite, vivid people. It is impossible to completely imagine a face from nothing. At the very least, there is some melding, some combination of features of the faces you have known, built up into the semblance of the imagined person. But this was different. These faces were all new, yet all remembered, as though she recognised them without ever having seen them. She knew, without knowing how it was possible, that these faces were all part of the future, Luke's future. But how could it be? Then there were the different emotions visible in the various faces. There was love, compassion, kindness, but there was also fear and danger. The problem was, she could not associate each face with each feeling aroused. The faces, clear though they were, had unreadable expressions. Fear and pain, love and caring, pulsed through them in a continuum. Even her own face, and Fran's, seemed to hide uncertainty – neither comfort nor threat could be found. This truly distressed her, and she pushed the faces to the back of her mind, telling herself it was all imagination, the ramblings of a distressed body. But at the same time, another part of her mind resolved to store those faces in her memory, to recall them when necessary, to avoid them all when she met them, lest she meet the one who bore the threat to her son.

The second incident was more explicit, yet it served only to confuse Avril. About a month later, she went for an ultrasound scan. Since the near-accident, she had been building up a lot of anxiety around this, and had put it off a couple of times. She was somewhat reluctant to go for the scan, afraid she would discover something horrific about Luke. At the same time, she longed to be able to see him, to pick out nose, mouth, eyes, ears, fingers, toes, knees, elbows, heart. She wanted to communicate with him, to say hello, as though he could see her as she would see him.

Besides, this was a point on which both grandmothers were in agreement, for once, as was Avril's doctor. It was Fran, though, who finally convinced her. Or rather, his enthusiasm finally infected her. The thought of seeing his son for the first time thrilled him skinny. He insisted on sharing the experience at least as far as hand-holding.

When she finally made the appointment, he couldn't sleep for days. The night before, he had to take a sleeping pill, as a result of which he slept like death, and Avril had to shake him violently the next morning so that they wouldn't miss the appointment.

As they pulled into the carpark of the hospital, Avril's apprehension returned to her. She felt a slight foreboding. Her hand on Fran's knee tensed, and he looked at her inquisitively.

"Do we have to do this?" she asked, smiling weakly. "It's just, I don't really know if it serves any purpose. It's a bit intimidating . . ."

Fran took her hand and squeezed it. "I know, love. But listen, we've made the appointment, and we're not going to find out anything that we won't find out later. I promise, it'll be fine." More reassuring for himself than for her.

She sighed reluctantly. "OK, I know you're excited about this. Let's just get it over with."

They had to wait almost an hour before they were called into the scan room, during which time the tension built behind Avril's eyes. She had to force herself to smile at the nurse. She tried not to look at the equipment arranged in the room, particularly the television-like screen. She let herself be helped onto the examining table. She watched the nurse; she watched Fran's face, ill-concealed concern behind his let-me-reassure-you smile. She held his hand and let her mind wander. She watched two magpies circling the air outside, and wondered if it was a mating dance or a war dance. Finally, however, she had to come back to the moment, and she braced herself. The nurse was speaking in soft tones, always smiling. They couldn't promise that this would show anything definite, good or bad, she was saying.

9

But the images they were about to see would give a very good indication as to the health and formation of the foetus. Beyond that, few certainties could be drawn from the scan.

As she spoke, the nurse had been rubbing Avril's bared abdomen with a clinical-smelling ointment – a sort of conductor, she explained. Avril watched in anxious fascination, as though seeing her navel for the first time. She looked like a cross between a basted turkey and a jelly blancmange. Her skin appeared almost translucent, and, for a moment – heartstalling – she almost thought she could see her baby. No – anticipation of the moment, and she realised she wasn't scared anymore. She was ready.

The nurse talked her through the process, she nodding, not really hearing the words. Then it began: the sonar instruments were switched on, she felt the cold detector against her skin. And there he was, on the screen, looking at her.

Her heart leapt, confusion swept through her like a bolt. The sudden thrill of seeing his body, registering it as a human being, was quickly superseded by the shock of realising that, not only did he have eyes, not only were they open, but they were looking directly at her.

She glanced quickly around the room to see the reactions of the others. The nurse was talking in a reassuring voice, saying something about fingers and toes, talking of heartbeat, all sounding positive, healthy. But there was no mention of eyes, nothing to suggest that it was unusual, this thing she was seeing. As for Fran, he was staring at the screen, fixed grin on his face, asking the nurse questions which sounded like numb, dull thunks on Avril's eardrums. Realising his wife was looking at him, he turned to her, squeezed her hand, beamed from ear to ear. She looked back at the screen, afraid he would read the fear and confusion in her eyes.

And there he was again, watching her still. His eyes seemed . . . what was it? Trusting . . . knowing, loving, sad . . . conscious? My God, conscious, aware of her, communicating with her. Then the nurse moved the detector around to the other side of her abdomen, and she felt him turning inside her, at the same time seeing him turning on the screen, keeping eye contact. She held her breath: she knew she wasn't imagining this, but she was unable to comprehend what she was seeing.

At that moment, he winked, and Avril almost fell off the examining table. Surely not . . . ? But yes, there it was again, a wink and a tiny smile. Speaking to her. Saying, trust me. Love me. But *shhh* – our secret. Say nothing. Not even to Daddy. *Shhh*. . . .

She began to laugh. Fran giggled, a little nervously. She looked at him, and he stopped, his face transforming into a picture of inquisitive concern. That was enough to set Avril off, and her laughter went out of control, over the edge. She had to hold tight to the sides of the examining table to stop herself falling off. The nurse stood back, appraising her, saying with a hint of irritation, "Please, Mrs Laverty, you'll have to lie still. The ultrasound won't work properly if you move around so much. Please."

At which Avril became serious again. Averting her eyes from the screen, she tried to pull her blouse down over her belly, suddenly self-conscious. The ointment on her belly frustrated her in her embarrassed confusion. "I'm sorry," she mumbled, "do you mind if we leave it at that. I . . . think I've seen enough. Could you help me get this . . . stuff . . ."

The nurse looked at her a moment longer, then shrugged, and began to clean her abdomen with a clinical roughness. "Whatever you say . . ."

Avril sat up in the chair, taking deep breaths, not wanting to think yet about what she had seen. Fran helped her down, and they got ready to leave. He said nothing until they were outside in the carpark. Then he blurted out, "What happened in there?"

Avril paused before answering. Taking another deep breath, she looked at her husband. "Did you see him?"

Fran was puzzled. "Of course I saw him." He smiled, trying to shake off a strange mood of melancholy. He put his arm around her. "Our beautiful little baby."

"No, that's not what I mean. I mean, did you see what he – " She broke off. It was obvious that he hadn't. Then she remembered the message she had felt reaching towards her from those tiny eyes on the screen. Say nothing. Not even to Daddy. "Never mind; it's just my over-active imagination again." She smiled and slid her arm around Fran's waist, although she felt her words dropping like fake pennies with a clunk, ringing false.

Fran opened his mouth, to press her further, to find out what it was she had seen. Because he didn't doubt that Avril had seen something. He hadn't forgotten the strangeness surrounding Luke's conception. There was something very unusual, something special about this baby, he knew. But, instinctively, he felt that if he was to be included in this particular moment, he would have seen what Avril saw. He could only trust. Besides, whatever it was, Avril's reaction had been positive; insane as it may have seemed at the time, her laughing-fit had an air of jubilation about it. So it must, he assumed, have been good news.

So Fran said nothing. In the car, though, Avril's doubts and fears rose again, and she was silent and pensive for the journey home. She tried to reason with herself, to persuade herself that everything would get back to normal after the birth, that the only adjustment Fran and herself would have to make would be to this new person in their lives, an adjustment necessary for every parent. But she knew in her heart that the strangeness, the magic, was only just beginning.

Exactly nine months after she first saw stars – nine months to the minute – Avril woke to a searing pain, cutting through her womb like a dagger, sending a hissing trail of fire up her spine. She jolted upright and screamed; Fran tumbled out of the bed with fright. As she screamed again, Avril's waters broke. The bed became a sponge, almost soaking the life from her loins.

Quickly, Fran recovered himself and went to help his wife who, after the initial shock, was breathing fast, quick, sobbing gusts, drawn in and spat out. Fran helped her to sit up properly, and snapped himself into autopilot, starting to play out the scene they had rehearsed a number of times already. In his mind, Avril had been the damsel in distress, he the chivalrous knight riding through the night in his Ford Fiesta. Now, reality threatened to throw him into a wild panic, and he had to act fast if he wasn't to end up gibbering on the floor. He quickly took out the carrybag containing her clothes, which Avril had packed almost a month ago in anticipation of this moment (she had to physically restrain him from packing it himself – she didn't relish the thought of having ten pairs of socks and no make-up in hospital). Fran threw on his own clothes, and grabbed his car keys. He headed for the bedroom door.

13

"Fran," Avril's voice drew him up sharp; in his frenzied performance, he had almost forgotten his wife's existence.

Now she was asking him, "Where are you going?"

He shuffled back to the bed and squeezed her hand. "Sorry love, I have to get the car. I'll bring it round to the front door, then we can get you sorted."

"No, don't leave me," Avril gasped, panic in her voice, gripping his hand harder.

"Avril, please, it'll only take a minute, then I'll help you put something on, and we can be on the road in five minutes." He kissed her softly on the forehead and released his hand. "Don't worry, we'll get you there in good time." Before she could call to him again, he was out the door. She heard the front door open, and then suddenly, she was alone, and it began in earnest.

Another shooting pain – less sharp, more localised – pierced her across the groin. She arched her back, feeling a great rip which she was sure would split her body in half. Then she felt the pounding, a dull throbbing at first, which she thought was her own heart; it built in intensity to a thumping ache, the muted offspring of the sharper pain. She realised then that it was her son. He was kicking and punching her from the inside. In the middle of all this confused bruising, Avril found herself once again in communication – how, she did not know – with Luke, this almost-born child. Nothing clear this time, a confused garbling, though she felt an apology for the pain he was causing her, a panic at the thought of going outside, a desperate clinging to the safety of her womb, though it was suffocating him now that the soft fluid atmosphere had ruptured under him like an earthquake, which was why he thrashed and thrashed, hit and hit her, and said sorry, abject and scared, desperate and enraged; and then, through it all, building, Avril felt a strange sense of well-being welling up inside her, growing louder and louder until she realised that he was laughing, through all the pain and confusion and fear, Luke was laughing. She giggled a little, but the sharp pain hit her again and he was gone, his telepathy vanished like a phone call cut off when the money runs out, and she lived again through the pain. Then more thumping confusion, no longer in communication, though. And another sharp pain, more thumping, more pain.

Fran came back in the room just as she screamed with another rip. He immediately rushed to help her. "Okay, love, it's okay. We can have you in the hospital in half an hour."

"I'M NOT FUCKING GOING ANYWHERE!" she screamed. Fran stared at her in shock. She pulled back from him, arching her back again. Between panting breaths, in a half-voice, she said, "Sorry, I mean . . . what I mean . . . it's too late for the hospital, he's coming. Have to be here. Help me . . . you have to . . . help me get this baby out . . ."

Panic flashed across Fran's face momentarily as the thought hit him: This wasn't rehearsed. I have to deliver my son. Then he gathered himself. He propped as many pillows as he could find behind his wife's back, muttering to himself ". . . hot water, towels . . . towels, hot water . . ." A thought struck him. "Jane O'Donnell!"

Avril looked at him maniacally. Who the hell was Jane O'Donnell and why should her husband pick this particular moment to think of her? Seeing her expression, Fran quickly explained: "The nurse. Across the road. She's a nurse. I'll go and get her."

"No wait, Fran, not again, don't leave me," Avril

pleaded for the second time that night, but she found herself grappling the air.

"Two minutes," her husband threw over his shoulder. "Just hold on."

"BASTARD!" she screamed, but she didn't have the energy to really mean it. Fran didn't hear anyway. He was already across the road, rapping frantically on Jane O'Donnell's front door. Two minutes later – no more – he returned with an unkempt woman in a dressing-gown, slippers, and, absurdly, a nurse's hat. Jane was carrying a small first-aid kit, but at least it was something. She had only been awake a minute. As she entered the bedroom, she took one look at Avril, and was suddenly wide awake, ready for action. She turned to Fran and said "Towels, hot water." She looked back at Avril and asked her, "Have you been timing the contractions?"

Avril gaped at Jane O'Donnell as though she was the gorgon Medusa, before spitting out, "There haven't been any bloody contractions, he's just trying to force his way out." Realising that she wasn't making any sense – the nurse was lost in a fog of bewilderment – she just screamed as another ripping pain clutched her to herself.

Fran came back into the room and Jane turned professional. Despite Avril's protests – "I want to squat, let me squat" – they laid her on the soggy bed and put the pillows under her spread legs. They stood for a moment at the end of the bed, one at either corner. Time froze for that moment as they fixed themselves in this triangle. It was as though, suddenly, all purpose had drained from the room, taking all colour with it. Nurse Jane and Fran simply lost feeling – momentarily – while it suddenly struck Avril, ridiculously, that she wasn't pregnant at all, it had all just been an extremely stubborn case of trapped wind. For the tick of a clock, they stood and lay in that tableau of grey, and then it happened. Time cracked, and a galaxy of light spilled into the room.

Avril felt it coming in a rush. A river flowing downstream suddenly became a quickening current. She felt herself dashing headlong into the rapids. She screamed again, but not in pain. The other two shook themselves out of their stupor and rushed to help her. She saw them appear in her peripheral vision, like foggy trees on the banks of the river. But before they reached her, they felt themselves pushed back, as though buffeted by the current, or a sudden gust of wind. They fell back on their backsides, and stared.

Avril was breathing heavily, squirming up the bed, trying to get away from whatever was happening to her. Strangely, she wasn't in pain any longer, she realised. She had reached some numb plateau from which she could survey the strange events being played out in and around her body. But it didn't seem like her body any more. She stared in awe as her baby began to emerge.

Or rather, her baby's emergence was heralded by an extraordinary procession. It could have been a band of angels, it could have been a brass band, it could have been anything and everything and nothing. The three adults who witnessed it could not describe it afterwards, because even as they thought they recognised it, it swirled and flowed into something different. Always at the edge of recognition, always defying recognition. Always nearly something.

What it was, was this: a flow of air and colour, flooding out from between Avril's legs, from the depths of her stretched-taut womb. Avril herself, not recognising them as her own legs, not willing to accept that this originated in her womb, giggled nervously. The river of colour, so thin and insubstantial, but definitely there, wound around her legs and wove its way up, surrounding her body, drawing her back into herself, back to sensuality. She had the feeling of being draped in silk, and indeed, the colours flowed like silk. She felt an unearthly calm descending around her, she felt safe and protected.

The colours flowed out, spreading, light gradually entering every corner of the room. It drew in Fran, until he had the feeling of drifting into sleep, being wrapped around his wife's sleeping body, as though they had somehow soared together into dreamtime; he felt, as Avril felt, that they had never shared such intimate space, that no two human beings could ever possibly intertwine their souls so deeply.

Jane O'Donnell also felt the silken embrace of light, although she, of course, was not part of the intimacy, the intricate envelope. Instead, she just closed her eyes, and let herself drift through the folds of time and space; she thrilled to the swirling light, which trickled into her bloodstream, driving her into an ecstatic rapture. Afterwards, she realised with amazement that she must have reached orgasm.

The light, the light . . . such extraordinary colours, blinking and flowering in random pulses. Every imaginable hue and tone danced through the room, and some unimaginable. Colours that had no right to be visible – as though they had slipped off the spectrum in primeval times – revealed themselves before the eyes of the stunned watchers.

Patterns formed and dispersed before they could be distinguished. Shadows crept in and out of the light, threatening to pin them down, to give them form, to solidify them. But the patterns never rested, never settled.

And then, gradually, the swirling slowed down, the lights stilled. The constellation of colours hung in the air for a few more seconds, and then slowly faded away.

The early morning light in the bedroom seemed strangely dark and monochrome after the fireworks. Fran and Jane still sat on the floor, blinking, trying to remember where they were. They slowly came to their senses; but before their eyes could completely adjust to the light, they could hear Avril's voice, small and wonderfilled, gasping, "Oh my God, oh my Lord," over and over again. And then they saw him.

While the extraordinary display of light and colour had held the three of them in its thrall, unnoticed even by his mother Luke had slipped quietly into the world. After all the struggling, all the pain, his final birth had been so simple, easy. Literally, he had floated home. And now he lay on the bed, bloody but unbowed, still attached to the messy afterbirth. A shock of black hair, and huge staring brown eyes, full of solemn curiosity. Avril, pain and struggle forgotten, stared in awe, muttering her mantra; the other two witnesses hunched over to watch. Luke didn't cry or gurgle. He stared back in complete silence.

Chapter Two

Jimmy McGinnity wasn't used to getting a scoop. A year after completing his journalism course – he'd passed, but not very spectacularly – he was still without a job. He'd made contacts, sure, but nothing solid. He'd survived on the scraps dropped from the tables of the tabloids, and they usually left an aftertaste which he didn't relish. He was seriously considering changing his name to Nancy and trying to sell himself as an agony aunt, though his goateed bullet-head would not look good beside a column called *Dear Nancy*. He had even written a plethora of whingeing letters to himself, which he had answered with a knowing self-satisfaction; but he couldn't bring himself to send them in to any of the papers. Ultimately, he felt he was meant for higher things. If the call from *The Irish Times* didn't come through soon (or if he was out when it did), he'd probably have to move to England. In the meantime, the tabloids would have to do.

He had asked most of his friends to keep their ears, eyes and noses open for any whiff of scandal, any twisted tragedy, any hint of human interest. But most of his friends worked in computers, banks or accountancy firms. One worked in the Department of Finance, but any time Jimmy went fishing, he would tap his nose enigmatically and mouth – not speak, mouth – the words "Official Secrets". Smug git.

Another mate worked behind the bar in Doheny and Nesbitt's, a sure goldmine – but he was either too deaf or too stupid to pick up on anything that went on there.

So it came as something of a surprise to Jimmy when his girlfriend came home from the hospital one evening to say that she'd heard from one of the nurses who'd heard from another one of the nurses . . . Jimmy laughed at first – I mean, a baby possessed by some spirit was pure 1970s B-movie stuff – but Siobhán insisted that all the nurses were convinced that there had to be something behind it, because Jane O'Donnell had suddenly resigned. Jimmy felt the first stirrings of excitement – his first scoop. He would write six versions of the story, he decided – *The Times*, *The Indo*, *The Press*, *The Herald*, *The Star* and *Hot Press* – and submit them under different names. He doubted they would all get printed, but at least one should take the bait, he reckoned. But he was getting ahead of himself.

He grilled Siobhán for all the details, but all she knew was that this Jane O'Donnell had helped deliver a baby for a neighbour at home. They had brought mother and baby into the hospital, and everything was fine and dandy; it was a normal, run-of-the-mill birth, apparently. Except that Jane O'Donnell had immediately afterwards handed in her resignation. Some of the other nurses heard her muttering something about angels and fireworks, repeating over and over, "It's not natural, there's some witchcraft going on".

"Did she file a report? Is that what happens with home births?" Jimmy wanted to know. Siobhán wasn't sure, but promised that she would try to find out. The story grew in Jimmy's mind until he began to rehearse his acceptance speech for the Pulitzer. He rubbed his hands together in glee.

* * *

That first morning, time seemed to have frozen as Luke Laverty lay on the sodden bed and watched his parents and this other woman watching him. None of them appeared particularly interested in doing anything about him. Luke tried to tell them with his eyes: I could do with a clean. Look at me, I'm covered in blood, I'm still attached by the cord, and I have goo up my nose and in my mouth. In fact, I think I'd better breathe soon. He tried to say all this with his eyes, but they kept wandering out of focus, out of his control. In frustration, he kicked the air a few times.

Jane was the first to move. She had gone into shock without realising it, and her professionalism took over. She rummaged in her small kit, emerging with a surgical scissors and some clamps. In a couple of swift movements, she had snipped the umbilical cord. Then she picked Luke up, turned him upside down, and gave him a tap on the behind. Some of the goo dribbled out. She wiped the rest away and then cleaned him, from head to toe. She gave a quick check that all limbs and bits and pieces were present and correct. Luke sneezed silently at her in gratitude. Then she held him out to Avril, but Avril drew back, uncertain. It wasn't that she didn't want to hold him, to feel his small body against her. In fact, her breasts ached with the need of him, and tears stung the corners of her eyes. It was a sense of awed respect that held her back. He looked like a golden god, and to touch him felt like sacrilege.

Jane shrugged, looking at Fran, whose jaw was making strange movements, like a stranded fish trying to gulp air. She finally arranged a couple of pillows and lay the precious bundle gently down. Luke looked gravely at her, and then fell promptly asleep. Jane went to the kitchen and made tea, humming to herself so that she didn't stop to think: Hang on a minute, did that really happen? When she returned to the bedroom, the parents had not moved. She offered a cup of tea to Avril, who took it distractedly. She gave another one to Fran, and took a long, hot drink from her own cup.

Fran and Jane sat down at either end of the bed, and the three of them began to discuss what to do. As they talked, they kept glancing at the baby, but nobody dared touch him. Avril insisted that she was fine, there was no need to go to hospital. Amazingly, all the pain had vanished. She didn't feel as if she had just given birth. Both Fran and the nurse insisted that she and the baby go to the hospital. Avril was stubborn, though. They argued what they would do, skirting around what had happened, until Avril had finally insisted, "I don't want this to get out. I don't want Luke turned into some sort of guinea pig." Jane reassured them that she wouldn't talk to anybody about what she had seen, if Avril would promise to go to the hospital. "They'll probably only keep you in overnight, if everything's OK," Fran said, while Jane nodded vigorously. Avril finally gave in, reluctantly agreeing that it would be for the best. "But give us a couple of hours, please. I think we need to introduce ourselves."

So Jane had left them alone, promising to call an ambulance in a couple of hours. She walked across the road and in her front door. There, her professional demeanour finally caved in. She began to shake uncontrollably as the feelings of that early-morning birth came back to her in a flood. She had to drink several gins before she could stop shaking.

23

Avril and Fran had turned their attention to the new addition. They still hadn't dared touch Luke, despite the yearning need they felt. Once they were alone, just the three of them, they stood for a while looking at him. He had fallen asleep quite calmly, and was already sucking his thumb. The two adults found it hard to believe that he could be a normal, healthy baby, but that was exactly what he looked like. Clean now, all blood and amniotic remnants consigned to the bin with their towels. Even his thin, wisping, jet-black hair had dried to a soft cottony tuft.

They must have watched him for a good hour, breathing calmly, without a concern. His skin glowed with the promise of life, and Fran and Avril both felt this glow welling up inside them. Their instincts, paternal and maternal, grew in them, before they even had the courage to touch him. Finally, Avril plucked up hers, and, bending down, lifted him gingerly, her hands carefully supporting him, head and bum. He did not break into a million pieces. She held him close, and Fran caressed his head. They both looked him over carefully; everything in working order. They stood together then, looking at their child again for longer, the morning's startling events almost, but not quite, forgotten. Their sense of awe choked in their chests as they held their son and each other. Luke awoke, without a fuss, and gazed up at his parents, ever silent, recognising them.

A deep longing welled up inside Avril, a strange pulling of her soul, which she had never felt before. She sat down on the bed, and, with her free hand, unbuttoned the front of her nightdress. Slowly, gracefully, she bared her left breast, and held him to the nipple, which he found without a fuss. As he began to suck, the tugging at her very essence took hold of her. It threatened to tip her over – into pain, ecstasy or insanity; she couldn't tell which. She felt herself unable to breathe with the strength of her love. Every nerve impulse in her body seemed to rush to her breast, and she was numbed again. She had to close her eyes to stop the tears from spilling down her cheeks. Gradually, the swelling inside her subsided, and she was able to fix her breathing to the steady rhythm of his tiny, soft mouth around her nipple.

Fran watched all of this in fascination. Luke drank gravely, silently. A small dribble of her milk escaped and ran past his ear. Fran reached out a finger and wiped it gently away. He felt such a great love for these two people. But he felt himself outside the circle which was the crook of her arm; he was shocked by the force of the jealousy which followed the love like a shadow. He bit his lip and swallowed hard. Eventually, coming out of the numbness, Avril noticed him, and the half-pained look on his face. Slowly, caressing Luke's cheek, breaking the suction with her little finger, she removed her nipple from his mouth, and gestured to her husband. Fran sat down beside her, reached across with gratitude and took his son in his arms. The soft warm body sent a thrill up his spine. He rubbed Luke's back gently, cupping a hand under his chin, until a small gushing of milk came back up. He cleaned his hand, resettled his child in his arms, and rocked him gently asleep.

The morning passed, until they finally saw the ambulance pulling up outside, and Jane coming out her door. She looked pale as a sheet, and she refused to travel with them, getting in her own car instead. The gins she had drunk appeared not to have affected her in the slightest. When they reached the hospital, she went straight to the matron's office, handed her a written report, and calmly offered her resignation.

Once settled in the private ward, Avril finally began to think of the strangeness of it all. Maybe, she thought, just maybe it has all been a dream, that this little child is just that and nothing more. When the doctor came to examine her baby – and the curious looks that he gave her and Luke convinced her that Jane must have said something – he asked her many questions. She calmly answered them, reassuring him that nothing strange had happened. And Luke was a model of discretion. They got a clean bill of health the following morning, although the doctor insisted she stay for at least one more night.

She was reluctant to let their own parents visit, unsure how much they should tell them, but Fran persuaded her that it would be better for them to see their grandchild, and to explain everything else later. There was little point in mentioning strange lights or other unusual happenings. That could wait. So Fran had contacted them and told them the good news. When they came to visit, Avril, glad of the distraction, forgot her reluctance and marveled at the idea of her own parents, and Fran's, as grandparents. They ogled Luke, drinking him in with their eyes, fascinated with tiny toes and fingers, holding him, passing him around delicately, tenderly. Avril's mother said she had never seen anything more beautiful in her life. Fran's father made *coochy-coo* noises, and tickled the radiant child under the chin. Luke dribbled on his finger.

For their part, Fran and Avril stared at the transformation that seemed to be coming over the new grandparents. Where they had looked tired and weary a couple of weeks earlier, bridging the gap between late middle and old age, now they looked fresh, refuelled by this new life. The creeping signs of old age had suddenly retreated. Their eyes, which had lost much of the brightness of youth, glowed anew with wonder, as though they had just discovered they were well after a long illness.

The following morning, the hospital confirmed that both Avril and the baby were healthy specimens, and they let them go home.

And so began the wonderful simplicity of those early days, the feeling that their lives had changed immensely, and that everything was going to be all right. However, for the first few days, they were still uncertain, and treated Luke as though he sat on the thin-ice surface of this world, and would drift from it as silently as he had drifted in. They tiptoed around him, unsure whether he would vanish in a puff of smoke, shatter like porcelain, or turn into a many-headed sea-monster. They whispered softly, whether or not he was sleeping. Avril fed him delicately, he sucked contentedly. They patted his back with a feather's touch, he burped happily. When they were sure that Luke was here to stay, they gradually began to relax. They realised that he was not going to give another performance – not just yet, anyway – and they began to settle into their normal routine; or at least the normal routine of a freshly created family.

Never once, however, did they hear him crying out in hunger or pain; in fact, no sounds uttered from his tiny mouth at all, other than the soft grunts as he fed. They woke instinctively when they felt his need, but it was silence that called them.

The grandparents called many times in those early days, providing a link to the outside world. Their myriad words of advice rooted the new parents to the practical, so that it became easier to forget the details of the birth. Fran and

Avril resolved to tell them the truth some day, but it would have to wait. There was enough for them to adjust to themselves first.

Fran had called the library that first day to say he would be taking his annual leave, and wouldn't be in for three weeks. Avril had taken her maternity leave from her job in the hotel about a month before, of course. They might have gotten under each other's feet, but they both quickly realised that Luke ruled the roost. He drew them in, as he had drawn them together at his birth. Whenever either of them was in the same room as Luke, they could feel him constantly watching them, with an open expression of curiosity.

Sometimes, it was stronger than curiosity, though. He seemed to be consciously tuning himself into their world, picking up their rhythms – as he had picked up the rhythms of her womb, Avril thought, and she knew he was an intelligent baby. She felt the same tingles of anxious excitement which she had felt as she watched him watching her on the ultrasound scanner. Fran felt that he was weighing them up, deciding on their worth as parents. Happily, Fran believed, he liked what he saw.

As he watched them, they would move about a little self-consciously. They would pick him up, feed him, burp him, change his nappy, and always those pool-deep brown eyes would gaze openly at whichever parent was taking their turn. Only when he was asleep could they escape that stare – almost brutal in its frankness. Even then, they found themselves drawn to Luke. They would take the opportunity to watch him in return. They would stand there, the two of them, and gaze down at his tiny, pulsing chest, his fingers and toes curled, almost in a beckon, his heart-melting face dreaming silently to itself. They wouldn't notice the time passing, until they realised from their own aching muscles that they had been immobile for up to an hour or more.

They had relaxed after the first few days, but they were still both fully awake to what had happened, though they found they could not speak about it; not yet, at least. They silently agreed that it would be almost a sacrilege to shatter the peace that they felt shrouded in since Luke's birth. But, at the back of their minds, expectations of strange events played havoc. Each time they watched him sleeping, they half-expected him to levitate, or change colour, something to follow up on the extraordinary heralding of his birth. But nothing happened. Apart from his silence, and the magnetic power he held over them, he was a perfectly ordinary newborn.

If anything, though, Luke's silence unnerved his parents far more than any magical display could have. Not once did he cry. When he became more confident around his son, Fran would tickle him gently; Luke would act like any happy child – but silently, just squirming and kicking his little legs. No whimpers, no whinges, no screams, no coughs, no sneezes (well, only quiet ones), no *goo-goos*, no *gaa-gaas*, no *aaaAAAaaahhhs*, no *bliblibliblilis* . . . the occasional, very soft, strain-your-ears-or-you'd-miss-it, gurgle as he fed. And farts. Luke was a good farter. What his mouth wouldn't do, his backside made up for in part. "He must be anal," said Fran, pop-psychologist.

"He takes after his father then," replied Avril.

"Seriously, though, Avril," Fran said, his expression solemn, "We may need to take him back to the hospital for a check-up. I'm worried that there might be something wrong. He's just unnaturally quiet. I'd like to know if there's anything serious."

Avril knew that he was right. The first visit had gone so smoothly, but now she was reluctant to let anybody else near him again. She just had the irrational feeling that she could best protect Luke by keeping him away from other people, even doctors. She hadn't forgotten the parade of faces that she had experienced during the pregnancy, and she still sensed some threat waiting out there for her child. Besides which, neither Avril nor Fran wanted to share this beautiful baby with the outside world, other than within their immediate families; they were too much in his thrall to even consider that as a possibility yet. As they discussed the options, the doorbell rang.

The fact that there was no sign of a report for the birth gripped Jimmy's mind. "You mean, there isn't one, or you can't find it?" he asked Siobhán when she reported her lack of progress. "Have you any way of finding if it has been filed away somewhere – maybe it's locked up because whatever it says is classified information!"

Siobhán threw her eyes to heaven. She was sorry she had agreed to help Jimmy in this. She had helped him with a story before – had risked her job for him – and had received little thanks. This time, he seemed even worse. He was becoming obsessed with finding out more about this mysterious baby. She stuck her ground now, refusing to delve deeper into something which might be classified. But Jimmy wouldn't be shaken that easily. He tried another route.

"This Jane O'Donnell. You say she's resigned? Is she working her notice, or did she just go?"

"No, Jimmy, she's gone. Vanished. Somebody said they think she went straight on a holiday. And no, I don't know where."

"That's OK, that's OK. What about her address? Have you any way of finding that?"

Siobhán reluctantly agreed to check this out. It was the only way of shutting him up. Even so, it took her the best part of that week to find Jane's address. None of the other nurses knew where she lived; at least, none of them were telling her. She only knew Jane to see, and had never talked to her personally. A couple of Jane's friends were a bit suspicious when she said Jane had asked her to water her plants while she was away, but that she had lost the exact address. Siobhán realised then that she was not a very good liar, but it was too late at that stage. Somebody must have passed the word around that she was snooping for something; they'd been told not to talk to her, she felt sure. She wanted to give up after a couple of days, but Jimmy wouldn't hear of it.

"How hard can it be to find out somebody's address?" he asked her in exasperation. "I mean, she isn't exactly a celebrity or something. It's not like I want to find out where the Pope lives, is it?"

Siobhán made a mental addition to her list of reasons for wanting to break up with Jimmy: sarcasm. It fitted in nicely with his totally inappropriate vanity, which, try as she might, she had been unable to shake. Then she answered him calmly with another question: "Have you thought of looking in the phone book?"

He hadn't. "Of course I have. But she must be ex-directory, or something." A flash of inspiration hit him. "Anyway, she's away at the moment, isn't she? So even if I got through to her, she wouldn't be there."

Siobhán couldn't argue with the faultless logic of that, so she sighed, "OK. I'll try again. But this is the last time I do your dirty work for you." Jimmy beamed at her in gratitude.

The following day, while Siobhán was at work, Jimmy went through the phone book; there were only three Jane O'Donnells, and two of them picked up their phones. There were also three J O'Donnells whose telephones remained unanswered. He made a note of them, and tried again later, in case some of them had been at work earlier in the day; only one answered, and that was a John. He had just finished jotting down the three remaining addresses when Siobhán walked in.

"Tomorrow", she answered his question before he could ask it. "I've made an excuse to visit Personnel tomorrow, so I'll try and find out then. I can't promise anything, mind."

Jimmy, afraid he would miss his opportunity, spent the following day lurking around three different areas of Dublin, trying to find where the real Jane O'Donnell lived. He took to loitering on the streets of the three J O'Donnells, in the hope of spotting a newborn infant. Any newborn infant would do, but particularly one with magical powers, though he had no idea how he would recognise such a child. His only other hope was that the parents would have a suspicious look about them. This was as forlorn a hope as trying to spot a miracle child. He gave up, having had the populations of Finglas, Sandymount and Lucan mark him as a pervert. One kindly neighbour had told him to "fuck off or I'm calling the guards". Besides which, he was drenched by the time he got home. He soaked in a hot bath while he waited for Siobhán to come home. When she did, he knew by her expression that she had good news.

Siobhán had gone to Personnel for her appointment at

a quarter to one, supposedly to discuss the possibility of being transferred to a different department. She didn't have a firm plan in mind for searching for Jane O'Donnell's address in the files. She was just winging it. She was amazed, therefore, when the secretary in the personnel department asked her if she wouldn't mind waiting by herself for a few minutes, because the personnel manager was in a meeting, and she (the secretary) had to meet a friend for lunch; Siobhán found herself alone in the office. For a couple of minutes, she didn't dare move. Realising that her luck was definitely in – some angel of destiny was looking her way – she scanned the room. She ignored the computer. There was sure to be some sort of password, and anyway, computers frightened her a little. So she turned her attention to the filing cabinets against the wall. Checking to make sure there was nobody around, she sprang to the cabinets and checked the "O" drawer. It was unlocked. Somebody was certainly looking her way. Maybe she'd try to keep up this winning streak for a while – yes, that's it, she'd break up with Jimmy this evening, as soon as she gave him what he wanted. She wouldn't even bother to offer him any excuses, she decided. He wasn't worth it.

She turned her attention back to the files. It only took a few seconds to find Jane O'Donnell's, and she had memorised the address and was back in her seat less than two minutes after leaving it. A few minutes later, the personnel manager walked in.

"Sorry for keeping you, Siobhán," she said. "I understand you'd like to be transferred to another department?"

Siobhán had forgotten her excuse for being here, but she had such a strong feeling of self-confidence that she decided she might as well go for it. "Yes, Ms Ryan. While

I'm happy where I am, I've always really wanted to work in paediatrics . . ."

By the time she got home that evening, Siobhán thought she would burst, she was so on top of the world. She almost laughed in Jimmy's face when she saw his overweight, stocky torso with its comical twists of hair sticking out of the bath. She restrained herself, gave him the address in Stoneybatter, and told him she was moving out, and would be back the next day to pick up her stuff. Then she turned on her heel, not even waiting for his pleas. She was almost running by the time she reached the street. Life was good.

The following day, Jimmy's head felt like somebody had drilled a hole in it. He had tried unsuccessfully to contact Siobhán through her parents or one of her friends, and had eventually sunk into a bottle of whiskey. He knew she was serious, and he knew there'd be no point in trying to persuade her otherwise. He had fallen asleep cradling the empty whiskey bottle. In the harshly bright morning, every movement was a penance to him. He struggled out of bed and tried to remember what he had to do.

He remembered then about Jane O'Donnell's address, but it took him a few moments to remember why he needed it. Oh yeah, miracle kid. He carefully manoeuvred his clothes onto his fragile body. He glanced in the fridge, but his stomach somersaulted at the thought of food. He swallowed a handful of tablets, grabbed his tape recorder and headed out the door.

By the time he reached Stoneybatter, his sweating body was almost ready to collapse. He dabbed at his sickly, shining face with the cuff of his shirt and breathed deeply.

He turned into the street of terraced two-up-two-downs and pulled up outside Number 11. The place looked deserted; there was no answer, as he suspected. But he hadn't come to see Jane O'Donnell, though he still wished he had some way of contacting her. He stood at her door, surveying the neighbourhood, looking for likely suspects. All the houses looked the same, their solid brick fronts staring blankly back at him. No clues jumped out. He would just have to do the door-to-door thing.

Avril and Fran looked at each other. Who could be calling? The cogs of suspicion began to turn in their minds; it could have been a friend, a parent, but something caused them to freeze, to think otherwise. It wasn't just paranoia. Something struck fear into their hearts, told them not to answer; at the same time, they both felt compelled to answer. Instinctively, they glanced over at Luke's pram. Neither of them spoke, but they both simultaneously felt an insight. This was part of his destiny calling. There was nothing they could do to prevent what had to happen. Fran stood up and went to answer the door.

The man who stood on the doorstep looked anything but a threat. He leaned against the wall, his breath coming in short gasps. His bloodshot, bleary eyes looked up at Fran from the centre of his greenish-white face. Fran's instinct was to close the door before the man threw up on their doorstep; but he hesitated, realising the man was working himself up to speak. Fran relaxed somewhat, but his guard stayed up. Finally, the man spoke.

"Mr Laverty, is it?"

"Yes," said Fran, "that's my name. Who are you?"

"Jimmy McGinnity's my name, Mr Laverty."

Fran reluctantly shook the proffered hand. "What can I do for you, Mr McGinnity?"

Jimmy, trying to glance over Fran's shoulder, almost forgot his cover story. "Hmm . . . ? Oh, excuse me, please excuse me. I'm doing a survey on household consumption. I wonder could I ask you a few questions? It will only take a minute." Jimmy had spent the last hour asking pointless questions of the neighbours. Finally, a Mrs Minahan had told him all he wanted to know, and much he didn't – her tales of varicose veins and hormone-replacement therapy had mixed like a bad cocktail with his feverish, addled thoughts. By the time he had made his excuses and run, he was feeling seriously queasy. However, he also knew the name and house number of a young couple who, Mrs M. suspected, had quite possibly, maybe, she thought, had a new babby.

Fran knew he was lying; there was no way somebody like this would be allowed to doorstep. The man was drunk. Yet he heard himself saying "All right" before he could stop himself. At least he had enough willpower to prevent McGinnity from passing the threshold which he had been edging towards. Inside, Avril watched it all with growing anxiety.

Jimmy cleared his throat. "Could you tell me, Mr Laverty, if you have any bab – . . . any children?" Subtlety raised its hands in exasperation as Jimmy launched straight in.

Fran shook himself and began to close the door, muttering, "No, no children. If you don't mind, I'd rather not answer any more ques – "

McGinnity's foot shot in. Out came his tape recorder. He knew there was no point in pretending now. He also knew from the look on Fran's face that he had struck gold.

"Mr Laverty, I work for *The Irish Times*," Jimmy grunted into the gap in the doorway. He may as well claim it now. There was nobody to contradict him. "I believe your wife has recently had a baby. Did you know that her file in the hospital has been put under lock and key? Could you tell me if it's true that there were certain unexplainable circumstances surrounding the birth?" As he spoke, he heaved against the doorway, catching Fran off balance. The door swung open as Fran tumbled heavily to the ground; Jimmy hopped over him and was in the front room before Fran could recover himself. He halted in front of the pram, and looked in, quailing anxiously as he expected to see two heads staring back at him, or some other unimaginable horror.

Luke looked back at the intruder with the same open curiosity-cum-knowingness which had already become a hallmark of his young life. For a split second, they each held the other's eyes, and then Luke let loose one of his huge farts. Despite himself, Jimmy felt himself smiling, and a wonderful feeling of peace welled inside of him. He muttered, not even realising that he was speaking aloud, "Sure, there's nothing wrong with this child. An ordinary, healthy baby . . ." He looked up to see a woman's red, angry face looking at him over the top of the pram. He grinned at her, his all-embracing love of the world extending to her. "And you must be the mother. Mrs Laverty, is it?"

Avril hit him solidly on the nose with her fist.

"Get out of my house," she yelled at him. "Keep away from my baby. I'm going to call the police if you don't leave NOW!"

Jimmy, blood oozing between his fingers as he clutched at his nose, cringed away from her. He half-stumbled, half-crawled to the door. Fran stepped out of his way as he fell out the front door. He got to his feet, and started to run across the street, although he could scarcely see through his streaming eyes. As Avril followed him out, Fran saw McGinnity's tape recorder in her hand. As she raised her arm, Fran read her intention, and grabbed hold of her waist from behind, surprised by the massive strength in her body. "Jesus, Avril, don't! We don't want murder on our hands. It's bad enough as it is." She stopped struggling against him. They watched the reporter weave his way to his car, fumble with the handle, and climb in. They kept watching until he had driven erratically out of the street and the sound of the wheezing engine had faded.

Avril turned on Fran, rage swelling her face. She raised her hand. For a moment Fran thought she was going to hit him as well. Instead, she flung the tape recorder to the ground, where it smashed to smithereens. She stormed back into the house. Fran followed her inside, glancing around; a few neighbours were looking out their windows. He waved at one of them, and closed the door.

"What are you fucking playing at?" demanded his wife. "Why did you let that madman into our house? He could have kidnapped our child! He could have killed me!"

The thought crossed Fran's mind that if there had been murder, Avril would not have been the victim. He was about to protest that he hadn't actually *let* the reporter in, when the doorbell rang again.

They paused for a moment. "It couldn't be him again, surely?" whispered Fran. They both tiptoed to the net-curtained window and looked out. An old man stood on the doorstep. There was something unusual about him, but neither of them could place what it was. Suddenly the man turned to the window. There was no way he could see them but he waved and smiled through his white beard, looking directly at them. He had something in his hand, something small and fluffy.

Avril went cold as she recognised him as one of the faces from her pregnant dream, and fear took her by the hand.

Was he here to harm Luke? Or was he one of the compassionate ones?

At the same moment, Luke let out a cry, followed by a gurgling laugh. They looked at each other, not recognising the sound at first, and scarcely believing their ears when they did. They ran to the pram, and looked in. He laughed again, uncontained joy rippling his tiny features. He kicked his feet in the air. The doorbell rang again, and Luke kicked his feet in the air.

"Who is he?" Fran finally voiced his curiosity.

"I don't know, but Luke seems to know him," said Avril, uncertain why she was so relieved. "That's the first time anything has set him off. I suppose I should answer it."

Avril opened the front door carefully, afraid she was wrong and that the old man would turn out to be another reporter, or worse. But she need not have feared. There was nobody there. She looked up and down the street, but he had vanished completely. She was about to close the door again when she noticed something on the doorstep. It was the object which he had been holding. She picked it up and came inside.

Fran had Luke in his arms. "He's gone quiet again," he said, tickling the baby to prove his point.

"He's gone – the old man," said Avril, by way of explanation. "He left this behind." She held out the small object to Fran.

Fran saw that it was a child's toy, a little fuzzy brown dog with a sad expression. When Luke saw it, he almost jumped out of Fran's arms trying to reach for it. Avril handed it to Luke, who hugged it to himself, sucking on an ear. Fran noticed something – a tag, attached to the dog's tail. He turned it towards the light, and read out loud:

"*For Luke. For now, a toy.*"

Chapter Three

For a while, it all seemed to fizzle out. From the day their lives were first invaded by the hounds of the press (well, one very sick dog, at least), Fran and Avril expected that the world would begin to crash down around their ears. They went to ground instinctively, unplugged the phone, didn't answer the door (they rang both sets of parents to assure them that, yes, everything was fine, and that, no, they'd prefer if they didn't call around for a few days; they would explain later) and went out as little as possible, stocking up on nappies and other essentials. They were quite taken aback when nothing happened. The world remained intact.

They scanned the newspapers for days, expecting some grand exposé from McGinnity, maybe featuring an interview with Jane O'Donnell. They were beginning to believe the whole thing had just been a bad dream, when they finally saw the article – in *The Star*, not *The Irish Times* as the reporter had led them to expect. A few lines, written in a jokey fashion.

Miracle Baby

Residents of Stoneybatter in North Dublin reported seeing "strange lights in the sky" at about the time a neighbour, Mrs Avril Laverty, gave birth to a baby boy. "It was like a flying saucer," said one. No doubt the three wise (little green) men will be around soon for a visit!

Nobody had taken it seriously. Avril just wondered who the neighbour was, or if they had actually interviewed anybody at all. McGinnity certainly had no chance to get anything out of either Fran or Avril; and, as far as they were aware, nobody from the press had attempted to call on them since. They stayed in a state of siege for a few more days, in case there was any reaction to the article. But nobody came, nobody called. Not even a curious neighbour. Maybe they had got so used to reading of strange events happening to other people in other countries that a miracle baby in their own would be simply another case of the ripples of fashion reaching Irish shores six months after everybody else. "Mind you," pointed out Fran, "we're lucky we don't have pilgrims camping on our doorstep."

As for the mysterious old man, he had not returned. To Avril's mind he *was* a pilgrim of some sort – that was what had struck her about his appearance. He looked exactly as she imagined a hermit must. The incongruity of the fluffy dog only added to his mystical air. And the message on the toy baffled them. How could he have known of Luke? How could he have known his name? And what did he mean by *"For now"*? They were unable to come up with any answers; however, Luke loved the dog, and sucked it contentedly at every opportunity. Fran fretted a bit over the fur, fearing the child would choke on it, but Luke took no notice. He had found his first friend.

Eventually, they decided it was time to come out of hiding and introduce Luke to the world. They had made their appointment at the hospital for a check-up, and they

41

would have to pay a visit to the grandparents if they weren't to cause a permanent rift. Besides, they all needed a little exercise.

Jimmy knew that he had messed up. He had no hard evidence, no quotes, nothing but a broken nose, a major hangover and an empty flat (Siobhán had collected her things; she wouldn't be back). He had seen the baby, sure, but it looked perfectly ordinary. Not that he knew much about babies. Jimmy shivered as an image of himself changing a nappy passed swiftly through his consciousness.

He would have believed that there was nothing in the story at all, if it hadn't been for the look on Fran Laverty's face. They had something to hide, he was sure. He had written his story, hoping it would flush them out. There would be a nationwide sensation, they would have to come out and tell the world about their child, and Jimmy would get all the plaudits for breaking the story.

But none of the newspapers would take it – nobody believed him. He tried to persuade them to check it out, to verify it. Mostly, they just laughed at him and hung up. It was a bitter blow, but Jimmy knew it was all his own fault. He eventually cajoled a friend of his in the *Star* to accept it; even at that, they cut it down to a fraction of its size, and turned it into a joke. His anger was only outweighed by his self-loathing. He made a resolution: he would bide his time, keep his eye on the Laverty family. Someday, he was sure, the truth would come out, and he would be there to capture it.

The paediatrician, Dr Fiona Menton, pushed her metal-framed glasses up her nose self-consciously. "Well, he's a perfectly healthy, strong baby," she told Fran and Avril.

Luke lolled on Avril's lap. "There's no sign of any breathing problems, heart problems, his reflexes are quite fast, his eyes are sharp, his hearing's fine, his co-ordination and head control are well advanced, no skin problems, no digestive problems . . . in other words, his health is – well, above average for a child. He's also extremely bright; my guess is he will be a very intelligent child. Plus, he's a little dote." Dr Menton smiled at Luke the charmer, whose face lit up as she spoke. He stared back at her openly.

Within two weeks of his birth, Luke had already become a personality of his own. He had Avril's colouring – her deep brown eyes and dark hair – but his features were more Fran's – less sharp than Avril's, softer. But his spirit was all his own. Fiona had to look back at the parents eventually, to break the spell.

Avril cleared her throat. "We're still a bit worried about how quiet he is." Luke looked up at the sound of her voice. "I mean, I think he's *able* to use his tongue – he did cry when . . . on one or two occasions. But, for the most part, there isn't a peep out of him. It's a bit frightening actually. If I didn't *feel* he was there, I think I'd be worried that somebody had made off with him."

Dr Menton found Avril's last words a little strange, but made no comment. She reassured them, "Well, not all babies scream their heads off, although that's the popular image. Still, Luke is certainly very quiet. But some babies are like that for a while. They usually grow out of it as they get older. His vocal chords are fine, and there are no mouth defects. So I don't think there should be anything to worry about. I should say to you, though, that it's impossible at such an early stage to say definitely whether there could be speech problems. Most speech disorders and defects don't manifest themselves until such a time as the child is reaching speaking age. If there are any underlying disorders of the parts of the brain affecting language, speech, a child may seem to be completely healthy until that time." Luke was nodding enthusiastically at her explanation. They all smiled. The doctor concluded, "Anyway, there's no reason to think Luke may be suffering from anything like that. Chances are, he'll be raising hell in a few months!" Fiona Menton giggled self-consciously at her own humour, and pushed her hair out of her eyes. She loved children, but hated having to talk about them.

Fran and Avril looked at each other. There wasn't much point in insisting that Luke was *unusually* quiet. The doctor was probably right, and it was useless worrying about it for now. The important thing was that Luke's (and Avril's) health was good.

The doctor was still talking. "Well, unless you have any more questions, we'll leave it at that. I'll see you again for his six-week check-up. And, if he's still as quiet in a few months, we might try a few further tests. But for now, there's nothing to worry about," she repeated, standing up to signal the end of the appointment.

Luke looked seriously at the doctor as she shook hands with his parents. He knew they had been talking about him, but he wondered what all the fuss was about. He felt perfectly fine. Inside, though, he felt a bubbling: something trying to rise to the surface, bursting to get out. He knew it had something to do with what his parents had been discussing. He knew he wanted to connect with them, to talk to them in some way, but somehow he felt his language was different. This bursting excitement inside him was his language, but it wasn't formed of words at all. He didn't know what it was, it confused him. He was happy, though. He liked what life had given him, so far.

Fran's parents had lunch ready when they called around to their house in Harold's Cross the next day. Fran apologised for their being incommunicado for the previous week. Avril took Luke in her arms for his feed. For a few minutes, they all watched the baby's cheeks as he sucked, his chest as it rose and fell, fluttering eyelids as he sank into a haze of well-fed drowsiness. Finally, Margaret, Fran's mother, broke the silence.

"So, Avril, have you decided yet about returning to work?" It was Margaret's great regret in life that she had chosen to stay at home after Fran was born.

"Well . . ." Avril hesitated. It had been her intention to go back to her job as a hotel receptionist when her maternity leave was over. But now, they weren't really sure what the next few months would bring. She was uneasy about the idea of somebody else spending time with Luke. He was an unknown, in so many ways. Besides which, she thought, looking down at the baby at her breast, I'm not sure I want to give up this pleasure.

Fran and herself hadn't really talked it over. Fran sensed her hesitation, and continued for her: "We're not sure, really. We'll have to see what the next few months are like. Then, if Luke needs it, one or other of us could stay at home." He left it at that; he wouldn't be drawn by his mother.

The following day they travelled to the house of Avril's parents, the Randalls, outside Avoca in Wicklow, where they stayed for a few days. Same scene, different house. Luke was again the centre of attention, and they were both left feeling a little uncomfortable. It was as though Luke's birth had cut them off from the rest of the world. He defined their world, and anything outside was a potential threat. A sense of isolation crept into their hearts.

Days became weeks and months. Luke grew in their lives as he grew in life, filling it as it filled him. They finally began to believe that, just maybe, this was an ordinary child after all. Nothing strange happened to them. There were no more strangers appearing at their door. The neighbours accepted Luke as they would any child of the neighbourhood. They would stop the nervous parents as they brought him on his increasingly frequent walks, eager for a view of the baby. None of them gave any indication that they considered Luke to be in any way strange or alien, confirming Fran and Avril in their suspicion that the reporter had made up the "quote" about the flying saucers.

Avril was still uncertain about returning to work. When she finally decided that she would, it wasn't so much that they needed the money. They had put away a large pot of savings, although with Luke on the scene they had less to play around with. Nor was she particularly concerned about losing her "career". She never looked on her job in the hotel that way. Besides which, Fran's job was permanent while she had been on temporary contracts for the past five years.

No, the real reason for Avril's return to work was to get away from Luke. Admitting this to herself wasn't easy. It made her feel very guilty. But it was the truth. It wasn't that he was difficult to look after; in fact, she was surprised at how easy that part was. Luke was far more independent than she had expected he would be, and he was never demanding. She knew instinctively when he needed feeding, or changing, and she put him to bed at exactly the right moment. This instinct grew from necessity; a child who never cries must send out signals in some other way, she decided.

Getting away from Luke was really a matter of pulling herself out of the magnetic orbit in which he held her. She had found herself sucked in by her baby. He became the absolute centre, not just of her world, but of her self. Everything outside the circle lost meaning as it blurred at her peripheral vision. Even Fran, who occupied some similar trajectory, appeared to her as a ghost at times, a dulled presence against the bright clarity of Luke.

Her own body, if anything, was completely invisible to her. After feeding Luke, she could not look at food herself. She avoided mirrors, frightened of the shock that could await her. She lay awake long into the night, straining for some sound of him, telling herself she could hear his breathing. She resented those people whom they met on the street, who would insist on looking at the baby. Anything that reduced Avril's time with him was to be shied away from.

For his part, Fran felt the pull too, but less forcefully. He had returned to work after his three weeks of leave were over. He tried to spend as much time with Luke as possible, but he sensed that Avril resented this. It was this, along with a concern about her health, which finally prompted him to have it out with her.

"I don't know what to make of you these days . . ." he appealed to her with open hands. "You only seem completely happy when you're with Luke."

"Nobody can be completely happy all the time, for God's sake," she answered testily.

"No, but the alternative isn't complete unhappiness. I'm worried about what's happening to you. It's like you've built a cocoon around yourself and Luke, where he's getting bigger and stronger, and you're wasting away. Life is still going on around you, Avril; you've got to trust that it's not going to kill our child. You've got to trust yourself, for a start, and then maybe me."

She turned to look directly at him, and he was surprised at the fearful tears he saw welling in her eyes.

"I do trust you, Fran, and I do love you. I just don't know what to do." She threw her arms around him and sobbed. Her strength and vulnerability scared him. He held her small frame awkwardly for a few minutes, unsure what to say. Eventually, it was Avril who eased herself out of his arms, and spoke, her voice firmer, a hint of her dancing spirit behind her eyes.

"I think I've got to go back to work. Even if it's just for a few months. I need a break from all this." Her gesture took in the whole house, but most specifically Luke and herself. Fran understood.

"So . . . what then? Would you like me to take more time off work – work part-time or something?" Fran asked gently.

"No, love, I think we both need to give him air – and give ourselves some, too. We'll find someone to look after him in the daytime, a crèche maybe." She perked up. "I've been thinking. There's a crèche in the hotel, for guests. I wonder would they allow me to bring Luke in?" It was an ideal solution; she would be able to continue breast-feeding him without disrupting her work much, and she wouldn't have his constant presence to draw her in.

A week later, Avril returned to work; Luke lay happily in the car-seat beside her. When they got to the hotel, she hesitated at first. It's for the best, she said to herself, heading for the crèche. Before she got there, many of the hotel staff crowded around her with congratulations and curious eyes. She didn't mind their questions and compliments so much now; she felt herself climbing out of a trough, and knew that things were going to get better now.

The crèche was run by Caroline, a young woman barely in her twenties, who had a wonderful effect on the children. Avril had seen how she kept them occupied, always playing, or listening to her read them a story in relative silence. It would probably be an ideal place for her bright but quiet baby. There were few tears, and no screaming, coming from the large room as Avril brought Luke in. Caroline smiled at her, congratulating her on producing such a beautiful child. Avril warmed to her. She seemed very sincere, and Luke kicked his legs in the air and grinned at her. "I think we'll get on very well, won't we, Luke?" she said, pretending to shake his tiny hand formally. If Luke were a squealer, he would have pierced the room.

Avril left him in her care, kissing him quickly on the head before she could change her mind. She felt such a fierce urge to grab him back, to run from the hotel and hide some place where no one could find them. The pull was so strong. She felt physically weak as she forced her legs to carry her out of the crèche without looking back. She told herself, reassured herself, that she would be less than fifty yards from him for most of the day. Nevertheless, the morning passed so slowly until the time for his first feed that she had to stop herself from checking on him every half-hour. She felt the same tug at her spirit when she had to leave him back after lunch, and she was so glad when her day was over and he was all hers again.

However, things got easier as the days wore on and she began to settle into a routine. Her fears abated as she saw how well Luke was getting on with the other children. He was the star of the show for a while, nobody could resist his charms. Caroline had put him in a cradle with bars, so that he could see everything going on around him. He lay there like a king holding court; they were his loyal subjects to whom he deigned to grant an audience. Avril was finally able to let her mind turn to other things. She began to enjoy her job, knowing that her baby was being safely cared for just across the lobby.

Luke was certainly enjoying himself. His horizons had gradually expanded over his few months of life when he realised the great variety of human beings that were available, all the shapes and sizes that they came in. They fascinated him. He knew he could love all of them as he loved his mother and father. There was something different about these ones, though. They were smaller, for one thing. And they were having a lot more fun. He watched them play, wanting to join in. He wanted to ask them so much about their lives, and whether they would mind if he loved them. He was sure they wouldn't, because they were all in love with life already.

One of them in particular attracted his attention. She was a little baby, the same age as himself, with a great head of bright red curls, and she lay in a cot beside his. He could see her if he turned his head to the right. She looked back at him. They stared curiously at each other through their bars. Luke recognised that she was closer in size to him than any of the others in the room, and felt an immediate need to know more about her. The little girl – whom Caroline called Sandy – felt the same need. They lay there staring across, straining toward each other, reaching out their hands as if they could touch across the great distance. Luke's brow furrowed as he frowned in concentration. He felt the need to talk with Sandy, stronger even than with his parents. He threw all his energy into trying to communicate. He felt blood and adrenaline pumping through his veins. He knew he was reaching some point where he would either scream or explode. He felt a superhuman strength tighten his muscles so that he could almost have got up and danced, and then he relaxed and it was released. And, for an instant, a spark of something moved between them, and in the same moment, disappeared.

The other children in the room stopped their play and looked around in curiosity. They could see nothing happening; strange how they had all felt something at once, though, like a tiny earthquake which people sense more than feel or hear. Caroline paused in the middle of showing a three-year-old how to hold a stick of crayon, and looked at the two cots. Nothing. She stepped over and looked in. The two babies were reaching towards each other, each gaze caught in the other, but there was no hint of anything unusual. But she had felt something, a tingling, and had sensed it coming from this direction. She watched them for a minute, and then she moved Luke's cot closer, until the two cots touched. Their stretching hands almost touched. They seemed to be greeting each other.

In fact, they had already exchanged greetings. Straining, unable to express himself, Luke had reached the point where he was ready to burst. His hand had clutched tightly at his little toy dog. That was the moment it had happened.

Everyone else in the room sensed the spark that had shot

51

across the gap, but only Sandy saw it. It was like a tiny snapshot of colour, abstract, unformed, but it held so much in it. She could see in it the love which Luke was trying to give; she knew in that moment all there was to know about him. And as the minute keyhole of space opened between them, she felt her own self opened to him, so that, when it closed, he knew all about her.

That was it. An instant, a brief flash, and nothing more.

Caroline moved the two of them closer together. Luke strained and strained, but he was unable to release any more. He knew it was there now, though, a huge well of need inside him, threatening to burst its banks.

"I think he wants to talk."

At home that evening, Avril was watching the great effort which Luke was putting in; she was a little afraid he would burst a blood vessel. She could see a little pulse pounding in his right temple.

"He's a bit young for that, surely," said Fran, coming to stand beside her, drying his hands on a tea-towel. He peered in at Luke.

"Well, either that or he's constipated."

Fran sniffed the air, and waved the tea-towel in front of his nose. "I don't think constipation is a problem."

Over the following days at work, Avril felt strangely tense. A headache dogged her as she went about her daily routine at the front desk. Try as she might, she couldn't shake it. When she went to feed Luke, it just got worse. He tugged at her nipple fiercely, and for the first time, it was physically painful. Her head throbbed as he sucked the very life out of her. She could see the pulse in his head, and was convinced that he was the source of her headache. It was a relief to leave him back in the care of Caroline, and return to work.

On a Thursday morning in late November, when Luke was four months and eighteen days old, Avril was sitting at the hotel reception as usual when the headache returned. This time, though, it caught her like a blow across the back of the head, it was so sharp. She was blinded momentarily, her eyes dazed, unfocused. She reeled and would have fallen if she hadn't been caught by one of her colleagues. She was helped to a seat, where she sat in confusion, trying to steady her trembling. The pain was intense. She felt as though her head was in a vice.

And then suddenly it stopped. The pain lifted so quickly that her eyes flooded with light as they cleared. She felt light-headed, a floating sensation, as though she had been tied to the ground by the sheer weight of her own body, and had now slipped her moorings and drifted free of it. Her balance returned to her, and she found herself still trembling, gripping the sides of the chair, but buoyant.

At almost the same moment – split seconds having ticked past – a series of screams came from the direction of the crèche. Some of the children who could run were scattering, rushing away from something inside. Caroline came out, her face blanched white, her movements jerky, uncertain. She looked around frantically. Her eyes met Avril's, and held.

Avril was out of her chair like lightning. Pictures raced through her mind of her son's mangled body, or some horrific accident in which he was scarred for life. She scarcely noticed Caroline's appealing face as she brushed past her and entered the crèche. What she saw there froze her in her tracks.

Of those children who were still in the room, some had tried to hide in the darkest corners, burying heads in blankets; others were milling about without purpose, some screaming; others simply sat on the floor, staring in awe. Luke's cot was in the same place it had always been, beside the little girl, Sandy, who was gurgling with joy as she looked at her friend. He was lying there, perfectly safe, looking at her, unbothered by the chaos he was causing.

In a spiral which appeared to be emanating directly from the soft vulnerable part of Luke's head – or from somewhere just above it, it was impossible to say – a kaleidoscope swirled. Avril was jolted right back to the moment of his birth again, and the incredible mix of emotions which had accompanied it. The colours seemed to form from nowhere, ebb and flow, eddy and swirl, but they were definitely focused on some point in or around Luke's head. There was no form to them; even less than Avril remembered from the time before, when there was at least a hint of something real in the light. She realised, with a sudden flash of insight, that this time Luke was on his own, more fragile than when he had the strength of her womb to support him. He must have taken strength through the umbilical from her, and used it to push out what he was trying to say – because she was convinced that he was trying to say something.

This, though – this was pure chaos. Unstructured, uninhibited by anything resembling shape or shadow. Pure light. She could almost see individual photons of energy pulse in waves. Again, the strangest, unimaginable colours mingled like lovers. Avril felt the back of her retinas sear in incomprehension; nothing could have prepared her for this the first time it had happened, and nothing could have prepared her now. And she knew, if it happened again and she was convinced now that it would, she would remain as dumbfounded, awestruck.

The room was lit in every corner, flushing out the cowering children who were trying to hide. But in the centre lay the two small babies, absorbed in this one-way conversation of light, oblivious to the hysteria around them. They knew all there was to know about each other already, and they were just on the small talk now. Neither of them seemed to be aware of how strange their words were. Luke, who had opened up the channel, felt that he was just learning to talk. For Sandy, this was simply the first time that anybody had understood her, and she them. They were like a couple of lovers who think they are whispering, unaware that they are whispering through megaphones.

Then it stopped. Luke simply drifted off to sleep. The room looked pitch black in the hazy aftermath. Avril shook herself; she looked around, suddenly deeply anxious for the safety of her child. She wanted a refuge, somewhere to hide. She strode to her sleeping son, picked him from the cot, ran from the room, from the hotel, into a life that scared her to death.

Chapter Four

The most immediate refuge Avril could find was in Fran's arms. She told him all that had happened in a rush of words, her tongue loosened by fear. "We have to do something, Fran, we have to get out," she concluded.

Fran hesitated. He was unsure what she meant, how they would "get out", where they would go. He knew she didn't want to return to work now. She had made that clear. She answered for him.

"Remember, love, how we talked about maybe buying a B&B in Wicklow someday, near my parents?" Her eyes pleaded with him. "Maybe now's the time. We have some savings, and the house has shot up in value. You could leave your job, we could sell up and buy something near Avondale. It's always full of tourists. We'd only need a few months to set everything up just right." Her face lit up as the idea took flight in her mind.

Fran hated to burst her bubble.

"Well, I suppose we could. But let's not rush into things. Let's give it a few weeks, see if anything more happens with Luke. Besides, I couldn't just leave my job. I need to give notice. We don't have to make a decision yet, do we?" He hoped she wouldn't notice the note of panic in his voice. The thought of sudden change unnerved him.

Avril looked disappointed. She had visions of the three of them fleeing like refugees, crossing the desert to some oasis where nobody could find them. She realised, of course, that nothing could be that simple.

They looked at their son. He looked so peaceful now, the world couldn't disturb him. But they knew that he was capable of wreaking havoc in their lives. They knew it wouldn't be long before the media heard, before they were invaded by the curious and the insane.

It happened even sooner than they had expected. When Avril turned on the radio the next morning, she couldn't believe her ears.

"I'm telling you, Gerry, it was an amazing sight," the voice crackled on the telephone line. "The whole room was lit up, it was like something out of *Close Encounters*. And then, the mother – I think it was the mother – just grabbed the baby and ran."

Avril stood, the kettle balanced in her hand, afraid to move. She stared in fascinated horror as the scene was played out again in her mind.

Gerry was digging for more information from the caller: "So, when you say this light came from the child, where did you mean exactly? His mouth? His eyes? His belly-button?" He was baiting her, of course, half-joking.

But the caller had obviously lost her sense of humour. "This is not a prank, Gerry. I'm serious. As a matter of fact, the light came from his head."

Avril broke her trance; in three steps, she was at the table and the radio was off. She sat down, waiting for the world to crumble.

It was a pity that Avril had turned off the radio. She didn't hear a few minutes later when a gruff voice spoke to Gerry over the air. "I know who this woman is," said Jimmy McGinnity. He sounded like he possessed the secret of the Holy Grail. "I'm a reporter, I contacted this woman after the baby was born. Her name is – "

In another part of the city, another woman sat listening to the story unfold on the radio. She sat in thought for a few minutes. Then she went to the phone and picked up the receiver. Her red-headed baby gurgled at her.

Avril pulled her chair over to the cot and sat looking at Luke's sleeping form. You look so peaceful, little one, she spoke in her heart. Do you not feel the earth shaking under you? How can you sleep when you are such a stranger in this world? Why is there so much we can't know about you?

She didn't know where it would come from first. The doorbell rang. She looked out the side window. It was that reporter, again. She couldn't believe it. Hadn't he had enough the last time? She wanted to ignore him, but he kept ringing the bell. She was afraid he'd wake Luke, that it would set him off again. So she opened the door a chink, keeping the chain across it.

"Mrs Laverty? Jimmy McGinnity. We met before." He was keeping his distance this time, making no effort to barge in as he had before. In fact, he looked – well, sheepish, actually.

Avril would have felt sorry for him, if the tracks of anger she felt from the last time weren't still imprinted on her heart. She said nothing, letting him stew.

Finally, he spoke again. "I am truly sorry about my behaviour at our last meeting. I'm afraid I wasn't really myself. My girlfriend and I had just split up, and I'd had a little bit much to drink. I hope you'll find it in your heart to forgive me."

Avril knew he was trying his best to sound like a gentleman, but she sensed that his cringing was just another act. She drew herself up to her full height, all five foot four of her. He wasn't a small man, but she seemed to tower over him. "Mr McGinnity," she said, as saccharine-sweet as she could muster, "I don't see what there is to forgive because, as far as I'm concerned, you meant nothing to me then and you mean nothing to me now." She made to close the door.

He spoke up quickly. "Wait, please, Mrs Laverty, please hear me out." She hesitated. He went on, "You see, I think I can help you. I know all about Luke now. I know that he has some strange ability, that he has visions. I'd like to help you find out what they mean. I know some people who might be able to help."

Avril was sceptical. "What would you get out of this, may I ask?"

He went for it. "Exclusive rights to your story. A chance to put the spotlight on a human story, something beautiful."

"And what makes you think I want a spotlight blinding my son?" Her anger was beginning to boil again.

"Thing is, Mrs Laverty – can I call you Avril? – thing is, Avril, a spotlight is going to be shone anyway. Your baby is big news already. It won't be long before they're all beating down your door. You could lose control of the situation very quickly. It would be much easier if I helped keep things under control. I could tell the world your story the way you want to tell it, not some twisted version."

"What, like 'Miracle Baby', you mean?" Avril sneered. "Thank you for your offer, Mr McGinnity, but no thank you. I don't have a story to tell. There is no story. My son is a perfectly ordinary child. Now, if you don't mind, I have better things to do than to stand here talking to you." She slammed the door in his face.

Jimmy knew there was no point in trying the door again. He would just have to do it the hard way – flush her out. He had already started the ball rolling that morning on the radio. But he knew it would take time. He walked back to his car, making plans.

Inside, Avril sat down and cried. It was all getting too much for her. What he had said had frightened her. She knew it was true – her child would be public property soon, and she wasn't sure if Fran and herself would be able to keep control of the situation. Despite herself, she found herself thinking through what McGinnity had suggested. She shook her head, trying to shake it. She wanted to run, *now*, and deal with the consequences later.

The doorbell rang. Not again, she thought. She looked out the window, expecting McGinnity or some other reporter. A woman stood outside, a baby in her arms. She was tall, blonde, dressed in a neat blue skirt and jacket. Avril recognised her. She was one of the managers in the hotel. Avril wondered why she would be calling, as she had never spoken to her and never had any dealings with her.

Avril opened the door. The woman smiled at her, and Avril knew almost immediately that she could trust her. Her eyes were open and honest, strong, but there was something else behind them, some pain. Avril felt a strange affinity for her from that first glance. Afterwards, she would not admit how much the woman's vulnerability and strength reflected her own. The woman shifted the baby onto her shoulder and held out her right hand. "Avril Laverty? I'm not sure if you know who I am . . ." Her accent was middle class, unashamedly so.

Avril shook her hand warmly. "Mary, isn't it? Mary Cullen?"

The woman nodded. Avril invited her in.

"Please, sit down. Can I get you something. Tea? Coffee?" Avril knew that Mary had called for a particular reason; she would get to it. She assumed it was something to do with the hotel. In the meantime, she busied herself in the kitchen. When she returned to the living-room, Mary was bending over Luke's cot; her own child was reaching in. Avril felt a moment's anxiety, quickly dispelled when Mary looked up and smiled.

"I'm sorry," she said, "They always seem to get on so well. I thought I'd re-introduce them to each other." She looked in at the sleeping Luke again. "He's so beautiful."

They sat down with their tea. Avril sensed that Mary had something to say, her reason for being here. She didn't want to push her, but Mary was eager to talk. "I just wanted to re-introduce them," she repeated. "This is Sandy, by the way. She was in the cot beside your baby in the crèche when . . . eh, yesterday."

Avril smiled at the five-month-old redhead. "She's a lovely baby. You must be very happy."

Mary sighed, and a dark cloud passed over her eyes. "That's just it, you see. She is a very sad child, very sick. Sandy was born with cystic fibrosis. It gets pretty bad sometimes. The doctors say she's strong, but they don't always see her when she's at her worst. She can be so, so sick. She could go at any time, or she might live five, ten, twenty years. My husband died last year, before Sandy was born, and I hate to leave her alone. The terrible thing is not knowing . . ." Her voice had faded as she told her story. She paused for a moment, gathering strength. "I don't know what happened yesterday. All I know is that, for the first time in her little life, my baby had real strength, vitality . . . I don't know, it's very hard to explain. It was nothing definite, just a feeling. A shadow always seemed to hang over her, and yesterday, it just lifted. Do you understand?"

Avril nodded gently. "And you think this has some connection with what happened to Luke."

"I know it does. I know that they've been getting to know each other over the past couple of weeks. I know that I came into the crèche yesterday when I heard all the commotion. I saw what happened. I know that Luke was trying to reach out to my Sandy, and that he had . . . comforted her, I suppose." She paused, taking a deep breath. "I don't understand what happened to your son, I don't know how he did what he did. All I know is, it made my child happy. So when I heard them talking about you on the radio this morning, and I heard your name, I had to find out where you lived. I checked it out with one of the other managers – I hope you don't mind – and . . . well, here I am. You probably think I've been too forward coming here."

Avril didn't mind. She felt that Mary was a friend already. What she was more concerned about was the fact that somebody could get her address so easily. She was growing more and more uncomfortable with the idea of staying in Dublin. But she put those thoughts out of her mind for the moment. They chatted easily for a while.

"So you think Luke and Sandy could be friends? I'd like that, all right. I think they'd be good for each other." She hesitated, wondering how much she could take this woman into her confidence. "These . . . attacks that Luke has. Has Sandy ever shown signs of anything similar happening?"

"No. I think Luke just needed to talk to her, and, for some reason, what he did is his way of doing that." As she spoke, she noticed a movement from the corner of her eye. Luke was waking up. As he focused, he turned his head to the side, and saw Sandy. And suddenly, there was bedlam.

The room erupted in a fit of colour. Teacups shattered on the ground as the two women reeled backwards in surprise. The riot of light spread up and out over the room. Experiencing the intensity of the feeling for the first time, all the tingles in Mary's body came together in one point. Avril, who was getting used to it by now, nevertheless felt a rush of health coursing through her veins. They looked at each other, and then at their own babies. Mary's disbelief and confusion was turned into joy as she noticed the transformation that came over Sandy. The child wallowed in the light, bathed in it, floated through it. She held her in her arms, fearful that, if she let her go, she would simply drift to the ceiling. The child was so light.

Avril quickly ran to close the curtains. *I'll be damned if I'm going to let the world in yet*, she said to herself. Then she sat back beside Mary and they watched the show.

When it was over, scarcely two minutes later, they sat in silence, afraid to break the spell that still hung in the air. The two babies were quiet now, oblivious to the current that ran through the room.

Finally, it was Avril who spoke first. "I don't know what to do – tell me what I should do?"

Mary looked at her and realised she was crying. She reached out and touched her shoulder in comfort. She had no words, but this simple gesture of solidarity strengthened Avril.

"Thank you for coming here. I shouldn't be burdening you with all of this. But I feel like I've known you for a long time. I'd like if we could be friends."

"Of course we will," Mary reassured her. "What about your husband? How's he coping with all of this?"

"Fran's a good man. But I think he's even more bewildered about this than I am. I want to move away, but he's reluctant. I think he feels it'll all blow over, but I know it won't."

There had been no mention of Avril's job in the hotel. Without anything being said, Mary knew that Avril didn't want to go back. "Where do you want to move to?"

"Ideally, I'd like us to get a guest-house somewhere in Wicklow. My parents live down near Avoca. Nothing too big, nothing flashy. Just peace and quiet."

Mary thought for a few moments. "Listen, I know a few people, contacts in the business. If you'd like, I can make a few enquiries for you. There's sure to be somebody hoping for a quick sale."

Avril brightened. "Could you do that? I'd be really grateful." Avril felt better, if a little guilty for talking about it behind Fran's back.

They chatted for a while longer, Avril's eyes nervously straying to Luke for any sign of a repeat performance, but the children were quiet as mice.

As the door opened, a pair of binoculars attached to a pair of eyes swung in its direction. Two women stepped out the door; the one carrying the baby turned and waved as she walked towards her car. The binoculars remained transfixed on the woman in the doorway. Finally, she went inside. The man put down the binoculars, made a note, and drove off.

A few minutes later, the doorbell rang again. Avril cursed, switched off the bathwater, and put her shoes back on. She came downstairs. Three strange women stood on the doorstep.

"Is this the house where the holy child lives?" asked one of them, her accent thick with piety.

Avril stared at them, stunned. "What?"

"We just came to see him, to say a prayer," said one of the others, clutching rosary beads.

"You must be very happy to be the mother of such a blessed child," said the third.

Avril stared at them, hardly believing what she was hearing. She felt frozen to the spot, afraid to move.

The first woman spoke again.

"It must have been a truly wonderful moment for you."

Avril frowned. "What moment?" Get rid of them, she told herself. But something prevented her from acting.

"Why, the miracle, of course!" The three women said in chorus, looking at each other and smiling knowingly.

Avril muttered, "I'm sorry, I don't know what you're talking about. You must have the wrong house." She knew she didn't sound convincing, but there seemed little else to say. Something in her head kept saying, *Invite these women in, show them your child, offer them food and hospitality*. She shook her head, trying to dislodge the voice, and started to close the door. "Please excuse me, I have work to do."

Luke chose his moment. Before Avril could close the door, a burst of light exploded inside the house. A trail of it wound its way around the front door and swirled around the three women's heads, licking their ears. They gasped and fell on their knees.

Avril slammed the door and raced in to where Luke lay. She picked him up and screamed into his small face, "Stop it, stop it!" The light suddenly vanished. A look of pained confusion crossed the baby's face. Avril realised what she had done, and immediately held him gently to her. "Oh, Luke, I'm so sorry, oh God, I've hurt you," she whispered, tears rolling down her cheeks. She clung to him, craving his forgiveness. But there was nothing to forgive. She looked at his face again, and he was smiling. He seemed to be saying, *Don't worry, everything's going to be fine.* She wanted to believe him. "My baby, my love, what are we going to do?"

The women were knocking on the front door, begging to be let in. Avril ignored them; eventually they stopped, but they didn't go away. They knelt on the path outside the house, muttering prayers. As the afternoon wore on, there were more knocks on the door. Avril ignored them all, and a small crowd gathered on the path outside: some curious, some pious. Avril watched them from the side window. She could see the face of Jimmy McGinnity moving among them, talking to them. A couple of others struck her as possible reporters. Neighbours watched surreptitiously from their own windows.

She called Fran and asked him to come home. He was there within half an hour. There was a flurry of activity as he raced from the car and Avril opened the door to let him in. A couple of the more wily reporters were barely a step behind him. "Excuse me, Mr Laverty, could you comment on the stories about your son? It has been claimed that he's able to perform miracles. What do you have to say about these reports?"

Fran kept his mouth shut. He felt like a criminal as he

ducked awkwardly under Avril's arm and she closed the door. He swung round. "Call the police."

"I already have. They should be here soon. But they say they can't do much. They can tell the people to leave us alone, arrest anybody who stays for loitering, but they can't stop them from coming back. We'd have to get a court order, and that would have to be against particular people, and it would take ages. And we'd have to prove that they'd been harassing us."

"You don't think this *is* harassment?"

"Well, they're just standing out there. If they were trying to break down the door, then maybe – but I'm not waiting around for that to happen. I'm getting out of here."

"What? Where will we go?"

"Well, I think we should stay with our parents – yours are closer, for now – until we can sell the house and buy the guest-house. You can give up your job, we can move down the country where nobody can find us." With a wry smile, Avril added, "And we'll all live happily ever after".

Fran was silent. He knew there was no point in arguing. Avril had taken the idea into her heart, and he knew she wouldn't waste a breath until she had made it into a reality. So he said nothing. Anyway, he had been thinking it over all day, and realised that he was quite fond of the idea of retiring down the country. He just hadn't expected it to be so soon. He knew it would be up to him to sort out the details.

In the living-room, Luke woke up again; he recognised his daddy's voice, and wanted to greet him. The stunning flash of light he produced was almost matched by the sudden flurry of camera flashes from outside.

Fran reached for the phone and dialled his parents' house.

* * *

They moved out in the dead hours of the early morning, carrying only the bare essentials. Even so, there were a few lingerers in sleeping bags, who had drifted back soon after the police had made everybody leave. They came awake as soon as they realised something was happening. As soon as they saw Luke, they all struggled to their feet and tried to rush the family. Avril and Fran quickly got into the car, slammed and locked the doors. One of the more enthusiastic of the fanatics launched himself onto the bonnet of the car, mumbling about benediction as he reached out for Luke.

Luke, sensing all the excitement, judged his moment to perfection. He responded to the small group with a short sharp burst of colour, over as soon as it had begun. The craggy individual on the bonnet fell off, landing on his knees, where he stayed, babbling. He was joined by the others, who finally felt their reward had come. Fran took the opportunity to throw the car into gear, and they raced off down the road before any of the fanatics could get off their knees.

Fran's parents had been expecting them. They welcomed them in. Fran and Avril knew that they would ask no questions; so they chose to tell them everything that had happened instead. "Better you should hear it from us than to read it in the papers tomorrow," Avril said, after the two of them, in fits and overlapping starts, had spluttered out the whole truth – that Luke was no ordinary grandson. Fran's parents were struck dumb. When they looked at the child, Avril recognised the same trepidation with which she and Fran had greeted him in the first weeks. Now, she realised how much they had adjusted him in their sights.

Finally, Margaret reached a verdict: "Well, I don't know anything about miracles, but he's my grandson, and as long as he's in this house, he's safe." Avril hugged her.

They went to bed then and slept for much of the morning. When they emerged, Fran rang in sick, then, turning to Avril, he said, "I'm going to go in tomorrow, and hand in my notice. In the meantime, we have to talk to an estate agent, see what they can do about a quick sale of the house. Once we've found somewhere suitable, we can move our stuff down. If we have to put it into storage in the meantime, we will." Truth to tell, Fran was beginning to enjoy himself. He felt that he worked best under crisis, and he knew he was in control of the situation now. An image of himself flying a helicopter into a war-zone in Vietnam floated through his head from nowhere.

His father, Ray, came into the kitchen. "Have you seen this?" He threw down the newspapers – three or four different ones, but in each one a photograph of a house that was so familiar to them, but which they knew now they would never be returning to. Outside the house stood a pathetic, huddled crowd, some of them holding candles. The house itself looked like a candle, lit from within.

Avril walked out of the kitchen in disgust. "I don't want to read any of that crap."

Fran read a few lines under one of the photographs:

Reports of bizarre events in Stoneybatter in Dublin's north inner city have been confirmed by many eyewitnesses. These "happenings" – unusual patterns of light coming from the house of Francis and Avril Laverty – have been linked to their baby son, Luke. It is believed that these strange occurrences are connected with similar events which happened on Thursday in the Castle Lodge Hotel – which is where Mrs Laverty works.

The Lavertys have refused to answer reporters' questions, and had not emerged from their two-up-two-down house by the early hours of this morning. Neighbours say that the Lavertys are an "ordinary couple", who are quite friendly but who "generally keep to themselves". A small crowd of people have gathered outside the house, many of them in the belief that the strange lights are some sort of religious sign.

Jimmy McGinnity, the journalist who first reported the circumstances surrounding Luke Laverty's birth a number of months ago, was at the house yesterday, and had this to say: . . .

Fran threw down the paper in disgust. He couldn't read any more, his head filled with words. *They're going to find us. We can't keep on running. We can go down the country, but then what? We have to do something – to cure him. Otherwise, we'll have to go public ourselves, to do it our own way.* The idea frightened him, but he knew it was something they might have to consider.

Meanwhile, there was a commotion coming from the room where they had put Luke's cot. It was, of course, Luke greeting his grandmother in the only way he knew how. Fran and his father ran to the room. Avril was there already, her arm supporting her mother-in-law, who was shaking her head in awe, muttering, "Beautiful, beautiful," over and over.

The next few days were a welcome respite for Fran and Avril. Fran's parents accepted Luke's little quirks with good grace. In some way, Avril felt as though maybe their age had given them a greater glimpse of life's possibilities, and Luke was simply an extension of this beauty. Thinking along these lines, she remembered the old man who had called to their door a few weeks before, and given Luke a gift. Who was he? What did he know about Luke? Maybe Luke was able to connect with the old and the young in a much stronger way than with those inbetween.

And maybe, just maybe, those people who came to see Luke were right. Perhaps he was some sort of "sign". But a sign of what? He was just a baby, after all. She didn't know what lay ahead for him; she had no way of telling if he knew that the light he was creating was like nothing else ever seen; she could not know whether it would draw in good or evil, or who would twist his destiny next. There were so many things that Avril did not understand, but the one thing which overrode all fears was her need to protect him, and that she would do whether or not she knew the reason why.

Avril pondered these things as she walked through the unfamiliar streets of Harold's Cross, where Fran had been brought up. She was enjoying her freedom for the first time since Luke's birth. Margaret insisted on looking after Luke while she went for a walk, while Fran was at work. She breathed the fresh air deeply into her lungs, and thought of the countryside. That was still what she wanted. She knew she had pushed Fran a little on that, but she really needed to get out of Dublin, for her own sake as well as Luke's. She had begun to feel a creeping claustrophobia that went beyond urban paranoia. The dark shadows she felt clutching at the edges of her psyche were more than just shadows, she felt sure. They were the faces from those dreams, the unknown echoes of Luke's footfalls, guiding his future.

To run free through fields where shadows could only be rainclouds passing overhead felt like a dream of heaven to Avril. She turned the corner and almost ran into the photographer.

"Oh, excuse me," he said, "I'm looking for Ray and Margaret Laverty. I don't suppose you know where they live?"

That night, they were gone again, running again. Avril's parents warned them that reporters had talked to them as well, and they would easily be found there. So she contacted Mary Cullen in Glasnevin, and that was where they were headed.

Mary was happy to put them up – she shared her large Victorian terraced house with Sandy, her baby, and nobody else. There were lots of empty rooms, and she was thrilled to have company. She was even happier to keep quiet about it.

They were to spend the next month there, while the sale of their own house went through and they searched for a suitable place in the country. Mary was an enormous help; she identified three potential houses. Unfortunately, they were all beyond their budget. The Lavertys were beginning to despair, when Mary again came to the rescue.

"Tell you what," she told them. "My husband left me a small fortune when he died last year, and I've been looking around for something to do with it. This could be perfect. Would you consider going fifty-fifty on the guest-house?"

Fran was uncertain, but Avril leapt at the chance. She knew she could trust Mary, even though they had only known each other a few weeks. They worked out the details: Mary was happy just to be a sleeping partner for the moment. Sandy needed regular visits to the hospital. So Mary would continue to work in the hotel, and take half the profits in the guest-house until her investment was recouped. Then she would continue to take a small part of the profits, with the idea, perhaps, of eventually moving in and helping out herself.

The deal was struck.

Eventually, Avril and Fran settled on a beautiful house outside Arklow, just a few miles from Avril's parents. Once they saw the house, they knew it was right. It was hidden from the road – which itself was hidden in a wide valley – by an avenue of evergreen trees, and a field of long grass sloped up behind it, creating a green canvas framing the house below. The house itself looked small from the outside – an ordinary, white-gabled bungalow, half-overgrown with ivy and rosebushes. Inside, the space seemed to open with the light that shone through. There were six guest bedrooms, a huge kitchen, and their own rooms were set off as a separate apartment.

Despite Mary's money, Fran still had to arrange a bridging loan, which would keep them afloat while they waited for their first guests. Their own estate agents had been granted complete autonomy on the sale of their house in Stoneybatter, on condition that they didn't reveal their whereabouts to anybody.

There were few visitors to Mary's house in Glasnevin during their last days there. Only those they told knew where they were. To everybody else, they had vanished. The media, whose initial frenzy had died down when they had disappeared, soon forgot about them; there were plenty of other freaks out there. Only one journalist kept searching for them, but nobody wanted his opinions any more. Still, he was persistent. As for the people who saw Luke as some sort of sign from God, they had all gone back to their homes, many of them happy in the knowledge that a living prophet had brushed against their lives. Fran went back to their old house a few times, sneaking in like a thief under cover of darkness, to check that nobody had broken in, to make sure everything was as it should be. He need not have bothered; there were no stragglers left. Life had returned to its former rhythm.

Meanwhile, Luke and Sandy were getting to know each other properly. Their friendship easily overcame the restrictions on mobility that their small bodies imposed. When possible, their mothers would place them side by side, where they could touch and play with each other. And, of course, they had no need of words.

Luke found he was able to focus his thoughts and the images in his head so much more easily when Sandy was around because he knew she would understand him. He no longer had to concentrate all his energy on the one thought in order to express it. The channel of communication between them had formed into a firm bond, in which they exchanged thoughts and feelings as freely as those around them exchanged words and gestures. Sandy found herself feeling truly well for the first time in her short life. The images which Luke showed her soothed her delicate, vulnerable body and soul. She was safe, cocooned in the web of colour which he wove around her.

Fran and Avril, and Mary who was growing more like a sister to Avril every day, watched their tiny courtship in wonder. Although they knew Luke's imaginings would eventually draw him into the world, for now he seemed detached from that world, unconnected to its meanderings. The adults were also growing more familiar with his increasingly frequent "episodes". They were so much a part of him that to do anything to disturb them felt like an amputation; they had discussed visiting a doctor again, but now that felt more like an intrusion into a body that was more whole than they could possibly imagine.

There was something else different about Luke's visions now; they were more focused, they held form and shape where before they had been pure abstraction, chaos. It was still hard to pin down what these forms were, but there were definite patterns.

"It's like looking at clouds," said Mary, watching him one day. Fran and Avril both looked at her, puzzled. She smiled at their confusion. "Did you ever look at a cloud, and you could swear you saw something – a map, or some sort of patchwork pattern? And you ask somebody else if they can see it, and they say yes, but what they see is a dog or an eagle or something. Well, I think Luke's pictures are like that. They're clouds, shifting patterns of light and shade and colour, and everybody sees something different in them."

Luke's parents looked at each other in amazement. Mary's insight suddenly struck them as just right. From then on, Luke's patterned tricks of the light became, for them, his clouds. He was drawing maps in light, but everyone matched their contours to whatever landscape they knew.

Chapter Five

Luke loved the long grass. He sat down now and watched his mother peering around, looking for him. She called his name a couple of times. She held her hand to her eyes as if she was a sailor on lookout duty, searching for land. Luke loved this game. He giggled softly to himself, making no sound. He knew she could see his small shape among the soft green grass a few yards from where she stood. He could see her smiling to herself. She looked so lovely in the bright blue summer dress, which he loved to touch.

Finally, she pretended to see him, saying, "Aha!" in a surprised voice. He jumped up and began to run in his three-year-old scramble. Avril scuttled after him, imitating his run, to his great delight. She caught up with him and swept him up in her arms. He giggled silently in her face, and she thought her heart would burst. She smiled broadly at him, and they rubbed noses, but a shadow passed over her.

Why won't you speak, or make a sound, any sound? They had tried everything; the doctors couldn't understand it. As far as they could see, Luke was a normal, healthy baby. There was nothing to indicate that he was brain-damaged or learning-impaired in any way. They had performed all sorts of tests, and they all showed the same thing: a happy, intelligent child, who, in theory, had all that was required for him to be a chatterbox. The only explanation that any of them were able to come up with was that Luke simply didn't want to speak, or didn't feel the need.

They had decided to stick with Fiona Menton as their paediatrician, even though it meant travelling to Dublin every few weeks. They had come to trust her, but not yet enough to tell her the full truth. Dr Menton recommended that they take Luke to a psychologist whom she had talked to, Dr Gordon Richardson. He had asked if he could do some further study and tests on Luke. Avril and Fran said they would think about it, but in their hearts they felt it would solve nothing, and would just cause further disruption to what was turning out to be quite a good life. If Luke didn't want to speak, but was otherwise perfectly healthy and content, then so be it. They never mentioned to any of the doctors what Luke did instead of talking, and, thankfully, he had never given them a demonstration. He probably knew they wouldn't take it lightly.

Avril put away such thoughts for now.

Luke had been very "quiet" for the past few days. There'd been no visions, no incidents, no clouds. In fact, a cloud of another sort had seemed to be hanging over him. He had sat with a couple of the guests and watched television for most of the evening the night before. Avril hovered, watching anxiously, afraid he would suddenly burst into a magnificent display, like a peacock spreading his plumage. But she needn't have worried. He was more interested in what was happening on the television. The guests, a young couple, smiled at her, happy to see such a quiet child when their world was normally full of screaming tykes – they had palmed theirs off on grandparents for the weekend.

Avril had not been able to work out what was wrong with Luke, but there was definitely a tinge of sadness around him. And then, the following morning, Mary rang to say that they were coming to stay for a few days. Mary had been down to the guest-house every few weeks, checking on her investment, but this would be the first time she would be staying as a guest. When Avril told Luke that Sandy was coming, the dark veil lifted from his eyes, and a broad smile lit his face for the first time in ages. He took her hand, and dragged her up to his favourite place in the world, where they chased after each other until they were both exhausted.

Now she was walking down through the field of long grass with her child in her arms. In the distance, she could see Mary's car crawling along the road. Luke saw it too, and wriggled to get out of her arms. Avril held him tight.

Mary's car pulled into the driveway just as mother and child reached the front of the house. Fran came out to greet the visitors too. Mary waved broadly at them, "So, how are the exiles?" She had started using that name when Fran, Avril and Luke had first moved down here, and it had stuck. Avril had grown fond of it, and eventually they had adopted it as the name of their house. But, for Avril, "Exiles" was more a place of refuge than banishment.

They all hugged. Sandy greeted Luke with a squeal of delight and a big kiss. Luke greeted Sandy with a brief flourish of his clouds, which quickly dispersed in the open country air. Avril watched them indulgently. Although she now took Luke's displays for granted, she still glanced around to see if any of the guests or neighbours had seen it. No shocked faces were visible behind net curtains.

Amazingly, in the two years they had been running the

guest-house, Luke had never once "showed off" in front of the guests. Avril could only assume that he knew he shouldn't. Just to be on the safe side, Luke would go to stay with Avril's parents every couple of weekends, which were usually the busiest times for the guest-house.

That wasn't to say he hadn't been projecting much – in fact, in the freedom of the countryside, his projections had become more frequent, more free. His visions had also become more distinct. What had seemed like drifting clouds had now firmed their outlines, become true shapes. It was still hard to tell exactly what they were, though. Memories, faces, reflections of all he could see around him, or dreams of how he wished it all could be – Avril doubted that even he knew.

The business had taken off more quickly than they expected. They had a couple of months of anxiety, when the bridging loan seemed to be sliding downhill rapidly, and only Mary's money had kept them afloat. But there were a number of people who had been regular guests of the house under its previous owners, and when they discovered that the new owners had no plans to make major changes, they decided to continue coming. From that point, they gradually began to build their business. They had to hone their own skills very quickly. But Fran had a good head for business, and managed to keep everything running smoothly when there were fewer guests around. Avril had taken a part-time catering course. Their nervousness soon gave way to a feeling that they had made the right choice. They always seemed to have just enough guests to keep their heads safely above water. By the end of the first year they had paid off the bridging loan and were heading into a healthy profit.

In these two years, Luke's brief fame seemed to have evaporated as quickly as it had arrived. Nobody came to disturb their peace. None of the guests knew that they were the young couple with the miraculous baby who had caused a small flurry of excitement in the media. They had left no forwarding address at their old house in Stoneybatter. When Fran went back a few more times to check on messages, he had to apologise to the new residents who had been disturbed on a number of occasions by a certain journalist. The rest of the media, and all the curious onlookers, had disappeared after a couple of weeks. And McGinnity himself appeared to have given up after about six months.

One thing disturbed Fran, so much so that he hadn't mentioned it to Avril. The old house was actually broken into about six weeks after they had left, before the new residents had moved in. Post had been opened, drawers turned out. They didn't seem to have taken anything, but they must have been looking for something. Fran guessed that it was more likely to be connected with them than with the new people, and he assumed that whoever it was had wanted to find out where they had gone. He had reasoned it out: if somebody really wants to find us, there are plenty of ways of doing so. None of the journalists, McGinnity included, had found them yet. If somebody is desperate enough to break into the house, they will be clever enough to persist, and will eventually find us. But there was no point in running from an unseen, unknown enemy, who might or might not exist. The best thing to do was to bide their time, not feel hunted, because nothing had threatened them yet. At least, that is what Fran convinced himself to believe. Two years later, there was still nothing to ripple their pond, and Fran had all but forgotten his fears.

* * *

Jimmy McGinnity had not given up. He had simply gone to ground, shifted perspective, changed career. He realised that he was never going to make it as a journalist, so he decided to become a private investigator instead – a dick. It wasn't really a spur-of-the-moment whim, because he had always harboured thoughts of dark alleyways, secret rendezvous, long trenchcoats. It suited his ego to think of himself as an observer of the seamier side of life. It wasn't easy to start off with. He was making even less money than he had as a journalist; his dole money barely kept his head above water. But gradually, he learned his trade, often through failure, and he soon found it was working, he was actually solving cases. Most of the cases, of course, were jealous husbands, embittered wives, the odd shady business deal. Nothing spectacular. Jimmy never went further than his job description. He was never one for the real dirty work. He just found out what he was being paid to find out, reported back to his client, and took his wages. He didn't care what happened afterwards. He chose to remain morally aloof.

Always somewhere in his mind, however, a constant floating cloud, lay the one story which would have kept him in journalism, and which sustained his thoughts now through many a long night's stakeout. What had happened to that baby? Jimmy couldn't understand his own obsession, but he was constantly drawn back to it. Whatever case he was working on, he always had half an ear open for news of the Lavertys. He picked up on any morsels dropped, hoping they would lead him somewhere, but there seemed to be nothing but dead-ends. It was almost as though somebody was trying to obstruct his view. After two years, he had pushed it to the back of his mind, so much so that he might have been prepared to forget it. But forces were gathering that would put him back on the trail.

Luke watched the two men gravely from his vantage point in the long grass. They knocked at the front door of the guest-house; when they got no answer, they began to look in windows, and finally walked around to the back of the house. Luke looked at his parents and Mary. They were happily engrossed in their picnic, out of sight of the house. He looked back at the two men, who to him definitely didn't look like guests. They had stopped outside the back door, and were discussing something. One of them lit a cigarette. He dropped the match on the ground and the two of them, having decided on some course of action, walked away. Luke watched the spluttering match, his clear eyesight following its self-destruction as the tiny flame blackened its length, millimetre by millimetre. When it had finally extinguished, Luke looked up. The two men were halfway down the road. Luke looked over at his mother, trying to signal that something was wrong, but nothing would come out. Finally, the men disappeared behind a bend in the road, just at the moment that Avril came over to him and picked him up. She brought him over and sat him down at the edge of the rug where they had been enjoying their meal.

Mary sighed, "This is so beautiful. It's so lovely to have all of this as your back yard."

Avril smiled at her. "Thanks to you, Mary. We wouldn't be here if it wasn't for you. Listen, the business is flourishing now; why don't you move down here? We'd love to have you, and I know Luke would love to have Sandy around."

Mary shook her head, avoiding Avril's eyes. "I'd really love to. But not yet. I don't want to risk giving up my job, not with Sandy . . ." She left it at that, firmly signalling that she didn't want to think any more about it. "Right now, I'm just happy to see all of you so happy."

Luke wanted to tell them all about the men, to warn them that something wasn't quite right. He struggled, trying to form the words in his mouth. All that came into his head was "MEN". He swallowed hard, gulping the word into his lungs. Then he pushed, hard as he could, so that it might rush up his tongue and cause it to flutter in his mouth. Then he would speak.

That was the plan. What happened was, he pushed it and pushed it, his fearful mind in turmoil, and what came out was not a word but a picture. The image of a man sprang from Luke's head, the most fully formed, identifiable figure he had produced yet. And not just an Everyman, but a man built from fear, a Dark Man, a man clothed in shadows. While before, Luke's images had been swathed in light and colour, this one was black, shades of black – non-colour, in fact, a black hole of a man, sucking in light, draining the landscape around of its vibrant colours.

The others at the picnic saw it and felt Luke's fear, felt the pulse of pain from which this demon had grown. The three adults drew back, horrified. The wonder of his previous "clouds" was replaced by a more stunned revulsion. But Sandy's reaction was different. She sensed that Luke's fear lay in something he had seen. She quickly moved over beside him, her legs more sure than they had ever felt before, and she wrapped her arms around him, holding his head to her chest. She muttered to him in the few words she had, "Gone, Luke, no fright, gone. OK?"

And the black cloud dispersed, slowly. Luke's breathing calmed, and the racing of his heart slowed. The two of them sat there, taking warmth and comfort from each other, while the adults sat and watched, excluded from their small world of understanding. Within five minutes, Luke had forgotten the dark men, whose dark purpose he could not guess. The picnic returned to lighter matters, although the three adults felt slightly colder, their hearts that bit heavier. Avril remembered the foreboding which had iced her soul that time when she was pregnant with Luke. The half-formed monster that Luke had just envisioned seemed to be a combination of all the faces from her dreams of those times, drained of all kindness and trust.

That night, Luke dreamed that a man came into his room. He wasn't afraid, because he recognised the man. He was a good man, not like those two who Luke had seen earlier in the day. An old man, long grey beard, flowing robes hemmed with moonlight. Luke remembered that this man had given him his favourite toy, Lenny, who he now hugged tightly. The small dog hugged him back.

The old man came up, bent over Luke and looked into his eyes. Luke returned his gaze, seeing smiling eyes, deeper and warmer than a tropical pool, a mist of light covering their innermost sanctuary. Luke recognised this misty light; he saw in it everything that was in his head. The old man spoke to him. His voice seemed older than the stars.

"I see you still have my gift, Luke."

Luke held out the toy puppy to the old man. "His name

is Lenny," he said. The sound of his own voice shocked him, until he remembered that he was in a dream. He wished that it was not a dream, that he could speak like that in the real world, and that this kind old man would stay to look after him.

The kind old man reached down and touched Luke lightly on the cheek. His hand was warm, and Luke felt a great power flowing between them. "I will always be around to look after you, Luke," he said, answering Luke's thoughts. "Just remember to keep Lenny by your side, and you will be safe." He paused, and his brow furrowed deeply. Luke was shocked at how old he looked. He continued, "I will be with you whenever you need me, Luke. But there are difficult times ahead. You must be careful, and you must look after your mother and father. Never forget their love for you."

Luke spoke again, each word ringing like a gold coin. "What is going to happen? Should I be afraid of it? Is there some danger ahead? How can I avoid it?"

The old man smiled, and as he did, he seemed to grow less substantial, translucent. Luke could see the bedroom wall through him. The old man's voice came to him, but from a distance now. "You have so many questions. Your first words, and they are all questions. But no, Luke. You cannot avoid what is to happen. Embrace it, because it is your life. Do not fear it. And remember, I am watching."

The old man flickered and faded. Luke reached out, wishing he could drag him back, but the last of his shape dissipated.

Luke woke up to see his bedroom door softly close. He strained his ears, thinking he could hear, very faintly, the swish of soft cloth against the wall. He tried to speak, but the words were gone from him again. He clutched Lenny tight in his arms, and a silent tear trickled down his cheek.

In a dim snug in a dim pub in a dim street somewhere in Dublin, two men were sitting anxiously waiting for a third man to speak. The third man bided his time, his face hidden in the smoky shadows of the corner. He took another long pull on his cigarette, blowing the smoke into the face of Alfie, the younger of the two men, who was barely out of his teens, his face still spotty and naïve. Alfie coughed and spluttered for a moment, tears starting in his eyes. The Dark Man in the corner watched him coldly while he tried to compose himself. He stubbed out his cigarette, turning to the other man, speaking in a soft, unhurried voice that seemed to carry a huge weight of violence.

"Tell me again. Why did you try to call to the door?"

The elder of the two flunkies, who called himself Banjo, tried to hold the other man's gaze, but he couldn't see his eyes in the shadows, so he spoke instead to his hands. "Well, we thought we could pretend we were hikers, looking for a bed for the night, and we might get a chance then to do it in the night, you know, when everybody else was asleep. Only, there was nobody in. So we had a quick scoot around, and then came straight back here."

"And nobody saw you?"

"No, they had all gone out."

"How do you know nobody saw you?"

Banjo was silent. The image of a small lonely kitten walking delicately across a pond of thin ice passed briefly through his mind. His boss lit another cigarette. He craved one desperately, but he said nothing.

"Next time," said the Dark Man, as softly as before, but with a knife-turning menace edging his voice, "when I ask you to get me information, I want you to report back to me with information only. When I want you to act, I want you to act, and only then. Now get out of my sight."

The two of them stood up, Alfie knocking over his stool in his haste to be out of that place. His bladder was bursting, but he didn't want to spend another minute in this pub. He'd hold out until he got home.

They didn't even know the Dark Man's name. He had contacted them out of the blue for this one job, as he described it, and he had made it clear that he would tell them only as much as he wanted to tell them. Besides, Alfie wasn't inclined to ask any questions. The money was all the answer he needed, and, for this one job, it was more than enough.

When they were gone, the man in the shadows tapped softly on the partition leading into the bar. The barman slid it open, a quizzical look on his face. "Another pint there, Paddy, like a good man."

Chapter Six

Luke stared in fascination at the black-and-white images on the screen. The grainy film held him in its thrall, the doomed lovers waiting at the border for the end to come. His eyes took in every detail of their faces, their gestures, and he sensed the great tragedy that awaited them on the other side. Their story was written in their bodies, and he felt his young soul ache at their sorrow.

The winter afternoons had given Luke his love of films. Now that he could no longer play in the long grass, his days centred on the early afternoon films. They were all he would watch on the television; Postman Pat and Bosco held no attraction for him, because they were never real. Luke was surrounded by adults – his parents, the guests. Sandy was the only other small person in his world, and he only saw her every couple of weeks. When he saw the grown-ups who populated the films, who looked like his parents, moved like them, talked like them, he knew that they were real. Puppets and cartoons were not. It was as simple as that. More than that, though, was the thrill of learning the language of pictures, seeing them move, telling more of a story than the words alone could.

So he filled his afternoons with thrillers and melodramas and gangsters and musicals, in black and white, in colour, in glorious Technicolor. His favourites, though, were the westerns. Those rough-hewn men riding across desert landscapes held a promise of a life of richness carved out from a solitary path which echoed of destiny to Luke. John Wayne, Jimmy Stewart, Alan Ladd, Lee Marvin, all crammed into his head with their mythic eyes, their sullen frowns, their stubborn jaws. As the camera caressed their weather-beaten faces, Luke breathed the same hoarse breaths they drew. For the first time in his short life, he began to see, through eyes not his own, the great expanse of life stretched before him.

In his mind, a Cowboy grew, a true hero. In his dreams, Luke saw him, a hazy figure standing in the sunlight in the distance, the only break on a borderless red horizon. He knew that he only had to call on him when he needed him, when life confused him, when fear threatened to overtake his small soul.

He looked up now at the sound of his mother's voice. She was talking to Fran, and Luke knew by her tone that they were discussing him. "I'm worried about him watching all of this," she said; though in truth she was feeling a little guilty, because they provided her long-winter-afternoon pleasure too. The guest-house was closed up until March, so she had begun to indulge herself in the matinees. Fran was usually occupied in the afternoons now; he had taken up fishing, and would spend many afternoons in tranquil isolation by the Avoca River. So she really blamed herself for getting Luke hooked on these films.

Fran was with her now, though, because she wanted to talk about Luke. "Maybe he needs some more stimulation," Fran suggested.

"What, though? The only toy he's interested in is that puppy." They looked at Luke sitting on the floor in front of the television. Lenny the puppy was sitting beside him, watching. The rest of Luke's toys were abandoned in a box in his bedroom.

"Maybe it's time we started him on reading. I think he's bright enough."

Avril picked out the obvious flaw in that. "How are we supposed to know if he is learning to read if he can't speak to us?" Fran looked disappointed, so Avril compromised. "Tell you what. We have to bring him in for a check-up with Dr Menton next week. We could take him around a few shops, and see if anything takes his interest. I've arranged to meet Mary afterwards, anyway."

"At least there's one good thing about him watching all these films. His clouds seem to have stopped for the moment."

Avril looked uncertain. "I don't know if I'd call that a good thing." They watched their son's shoulders lift and sag as the film ended. He continued staring at the screen. Avril sighed. "He just isn't himself. In fact, I don't think he has really been happy since the day we had that picnic. I wonder should I mention anything to the doctor?"

"Do you think we can trust her?"

"What?" Avril looked at Fran, a little bewildered by his question. "What do you mean?"

"Well, how do you tell somebody that your child has magical powers?"

Avril was startled. "I wasn't talking about Luke's . . . powers. I was talking about him being unhappy." Fran wouldn't meet her eyes. "Is there something else, Fran? Do you think we should tell somebody?"

Fran hesitated, so long that Avril thought he had switched off. He stared at the television. She was about to ask him the question again when he spoke. "I don't know any more, to tell the truth. It just seems as if we have accepted that Luke's . . . behaviour is natural. Strange, certainly, but natural. And we know nothing about it – what causes it, if it's ever happened to anyone else, why it's happened to Luke, what could happen to him in the future. The truth is, I think we've been running away from all these questions ever since he was born. If he's unhappy, maybe it's because he senses our own fears. The best way to find out is to talk to a doctor."

Avril looked down at her son again. She knew Fran was right. They had gone into denial, pretending that Luke was just a normal boy with an unusual way of expressing himself. But beyond that, they knew nothing. For all the love they had given him, their son was still something of a stranger to them. Maybe it would be for the best. It was time to come out of hiding.

Dr Fiona Menton swung her head from side to side in disbelief, looking at Fran and Avril in turn. Finally, she settled on looking at Luke, sitting silently between them. She stumbled over what she had to say, finally releasing her words in a rush.

"I've never heard anything like that before. I mean . . . surely it isn't possible?"

"I wish there was some way of proving it to you," said Avril, all apologies, "but it's as if he knows not to do it in public. Anyway, it's a few weeks since his last episode. So we can't show you exactly what we mean."

Fiona's mind was doing somersaults. Her natural scepticism was being assaulted on all sides. She wanted to shout out "I don't believe a word," but doubt rained down on her. Somehow, she knew these people were telling the truth. They had been coming here since Luke was born, and she realised now, in hindsight, that their visits always made her feel uneasy, as if there was something they weren't telling her.

His silence had intrigued her, leading her to believe that maybe there was something psychological. But, up to now, Fran and Avril had become evasive whenever she brought up the possibility of referring them to a psychologist. Now, she was no longer sure whether a psychologist would be enough. She decided to go for the gentle, probing approach.

"OK, let's suppose I wasn't looking for proof. Just say I believed you. What do you think the next step should be?" She wanted them to do most of the talking, because she herself really didn't know what the next step would be.

Avril and Fran looked uncertainly at each other. Had they made a mistake coming here? Avril finally spoke up. "We had hoped, I suppose, that you might know something . . . but – you've never come across anything else like this?" Fiona shook her head. Avril went on. "Well then, I suppose what we're hoping is that you might come to believe us, and that you might be able to help us."

"I see . . ." Fiona spoke slowly, uncertain whether to trust her own voice. "And what sort of help do you think I could give you? Do you want me to get some tests done, some sort of experiments? I know some people."

"No, no tests. I don't want Luke prodded or probed for the sake of a few scientists."

Fiona could see how strongly Avril felt about this, and decided it was best not to push it. "OK, what then? How can I help?"

Avril was losing confidence. "Well, I don't know. Maybe there's some way of finding out more about Luke?"

Fiona thought for a few moments. "Have you checked back with the hospital records on your son's birth?"

Another meaningful glance between the couple. This time, Fran answered her. "We rang them, and all they would say was that there were no complications, other than the fact that it was a home birth. But there was no report from the nurse, Jane O'Donnell. They said that was a little unusual, but they had no other information in the file. Which made us wonder if there had been something, but that it had been hidden or destroyed."

Fiona pondered this possibility. She knew of cases where hospital records had been held back from patients, but not in the case of a simple birth without complications, even if it was a home birth. She realised there must be some truth behind what these people had told her.

"I'll tell you what. I'll have a go at trying to view Luke's records in the hospital. I'll also do some research, to see if I can come up with anything, anything at all. In the meantime . . ." she hesitated, trying to put it delicately, "I know you don't want Luke tested, but . . . do you remember I mentioned that psychologist friend of mine, Gordon Richardson? Maybe you should contact him. He's a specialist in child psychology, and he may well come up with some answers." She paused, half-expecting an abrupt "no". She was wrong.

Avril nodded her head enthusiastically. "That sounds like a good idea. I'm not sure if it's connected with . . . the other thing, or with the fact that he is so quiet, but he has been a little out of sorts recently." She looked at Fran, who nodded encouragingly. "I suppose," she continued, "we have really just been avoiding the issue up to now. Maybe it's time we got to the bottom of it."

"OK, leave it with me, and I'll get back to you. I'll talk to Dr Richardson, and then I'll leave it up to yourselves to call him. Here's his number." She scribbled it on some notepaper. Then, looking directly at Avril, she said, "I'm not sure why, but against my reason, I do believe you. I hope I can help Luke." She offered her hand, and Avril shook it warmly.

"Thank you."

"Yeah, there they are now. Let's call in." From their beat-up Fiat across the street the two men watched the Lavertys leave the doctor's surgery. Alfie, who had just spoken, reached for the mobile phone on the dashboard.

Banjo got there first. "Jesus, will you wait till they get in their car. They might see us. They might get suspicious." Alfie went into a sulk.

When Fran and Avril reached their car, Banjo said, "Now!"

Alfie looked at him, puzzled.

"Now," repeated Banjo, "call the boss now."

"All right, all right, take it easy." He picked up the mobile phone and dialled as his partner started the engine with a rasp and a curse. When the phone was answered, he spoke in quick, nervous words. "Hello, boss? Yeah, it's Alfie. We're in pursuit again. Yeah. Yeah. Right. Okay, bye." He switched off the phone and laid it back on the dash.

Banjo, his eyes fixed firmly on the car ahead of them, said, "Well?"

The younger man said, "Well, first opportunity. Grab him and get him to the safe house. He'll meet us there."

Banjo grumbled. "I don't understand that man. We've had all this time down the country, and all he could say was, *don't act*. Now he wants us to do it right in the middle of the city, in the middle of a bleedin' crowd. Fuck's sake."

Mary waved across the department-store café to attract Fran and Avril's attention. Luke saw her first, saw Sandy on her lap. He struggled to get out of his mother's arms. Avril spotted them then, and set Luke down on the ground, where he immediately tried to run towards his friend. Avril kept a firm grip on his hand as he strained his body in the effort to reach Sandy. There was no way she was going to let him go; he would probably crash headlong into the nearest table. As soon as they reached the table, Luke and Sandy scrambled under it to renew their acquaintance.

Fran, Avril and Mary greeted one another warmly. As she always did when they met, Avril said a small mental "thank you" to God for Mary's friendship. She had, in many ways, been their main link to their old life, indeed to the outside world, since they had "gone underground". Avril had come to see her as a sister, to whom she could confide all her concerns. Mary always had some piece of sense to clear Avril's conscience. As they settled down at the table, Avril noticed an immense sadness in her friend's face, and was immediately worried for her. Before she could ask, a waitress arrived to take their order, and by the time she had left, Mary had hidden whatever troubled her behind her businesswoman's tight smile, though her eyes betrayed a well of emotions. She spoke first.

"So how was the visit to the doctor?"

Fran told her they were referring Luke to a psychologist.

Mary nodded thoughtfully. "That mightn't be such a bad idea. I suppose no harm has been done up to now, but none of us really knows what's going on in Luke's head. I presume, then, that you did tell the doctor everything?"

"Yes, more or less." Fran went silent for a moment, lost in thought. He looked straight at Avril next time he spoke. "I just wonder – assuming Dr Menton and this psychologist aren't able to find anything more – if we shouldn't . . . go public about Luke." Avril's face drained of its colour. Fran quickly went on, before he could be shot down completely. "Just bear with me for a minute. Mary's right. We don't know what this thing is, or what it could do in the future. But somebody out there might. If it is the only road open to us, maybe it's the one we need to take. Besides which, we have been incredibly lucky up to now that so few people know about Luke. But what's going to happen when he starts going to school? We can't shelter him forever. Surely it would be better to make everybody aware that Luke is a . . . special child, rather than having him suddenly burst into light in the middle of the classroom?" Fran thought of something else. "Anyway, maybe that's why he seems so down at the moment. Maybe we've been overprotective. Like, how many friends does he have, apart from your Sandy, Mary? How many of our neighbours do we know? How many of them have kids?"

Fran paused for breath while the waitress arrived with their coffees and sandwiches. It was a long speech for him, and he didn't want to spoil it by over-stressing the point. He watched a wave of confusion rippling across Avril's face. He could see her almost physically fighting off fear. When the waitress had gone, she took a deep breath and quietly asked, "And how exactly do you propose 'going public'?"

"Well," Fran was already losing confidence, regretting his outburst, but he had to make his point. "There are two things we can do. We can tell the relevant people – schoolteachers, neighbours, friends – but where would we stop? Would we tell all his classmates, their parents . . . ? How long before the rumours became public property? How long before we'd get all these half-wits camping on our doorstep again? The alternative is to do it ourselves, the way we want it done. To go to the press ourselves, instead of waiting for them to come to us. Send it out as a sort of appeal, to anybody who might be able to help us. If we do it right, it will work out better for Luke in the end – "

Avril cut him off with a question. "So how exactly would you go about making this 'appeal'?" Her voice was sharp, warning of the anger that was welling inside her. The thing was, her anger was not really focused on Fran. It was twisted inwards, at her own sense of uncertainty, at the glimmer of reality that told her Fran might be right.

"I don't know," her husband answered her. "Maybe we could go on the radio, or the television. Or that journalist, maybe we could use him. What was his name . . . McGinnity?"

"*What?*" Avril was incredulous now, suddenly snapping her anger into focus, pointing it directly at Fran.

"Well, I got the impression last time we met him that he really regretted how he had treated us. I genuinely think he could be helpful to us. Remember? He said something about telling Luke's story how we wanted it told."

"*Never!*" Avril flashed at him. "My God, Fran, I can't believe you would even think of letting that man near our son again. No way! I am not going to turn Luke into some kind of media freak, not through McGinnity, not through anybody. He's *my* son, and I will look after him."

Suddenly, Mary burst into wild tears. In the intensity of their argument, Fran and Avril had almost forgotten she was there. Now, Avril realised that she was in turmoil. She had never seen Mary's raw vulnerability so exposed. All their animosity vanished as they went to comfort her. "Mary, love, what is it?"

Between sobs, Mary managed to tell them what was troubling her. "It's Sandy. She's getting weaker. The doctors say that her best chance might be a lung transplant in a few years. She'll be put on a waiting list and in four, maybe five years, they might do the operation." Her voice had gone very small. "I don't think she'll last that long, myself. I don't think she'll make it." Her tears had dried up, and her face had become a blank mask. Avril held her, unsure what to say. Fran looked on helplessly, feeling as though he had been selfish, trying to claim too great a share of hurt for himself and his child. Mary's tears put it all in context.

Suddenly, Fran exclaimed, "Oh Jesus, where are they?" He ducked down, searching under the empty table on the off-chance that the two children might suddenly reappear, clinging to its underside. But they had vanished. The two women, startled out of their tears, jumped up from their chairs, spilling coffee, glancing around frantically. Luke and Sandy were nowhere to be seen. Avril called out to Luke, a note of panic gilting her voice. No response. By now, everyone in the department-store café was glancing around to see what the commotion was. The waitress quickly came over to see what was wrong.

Mary's tears dried quickly in the immediacy of the crisis. She was focused and determined again, and she told the waitress that the two children had gone missing.

The waitress, quickly switching herself into saviour mode, asked them for a description; Avril and Mary between them managed to describe Luke and Sandy, and the waitress managed to immediately confuse them. She cleared her throat, picturing herself in front of a vast crowd, and addressed the assembled masses.

"Excuse me, could I have your attention please? These two ladies have lost their children, a little boy called Luke and a little girl called Sarah."

"Sandy," interrupted Mary.

The waitress went on, scarcely missing a beat: "Sorry,

the girl's name is Sandy. They are both three years old. Sandy has dark brown hair, and Luke has red hair."

"No, it's the other way around."

"Sorry, it's the other way around. Sandy – the little girl – was wearing a pair of blue jeans – "

"No, that was Luke."

The waitress faltered. She was beginning to panic. A small bead of sweat sprang out of her forehead, trickled down her cheek, and across her upper lip. Her tongue shot out and licked it away. The salt taste brought her round. She swallowed and spoke again. "Did anybody see these two children leaving the restaurant?"

"Sorry, but don't you think you should make an announcement on the intercom?" asked Avril, but the waitress didn't hear her.

A few people muttered about seeing them under the table. A stout woman, who had been trying to speak throughout the waitress's oration, finally saw her opportunity. "Yes, I saw them over there, beside the electrical goods." She pointed a stubby finger into the main body of the shop, which was separated from the café by a wooden barrier. "They seemed to be playing some sort of game, hide-and-seek or something. There was another woman looking at some gadgets; I thought she was their mother. I didn't see where they went after that."

Mary was exasperated. It was time to take control of the situation. "Oh, for God's sake! Where's the customer-service desk? You have to make an announcement before they leave the shop!"

The waitress blushed. "Right. I was just getting to that," she said, all flustered. "And I'll get the security guards on the doors to keep an eye open. Don't worry, we'll find them." She gave them a smile that she hoped was reassuring, and went to perform her task.

Mary turned to the other two. "OK, they can't have got far. They're probably still on this floor, but we can't be sure. Why don't we split up? I'll look on this floor. Avril, you can try the ground floor. Fran, you go down to the basement. They're bound to show up."

As the three of them ran in opposite directions, the announcement came over the intercom. It was all so unreal; Avril felt as though she was moving through a dreamworld.

The sales assistant in the haberdashery department had been watching the two men closely for some time. They had aroused his suspicions after their brusque dismissal of his "Can I help you?" He made no secret of his suspicions, trying to stare them out, hoping they would go away. But they took no notice of him. They were intent on looking in the direction of the café, largely ignoring the fine silks which they were idly running through their fingers. The assistant was considering calling a manager but he remained rooted to the spot, afraid that if he moved, they would attack him. As he was thinking this, he realised that something was happening.

There was some commotion in the café that made the two men perk up. It looked as though a small group of people were in distress, and the sales assistant recognised Linda, the waitress he had asked out last week (he blushed now, remembering her excuses), who was talking to the people. When she turned to the diners, he tried to make out her words, but the distance was too great. He switched his attention back to the two men, who were also straining to follow the exchanges. The younger of the two men whispered, "What's goin' on?" but was shushed by his companion.

As Linda bustled over towards the customer-service desk and the three people she had been speaking to also left the café, the two men dropped the fine silks they had been mauling, to the considerable annoyance of the sales assistant, and began to walk away. As he hurried to rearrange his precious goods, the sales assistant heard the public announcement over the intercom – "... *two small children ... their names are Sandy and Luke, and they are wearing* ..."

"Shit!" The assistant distinctly heard one of the men say. "How could we have missed them?" Then they moved out of earshot, so that he missed the other man's reply: "This could be our chance. If we find them before the parents or anybody else, we might be able to do it. Let's split up."

The sales assistant followed them with his eyes until they disappeared behind the soft furnishings.

Luke had so much to say to Sandy. He wanted to tell her all about the Cowboy, for one thing. He wanted to show her how real he was, how much of a hero he was. Luke knew that Sandy was weak. He could see it in her eyes. They didn't dance as much as they used to. He wanted to tell her that the Cowboy could help her, could bring her to a place where her sickness would disappear when she let the light flow in, the nourishing light. He, Luke, could come with her to this place – he was her friend, after all. The Cowboy would do whatever he asked. When they got there, they would be happy.

All these thoughts jostled for space in Luke's head as he sat under the table with Sandy. He didn't know why he couldn't say them to her, not even through light. In fact, he didn't know why his "clouds" had stopped at all. He still had as much to say but for some reason, in the last while, he was unable to open the box of colours which he held at the back of his head. Try as he might, the lines of communication had closed down on him; that was why he was sad, frustrated by his own inarticulacy, and he didn't know why. All he knew was, he was bursting to tell Sandy all about the Cowboy but, for now, it simmered just below the surface.

Sitting under the table, they were just glad to see each other now. They watched the adults' legs for a while, fascinated by the way their feet shifted every now and then, as if they were trying to get away from the rest of their bodies. For a couple of minutes, they played a game of dodge-the-feet, trying to anticipate when each foot was going to move so that they didn't get kicked. When they got bored with that, though, they just wrapped their arms around each other and played a game of rubbing noses; then Luke put his right eye up as close as possible to Sandy's, so that their eyelashes tickled each other, and they stared deep into each other's pupils. They sat like that for what seemed like a long time. Luke thought he could see his own reflection in the very depths of Sandy's eye, peering back out at him. It looked so small and lonely. Sandy could just see a mist, unfocused, drifting, but in the middle of it she finally distinguished a figure: not herself, but a tall man with a big hat, riding on a big horse through the mist. She blinked as an eyelash stung the surface of her eye, raising a tear, blurring the image. She had to pull away.

Sandy thought she recognised the man. She had seen him just minutes before, she was sure of it. In this shop! She took a firm grip on Luke's hand and began to move. Luke sat still, puzzled. Sandy jerked on his hand, indicating that she wanted him to follow her. They listened for a minute to the muted sound of the adults talking intensely above them. Then they crawled out from under the table, straight under the wooden barrier and on to the shop floor. They stood up and looked back at their parents; they hadn't been spotted. Sandy looked around, uncertain of which way to go. They made a few false starts, running this way and that. Finally, she picked an aisle, and they disappeared down it.

Avril's panic was rising when each turn she took, each aisle she peered down, failed to reveal the two children safe and well. A million thoughts raced through her head, crashing into each other, making no sense. She blamed herself. Then she blamed Fran. She was an inadequate mother. She couldn't understand her own child. He'd been sent here to torture her. It had all been a dream, and he had never really existed.

None of her thoughts made sense to her. But something pulsed deeper, an older fear, a sixth sense of anxiety which overruled all her thoughts. She instinctively felt that Luke was in danger. Children went missing in shops every day of the week, she told herself. Luke himself had almost wandered off a couple of times previously when her vigilance had slipped. But this felt different. There was a quality of foreboding in the air. That sense of brooding uncertainty which had first arisen when she was pregnant, that time when she had caught a glimpse of her son's life-to-be; that had sprung up a few times since the birth, most recently on the day of the picnic, when something beyond her comprehension had traumatised Luke to the point where he had given them all that view of a Dark Man; that same sense of fear now clung to her like glue, slowing reality down until she felt as though she was moving in slow-motion, her legs heavier than lead, her heart a plodding rhythm.

Suddenly, a thought struck her. Just a few aisles away, the toy department began. Of course! Where else would a pair of wandering children head? All her thoughts of dread slipped away, the rhythms of her body returned to normal, a huge breath of relief escaped her lungs as she raced to where she knew they would be. And then her heart stalled.

Avril, like most people in the department store, had never heard a gunshot before, but the sound was nevertheless unmistakable. She paused for just a moment, and then began to run, a scream rising in her throat.

In the forest of hurrying legs, nobody had noticed that the two small children holding hands were not accompanied by an adult. When Luke and Sandy stepped on the escalator, their parents had only just noticed their absence. The harried Christmas shoppers didn't spare them a second glance.

Luke was happy for the first time in ages. He was on a great adventure with Sandy, and there were no parents to call a halt. The escalator both fascinated and sickened them. They clung tightly to each other as they stepped on, and lurched as they felt themselves floating slightly off-balance. To distract himself from the movement, Luke watched the funny brush-like thing at the edge. He stuck his foot out to it, thinking he could give his shoes a bit of a polish, but quickly withdrew it when it began to move in the opposite direction to the one he was going. He felt Sandy squeezing his hand, and he saw that they were approaching the end. They braced themselves and jumped just before they were swallowed up by the monster they feared might live under the escalator. They had done it! They were both dizzy after the ride, and they giggled, Luke silently as ever. Sandy looked around, and saw where they needed to go: the toy department.

Suddenly, Luke was aware of his name drifting across the air. He wasn't sure where it came from, but it sounded like somebody was looking for him. He thought it would be fun if they hid. He pulled Sandy's hand, and they dived in behind a rack of long coats. From there, they took quick, darting runs between hiding places. Gradually, they got closer and closer to the toy department.

Alfie stepped onto the down escalator. He patted the pocket of his trenchcoat nervously. He didn't like guns, and he certainly didn't see the need for one in this case. "If things get nasty," that's what the boss had said. Banjo, on the other hand, relished having a gun. It gave him a rush, he said. Some sort of power trip, thought Alfie. Himself, he had no such illusions. He glanced around fitfully now, worried that he was being watched, that somebody – everybody – would see the gun and know what he was up to.

A movement on the lower floor caught his swivelling eyes, something that didn't register as an ordinary shopper. He stared at the spot, and then he saw them: two children flitting across the shop floor, and merging again into shadow.

He thought, maybe I should go back and get Banjo. But the escalator was still going down, down, and he thought, I'll probably just lose them again. I'll have to try to do this myself.

Sandy and Luke emerged from behind a mirror, and scuttled across the floor to the toy department. Luke realised they had finished their little game. Sandy was looking for something. She pulled Luke along rows of fluffy pink bunnies, glamorous supermodel dolls, miniature prams and vanity sets; she began to slow her pace when they reached the toy guns, the model cars, the action men. Boys' toys. She stopped in front of the action men, stacked up in their plastic homes for what looked like miles above their heads, and she scanned the rows. Finally, she saw him.

She shook Luke's arm to attract his attention, and pointed up at one box. Its occupant stared down at them stoically, giving them a clear message: *Don't y'all mess with me.* His bright yellow shirt, ten-gallon hat, spurs, holster belt and gun were all familiar. Luke immediately recognised his Cowboy. A broad grin lit his face as he looked at Sandy gratefully. He leaned over and gave her a peck on the cheek. She squeezed his hand. He turned back and tried to reach up for the Cowboy, but the shelf was too high up.

A gruff adult voice from behind startled them. "Here, let me get that for you, little man." A hand descended, plucked the Cowboy from the shelf and put it in Luke's hands. Luke spun around and looked up at his benefactor. A chill of rec-ognition went through him, and he took a step backwards, still holding Sandy's hand. He looked around frantically for an escape route. He wanted to scream, but of course he couldn't. Somewhere at the back of his eye, the Cowboy was galloping. The man reached his hand out towards him, a glint in his eye. "Would you like to go for a walk, little man. I can show you a real gun." He grabbed Luke's hand roughly, and Luke exploded.

A searing flash of light sent Alfie reeling backwards. A million colours prickled the back of his retinas; for one heartbeat, he was blinded. He lost his balance and fell over. He blinked rapidly, his eyes desperately trying to focus. When he could see, at least partially, the first sight that awaited him was a giant. The Cowboy was huge, seven feet tall or more, and made entirely of light. It was as though all the constellations in the heavens had been refracted through a prism, projecting this concentrated wave of energy, which just happened to look like a huge Cowboy. His eyes shone with celestial vision. The wide brim of his hat spun like the rings of Saturn. His belt was the Milky Way. A billion stars glinted off his stubbled chin. His breath was a supernova of power.

The Cowboy took a step towards hapless, spreadeagled Alfie. The Cowboy's gun glistened in his holster like the mighty bow of Orion. The Cowboy's expression made no bones. The pathetic figure lying on the ground swore later that he heard the clank of spurs, the whinnying of a horse, and something deeper, some primeval growl of rage. Alfie pushed himself backwards on the ground and fumbled for his own gun. As the towering figure came closer to him, he drew it, aimed with trembling hands, and fired.

The bullet went straight through the Cowboy, registering only as a slight dimming of his brightness, which quickly flared up again as, behind him, the bullet passed through a giant panda and lodged harmlessly in the wall. Alfie scrabbled around on the floor, crablike, his arms flailing as the Cowboy took another step. Somehow, Alfie managed to find a shelf to grip, hauled himself to his feet and immediately began to run, waving the gun frantically around. He kept running as he reached the glass doors of the shop (the security guards steering a wide berth), which closed again behind him as he disappeared into the crowd.

The Cowboy didn't follow him. Instead, he turned his attention to the two children. They too had fallen to the ground in the flash of light. The scowl of anger on the Cowboy's face quickly melted. He grinned, showing a swirling nebula of teeth. He bent down and gently lifted the children to their feet. He looked around and saw Avril, who had just spun around the corner. Her first thought was to breathe a sigh of relief when she saw the children unhurt. Her second was, *Oh my God.* She stared in awe at this huge man, whom she knew instinctively to be a creation of her son's imagination, as he strolled unhurriedly to her, his knees comically bent so that he could hold the children's hands.

A small crowd had gathered, drawn by the gunfire and the commotion, and they stared dumbfounded at the giant pillar of light dressed in the Cowboy suit. He reached the place where Avril stood rooted. He let go of the children's hands and gently pushed them from behind. Avril, as though in a dream, reached out and pulled them to her. She muttered a "thank you". The Cowboy tipped his hat to her. He grinned and winked at Luke, and Luke grinned back. And then he was gone. Vanished. The lights in the shop dimmed for a moment, and everybody blinked, unsure they had seen anything.

Fran reached the scene, quickly followed by Mary. He ran to Avril, and together they lifted their son and hugged him. Mary picked Sandy up and kissed her. They stood like that for a few moments, until they gradually became aware of the stunned crowd of people, who stood in a circle around them. Fran glanced at Luke and asked his wife, "Was he . . .? Did he . . . ?"

"Yes," said Avril. She smiled at him, and Fran was surprised at the mischievous look on her face. "Well, what's that you were saying about going public? I think Luke has decided that for himself."

Chapter Seven

Avril and Fran crouched over two cups of hot chocolate in the waiting-room of the Garda station. They were watching Luke, who was quite unconcerned with all the trouble he had caused. He was playing with the plastic cowboy which he had begged Avril to buy for him before they left the shop. To look at him, he was an ordinary boy playing an ordinary game.

"At least he seems happy now," Fran whispered softly, almost afraid to break the fragile peace that surrounded his son.

Earlier – it felt so long ago – the police had arrived at the shop within a few minutes. There seemed little point in trying to disappear. Everybody was aware that the small group huddled together was the centre of attention. The gardaí quickly questioned all the witnesses, of whom there were many among the Christmas shoppers. Somewhere between garbled versions of events, in which talk of giant cowboys and dazzling lights seemed to play a major part, they got the gist of what had happened. They decided to bring the parents down to the station to make a fuller statement. There, things got a little complicated.

"So you have no idea why this man was after your son?"

Avril hesitated, looking at Fran for support. "Well . . . no, not really."

The desk sergeant who was taking their statement was a sceptic. "Not really?" he repeated.

"No."

"Okay, then, Mr and Mrs Laverty. Do you know who this other individual was, the one dressed as a cowboy?"

"No." Avril was miserable. Her emotions were in turmoil. She felt as though the world was about to claim Luke for its own purposes, and there was nothing she could do about it, but she wanted to fight it stubbornly to the end.

The fruitless interview was interrupted just then by the Inspector who was heading the investigation. He was a tall man with a grandfatherly face and greying sideburns. He played his role as guardian of the peace with an old-fashioned relish, rubbing his hands together. "Sorry, Seán, could I borrow the Lavertys for a minute? There's something I'd like them to have a look at."

Mary was already waiting in the small conference room. Inspector Alan Moroney began, "We've recovered the closed-circuit video from the shop. I'd like you to see some extracts from it." The video was poor quality, but it was clear enough to make out the main actors. The first extract showed two men standing in the haberdashery department.

Avril immediately reacted. "That's him, the one on the right. That's the man who attacked my son."

Inspector Moroney made a note, before looking up and asking Avril, "Have you ever seen him or his companion before?"

"No."

"OK; let me just change the video here." The Inspector laboriously switched between videos each time the relevant section had finished. The result was a sort of delayed montage of images, but the effect was as mesmerisingly scary for the watchers as a finely edited horror movie. The scene built up before their eyes: themselves sitting in the café, the two children sneaking out from under the table, the escalator, the two men splitting up, glimpses of the children flitting between coat-racks, one of the men again in pursuit, and then finally, the reason why the Inspector was showing them the tapes in the first place.

The two children looked so small on the screen, dwarfed further by the angle of the camera, as they arrived in the toy department. A brief pause, and then the man appeared, looking around him anxiously before approaching the children from behind. The sense of menace was unmistakable as he reached his hand out for Luke. And then the explosion happened. The camera reeled in the burst of light. It took a few seconds for the video to recover from this major over-exposure, and then the figure of the Cowboy materialised on the screen. Even in the harsh, slightly blurred black-and-white of the closed-circuit system, his appearance was dazzling. He appeared to have his own light source, pulsing and sparking. And, given the angle of the camera, his seven-foot frame was even more intimidating, the head and shoulders disproportionately large. In fact, the wide brim of his ten-gallon hat, with its swirling stars, blocked out a large section of the screen. The two children were hidden from view, and all that was visible of Luke's potential assailant was a horrified, bewildered face. He scrambled back, and his full body became visible as he fumbled with his gun. The silent screen didn't register the sudden explosion of the shot, but the gun jumped in his hands, and a brief disturbance ruffled the Cowboy's check shirt. The man with the gun was on his feet and running. He disappeared from the screen. Avril's startled form appeared in one corner of the screen, and the last shot was of the Cowboy handing the children over to her before vanishing. Inspector Moroney pressed "pause", and Avril stood there, wavering, with the children at either side. Luke had his hand raised in a farewell gesture to the barely discernible, ghostly after-image, all that remained of the Cowboy.

They stared at this flickering image for a full minute. The Inspector drummed his fingers loudly on the table, his eyes darting between the screen and the faces of the others. Finally, he broke the spell, asking gruffly, "So, do any of you people know what the hell happened there?"

Fran and Avril looked at each other, long and hard. Avril nodded, a tiny, almost imperceptible gesture, which only Fran was meant to notice. He nodded in reply, and, looking up at Moroney, began. For the second time that day, he told the whole story, right from the beginning. The Inspector proved less willing to believe that Luke possessed magical powers than Dr Menton had been, but he at least had evidence before his eyes of something beyond his understanding. This kept his attention fixed on everything Fran had to say. When Fran had finished, Moroney sat for a long moment, everything he had believed in, and many things he had not, clashing swords in his head. Eventually, it was the pragmatic compartment of his brain that caused his mouth to move.

"Listen," he said, measuring every word, "I don't know whether to believe what you've just told me. But I do know that you believe it yourself. The thing is, I have an investigation to run, and I have a criminal – possibly two – to track down. Two things: if your son can do all the things you say he can, then we may very well have a motive for his near-abduction." Avril started. The word had thrown her offbalance. Inspector Moroney held up his hand, indicating that he wasn't finished yet. "I believe, from witness statements, and from the evidence of this tape, that that man was trying to kidnap your son. For what purposes, I don't know; but if what you say is true, or rather if you believe it is true, then it is possible that this man, or somebody he works for, may have got wind of it, and, for reasons of his own may want to use your son for some ulterior purpose." The Inspector hammered the air with a fingertip, emphasising every word of the last sentence. Then he leaned back in his chair, impressed with his own powers of deductive reasoning.

Fran spoke up. "Two things?"

"I beg your pardon?"

"You said 'two things'."

Moroney brought his chair to rest on the floor, and began again. "Number two. We're investigating a shooting incident, which is what you might call a newsworthy event. It's very likely that it will be reported on the TV news tonight. We appear to have two criminals at large, and we have a videotape which makes them clearly identifiable. My gardaí are currently looking at freeze-frame photographs of these two men. It is possible that we will be able to identify them within the next few hours, or even make an early arrest. But if this doesn't happen, the next step may well be to broadcast these extracts on the news, and appeal for anybody who knows the men to come forward." He paused, looking for reaction from the others, but they kept their counsel, so he continued, "Now, it's quite possible that we could simply show some of the earlier pieces, and leave out the last extract, the one with your son and the . . .

113

Cowboy. But there were a lot of witnesses, and my feeling is that it's bound to come out sooner or later. Maybe it would be as well for you to talk to the media yourselves, give your version of events, before they come after you."

Fran was nodding. He looked at Avril, leaving it to her to decide. She looked downcast, resigned. She shrugged. "Maybe this is the right time."

The Inspector left them in the waiting-room to talk things over. Mary left with Sandy shortly afterwards. She offered them her full support, but they could tell she was reluctant to share the limelight with them. Sandy wasn't well, after all, and she'd had enough excitement for one day. So Fran and Avril were left alone with Luke for the first time in hours.

Avril yawned. "I'm so tired, Fran. I wish we could just go home."

"We can, if you really want to. We can forget about all of this and just leave."

Avril was sorely tempted, but she sighed, looking at Luke playing on the floor. "No, you're right. I think it's time we faced up to this. What do you think is the best way to handle it?"

Fran took a deep breath and told her the plan he'd been formulating all afternoon. They'd contact Jimmy McGinnity, who could write their story. (Avril shivered once at the name, but said nothing.) Then they would hold a press conference. Fiona Menton, in the meantime, could keep checking for medical precedents.

"I reckon Luke will be in the news for a week, two weeks at most. Then they'll find something else to talk about. In the meantime, hopefully, they'll catch those two men. And we may know more about Luke's condition. Who knows, we might even hear from somebody just like him."

* * *

They finally trudged home about six o'clock that evening. Fran set about trying to trace McGinnity. Most of the newspapers had never heard of him. Finally, he found two who only had old addresses. He tried the two phone numbers he got from these sources. Both were flats, and neither had ever heard of McGinnity. He had obviously moved on. Fran tried the phonebook, but neither of the two McGinnitys listed had any connection with Jimmy. (He never thought of looking in the Golden Pages under *Private Investigators*, of course, where he would have found a small ad: *Matrimonial investigations, covert surveillance, mysteries solved: Call J McGinnity at – .*) Eventually, Fran decided to give it up, just as Avril called him in to see the news.

Sure enough, the story featured prominently. The shooting in the Dublin department store and the mysterious stranger who vanished from the video footage, which they duly showed. "Garda sources told us they are following a number of lines of enquiry," said the newscaster. "They have appealed for anybody who may recognise either of the two men, who are both clearly visible in the closed-circuit video footage, to come forward. Anyone with information should contact the gardaí at Store Street. As for the mysterious man dressed as a cowboy, the garda sources say that they hope to make a statement at a press conference on Thursday regarding his identity. However, they have ruled out the theory that he was part of a new elite crime-fighting branch of the force . . ." That was pretty much everything. There was no mention of Luke, or of a possible kidnap attempt. Inspector Moroney was obviously leaving all that to the press conference, which he had arranged with Fran and Avril for the following Thursday.

Within half an hour of the news item, the telephone rang. Fran went to answer it. When he returned, a look of bemusement etched his brow. "That was Inspector Moroney," he told Avril. "Apparently, McGinnity saw the news, and called Store Street straight away. He wants us to call him."

McGinnity had recognised Avril the moment he saw her face on the screen. At first, he couldn't think where he had seen her; then she was reunited with Luke, and it all came together in his mind. And what's more, here was evidence of that very thing which he had been pursuing for so long: a magic child. The seven-foot man of light might have been a mystery to everybody else watching the news item. But to Jimmy McGinnity, it made perfect sense. Why not a cowboy?

After all this time, he almost laughed at how easily the story he had vainly pursued had suddenly burst into the public domain. Nobody had believed him then; surely nobody would believe his claim over this story now? He'd be just another washed-up hack journalist jumping on the bandwagon. But he wasn't a journalist anymore. He was a private investigator. He was no longer just somebody who chased a story; his new role was to piece together the links so that a story made sense. It was with this in mind that he reached for the phone and dialled Store Street.

By four o'clock that day, Alfie and Banjo had reached the rendezvous, where they waited for the boss for a good half an hour. That was just enough time for Banjo to give Alfie a black eye. "Jesus, you're fuckin' lucky we aren't both in the nick right now – or worse, lying dead after a major gun battle with the cops."

Alfie, nursing his wounds sulkily in a corner of the room, grimaced at his former partner's vivid imagination, but said nothing.

"Mind you, lucky is not the word for it," Banjo continued. "The boss'll fuckin' kill us after that fiasco. One of us, at least, is for the chop, and I'm making damn sure it's not me." He stood across the door, ready to block any sudden attempts at flight by the pathetic heap in the corner.

Alfie was going nowhere, however. After what he had seen that day, the thought of the boss's wrath was almost a blessing to him. The glint from that Cowboy's gun would be forever etched at the back of his eyeballs.

Suddenly, the boss was standing between them, appearing from nowhere. A bewildered Banjo looked quickly at the door, wondering how he had got past him. Alfie had no such curiosity. The expression on the boss's face was sufficient: he knew, somehow, he already knew. Maybe he was checking us out; maybe he had somebody spying on us, to see if we cocked up. Which we did. Alfie had no illusions about how "close" he and Banjo were to the boss. He was still nothing but a shadow to them. But he certainly paid well, for a shadow.

The boss stood there for a long minute, looking calmly at each of them. His eyes were black holes of untold rage. When he finally spoke, they had to strain their ears to hear his words, which came out in a low whisper. "I don't want to know. I don't want any excuses, and I don't want any pleading." He reached into his pocket. Banjo's hand instinctively went for his gun, prepared, though he knew it was crazy, to defend his last scrap of life.

But the boss pulled out two bundles of documents, handing one to each of them. "Two tickets for the next boat from Dun Laoghaire, and some false papers, including two passports," he told them, his voice a knife-edge of control. "And this is what I owe you." Two thick wads of notes. "You failed me. By rights, I should kill the two of you. But I'm a generous man, and I don't like to waste resources." He paused, and a weary look passed briefly over his normally expressionless face. Then he went on, "Anyway, I think it's probably for the best. I think I acted too soon. He isn't ready."

The two thugs looked at each other, not understanding what he was talking about. The Dark Man continued, "You might be valuable to me in the future. So I'm putting you on the boat. In an hour's time, you'll be out of the country. I want you to disappear. If you're caught, your lives will be worthless. If you try to contact me again, I'll see to it that you never set foot in Ireland again. If I need you, you'll hear from me. Don't worry, I'll find you." With that, he turned on his heel and walked out.

Alfie and Banjo looked at each other again. Their mutual animosity vanished in the suddenly chilly air. They looked down at the money, and then at the tickets. One way. Alfie noticed that they'd been bought the day before.

Fran held off from calling McGinnity for as long as possible. Now that the time had come to make a move, he had serious doubts about the course of action he had decided upon. Not least of these was the unpredictability of McGinnity, a man he and his wife had only met on a couple of occasions, and then hardly under the best circumstances.

In the end, it was Avril herself, who had been so reluctant to even hear the man's name mentioned, who spurred him to it. "Look, if you aren't going to call him, then give me the number. Maybe I'll call him. Or maybe I'll rip it up."

The phone had almost rung out when McGinnity answered it. When Fran announced who he was, the world-weary voice at the other end of the line sounded unsurprised. "Ah, Mr Laverty. I've been expecting your call. For quite a while, in fact."

Fran didn't waste any time, but got straight to the point. "I take it you saw this evening's news, Mr McGinnity?"

"Indeed I did, Mr Laverty. Your wife is looking as lovely as ever."

Fran ignored this last remark. "You'll have seen, then, some of the strange things that happen around my son, Luke? Things you once described as 'miracles'?"

"Yes?" McGinnity answered cagily. He had scarcely expected the Lavertys to ring him back at all. He certainly hadn't expected them to be so forthcoming. There had to be a catch, surely.

Fran went on, "Mr McGinnity, I know we haven't exactly seen eye to eye in the past, but we're now in a position to make you an offer."

"Offer?"

"Yes. You told us you'd like to have an exclusive story. Luke's story, the way we wanted it told. Well, we'd now like to meet up with you, to discuss you writing this story."

"I see . . . and why, if I might ask, have you suddenly decided to come to me with this after all this time?"

Fran was a bit taken aback. He'd expected McGinnity to jump at the chance. Instead, he sounded wary, unconvinced. "Well, we just realise that it isn't going to go away, and we'd like you to put the record straight before everything gets out of hand."

There was a long pause at the other end of the line. A battle was raging in Jimmy McGinnity's head. He was sorely tempted to take up Laverty's offer. It was, after all, what he had wanted for so long. And yet . . . he had abandoned journalism, and felt quite content with his life as a private dick. He was doing better now. The thought of going down that road again frankly sickened him. Fran heard a reluctant sigh. "Well, now, Mr Laverty. The truth is, I'm not in that line of business any more. I've given up journalism. I'm a detective now, a private investigator. I'm actually quite good at it. So, I'm not really interested in writing your story anymore."

Fran experienced a strange mixture of disappointment and relief. A thought struck him. "You might still be able to help us, then. We'd like to find out more about Luke's condition. We already have a couple of people checking it out for us. But somebody like yourself might be able to find out more – if you're as good as you say you are. We'd pay you at the going rate, of course . . ."

They talked on for a good half an hour. Fran filled in the gaps in Jimmy's patchwork knowledge of their story, and Jimmy suggested a number of possible leads he could follow. By the time he rang off, Fran was feeling more confident they had made the right decision.

Inspector Moroney called the following day to say that they had identified the two men in the shop as Ben "Banjo" O'Reilly and Alan "Alfie" McCabe. Unfortunately, neither man had returned to his home since the shooting incident. Interestingly, while both had criminal records as petty thieves, neither had, to the knowledge of the gardaí, been involved in anything for a number of years. In fact, both wives claimed that their husbands were "clean", and, as Moroney said, "They sounded like they believed what they were saying". There was no evidence of links between them and any other known criminals, major or minor. Nobody had seen or heard from them since the previous day. "We suspect," said Moroney, "that they may have left the country. We'll continue our investigation at this end, and we'll put the word out internationally."

Inspector Moroney hesitated. At the other end of the line, Avril sensed what he was going to say next and prompted him. "What about Luke? What's happening with this press conference?"

"Well, Mrs Laverty, I should say to you that we have had a number of phone calls. Enquiries. Some people claim they saw John Wayne. Some say Jimmy Stewart. But mostly, people are just bewildered, wondering if it was some sort of optical illusion, or in-store promotion. And we've had a number of newspapers asking who or what the Cowboy was. I just told everybody that all would be revealed at Thursday's press conference. That is . . . if you still want to go ahead with it?"

Avril paused to think for a heartbeat. "Yes, we do. But we'd appreciate any advice you can give us."

For the next three days, Fran and Avril felt as though they were at the eye of a storm, which they knew was going to hit them on Thursday. The rumour machine hadn't yet identified who the Lavertys were, so, for now, there were no reporters, nothing to disturb their relative peace. Just in case, Inspector Moroney had placed them under police protection, ready to intercept anybody who got too close before they were ready for them. But there were pictures in the papers, speculation, repeats of the video footage over and over on the television. Luke was an undiscovered treasure, lying in wait for the chosen moment when he would shine. In this relative calm, Fran and Avril grappled with their conscience, and asked themselves the same questions over and over.

What would happen to Luke? Would their deepest wishes be granted – that, after a flurry of interest and publicity, life would return to normal, and Luke would be accepted by the world for what he was, and maybe would find somebody who shared his abilities – or were they completely misjudging the situation? Would he become a freak, an anomaly of nature whom nobody would ever accept? Would his moment of fame simply lead to a deeper sense of despair? Once the "newsworthiness" had dissipated, would Luke be left with nothing but curious faces staring at him as though he belonged in a zoo?

On Thursday morning, they awoke with more questions hovering in the air than answers, and they headed into the press conference with heavy hearts.

Chapter Eight

Luke sat between his parents at the long table. He was quite happy. He had his cowboy, whom he had decided to call Jake, in one hand, and Lenny, the toy puppy, in the other. He had introduced them to each other, and they had immediately hit it off. At the moment, Lenny was giving Jake a piggy-back, which he didn't mind doing. The table made a good desert for the two of them to ride across, and Luke made the most of it. He was a bit hindered, though, by the large mass of metal objects, with all the wires stuck into them, which were set in front of him on the table. They blocked the way.

Avril leaned over to Inspector Moroney, pointing at the microphones. "Are these really necessary? He can't speak anyway." Moroney grunted and moved the microphones to the other side of the table. Luke looked up at him with a grateful smile. The Inspector cleared his throat, avoiding the child's eyes.

"Ladies and gentlemen, I have called this press conference as a result of the speculation that has arisen regarding the circumstances surrounding Saturday's shooting incident." He went on to describe the two men wanted in connection with the shooting, and the progress that had been made in the investigation. Then he took a deep breath, and continued. "In the course of the incident, a highly unusual, mysterious perhaps, event took place. It was captured on closed-circuit camera. Most of you will have seen this footage on the television news reports. However, I would like to replay the relevant portion of the tape, if you would bear with me for a moment." He proceeded to do just that. When the clip had ended, Moroney cleared his throat again and picked up where he had left off. "Now, before I take your questions, I'd like to hand over to Mrs Avril Laverty, the mother of the little boy, Luke, whom you saw in the clip and who, we believe, was the target of a kidnap attempt. Mrs Laverty has a prepared statement which she would like to read."

Avril looked around at the faces massed in front of her, trying to gauge what they were thinking. A few eager beavers leaned forward, tape recorders in hand. But most of the reporters were slouched in their seats, looking bored, oozing a seen-it-all casualness. For the most part, their faces were impassive, unreadable. Avril saw them as disinterested scientists, come to work their alchemy, to build a narrative structure around the shaky foundations of her son's life. She glanced at Fran and then at Inspector Moroney. Both of them gave her a bright, encouraging smile, which didn't help her nerves one bit.

Avril looked down at Luke, who had stopped playing when Inspector Moroney had begun to talk. He appeared to be listening intently, as though understanding that his life was under discussion. Like Avril, he stared out at the people who had come to hear his story, and he was frowning slightly. For the umpteenth time that week, Avril was on the brink of changing her mind. For one mad moment, she thought of just standing up and walking out. Instead, she took a deep breath, and read calmly and clearly into the microphone.

"From the time our son, Luke, was born, we knew there was something unusual, something special about him. Not in the sense of looking different physically, or even behaving differently. There was something deeper, something spiritual, if you like, which marked Luke out from the rest of us. It is very difficult to describe exactly how this manifests itself. The best I can do is to describe it as magic. Luke possesses a certain ability which allows him to create light and colour out of thin air. At first, these occurrences resembled a sort of coloured mist, without form, which is why we began to call them his 'clouds'. But, as time went on, these clouds took on more formal shapes and patterns. I suppose it's similar to the way a child learns language, gradually discovering how to make connections. In fact, these images are Luke's only language, as he can't – or doesn't – speak. But he understands everything we say. What happened on Saturday – what you just saw from that clip – was the most solid formation he has yet created. The 'Cowboy', we believe, was Luke's first complete sentence."

Avril went on to describe their life with Luke, how they had struggled to keep him out of the public eye, running away all the time, fighting the inevitable.

"So, the obvious question is, why now?" she continued. "And why do we think the world will believe us now, rather than before? The answer to the second question is: we don't know, but we hope. We hope we can trust you, all of you, to tell our story straight, as the truth should be told.

"As for the first question: why now? I think that recent events have brought things to a head, and Fran and I have come to realise that we could not go on pretending that Luke could survive, cocooned, forever. He will have to go to school, meet friends, integrate in society; it would be unfair and entirely selfish of us to deny him these things.

"Last Saturday's attempted kidnap brought all of these questions forward before we had fully thought everything through. We have no idea why anyone would want to kidnap Luke. We can only assume that it has some connection with his powers. Somehow, these people know about Luke – perhaps they know more than we do – and they have some ulterior motive for abducting him. Until they are arrested or somebody comes forward with more information, we will not know the real reason.

"We would like to appeal to anyone who may have more information about the two men who tried to abduct Luke, or indeed about his condition, to contact us, through Inspector Moroney. We also feel that, in going public now, we might prepare the world to accept Luke, so that when, for instance, he eventually goes to school, he will not be an object of curiosity, or scorn, or bullying, but will be accepted as just a normal child.

"Again, Fran and I appeal to you to report what you have heard and seen here with honesty and open-mindedness. We cannot force you to believe us, but we sincerely hope you do."

Avril fell silent. She was afraid to look at the array of faces before her. She looked down at her son, and he nodded, almost imperceptibly, as though to say, *you have done the right thing*. Fran, silent and pensive, *had* been watching the faces of the journalists. Many of them remained as impassive as ever. However, he noticed a change coming over the others. The cynical expressions had melted. There were no longer any slouchers in the room. Most of the reporters sat forward on the edges of their seats. There was a distinct air of wonder and open amazement in the room. *They believe us*, thought Fran, *they actually believe us*.

At the back of the hall, Fran spotted a familiar face. Jimmy McGinnity. Dressed in a long trenchcoat and a felt hat. He caught Fran's eye, and nodded sombrely.

The press conference continued. Inspector Moroney invited questions, which came in a quick barrage. Fran and Avril answered them between them; the questions were surprisingly generous. How often do these visions happen? Do you think Luke will ever speak? Did you talk to the Cowboy? Where do you think these visions come from? Who is the little girl in the clip we saw? Do you believe there's some sort of supernatural cause behind Luke's condition?

Then, one reporter stood up and asked in an authoritative voice, "Mrs Laverty, you've asked us to take you at your word. The only evidence that has been presented as proof is this clip apparently filmed by a closed-circuit camera. How do we know that it wasn't faked? Some sort of optical illusion, maybe, or a hologram or something. What I'd like to know is, how do we know this isn't an elaborate hoax? Can Luke give us a demonstration of these so-called magic powers?"

Avril hesitated. She had been dreading the question, though she knew it would be asked. She looked around the room; a few of the reporters nodded. With every second she hesitated, she knew that she was losing confidence, and with it would go their story's credibility.

Luke had been listening to the barrage of questions with a quiet fascination. He had never heard so many people apparently talking about him – except perhaps on the television – and he struggled to understand what they were saying. There were also a lot of strange metal eyes being pointed at him, and flashing lights. He blinked at each flash. They were blinding him, and he felt hot and confused. Why had his parents brought him here?

He looked up as his mother began to speak. "This is why I ask for your trust. As far as we can figure out, Luke's episodes seem to occur at moments of stress, or when he desperately wants to communicate something. As far as we know, he can't just do it at will. We don't even know how much control he has – "

At that moment, one of the photographers moved in close to the table and pointed the camera straight at Luke, who looked at him just as the flash went off. The light passed straight through his pupils and pierced his very brain. It was like a short circuit. All the light in his head came spilling out at once, a tumbling galaxy of it. Flashes of chaotic colour, occasional waves and patterns, hints of shape and shadow, and riding through it all, the Cowboy on his fiery stallion, throwing dust like stars behind his hooves. Everything, in fact, that Avril had described.

In the ensuing mayhem, photographers crashed over chairs and each other in their attempts to capture the spectacle (those with only black-and-white film loaded, scrambled, cursing, for their bags). Everybody was on their feet, straining to identify patterns and shapes. Everybody, that is, except Luke, and Fran and Avril who looked at each other and smiled. The perfect demonstration.

Moroney quickly ushered them out of the room before they were mobbed. As they waited for a car to pick them up, Jimmy McGinnity approached them. He shook hands with Fran, and looked sheepishly at Avril, who nodded frostily to him before turning to talk to Inspector Moroney.

"I take it you were the one who decided to contact me?" asked Jimmy, raising a bushy eyebrow.

"Well, it was my suggestion, but we both decided," answered Fran. "Don't worry, Avril will get used to the idea."

"As long as we understand each other."

"My advice to you," Moroney told them, "is to take a holiday. Or, better still, we can take you to a 'safe house' until the hysteria dies down. And believe me, there will be hysteria."

"I feel like a criminal," said Avril. "I feel like we've been running ever since Luke was born. Can we not just try to weather it this time?"

Moroney sighed. "Well, I can't force you to go into hiding. But I think it'd be a wise move. After a few weeks, people will lose interest, move on to other things. Then you can get back to your lives."

Fran shook his head. "Thank you for everything you've done. But we'll stick with it for now."

"Well, if you change your mind . . . I'll keep in touch. And I'll leave a couple of officers with you – that, I insist on."

They lasted a week.

Jimmy McGinnity disappeared into the background, but their own lives became an intense focus of speculation and attention. They were all over the newspapers and television. This time, though, there were no "Miracle Baby" mock-serious articles. The word was out: this was for real.

At first, everything was reported as it happened. Most of the newspapers printed Avril's statement word-for-word, with a number of photographs of Luke's light display. The greatest impact was on television, however; the press conference was shown over and over, and, within a few days, the entire country had seen it – seen it and believed.

Then the rumours spread further afield. Their address could no longer be kept secret. Journalists flocked from all over Europe and the States. CNN got wind and sent over a film crew. For the second time in their lives, Fran and Avril found themselves swamped. The house was surrounded by a massive crowd, a mixed bag of journalists and hangers-on. Rival television crews set up camp in some of the other local guest-houses. A few of the neighbours resented that their community had become the focus of world attention. However, as most of them ran guest-houses themselves, they were happy to avail of the sudden influx of guests. It was off-season, after all.

Besides the media, the biggest group were habitual pilgrims. Many of them were tired of traipsing from one report of mysterious happenings – moving statues, stigmata, bleeding stones – to the next, and were relieved to find a miracle that everybody else believed in.

Strangely, there were also a large number of cultists, UFO freaks and conspiracy theorists, who had various theories about Luke's reasons for choosing our planet, and Ireland in particular. They had no doubt that he had chosen. It was just a matter of deciding what his mission was. The more reasonable among this group believed that he was a superior life-form from a distant galaxy, or the reincarnation of Shiva, or Ammon-Ra, or Lugh, or any number of other gods. Some of the others believed he was a genetic experiment, a newly evolved form of humanity, which had been covered up by the government (the denials by one rather foolish government minister added fuel to their conspiratorial fire).

There were the Hollywood agents, each with a more ludicrous bid to buy Luke's story. One company told them that Luke would be perfect for a part in a new comedy, and would save them millions on special effects, if he were able to project at will. Each day, they received at least two or three phone calls asking if Luke would sponsor their products, everything from nappies to sunglasses to mobile phones.

Then there were the scientists, doctors and academics, all of whom claimed that they knew what Luke's problem was, and if they could just perform a few tests . . . The Lavertys were determined, however, that their son would not be turned into a guinea pig. There were other ways, other avenues of investigation which they could try, without Luke becoming a science experiment.

All of this was filtered through to the Lavertys by the couple of police officers assigned to protect them, and by the friends who surrounded them, trying desperately to keep them out of the public eye.

There were a few of the "disciples" whose persistence had to be watched, however. After a couple of fanatics begged that they be allowed to touch Luke – a piece of his clothing, a limb, any part of his body would do – Fran made it clear that there were boundaries. One night, one of them even managed to prise open the window of Luke's bedroom, but got stuck halfway. His muffled groans attracted the gardaí.

Subterfuge was required whenever anybody had to leave the house. Avril learned this to her annoyance when she tried to creep out for a breath of fresh air without telling anybody. She got as far as the field behind the house, when she was suddenly confronted by three grinning old women clutching rosary beads.

Avril recognised them even before one of them greeted her cheerfully in a piping voice. "Hello, dear! Do you remember us? We came before to see your son, when he was just a little baby. Do you think you could let us meet him today?"

Avril turned and retreated to the sanctuary of the house.

On another occasion, Fran had to drive up to Dublin. As usual, he had to sneak out the back door with the aid of one of the gardaí. Suddenly, a man in a suit seemed to appear from nowhere and stood before them, his hand in his pocket. The garda was on him immediately, wrestling him to the ground. After a brief struggle, punctuated by the man's muffled protests, it was established that he was not, in fact, reaching for a gun, but for a business card. The garda apologetically helped him to his feet.

The indignant man brushed the dirt off his suit. Then, taking advantage of the situation, he side-stepped the garda, beamed, shook a bewildered Fran by the hand, and handed him his business card with the other. His name, according to the card, was Peadar Monks, and he wanted to make a business proposal: to use Luke as a sort of fortune-teller-cum-faith-healer, with him as manager.

Monks was determined to be heard before Fran could make his escape. He had the sort of large moonface that Fran would have described as smarmy, if he was being kind. False teeth gave away the falsity of his smile. Nevertheless, he had a powerful way of arguing. "My idea," he said in a wide, generous voice, "is to take Luke on the road, to tour all over the country, to build up his reputation as a faith healer by word of mouth, and eventually to take the show abroad."

Fran looked at him in bewilderment. "But . . . this is absurd. Luke isn't a faith healer. And even if was, we'd never let him go 'on the road', as you put it. Now if you don't mind – "

Monks still held Fran's hand, and he spoke quickly before Fran could push past him. "Do you believe, Mr Laverty, that what your son sees is the truth?" When Fran hesitated, he went on, his eyes misting over. "Surely there can be nothing more pure than the visual image? Seeing is believing, yes? With words, we can lie. With pictures, what you see is what you get." His argument was that Luke's visions possessed a certain truth, although it was a truth that nobody could pin down. "What is faith, after all, but a belief in a truth that can't be seen?" He paused dramatically, holding Fran's gaze with his deep blue eyes. "Naturally, as his manager, I would be able to determine the best strategy for Luke's touring schedule. I would, of course, take a small percentage as commission . . ."

Before he felt himself sucked in any deeper, Fran, with a muttered apology, pulled his hand away and dodged past him. The garda took over, ushering Monks off the property still shouting "Think about it! Call me!"

The following day, they agreed to go into hiding once again. Gathering their essentials, they fled the guest-house, which was no longer a sanctuary for them, leaving it in the hands of Avril's parents. There was a flurry of flashing cameras and a rush of bodies as the garda car emerged from the garage. Then they were through; a couple of hours later, they sat in an anonymous house in an anonymous suburb of

Dublin, staring glumly at each other while their protectors guarded the doors outside.

They were to spend the next two months there – including a dull, uncomfortable Christmas – waiting for the storm to die down. Even closeted in the "safe house", they could not escape the nightmare. There was nothing to do there but watch television, and there was nothing on the television but their son, hours of speculation and analysis, for the first couple of weeks. Every channel regurgitated the same material: the closed circuit camera footage from the department store, the press conference, whatever glimpses of Luke or his parents had been captured on camera. He was everywhere – RTE, BBC, CNN, Sky . . . even Oprah had a show specially dedicated to "children of the light".

RTE broadcast a special programme on Luke about a week into their new exile. The press conference was aired yet again, and there was the usual footage of the scene outside the Lavertys' house. The reporter described the events as "one of the most astounding twists in modern Irish history" and "a watershed in the spiritual life of the country".

There followed a studio debate among a group of experts from various areas, including a psychologist, a scientist, a theologian and a "well-known commentator". After a brief introduction by the presenter, the psychologist began the debate.

"I believe that what we are seeing in Luke is an extraordinarily vivid imagination combined with a psycho-kinetic ability to project," he said. "We see here the most profound expression of the mind-body relationship that I have ever witnessed. There are some deep linkages between the internal imagination and his physical presence, as a person, in the world, which has caused a blurring of the normal boundaries. His physical ability to communicate is actually inhibited by the quantum leaps which his mind is capable of."

"So what you're suggesting," ventured the presenter, "is that Luke is a genius trapped in a child's body?"

The psychologist looked at him disdainfully. "That is not what I am suggesting at all. My fear for Luke is that the blurring of his boundaries will eventually result in a sort of pseudo-schizophrenic state in which his identity oscillates between a body-bound inarticulacy and a free-flowing but uncontrolled state of hallucination, in which his mind is his body."

The scientist interjected at this point: "I disagree. Obviously, we have not had a chance to study this phenomenon in any detail; Luke's parents are not amenable to experimentation. But I would tentatively suggest that the images we have seen are a result of a chemical imbalance in Luke's metabolism. It seems that, whatever Luke's chemical makeup, it is producing a massive build-up of electrical energy, which is being released in sudden bursts by some unknown catalyst. The extraordinary thing is, this energy is not being released as electricity, but as refracted light; Luke's body is effectively acting as both conductor and transformer. The images we see are the waste material, if you like, of this massive release of energy."

The presenter frowned. All of this was going over his head. "But how do you account for the shapes and patterns that we saw? What about the Cowboy?"

The psychologist answered: "These are repressed memories, twisted by Luke's mind into a sort of imaginary landscape on which his fears and anxieties are played out. I

135

would say that the Cowboy represents a figure of male authority, which Luke is, perhaps, lacking in real life."

"So you think there's some sort of . . . eh . . . Oedipus Complex at work here?" threw in the presenter, latching on to the one phrase he remembered from first-year psychology.

"That's bullshit," exclaimed the commentator forcefully. "Psychobabble! What we have in Luke is the culmination of the information society, the media domination of our hearts and souls as we head towards the new millennium. The greatest divide in the latter half of the twentieth century has been between the word and the image. The struggle between capitalism and marxism has been replaced by a struggle between the modern and the postmodern, the word which shows meaning, and the image which, ironically, hides it in its surfaces. Luke represents the victory of the image over the word."

Feeling more and more at sea, the presenter turned nervously to the theologian, who smiled magnanimously before beginning his own pontification. "I think you're all clouding the issue somewhat. I would agree that Luke is a product of our technologically led age. But it is my belief that what he expresses is actually a return to the spiritualism of our ancestors. Many people have talked of this as a 'miracle'. It is not a miracle in the strict sense, but it is truly a challenge to our sense of faith."

The presenter saw this as a good place to finish, and smoothly picked up on the last line to sum up. "Indeed, a challenge to our sense of faith, or perhaps a scientific enigma for our mass-media age. Luke's story touches us all. Next week, we'll be – "

But the theologian was having none of it. "Sorry, if I

could just finish what I was saying. This is a society where we talk incessantly of 'the supernatural' as something real, yet we scoff when this is couched in religious terms – as a miracle. I think it is important, therefore, to see Luke's visions as a bridge between this world and the unknown spirit world."

"That's bullshit," said the commentator.

And so it went on. Fran and Avril watched it all on the television in their secret hideout, their disbelief growing as the programme creaked on towards the end. When the credits finally rose, nobody was any the wiser, either in the studio or among the Lavertys. At least it appeared to have provided some entertainment for Luke, who, Fran and Avril noticed, was giggling silently to himself.

"What is it, Luke?" Fran asked, not sure why he was starting to laugh himself. "What's so funny?"

For an answer, Luke closed his eyes, and suddenly a giant television screen lit up over his head, quivering like a huge block of jelly. Inside the screen, the faces they had just seen on the real TV materialised, shaky but recognisable, and began jabbering in nonsense verse, their mouths growing wider and wider, their voices rising in a chorus of absurdity. The scientists and the theologians merged into one huge mouth, which continued to speak in tongues. As the faces melted into each other like a Salvador Dali painting, the hovering television began to expand, rounding at the edges, until it looked like a huge balloon. It got bigger and bigger, filling the space above their heads. Suddenly Luke sneezed, and the whole scene disintegrated into a rain of starry light, pouring down on their heads.

For a moment, Fran and Avril didn't know what to do, staring at their son who, once again, had surprised them.

Luke, recovering from his sneeze, looked up and grinned. They couldn't help themselves then, collapsing into each other's arms in a welter of laughter. Luke crawled in between them, happy to be the source of such hilarity.

That was probably the lightest moment they had in the whole time that they were public property. Luke would forever be the boy with the light in his head, but after two months in which nothing new happened, the world moved on, other events became news. People, in their odd way, got used to the idea of a child with magical powers, and eventually were bored with it. Other dramas, real and imagined, clamoured for their attention.

The Laverty family began to drift back to relative normality. The journalists, followers and onlookers moved on. By the time Inspector Moroney told them that they would be safe if they moved home, even the most fanatical had disappeared. On a crisp February morning, the Lavertys came home. Calm descended.

As they had hoped, Luke's fifteen minutes had been and gone. Now it was time to begin growing up. However, there were other concerns facing Fran and Avril, which made them feel their plan had only been a partial success.

For one thing, the police had hit a dead end in their investigations. It was now certain that the two men had left the country – they had been positively identified on yet another closed-circuit recording at Dun Laoghaire's passenger terminal. But there was no trace of them after that. International enquiries had so far proved fruitless. At home, nobody knew who or what they had been involved with. Their wives were genuinely distraught at their disappearance, according to Inspector Moroney. A tap had been put on their phone lines, but there had been no attempts to contact them.

The lack of news darkened the horizon for Fran and Avril. They had hoped the publicity would flush out whoever was after Luke. Now they could only hope that they had been scared away.

There was also a distinct lack of a positive response to their appeal for any information about Luke's condition. There were a few crank calls, and some leads which appeared genuine; they passed these on to the police and to Jimmy McGinnity, but they ultimately led nowhere. Jimmy, for his part, had opened up a few possible avenues, but had nothing of substance to report. Fiona Menton was delving deep into medical journals. She had, at least, discovered one thing; the hospital holding the records of Luke's birth let her see their files. There was no sign of a report by Jane O'Donnell. While the birth was described as unusual in so far as it had taken place at home, there were "no other complications", and mother and child were both healthy. A short note at the end, however, mentioned that the nurse who had "attended the delivery" had been "inexplicably distraught" and had resigned her position that very morning.

"You're certain the nurse didn't hand in a report?" Avril asked Fiona.

"Well, there's no sign of one. Unless it was stolen . . ."

Luke himself came out of the storm best. He seemed to know that he was the centre of attention, and he lost much of the melancholy that had dogged him for the past few months. He had been given a taste of fame, and it appealed to his need for communication. When the storm died down to a whispering breeze, he was still giddy with the excitement of it. Inside his imagination, new shapes and colours were forming, new possibilities emerging.

In a large house somewhere in Dublin, the Dark Man was in retreat. His plan had gone astray, but he had no intention of abandoning it completely. He had amassed a vast treasure over many years in the shadows of the city; but Luke would be his prize possession, the gateway to the pinnacle of his power. This was just a setback, a minor irritation, a pilot run, executed with just a little too much haste. He realised now that it was too soon. The child was too young. It was time to reflect, refine, plan again. He had plenty of time to wait. One day, Luke would be his.

Chapter Nine

Life settled back on its haunches to wait and watch. Apart from the occasional phone call, the odd over-zealous guest and one or two brief resurgences of media interest (along the lines of "whatever happened to . . ."), their lives moved on in heartbeats, regular, normal, unhurried. The guest-house maintained a steady profit, the seasons came and went. Three years passed.

It was a strangely, tensely uneventful three years. In the slow, measured flow of their existence, there were few ripples. Mary and Sandy were regular visitors, but Mary was still reluctant to give up her job and move into the guest-house full-time. Sandy's health continued to waver. She could spend weeks on end leading a normal life, but just when Mary began to hope that her daughter was fighting her disease successfully, Sandy would take a downturn. So Mary held her nerve, and made as few changes as she could.

Jimmy McGinnity and Fiona Menton both reported in regularly, though with reducing frequency and little news of any value. Jimmy had run into a dead-end in trying to trace who might have wanted to abduct Luke. Alfie and Banjo had effectively disappeared. He had spoken to most of the people who had shown an interest in Luke, but to no avail.

Fiona had managed to reach the doctor who had examined Luke on his first day of life. He didn't remember, until Fiona mentioned Jane O'Donnell and her resignation. "Hmm . . . yes, I think . . . I recall the case," he had said then. "Let me see . . . yes, as far as I remember, she did hand in a report, but I'm afraid I threw it away, because . . . well, frankly, it was all over the place. Nothing made sense in it. As far as I could see, she was raving. Drunk, I think. I believe she resigned the same day." Fiona questioned him about Luke's condition, and whether anything in Jane's report had struck him as familiar. He dismissed it with a patronising wave of his hand. "My dear lady, you must understand, this woman should never really have assisted at the birth. I examined the child, and he was in excellent health. I didn't want to distress the parents by letting them see the ravings of a madwoman. So, I destroyed her report." Fiona gave up. It was obvious she would get nowhere by that route.

Beyond this, she found nothing solid, but had discovered some potentially useful resources. She had researched medical journals going back decades. She had read numerous books on telekinesis, astral projection, psychic hallucination, and any other subject that bore any resemblance to Luke's case. In doing so, she was exploring a world which, to her, was contrary to everything she had previously believed to be the limits of the universe. Most of what she read – and she did read a vast amount – she ultimately dismissed as rubbish. But there were a number of gems which led her down different pathways, giving her a whole new outlook on life. She began a course in homeopathic medicine, with the intention of transforming her practice into a holistic one in a few years.

But she found nothing that exactly matched Luke's apparitions. There were a few attempts to describe the theoretical potential of some human beings to produce light energy, but it was all theory; there were no recorded cases of any actual projections. Then there were all those American-published "true-life" accounts of supernatural happenings, but Fiona was unable to relate Luke to any of the descriptions given. She did attempt to contact a few of the authors; of the few she managed to reach, only one or two proved in any way useful. Most of them had seen or heard of Luke's story through the media, but they tended to be sceptical. Only one man, Joshua Pitford, showed an immediate interest. He had written a book about the human body as an energy source. Unfortunately, he had not heard of any similar cases, but he promised to use his contacts and sources to see if he could come up with anything.

Despite these possibilities, however, Fran and Avril were beginning to feel, more and more, that Luke was just a one-off, unique. They would never call him a freak or an aberration.

For his own part, Luke continued to grow in silence. He never spoke, but to his parents' great relief, he took to their attempts to teach him to read and write. He loved it when they told him stories, building pictures of the characters in his imagination. He read voraciously, moving very quickly from Dr Seuss to story books, even novels written for children twice his age. His favourites, though, were comic books: *Asterix*, *Tintin*, *Lucky Luke*, *Calvin and Hobbes*, *Charlie Brown*.

Inside his mind, he stored all the faces and personalities he encountered in these books. They mixed and intertwined with the various film stars and characters who floated around his head. The Cowboy remained the strongest, most well-developed of them all, although his face had softened, so that it was now a cross between a John Wayne-style ruggedness and a Lucky Luke-style coolness: half-man, half-cartoon.

This remained Luke's favoured method of communication. When he had something big to say, the word-pictures would crowd his brain, and come tumbling out

143

in a rush of light. But it was a huge feat, an energy-draining expressiveness. More and more, he began to write what he wanted to say, in a chicken-scrawl hand; one word, two or three at most, were enough. He resented having to wield a pen, but he knew that ink was much more manageable than light. Eventually, he reached a compromise: he would write his word or two, the last letters trailing off into a simple drawing. As time wore on, he became more adept at drawing pictures of what he wanted to say. Sometimes, he would leave out the words completely. In this way, he discovered a new talent in himself: he was an artist.

In the meantime, Fran and Avril had decided to bring him to the psychologist recommended by Fiona Menton. It was a mistake.

"So, tell me: how long has Luke had this illness?" had been Dr Gordon Richardson's first question to the parents, after an hour-long, fruitless session with a silent, staring Luke.

Avril's hackles were raised immediately. "He's not sick. We just want to know if there's anything psychological behind his powers."

"Forgive me. It's my belief that Luke may be suffering from some form of delusional psychosis."

"He's six years old."

"Nevertheless, there may be some latent chemical imbalance. If I could just run some tests, I may be able to cure him."

"I won't let you turn him into a guinea pig," Avril retorted, her voice rising a degree. "Besides, I don't think there's anything for you to 'cure'."

Dr Richardson sighed. This was proving more difficult than he had expected. "Mrs Laverty," he reasoned with absolute patience. "Perhaps I should explain. My job is to analyse a situation fully, to seek out abnormalities where they exist, and ultimately to attempt a cure, if one is possible."

Avril flared. "Abnormalities? Don't you get it? Luke is completely normal!"

As if to prove her point, Luke, who had been following the conversation with interest, suddenly burst into light, producing a troupe of dancing candles which swirled around Dr Richardson's head. They formed an animated crown around his bald patch, looking at their reflections as they danced their jig.

He threw them out after that, declaring stiffly that he was unable to offer any explanations for Luke's verbal silence or his visual fluency.

Luke started school. His teachers had all been warned, well in advance. He was to be treated as a normal child, except for the fact that he would not be able to answer in class, and that he might, on occasion, turn the classroom upside down. Many of the teachers remembered Luke from his moment of fame three years previously. Some of them were apprehensive, all of them curious, but, for the most part, they were delighted when he joined the school. For one thing, the dark beauty he had inherited from Avril was becoming more pronounced as he got older. The teachers found him irresistible.

Nevertheless, there were some problems. Luke's silence isolated him from his classmates. Not that some of them didn't make an effort to integrate him into their games. Mostly, Luke chose the isolation himself. Truth was, he missed Sandy sorely. She had started school in Dublin and they saw less of each other now than before. Despite the fact that he now found himself surrounded by small people like himself, Luke did not want to make new friends. He usually spent his break-time playing with Lenny the dog (he wasn't a puppy anymore) and Jake the plastic cowboy.

And, inevitably, the day came when Luke finally had one of his "episodes" in the classroom. The teacher had, of course, been given plenty of warning of what might happen. She had endeavoured to explain to the rest of the class about Luke's "special ability". Still, when it happened, nobody was prepared for it.

It began when Luke found himself in class one day without his favourite set of colouring pencils. They were his lifeline; whenever he was called on to answer a question, his fingers would fly over the page, and the answer would emerge in multi-coloured words and pictures. On this day, though, the teacher asked him what colour the sun was. He had no yellows or fiery reds to scribble its brilliance. He looked around, at a loss; Philip Carty, who sat beside him, offered him an ordinary lead pencil. But he wouldn't compromise; the words "oh well" passed through his mind, and a magnificent, boiling sunrise burst through his head and spread quickly around the classroom.

The children screamed. One or two began to cry. The teacher dropped the piece of chalk she was holding and fell back against her desk. All around, the children were milling about, running in every direction. Gradually, when they realised that the fabulous crimson ball was not going to singe their eyelashes, they calmed down and stared in awe, as the teacher gathered herself to take control of the situation. She cleared her throat, and began to speak; her voice in her own ears was too high-pitched, too nervously squeaky.

"Now children, everything is just fine; Lu-Luke is showing us what the sun looks like. It's a very nice sun, Luke. And yes, you're right, it is yellow and orange and red, and very, very bright. So, I think we've all seen enough of the sun now. Maybe you could make it set now, Luke. Thank you."

Obediently, Luke slowly made the sun sink lower and lower. It darkened and spread out against some imaginary floating horizon which nobody could quite get a fix on. The red got deeper, and a great salubrious laziness drifted over the room. Just before the sun became one with the horizon, a solitary, barely discernible silhouette came into view; it was the Cowboy, riding high in the saddle. At the last moment, he turned, the horse rose and pawed the air, and then the sun disappeared, taking the Cowboy with it.

From that moment, Luke's position in the class changed. He was suddenly popular. Everybody wanted his friendship. He found he was enjoying himself and joined in the schoolyard games. And he realised something new: he could control his visions now. He was able to say what he wanted, in pictures, precisely and clearly. They also came much more easily to him. He no longer had to strain to create. His teacher was a pragmatist who quickly recognised his potential. Luke was the perfect educational tool. He could hold the class's attention without any great effort on her part. She worked out a system: she would read out a story, and Luke would visualise it for the whole class. Her pupils made huge strides in their reading and writing ability.

Now Luke could make up his own stories, using the stock of characters who lived in the vast space of his imagination. Sometimes he entertained his classmates between classes. At other times, he would keep Fran and Avril amused; and sometimes, he would tell the stories to himself. Whatever the source, the characters were free to roam and intermingle in their projected space. Thus, ET might find himself setting off on an adventure with Snowy the dog, or Inspector Clouseau might stumble on Calvin and Hobbes hatching a plot to kill Winnie the Pooh, or Marlon Brando would find himself Sumo-wrestling with Obelix the Gaul. Striding majestically through all of this was the Cowboy, the guardian angel of Luke's fantasies.

At first, Luke's stories only lasted a minute or two.

147

Despite the fact that it took much less effort than before to release his imagination, the experience could still be draining after a few minutes. Luke's energy would often start to fade quickly; the characters would lose their shine, grow sluggish and lazy, and eventually vanish, well before the story had reached its natural end. Afterwards, Luke would be left listless and exhausted, until he felt a fresh rush of energy and brightened up again.

But gradually, Luke's growing body gathered energy and strength. The stories began to lengthen, the characters grew stronger and more solid with each passing month and year. Sometimes he could go on for as long as an hour or more before he found his strength sapping. He even began to invent completely new characters, sometimes conglomerates of the people he saw on television or read about in his favourite books; sometimes pure invention.

Some of these characters were more firmly drawn than those he had gathered from outside himself; they were drawn from his deepest soul-feelings. They could be extraordinary in their beauty and complexity, their very realness.

Among the characters that Luke created around that time was a boy, fifteen or sixteen years old, with a quiet, pensive face. He appeared in just a few of Luke's stories, usually as a dreamer with a wistful smile, or a patient, waiting servant to some extravagant adventurer. Of all the characters he had created, he bore the strongest resemblance to Luke – an older, though just as silent, Luke. He remained the most closely guarded figure; the Cowboy often stood behind or near him, ready to protect. Luke rarely brought him out of his inner thoughts; he required too much energy, leaving his creator totally drained.

Although the cystic fibrosis meant that Sandy remained weak, she insisted that her mother brought her to visit Luke every fortnight. As she approached eleven years of age, Sandy spoke enough for both herself and mute Luke. She still understood Luke better than Fran or Avril; their telepathy seemed to grow stronger with the years. She would often "translate" his unspoken thoughts into words. When Sandy was around, Luke now had less need of his projected thoughts. Instead, he kept them for their play, their story-telling sessions.

That summer was filled with glorious days of hazy sunshine, and the children lapped it up. Mary tried to keep buoyant, but her mood slipped its moorings and began to float into despair. One day, as they sat in the garden of the guest-house watching the children playing, Avril touched her gently on the arm. Mary was startled, as though she had been sleeping. When she looked at Avril, Avril noticed that her friend's face was wet with tears. She didn't ask her what the matter was; she knew what it would be, even before Mary spoke.

"I wish it could always be like this. Sandy's so happy with Luke. He seems to give her strength and joy. But she's getting weaker. At home, she's just so listless. Every evening, she falls asleep in my arms, when most children of her age are still outside playing. I pick her up to put her to bed, and she feels so small and helpless, a bag of bones. There's no weight on her at all."

Avril said nothing. Mary looked away, her voice trailing off. She was silent for so long that Avril thought she was crying again. But Mary breathed deeply, and when she spoke again, her voice was firm.

"Sometimes I wake up in the night, with the awful feeling that she's died – the worst thing about it is, among all the pain and fear, there's this immense relief, as though her frail little body is the greatest weight around my neck, suddenly lifted. I feel free, unburdened. I rush into her

149

room, and there she is, warm, her chest rising and falling with her short, ragged breathing. And all I can do is cry, for love of her and for shame at my own selfish feelings."

Avril took Mary in her arms as the tears came freely again. She stroked her greying hair softly, and held her gently to her breast until the tears had run their course. Avril thought how much Mary had changed since the time she had first shown up on her doorstep, all vivid and businesslike. Sandy had drained her.

Finally, Mary pulled herself free. Avril asked her quietly, "What do the doctors say?"

Mary sniffed. "Well, she was doing great up to a few months ago. They were saying she had an excellent outlook. But then she got worse again – she's been coughing a lot, and she's very listless. I've brought her in for a lot of physio, but it hasn't done much good. This is the best I've seen her in ages, but I don't think it'll last. The doctors want to take her into hospital for longer. They say they can look after her better. But I don't want to let her go in, not yet anyway. I'm so afraid she'll never come out again." Her voice trailed. She bit her lip.

"But listen, Mary, you've got to trust these doctors. They know what they're doing. If she's properly treated, Sandy could be as right as rain by this time next year." Avril felt her own words echoing hollowly in her ears, small comfort.

Mary turned to Avril and gripped her hand tightly, telling of her old strength. "Thank you for everything, Avril. You're a great friend. But I just feel now that we do need a miracle for Sandy. I used never pray, but now I pray every night. I just feel I'm losing her." She paused for a moment, looking at the children. To Avril's surprise, a smile spread across her face. "Funny, to me, Sandy has already been given an extended life, through Luke. I honestly don't think she would have survived this long if she hadn't met him."

Chapter Ten

It was the full mouth of teeth that Fran recognised, although it took him another moment or two to place the memory accurately. He shook the proffered hand hesitantly.

Peadar Monks gripped firmly, sincerely. Man to man. Yes, the husband was definitely the weak spot, the one to work on.

"Yes, I remember you all right," said Fran, standing square across the door-frame at the front of the guest-house. "You came to us . . . when was it? Seven or eight years ago? With some hare-brained scheme to turn our son into a con-artist."

"Faith healer, please, Mr Laverty – may I call you Francis? The idea was a faith healer. There's nothing deceptive about a faith healer. But anyway, that's all in the past. That isn't why I'm here now."

"Whatever," replied Fran irritably. "We weren't interested then, and we're not interested now."

Monks winked at him conspiratorially. "Ah, but this is different. This, I know you'll be interested in." He said no more, folding his arms, the consummate tease.

"Oh yes?" said Fran, his eyebrows raised cynically.

"OK. This is my proposal. I understand that Luke's visions have developed so much that he's now able to create his own characters, tell stories and so on."

Fran nodded.

Satisfied, Monks went on, "What I'd like to propose is that you allow Luke to tell his stories to an audience. *An Evening with Luke Laverty*, that sort of thing. We could tour all over the country. People would flock to see him. I'd make all the arrangements, of course, for a small commission."

Despite himself, Fran felt his curiosity piqued. Peadar Monks saw the spark of interest, and decided to push it further. "The way I see it, Francis, Luke is already doing this. He's telling his stories to all his classmates. He probably loves the attention. It's only natural that the next stage would be to do it for a paying audience."

Fran considered this. It was true, Luke seemed at his happiest when he was performing in front of a group of friends. In an effort to pull himself out of Monks's field of gravity, Fran pounced on something he had said. "Wait a minute – how do you know all this? How do you know that Luke is telling stories in class?"

Monks held up his hands apologetically. "Oh, forgive me, I'm just assuming." He didn't mention the fact that his wife knew someone whose sister's daughter was in Luke's class. He merely smiled knowingly. "I am right, though, aren't I?"

"Well, yes, but . . ." Fran felt his will crashing around his ears.

Monks knew he had hooked his fish. It was time to give him some slack. "Listen, I don't want to put pressure on you. Talk to Avril. I'm sure she'll see things our way as well. Here's my card. Give me a call, and we'll go over the details."

* * *

It took Fran all of three days to work up the courage to mention it to Avril. During that time, he fought off the idea again and again, but he couldn't get it out of his head. When he eventually did bring up the subject, late one evening after Luke had gone to bed, it felt as though he wasn't speaking himself, as though he had a traitor's voice.

Avril was vehement. "No way! My God, I thought we'd got past all that, Fran!"

"It's not that, Avril. This is different. It's just, maybe something like this will help Luke. He isn't a little boy anymore. He'll be twelve in a few months."

"But how would performing like a freak help him grow up?"

Fran found himself dishing out the same arguments he had been trying to fight off ever since Monks's visit. "You've got it all wrong, Avril. He'd just be doing what he enjoys doing best, only in public. I mean, if Luke had a beautiful voice, you'd want him to get a chance to sing, wouldn't you?"

Avril refused to be drawn. "That isn't the point. He's only a child, no matter what you say."

"But he's a child with a talent. This could be the perfect opportunity to develop that talent."

"I can't believe you've been taken in by this guy . . . what's his name, Monks? I mean, who is he? What do we know about him? As far as I can see, all he's interested in is exploiting our son!"

"OK, so he's a businessman and, yes, he's interested in making money. That doesn't mean he's out to exploit us."

"Us? It's Luke I'm talking about, not us," retorted Avril. "And as far as I can see, you're exploiting him, too. How much money did he offer you?"

Fran had never seen Avril so raw, but he certainly wasn't going to back down now. "That's unfair. You know damn well that I have Luke's best interests in mind."

"Then why are you trying to make money out of him?"

They continued arguing, their voices rising. Luke, unable to sleep, came downstairs to see what all the fuss was about. He stood just outside the doorway, unnoticed, watching his parents' anger for five minutes, as a small corner of his soul was chipped away. He knew they were arguing about him; he knew it was all his fault. By the time Avril and Fran noticed their son standing there, his cheeks were sodden with tears. They immediately forgot their argument as they went to comfort him. By unspoken agreement, they said nothing more about it that night.

By the following morning, Avril had decided to compromise. "We'll try it once, and only if Luke wants to," she proposed. "And I don't want any money involved. If it works out well, if Luke enjoys it as much as you say he will, and if he's willing to give it a go, then we'll look again at Peadar Monks's proposal. OK?"

Fran was happy to agree, and they put the idea to Luke. At eleven years of age, Luke was getting bored with his old games. Besides, he didn't want to see his parents arguing anymore. So he jumped at the chance to do something different. So Fran contacted Monks.

Three weeks later, Luke sat in front of two hundred invited guests, friends and relations of the family for the most part. Avril had insisted. They were in a large hall, space and air all around, empty, waiting for Luke to fill it with some beautiful fantasy, like a blank cinema screen before the projector flickers into life.

154

The people waited, hushed, buzzing with anticipation. Everybody knew somebody else here, but nobody dared speak. Nods were exchanged, the odd tentative wave.

Luke looked at his parents, sitting close by in the front row, and they both smiled encouragingly at him. Luke was relieved that there had been no more raised voices or tense silences in the past three weeks. His grandparents were all there too, watching him dotingly. Peadar Monks sat at the end of the front row, showing his shiny teeth to Luke. Luke didn't like the man, and pulled a face at him, just quick enough so that his parents wouldn't notice.

The biggest disappointment was that Sandy was not there. Luke wondered what had happened to her. Maybe Mary had to bring her for more tests. Luke wished she could see him now. In his head, he silently dedicated his first public performance to her.

There was only one stranger in the hall, sitting unnoticed in a dark corner. Luke's gaze brushed over him without recognition. Just a shadow, a brief flurry that made him frown.

Luke took a deep breath. He felt a strange thrill rippling through the nerve-endings all over his body. It was something to do with the newness of it, the expectation of a crowd of people all here to see him, waiting for him. But it was also something much stronger, the feeling that this was only a start. This was a low-key, respectful piece of theatre, but Luke could hear the carnival calling.

The lights were dimmed. Luke closed his eyes and began. The hall seemed smaller in the darkness, with all the people in it. But as soon as the light began to spiral out of Luke's head, it took on new dimensions. The walls disappeared and were replaced by a great and shining light on all sides. The hall seemed to shudder with the brightness of it. Two hundred pairs of eyes shut in simultaneous shock, as pupils narrowed to pinpoints. Then slowly, tentatively, they were all opened, peering through protective fingers, squinting until they were fully adjusted to the brightness.

Something was moving in the light, a flitting shadow weaving through the circle of light. No, not one shadow – specks of dust, thousands of them, like a sandstorm pebble-dashing the white wall. They danced, and gradually they settled, coagulated into shape and form. Human form. Life reclaimed from dust. They were children, small children, silhouetted against the light, and they danced in a ring-a-ring-a-rosy around the group of adults who turned, following them in half-blind amazement. Gradually, the children moved closer, inside the perimeter of light, and each of them gravitated towards a particular adult – two hundred children, two hundred adults. Each child took the hands of each chosen adult and smiled up into their eyes. Glints of vague recognition sparked all over the hall. The adults were mystified, until Margaret, Fran's mother, spoke to her son in amazement.

"My God, Fran, it's you!"

The realisation rippled through the room as each of the adults knew that they held the hands of their own childhood – long-forgotten faces, or photographs recalled, or dream memories. The shock was almost too much for some to bear, but they were lifted up by the silent music that seemed to invade their every pore, and they let themselves be led, dancing, swirling around the floor, by the little children. The children's joy was truly infectious, and soon everybody twisted and turned around the room in ecstasy.

156

Everybody, that is, except the Dark Man, who sat brooding at the back of the hall. He had no child to dance with.

Gradually, the dancing slowed as exhaustion overtook everybody. The children slipped their hands free – although many of the adults tried in vain to keep hold of them forever – and moved back to the outside, gradually merging with the light. Soon, there was just the light again, and it faded softly until the hall was again in darkness.

Somebody brought the artificial lights back up too soon, dazing many people. Everybody stood in the position they had been in when they stopped dancing, their hands outstretched. Many faces remained in ecstatic joy, while others were clouded in a mist of sadness. A few wept openly. But there was no anger, and no regret.

Nobody applauded, nobody sat down again. They all looked at Luke – sitting calmly, peacefully as he had been – and smiled or waved their grateful respect to him, before filing slowly, nervously, out of the hall.

Peadar Monks walked out in a daze himself. At the door, however, unseen by anybody else, the Dark Man tapped him on the arm. "A word in your ear, Mr Monks, if you don't mind . . ."

Soon, the room had emptied, except for Avril and Fran, who sat in silence, watching their son.

After that, everything seemed to happen at once . . .

The Lavertys walked in the door of "Exiles" to the ringing phone. Mary's frightened voice told Avril that Sandy had taken a sudden downturn. She had been rushed to hospital, her lungs unable to cope with the demands the disease was

157

putting on them. She was in a coma, and the doctors weren't very hopeful.

Luke watched his mother's expression change as she listened to Mary, and he knew.

Peadar Monks was uncomfortable, though he wasn't sure why. The fresh memory of staring into his own eyes as a child didn't help him focus. He shook his head to dislodge his suspicions. He was, after all, a businessman, and he had dealt with plenty of shady characters before. And he knew a good business opportunity when he saw one. Besides, this man had such a persuasive tone – a man after his own heart. It was hard to resist.

It was just that he seemed so constantly shrouded in shadow.

"Sorry, what was your company's name again?" he asked the Dark Man as the car turned in beside a warehouse in Dublin's docklands.

"Oliver Fuller Productions," said the Dark Man; and again Monks felt a shifting discomfort, as though every word the other spoke was a deceptive trap. But he couldn't stop himself walking straight in. He felt as though he was in a trance, that this man owned his life now.

They got out of the car, and the Dark Man pulled out a set of keys, looking around cautiously. The warehouse looked much bigger on the inside. It was empty, windowless, and the air tasted stale. The Dark Man strode to the centre. Peadar Monks stood nervously beside the door.

When he spoke, the Dark Man's voice filled the space oppressively. "So, Peadar, what do you think? Would he fill this space with his dreams?" He stretched out his arms dramatically.

Monks, eager to please and be gone, nodded. "Yes, I can certainly see how well it would work. Where would you set up the camera?"

"All over! I'd shoot him from every angle."

"I see. And how long would you need?"

The Dark Man walked back towards Monks. "Oh, it's hard to say. Could take a day or two, could take a week. Depends on the boy. Ideally, if I had him by myself for a few hours . . ." He trailed off, fearing he would say too much, push his luck too far.

But Monks hadn't noticed. He was busy calculating. "So you'd pay me five grand initially, and – what were the percentages you mentioned?"

"I'd take fifty per cent on all videos sold; you could divide the rest whatever way you like between yourself and the Lavertys."

To Monks, it all sounded too good to be true. He quickly silenced the turning cogs of doubt and suspicion by clearing his throat and asking, "And all I'd have to do in all this is to persuade the Lavertys to let their son be filmed?"

"Exactly."

"OK, I'll do what I can. But I can't promise anything."

"That's all I ask. So we have a deal?"

They shook on it.

While their hands were still clasped, the Dark Man added, as though he had just thought of it, "Oh, by the way – it would probably be best if you pretend this is your own idea. No need to mention me at all."

Monks frowned. "Why not?"

"Well, they obviously trust you now; you could persuade them much more if you don't bring a stranger like myself into it."

159

Monks shrugged. "Sounds reasonable."

At about the same time, Fiona Menton was sitting in her newly opened homeopathy and reflexology clinic when she received a phone call from Boston. Half an hour later, she was on the phone to the Lavertys, excitement tripping her tongue.

"You remember I mentioned a man called Joshua Pitford a few years back? He wrote a book on human energy?"

The name was vaguely familiar to Fran. He waited for Fiona to go on.

"Well, he has found somebody who knows something about Luke's condition. This man's name is James Abbott, and he wrote about it years ago – way back in the thirties, I think. Anyway, turns out he's Irish. So Joshua Pitford is coming over here next week, and he wants to meet Luke and yourselves."

Fran was puzzled. "This man Abbott: he's still alive?"

"Well, I think so."

"And you say he's Irish? Do you think there might be something in that?"

"Maybe. Or it could be just coincidence. Pitford didn't seem to think it was important. I suppose James Abbott might be the only one who could answer that."

Fran was trying to take it all in. It seemed almost absurd, after all this time, that somebody in another part of the world would all of a sudden be able to provide them with answers to all their questions. They had almost given up trying themselves, and had reached a point where they would have been just as happy not to know what made Luke the way he was – as long as Luke himself was happy. Now this . . .

Fiona was still talking. "Fran? Are you there? Listen,

Fran, the other thing that Pitford told me was that this man Abbott had given a name to this condition. He called it Abbott's Syndrome. A bit egotistical, I suppose, but – "

"So there are other people like Luke out there?" Fran cut in, his excitement building.

"Well, I don't know, Fran. Don't get your hopes up. That's about all I know myself. Joshua Pitford said he'd tell us all the details when he comes over next week. Listen, I have to call him back, to let him know when you can meet him. When suits you best?"

Fran barely had time to relay all of this to Avril when the phone rang again. It was Peadar Monks, bringing them his proposal about the video shoot. He found the Lavertys less amenable, however. They were trying to come to grips with all the news they had received that evening.

"No, Mr Monks, now is *not* a good time," Avril told him. "No, not tomorrow either. Listen, I'm still not sure we want Luke to do any more of your 'sessions', never mind in front of a camera."

"But I thought we had an arrangement. Has something happened?"

"I don't want to discuss that with you, Mr Monks. Now, if you don't mind – "

"OK, Mrs Laverty – Avril. I understand. Think about it, and I'll call you again in a week's time. Talk to your husband, talk to Luke. This could be a great opportunity."

Avril stopped herself asking "For who?" and remained firm. "Two weeks. Give us two weeks. And *I'll* call *you*." She hung up. In two weeks' time, she thought, things may have changed.

* * *

Luke felt his heart ache. It was connected across thirty miles to another heart, which was struggling to survive. Luke felt the echo of every painful beat with his own beating heart. Sandy's soul slept in an uncertain truce with her body. As she drifted, over the following hours and days, through sleep and half-wakefulness, slipping in and out of a coma, her mind kept coming back to Luke. He was there, waiting for her, reassuring her that everything was going to be all right. But in his voice inside her head, he sounded less certain than usual, and she was afraid.

Sandy's condition stabilised after a few days. She was still very weak, and remained in intensive care, but she was awake, and missing Luke.

Avril noticed Luke's depression. She had seen it before, but now it seemed stronger, deeper in him. He was sullen and morose; he refused to eat anything, and he wouldn't even sit and watch his favourite films on the television. He spent most of the mornings in his room. In the afternoons he would sit in the long grass in the field above the house, moping, until Avril would come and pick him up.

She knew it was because of Sandy. She'd always sensed the connection between them, and knew that Luke's mood came out of Sandy's pain. Avril had been in touch with Mary, daily, since Sandy's health had deteriorated, offering what words of support and encouragement she could. She rang her now and told her how Luke was acting.

"Bring him in to see her," said Mary. "I'm sure it'll be OK with the doctors. She isn't fully aware, most of the time, but I know if Luke comes to see her, she'll respond to him. When she has been awake, she's been asking for him."

So Avril brought Luke in to see Sandy. She looked barely alive – whiter than snow, and thin – but when Luke touched her on the back of her hand, she opened her eyes and let out a huge smile. They remained like that for many minutes, not speaking, but in deep conversation. Then Sandy closed her eyes. Luke stood up, looking at his mother. Avril stood up and gave Mary a hug, and they left mother and daughter alone in the room.

The Dark Man was disappointed in Monks, and he let his displeasure be known. If only he could contact the Lavertys himself, he knew his persuasive powers would win them over. But he didn't want to risk exposing himself yet. He would just have to keep playing his game, using Monks as his blunt instrument. Two weeks wasn't long; after all, he had already waited over eleven years.

Joshua Pitford was a broad man, full of words and expansive gestures. He was bubbling over with excitement when he arrived with Fiona Menton at the guest-house, "Exiles". It was an unseasonably warm day, and Pitford had two broad patches of sweat under each armpit.

Fiona made the introductions. "And this," she said with distaste, "is James McGinnity, the private investigator I mentioned."

"Jimmy, please, call me Jimmy."

Joshua Pitford ignored the adults once he spotted Luke. "So you must be the young man I've heard so much about," he said, looking at the boy with admiration. "You seem a bit glum, Luke."

Fran explained. "A little girl, a great friend of Luke's, is very sick at the moment. He's taking it badly."

"Oh, I'm sorry to hear that, Luke." Pitford had scarcely spoken a word to Fran or Avril. He talked directly to Luke, looking down at him, his hand reaching for Luke's shoulder in sympathy. "I hope, Luke, that you'll be able to show me some of your pictures, or tell me some of your stories. Hm?" Luke hung his head.

"That may not be possible, Mr Pitford," said Avril. "Luke hasn't projected for over a week, since the little girl went into hospital. I don't think you'll be able to persuade him."

Pitford looked disappointed. "I'm sorry to hear that," he said again. "I hoped to experience some of Luke's visions first-hand." He sighed and stood up, slapping his hands against his substantial belly, and spoke directly to Fran and Avril for the first time. "Still, not to worry. I've heard a lot about this young man, and I'm hoping you might be able to fill in the gaps."

They settled themselves in the living-room with tea and biscuits. Jimmy McGinnity stood over by the window. Luke disappeared to the long grass again. Avril glanced at him every few minutes.

Pitford insisted on retelling Luke's story, his birth and childhood, as he had heard it from Fiona, prompting them to correct him if he got anything wrong. He was an expansive man, and Fran and Avril had to wait patiently while he went through every detail.

Finally, Fran found space to ask him, "What exactly is this Abbott's Syndrome that you mentioned to Fiona? What do you know about it?"

"Very little. Only that it's no more than a theoretical condition. There have been no recorded cases – at least up to now. I only heard of Abbott's Syndrome a couple of weeks ago, and I contacted Dr Menton here immediately.

James Abbott, the man who coined the term, is an Irishman. Abbott wrote a paper about the condition when he was a lecturer in the Medical Faculty in University College Dublin – this was a long time ago, the thirties or forties, I think."

"And this man Abbott is still alive?" asked McGinnity.

Pitford let out a loud bellow of laughter. "Well, I should hope so! I'm supposed to meet him in a couple of days! No, no, he's very much alive all right, but I think he's close to ninety by now. I haven't spoken to the man himself yet, just to his wife. Lovely woman, much younger, only in her sixties, I believe. Says the old man can be a bit forgetful sometimes, but I'm hoping he'll be lucid enough."

"But what exactly is this Abbott's Syndrome?" asked Fran. "What are the symptoms?"

"Well, it isn't really a matter of symptoms. As I say, this was purely a theoretical condition. Abbott's area of interest was similar to mine, apparently. His basic idea was that the human person is a very finely balanced combination of matter and energy – body and spirit, if you like. Abbott believed that this balance could become unstable in a particular individual. He speculated, for instance, that certain mental illnesses were the result of an overflow of energy through the neural system, something like a power surge in a computer, I suppose, resulting in a malfunction or a shutdown in certain parts of the brain."

Pitford was getting into his stride now, picturing himself back home in a huge lecture theatre, surrounded by hundreds of admiring students, many of them female. Fran and Avril were both remembering the television debate about Luke from all those years ago. Fran shrugged, as if to say, *What the hell, let's just go with the flow.* They listened, but

Pitford was getting more and more obscure, making little or no sense to them, talking, as far as they were concerned, gobbledegook. Avril turned her attention to Luke outside. He was moping about, kicking the grass.

Pitford finally got around to Abbott's Syndrome. James Abbott had written a paper in the 1930s, describing how, if a person with an "energy imbalance" was somehow able to channel the excess energy, they could transform it – into electricity, light, radiation. "He was a bit vague on this," Pitford apologised, pausing for breath.

Fiona Menton used the pause to get in her own question: "But, Joshua, there's one thing I don't understand. How come this Abbott's Syndrome isn't more widely known? And why did I never come across this paper while I was doing my research?" She sounded a little hurt that she hadn't been the one to unearth this evidence.

"Well," replied Pitford, digging in his briefcase, "the simple answer to that is, the paper was never published, and Abbott's Syndrome, as far as the medical community of the time was concerned, existed only in the mind of James Abbott. His paper was buried; nobody would publish it, and I can't say I blame them." He found what he had been searching for in his briefcase, pulling out a thin sheaf of photocopied pages and slapping them on the coffee table. Fran picked them up and glanced through them. Most of the words that caught his eye were obscure, scientific terms. Pitford went on, "It's completely speculative, with no evidence from case studies or experimentation, and, as I say, no firm conclusions. As you can imagine, Abbott's academic career took a nosedive after that."

"So where did you get this copy of his paper?" asked Fiona.

"Well, just by chance, two weeks ago I was at a conference, and I got into conversation with a retired professor of medicine, Séamus Ferguson. When I mentioned my area of study to him, he showed an immediate interest. Turned out he had been a student of James Abbott's in the early forties. He latched onto Abbott as some sort of mentor. Anyway, Abbott, for whatever reason, gave him this paper, told him it was a heap of junk that he had no use for anymore. Ferguson read the paper and thought it was a heap of junk too, but kept it for years in his bottom drawer, as a souvenir of his days in UCD. He made a copy and gave it to me. When I read it, I realised the possible connection with Luke.

"I did a bit of investigating and found out that Abbott is still alive, living in County Kerry. I got a phone number, I called and talked to old man Abbott's wife, Agnes. She told me her husband was wheelchair-bound and wouldn't talk to anybody on the phone. So I told her a little bit about my work, and I asked if they knew about Luke. Apparently, they're pretty reclusive people. They don't have a telly, never read newspapers. She goes into town once a week to get his medicines, post any letters, buy food . . . Anyway, she went off and told him about Luke, but he seemed pretty indifferent. His mind, she said, wanders a bit sometimes, he mightn't have understood. I talked to her for a few more minutes, I told her I was coming over, and she said it'd be okay to meet with her husband. She told me all the stuff I just told you about him. And that's about the height of it. That's all I know."

Joshua Pitford seemed to deflate once he had unburdened himself of all he had to say. He sank back in the armchair and pulled out a pipe.

* * *

Luke lay back in the long grass and closed his eyes. He tried hard to feel Sandy's heart beating across the miles; it came to him faintly, and he tried to whisper inside her head, to tell her he loved her, that he would be with her soon, but he was not sure she could hear him. He tried to breathe light into her head, so that she would see the Cowboy and know that she was safe. He tried to tell her a story, one of her favourites, to cheer her up.

But he couldn't get through, because she was fading, fading. A sad, kind voice spoke in his head, "Let her rest, Luke."

He opened his eyes. Above him, silhouetted in the bright sunlight, stood the old man who had paced him through his life, appearing when he needed him most. He bent down to Luke now, and placed a cool hand on his fevered brow. "Let her rest," he said again.

Luke found tears stinging his eyes, and the old man blurred in his vision. He blinked several times, and found himself breathing more calmly. The heat in his head slowly abated. He tried to speak, and suddenly found he could.

"Will she die?" His voice came back to him as though from a great distance. It seemed so small and defenceless when he compared it to the grand sweep of his visions, but he clung to its preciousness now. He wondered if he was dreaming, like the last time. No, he felt sure he was awake, conscious.

The old man didn't answer his question, instead repeating, "Let her sleep. It's you I'm worried about, Luke."

"Why?"

"Because you're entering a dark period in your life. You

must leave, to find your way alone for a while. I'll be watching you, and I'll be with you when you need me most. But what you do must be your own choice. I can't intervene."

"What's going to happen to me?"

The old man sighed. "I don't know these things. I can only read the signs. I just came to tell you that you only have to call to me. Now, I must go. Sleep, Luke." He stood up and started to walk away. He began to blur at the edges, to fade again.

Luke called out to him, but his own voice was fading again, disappearing under the surface. Still, he managed one final question, "Who are you?"

The old man seemed not to have heard him at first, as his wraith-like form swished through the long grass. But, just before he disappeared from view, he turned once and spoke softly, "Just think of me as the Druid, a wise friend." He turned then, but thought of something else. "Oh, and Luke, keep Lenny close to you. He is a faithful puppy." Then he was gone.

Luke tried to call out to him again, but his voice had gone with the old man. He closed his eyes again, concentrating, trying to find words, but the pictures had returned and there was no space for words. He went deeper, trying to find Sandy. Maybe she could draw the words from him. He found where she should have been, but there was nothing there except a stillness. He searched for her heartbeat, but found only silence. He tried to delve deeper, to find her life, but he drew back, because all he could feel was a cold darkness creeping across his soul.

Luke opened his mouth, and all that emerged was a silent scream. He curled up and hugged his knees to himself as the sky darkened over his head. Clouds were forming rapidly as he lay in a frightened whimper, his head filling with a darkness that he had never known before. He tried to find all his friends, some trace of the light in his head. Where was the Cowboy? He searched the depths of his mind and body, but he could not find him.

Then, as though looking in a black mirror, he saw a face, and recognised it as his own. It was the Lost Boy, the one who needed protection, Luke as an older child. Luke saw the fear on his face, and tried to reach out, to comfort him. But the Lost Boy cringed away from him in fear.

The first drops of cool rain hit Luke solidly on the side of his face, seeping through into his unconscious, and he felt himself slowly coming to. Before he opened his eyes, he could hear the rain pelting the grass with a numbed *tchi*. And behind that sound, another sound gradually filtered through to him. It was a small, whining noise, like a small dog in pain. He gradually opened his eyes, and as they came into focus, he saw him.

Lying about ten feet away from him lay a figure, dirty, cloaked in a dark cloth, curled in a ball just as Luke himself was. The whining noise was clearly coming from him, emerging from deep in his throat. Luke raised himself slowly to his knees and shuffled over to the figure. He was older, perhaps fifteen, sixteen . . . with a shock, Luke recognised himself, the Lost Boy.

He reached out a hand and touched the boy on his bared arm. Solid flesh. Human feeling. As he touched him, the boy stopped whimpering, and looked up at him with deep, sad eyes. He attempted a smile, but it came out lopsided, hurt-looking. He opened his mouth, and in a small hoarse voice, he spoke, "Hello".

Luke couldn't stop staring at him. The boy's face was filthy, his eyes shadowed and dull. The clothes he wore hid his body. Luke remembered seeing the Cowboy for the first time, how the light of stars and galaxies seemed his very essence. This boy was the exact opposite. He seemed to drain light.

Luke tried to answer his greeting, but no, his voice had definitely gone with the old man. Questions formed in his mind, but the Lost Boy seemed to know what they were, or anticipate them, without the need of hearing them.

"Yes," he said, "I'm real. But I'm not like the Cowboy, I can't disappear again. Your imagination was my home, but now I'm homeless."

Are you me? Luke felt the words in his head, and again the Lost Boy spoke in anticipation.

"No, I'm not you. But I am *from* you."

Are you . . . my future?

The Lost Boy frowned. "I don't understand. What do you mean?"

Just then, above the noise of the rain, Luke heard his mother's voice. "Luke? Where are you? Come in out of the rain, Luke!" He looked down towards the house. He could see her coming towards them.

The Lost Boy saw her too. "I have to go. I don't want to be seen." He stood up, but bent over behind the screen of grass. He broke into a crouching run. Once he glanced back at Luke, who was looking between him and his mother. "Don't worry. I'll be fine. I know how to survive. But you have to learn how. Go to your mother. She's worried about you. We'll meet again, soon, and we'll have more time to talk then. Now go on, go." He turned around and continued running, keeping well down in the grass. Luke hesitated a moment longer, watching to see if he would disappear, fade like the rest of them. But he knew that he wouldn't. Luke shivered then as he noticed the rain for the first time. He turned and ran down to his mother.

Avril cried out with relief when she saw him. She folded him in her arms. As she did so, a faint movement in the long grass caught her eye. She strained, but could see nothing. She looked down at Luke. "Was there somebody up there with you?" Luke shook his head. Avril looked back up towards the field. "I must have been imagining it." She felt Luke shiver. "My God, you poor child, you're soaked. Come on, I'll get these clothes off you and put you in a nice hot bath, before you catch a chill."

Chapter Eleven

The last thing Sandy knew was Luke's voice whispering in her head, *Don't go*, and the last thing she felt was his warm breath on her face.

Mary was inconsolable.

Two days later, they buried Sandy. The funeral was poignantly dignified. As the coffin was lowered, Mary laid a tiny pair of shoes on top. Seeing this, Luke let go of his mother's hand and went to stand beside Mary. He reached down and laid his own tribute on the lid: the plastic cowboy. He wanted Jake to go with Sandy wherever she was going. He knew that, with his protection, her journey would be safe.

When he looked up, he noticed a figure watching the funeral from a distance. It was the Lost Boy. He was hiding in some trees at the edge of the graveyard. He had found some more clothes and shoes, but he still looked a mess. When he realised that Luke was looking at him, he raised a hand in greeting, then turned into the shadows of the trees and walked away.

Luke looked around to see if anybody else had noticed him but everybody had their eyes downcast as the priest prayed over the grave. *I wonder if I'm the only one who can see him*, Luke thought. He saw his mother looking at him, signalling to him to stand beside her again. He put the Lost Boy out of his mind for the moment as he linked her arm.

He thought again of Sandy, and he felt a hole opening in his soul when he realised the loss of her. He wanted to just fall through the hole, to sink forever. He leaned closer to his mother, hiding in her long coat as his tears coursed down his cheeks, unhindered.

They tried to keep their voices down. They didn't want Mary to hear. It was her house, after all, and her child had just been buried. Avril had told Mary they would stay with her in Glasnevin for a few days.

Luke heard it all, however, sitting in the room next door with his ear to the wall.

"I don't see how you have to go now," Avril whispered tensely.

"Avril, it's probably the best chance we have of finding out. I have to go while Pitford is here," Fran tried to sound as reasonable as he could.

"Come on, we can go at any time. We don't need to do it while that man is here. Besides, I think he's a phony."

Fran was in a huff. "Well, I don't. I think we're on the right trail here. I don't understand you. Just last week, you were all enthusiastic about finding out everything we can."

"Well, this isn't last week. Anyway, what about Mary? She's devastated. She needs as much support as she can get."

"Sandy wasn't our child. Luke is." Fran regretted it as soon as the words were out, but it was too late.

Avril's voice had risen a notch. "Oh, Christ, Fran, what's gotten into you?"

"OK, I'm sorry, I didn't mean that. I don't want to sound heartless, but I want to do what's best for our son."

"So do I, dammit. And right now, he's in grief too. He

loved Sandy, you know that. He needs us, not some voodoo doctor! Can you not wait, even for a few weeks?"

"But what are we going to do about Monks and this video thing next week?"

There was a brief pause, during which Luke could hear his mother taking in a sharp breath. "You aren't seriously saying you still want to go through with that?" She was positively livid now. She didn't even give Fran time to answer. "Oh, go on, then, go! Go down to Kerry, find your fucking doctor. Leave me here to look after reality." Footsteps, and a door slammed.

Luke sat in silence, his head resting against the wall, listening to his father's uncertain noises from the other room. Tears wet his cheeks, and he wiped them angrily away. *It's my fault*, he thought, *it's all my fault*.

Fran travelled down to the Dingle Peninsula with Joshua Pitford that afternoon. He apologised to Avril, and said a guilty farewell to Mary and Luke. The truth was, he felt awkward, unable to offer great comfort to Mary. He felt somewhat outside of the bond that had formed between her and Avril. Besides, he was relieved at being able to get away from the mourning atmosphere of Mary's house in Glasnevin. He had never liked funerals; attending the funeral of one of his parents, whether in ten or twenty years' time, scared him even more than the idea of one of them dying.

Fran also felt it would be good to get a bit of space, for Avril and himself, and also for Luke. The last few weeks – between Monks, Pitford, and now Sandy's death – had been a strain, and they had sparked off each other in a way he had never felt before, and it frightened him. They all needed space. He said as much to Avril before he left, and she nodded – in agreement or indifference, he wasn't sure.

It was a great relief, then, to reach the Atlantic shore and feel the force of the sea in his hair. They found James Abbott's house, a small bungalow overlooking Clogher Strand. It was an appropriate place for the old man. As they got out of the car, they could see him sitting in a conservatory to the side of the house, staring out at the huge waves which crashed onto the black rocks below. His wife, Agnes, came to the door and welcomed them. She was a beautiful woman, even at sixty-six, with fine, unlined cheekbones and a soft mouth. She brought them into the conservatory and introduced them to her husband.

James Abbott was a very frail old man. The wheelchair which he occupied seemed much too big for his body, which looked like a withered prune. His skin was as dark and weathered as the rocks on the shore. His eyes, though, were cold steel, piercing his guests as he examined them, head to foot. And his voice, when he finally spoke to them, seemed stronger than his lungs could manage.

"Pleased to meet you. 'Scuse me if I don't get up." He opened his mouth in a gap-toothed grin at his own joke.

While Agnes Abbott went to make tea, Pitford explained again why he had asked for this meeting. He told Abbott about Luke, and that Fran was his father. He mentioned Séamus Ferguson, asked him if he remembered giving his paper to him when Ferguson was his student, but this sparked no recognition. Eventually, his voice trailed off. The old man didn't appear to be listening. He had gone back to staring at the sea. Fran wondered if his mind was out there. Fran began to suspect that the journey might have been a waste of time.

After a couple of minutes of tense silence, however, Abbott turned his head slowly and looked straight at Pitford. "Well? Go on!"

Joshua Pitford looked awkwardly at his fingers. "Dr Abbott – " he began.

"Mister – I'm retired, which I'm sure is obvious. Call me Mister. Or just plain Jim."

Pitford began again. "Mr Abbott, your wife said that you didn't hear much news these days, that you probably hadn't heard about Luke's case. I'm curious to know what you think of what I've described. If you think it might be a case of what you described in your paper as Abbott's Syndrome?"

"Rubbish!"

"Sorry?"

"It's all a load of crap. The whole paper. All in the past now, water under the bridge."

"You mean you don't believe what you wrote in that paper any more?"

"Bullshit, it was all bullshit. I was young and naïve. It was a lot more complicated than I made out."

"More complicated? How do you mean?"

But Abbott had gone silent again. His wife came in with a huge pot of tea and a plateful of fruit cake. Abbott picked up a large wad of the cake and shovelled it into his mouth, pushing it to the right-hand side where the teeth were, chewing laboriously. They watched him doing this for several minutes, as they awkwardly sipped their own tea. When he had washed down his cake, Abbott belched contentedly and closed his eyes.

Pitford tentatively tried to get back to the subject. "Do you not think that Luke's projections sound remarkably like Abbott's Syndrome?"

177

Abbott opened his eyes irritably. "I don't bloody know. Maybe they do. Maybe the child is psychotic."

Fran breathed out in exasperation. He felt his head pounding, the morning's argument with Avril coming back to him. It was a mistake coming here, yet he knew he had to get away. He just wanted to go for a walk on that beach.

Pitford was more persistent, however. "Mr Abbott, I know that you were only theorising when you wrote that paper, and yes, I can certainly see that it would be more complicated than you described. But the fact is, what we have in Luke is possibly the first real case of Abbott's Syndrome."

Abbott looked around him in disgust. "Hmph! Second."

Fran and Joshua looked at each other. "What did you say?" They both asked the question together.

Abbott put his hands to his mouth like a megaphone, and bellowed through them, *"Second!"*

Joshua Pitford leaned in close to the old man. "Are you saying there was an earlier case?"

"Of course there was. Long time ago. Thirties, I think. Water under the bridge. Forget about it."

"But why didn't you write about this case in your paper? My God, everything would have been so different if you had said that there was a real case."

"No proof, no evidence."

"What do you mean?"

"I met the man in the thirties, I told you. Kept it secret for years, he asked me to. When I went to write my paper, I couldn't find him, and I had no notes, nothing but my memory. No proof. Nobody would have believed me. They'd have said I was crazy. So I wrote the bloody thing without using the case, pretended it was just speculation. They said I was crazy anyway. Maybe I was."

Fran asked quietly, "Who was this man?"

"Look, why are you asking all these questions? It's all gone now. Why dig it up? I promised the man I'd keep his secret. I should never even have written the damn paper. None of it was true."

Pitford laid his hand gently on the old man's arm. "Please, Mr Abbott, if it was such a long time ago, then you've kept his secret very well. What can it matter now if you tell us about him? We're trying to help a young boy. We've come all this way, please tell us about this man."

They watched Abbott struggling with a vow made many decades before. Finally, he let out a sigh, and raising his eyes, he mouthed two words: *forgive me.* "His name was McAndrew, Thomas McAndrew."

"Is he still alive?" Fran asked excitedly.

Abbott let out another bellow of laughter. "Alive? Certainly not!"

Fran was visibly disappointed. "Oh. When did he die?"

"How would I know? Long time ago. All I know is, he was old when I met him, back in the thirties. About 1932, I'd say. He must have been sixty-five or seventy, even then."

"Where was this?"

"Connemara. Clifden. It was my first job. I was about twenty-three, I suppose. I'd just graduated, got a job there as the local GP. He came to see me, told me he had a troubled spirit. That was all. He wouldn't say any more. I told him he should try the parish priest, that there was nothing I could do for his spirit. He went away then. He came back about two weeks later, and just sat in my office, saying nothing. I asked him had he been to the priest, but he shook his head, and muttered something, I couldn't quite make out the words. 'I'm a monster – I've become a monster – Created a monster'. Something like that. I was getting angry with him at this stage, asked him to leave, that I had some real patients waiting. That was when it happened."

"What happened?"

"He shot a burst of light out the top of his head, nearly blinded me with it. The most amazing colours and patterns of light you could imagine. This went on for a couple of minutes, then it just stopped. He made me promise to keep it secret. Then he asked me to try and find some way of stopping it, of inhibiting his abilities. I told him I'd have to examine him, do some further tests. So he came back four, maybe five times over the following month. Each time, he would give me an example of what he was able to do with the light – a private show, I suppose.

"I was very excited by all this. I was bursting to tell somebody about this man, but I'd given him my promise, and I didn't want to scare him off. Besides, I didn't know anybody in the town at that stage, and I didn't meet Agnes until about thirty years later. So, I kept my counsel.

"I began to read up as much as I could find, which wasn't a lot, as you can imagine. That's when I hit on the idea that this light was a result of an excess flow of energy through the body, and I began to formulate my thesis. Most of what I wrote in that paper I worked out at that time. Unfortunately, I had no success in proving it. I performed all the tests I could think of on Thomas, but he seemed perfectly normal, other than having a very strong heart for a man of his age. He wasn't very interested himself in what was causing his visions. He just wanted them to stop. But, for me to be able to help him, I needed to find the cause. And I was having no luck there. I even had doubts then about my own thesis. I know now I was wrong. Still, I tried to persuade him to come up to Dublin with me, to let some experts see him. But he refused. When he saw I wasn't making any progress, he stopped coming. He just vanished. I went to the address he had given me, but it was an empty hovel. Nobody in the area seemed to know where he had gone. It seems I was the only person who'd talked to him for years. He was a complete hermit. Everybody thought he was, let's say, a bit eccentric. And then he was gone. Vanished."

"Did he tell you more about himself during his visits?" asked Fran.

"Oh yes, after he'd come to the surgery a couple of times, he opened up a little more. He was from that area, all right, born sometime in the 1860s. He didn't know anything about his father; he was born in a poorhouse, and his mother died giving birth to him, so he was brought up there. He realised his abilities at an early age because he found it was his own way of communicating. He only learned how to speak when he was sixteen or seventeen. But the other people in the poorhouse, and the people running it, thought he was some sort of demon, so they threw him out. He spent many years begging, moving around the country. There were still some fairy stories floating around, he told me, claiming that people saw all these lights, these colours. 'That was me,' he told me.

"Anyway, he didn't say much more about himself. I worked out myself that, after many years of travel, he'd come back to the area, and had lived in a hovel since. But any time I asked him why he wanted to get rid of his powers, he would just shut up, I couldn't get a word from him other than that first day when he talked about being a 'monster'." Abbott paused, remembering. A dark shadow crossed his face. "I never did find out, but it seemed to me that there had been some terrible crime, or cataclysm, for which he felt responsible, something connected with his magical powers.

"After he disappeared, I continued my practice for a couple more years. But all the time I was looking for him, waiting to get word of him. And I kept up my reading, and refining my theory. I decided to go back to university, and I got some lecturing hours. I finally got around to writing my paper – this must have been 1939, 1940 – but I shied away from mentioning Thomas, because nobody knew him, I had no proof except for a few notes and my own memory." Abbott waved a dismissive hand. "The rest you know." He lapsed into a complete silence. The effort at memory had been great, and he was exhausted now. He turned his attention back to the waves crashing in their relentless rhythm, always the same, past, present and future.

After making a few polite but futile efforts to ask him about McAndrew's visions, and about his own theories, they realised that he had given them all he was willing or able to. They quietly stood up to leave; Agnes Abbott brought them their coats. They talked to her briefly, but she was able to tell them nothing more. As they turned to go, however, Abbott spoke, his voice suddenly soft and sad: "Look after the boy." Fran glanced sharply at him, but he hadn't moved.

As they turned the car out of the driveway, they looked back once more at James Abbott. He was still with the waves. Joshua Pitford, his own voice hushed for once, said, "Well, for somebody whose memory is supposedly dim, he sure seemed pretty lucid to me."

"Yes," agreed Fran. "Whatever about Abbott's theories, this man McAndrew certainly had the same powers as Luke. I wonder what happened to him?"

Pitford raised an eyebrow. "If he ever existed."

Luke was miserable. Since Sandy's death, he felt more isolated from the world than ever before. She had meant more to him than he could have imagined. She was his connection to a reality from which he was otherwise detached; now, when he tried to find that connection, there was just an empty space.

If I could, he thought, I would give up all the magic, if only she were still alive. He tried it. He buried all the light in his head under a deep cloud, and he waited. But she did not come back. He felt he was to blame for her death, that there must have been something he could have done. Now, his parents were angry with each other, and it was his fault too. He cried himself to sleep.

His dreams disturbed him. He saw the Dark Man, his face a mask of horror, shrouded in mist. Sandy was there, smiling trustingly at Luke. The Dark Man crept up behind her, his hands claws to grip her throat and rend the life from her. Luke tried to call out to her, to warn her of the danger. He tried to summon the Cowboy, but the only picture in his head was an empty desert. He tried to find his voice, but he had no voice. His mouth was gone, just blank skin from nose to chin. It stifled his breathing. He struggled to catch oxygen, and awoke thrashing, his face covered with the blanket of an unfamiliar bed.

He looked around in the semi-darkness, fear still gripping his heart. He blinked, hoping he would find himself at home in his own room. Where was he? Was this

183

the lair of the Dark Man? Then he remembered. This was Mary's house in Glasnevin, and if he reached out and touched the wall, his hand would be inches from his mother's warm body. He lay still and imagined her there. His fear gradually abated. But the empty loneliness did not.

Something made him climb out of the bed and walk over to the window. The moon was a silver coin hanging over the earth. By its light, Luke could see the damp city streets below. Their emptiness echoed back at him. He wondered what it would be like to live out there, crouched in a cold laneway, wrapped in all your possessions. As he stared down at one of those dark gaps, a figure stepped out of it into the moonlight, and looked straight up at his window.

Luke recognised him immediately. The Lost Boy carried a sleeping bag under his arm, and a small rucksack on his back. He looked very small from that angle. Luke wondered how he himself must look to the boy. He raised a hesitant hand and waved. The Lost Boy smiled and waved back. Luke thought, *Maybe I could let him in*. He signalled to him, pointing downstairs. The Lost Boy understood, but shook his head firmly. They watched each other for a few minutes, and then the boy turned and disappeared down the alley again.

Luke stared at the dark space for a few more minutes, but the Lost Boy did not reappear. Eventually, the cold air in the room began to turn his feet to ice, and he hurried back to bed, rubbing them together rapidly until the blood started flowing. He picked Lenny off the bedside table, and hugged him close.

Avril was finding it difficult to cope with both Luke and

Mary. Her anger at Fran had abated, but she had a thumping headache in its place.

She tried her best to take Luke out of himself, to distract him, but he remained morose, closed off. She could only give him second place in her thoughts and efforts for the moment, because Mary demanded more of her time. Hence her need for Fran to return as quickly as possible.

Mary was shattered. Her world had collapsed, and she saw no reason to dig herself out of it. Two days after the funeral, she wouldn't move from her bed. She cried all day. Avril looked after the house in Glasnevin, tidying, making a dinner which nobody felt like eating, apologising to callers because Mary wouldn't see anybody. She shuttled between Mary and Luke, soaking up their grief in bucket-loads. She had to bottle up her own sadness. By the time she went to bed, she was a nervous wreck.

Avril found herself imagining what it would be like to lose Luke. She tried to picture herself like this, lying in bed, nothing but emptiness inside. She tried to think of Luke being lowered into the ground, and her own despair dragging her down with him. How would she live, how would she be able to adjust to a world without him? She found it impossible to imagine. A world without Luke was inconceivable. She felt as though she had always known him, that he had always lived and would live on forever. An unbroken line through time. No, it was impossible to think that Luke's life could be so easily snatched away.

Avril fell asleep, her head filled with these thoughts. She had no dreams.

In the morning, she awoke with a fresh sense of life. Fran wouldn't be back from Kerry until late afternoon, and she was determined to make the most of the day. She bullied

Mary out of bed, and forced Luke into his coat. "We're going for a walk," she announced, "to blow away the cobwebs."

The Botanic Gardens were nearly empty. It was midweek in June, and most people were working, unaware of the small pocket of grief out for a stroll. Avril decided she had made a good choice. The cool air on Mary's face seemed to revive her spirits a little. She began to talk, and found eleven years of memory coming back to her in a flow of words. It was a great relief to talk about Sandy, and she was grateful to Avril for listening. She picked out all the positive memories, the joy of Sandy's birth, watching her grow and play, the softness of her skin, the bright light of her eyes. The pain and uncertainty of her sickness were cured in this skilful editing of her short life, so that her eleven years seemed fuller, less of a waste. Mary found herself smiling as each new memory bobbed to the surface. For the first time, she even opened up to Avril about her dead husband, who had never got to see his daughter. Now, she said, they were together at last. He would look after her.

The transformation in Mary was remarkable. Strength she had lost through the years of looking after Sandy now seemed to return to her like a lost ghost, not defeating her sadness, but mixing it with hope. Avril knew she would be all right.

Luke was brighter too, though the heaviness remained on his soul. As he walked, he breathed clouds of vapour into the air. He amused himself by chasing after his own breath, trying to trap it again in his jaws, to suck it back into his lungs. He imagined Sandy beside him. They could have a contest blowing shapes from their lungs. Instead of light, air would be the new material of their words. He tried to blow a circle, a heartshape, a star, but all he got was clouds. After a while, he looked at Sandy, and realised she wasn't there, and the heaviness descended again. He hung his head and kicked pebbles.

They walked on for a few more minutes, and then sat down on a bench at the side of the path. Luke saw some ducks on the pond a dozen yards away and he looked up at his mother. Avril handed him the paper bag of bread she had taken from the house. "Go on, but don't go too far."

Avril and Mary sat with their own thoughts for a few minutes. Avril watched Luke pulling off huge chunks of bread and throwing it directly at the ducks. The ducks turned and tried frantically to get away, before realising that this was food and not stones, and they just as frantically tried to reach the bread first. Avril smiled, watching him.

Luke very quickly ran out of bread. He watched the ducks fighting for the last scraps. He looked up. The Lost Boy was standing at the far side of the pond, watching him. He waved to him. The Lost Boy didn't wave back, but turned and walked into the trees behind him. Luke took a step closer. He looked back at his mother, but she wasn't watching him. He felt in his pocket for Lenny. The dog was safe.

Mary spoke her thoughts. "Avril, do you remember, years ago, how we talked about me moving into 'Exiles' with you?" Avril looked at her and nodded. Mary went on, "Well, if you've no objection, I think I might finally take up your offer."

Avril was delighted. "Oh Mary, how could I have any objections?" They embraced warmly.

A chorus of quacking drew their attention.

"Luke? Where's Luke?" Avril was off the bench and running already.

187

"Oh God! Oh no, please no . . ." Mary followed her.

Avril looked around, expecting him to appear suddenly from behind a tree. "Luke? Where are you? Luke?" Her voice rose as panic began to grip. She looked around desperately. Nothing. Her eyes finally came to rest on the pond itself. Dear God, please don't let him have . . .

She waded in, scattering ducks. She reached down, feeling for she didn't know what. She kept going further in, but the water never reached above her knees. She swung around and around frantically. Something rushed past her ears. Air. Wind. Numb noise. Her vision blurred. She could see Mary faintly at the side of the lake, her arms windmilling, shouting something to her. Mary's voice finally filtered through to her: "Come back, Avril. He's not there. We've got to search the park. Come on, he can't have gone far."

Slowly, like swimming through honey, Avril made her way back to the path. Mary quickly found two or three more people, and they began a search. Somebody went for the police, and they arrived a little while later. They searched the Gardens and the surrounding area, but Luke had disappeared completely. Two hours later, a general alert was put out. Luke was declared a missing person.

Chapter Twelve

Fran's heart began to thump when he saw the police car outside Mary's house. The front door was opened by a young garda, and there were several other gardaí inside. "What's going on?" he demanded, looking around for a familiar face.

Mary, recognising his voice, emerged from the kitchen. She looked tired and dishevelled. Her eyes were bloodshot. "Oh Fran, thank God you're back. It's Luke. He's disappeared."

The shock of it hit Fran like a blow to the chest. He reeled and would have fallen, but somebody put a steadying hand on his arm. He sat down heavily and took several deep breaths. When he could speak again, he managed to ask, "Where's Avril?" He looked around the room. He recognised one or two of Mary's neighbours, and – yes, there was his own mother in another corner, looking lost and bewildered. Fran wanted to go over and talk to her, but he didn't think his legs would carry him.

The police officer with the steadying hand spoke. Fran looked up at him, and recognised Inspector Moroney. What was he doing here? Fran felt his grip on reality slipping. He felt as though somebody was playing a cruel joke at his expense, and he wanted it to stop.

"She insisted on staying out searching with my officers,"

Moroney was saying. "I tried to persuade her to stay here, that she needed some rest, but she's a stubborn woman."

Fran was in a fog. "But what happened?"

Mary told him. "We looked everywhere. He just disappeared. Oh God, Fran, I'm so sorry."

Fran looked up at Inspector Moroney, desperation in his voice. "Maybe he's just . . . hiding somewhere?"

Moroney shook his head. "We believe that Luke is either wandering the streets somewhere, or . . . there is a possibility that he was kidnapped."

"Kidnapped?" Fran's voice had gone very small.

"At the moment, it's the most likely possibility. Remember, it has been tried before, and we knew that those responsible might try again. The fact that he vanished so suddenly, and that we haven't been able to find him, suggests a possible abduction. Your wife told me about this man Peadar Monks. Do you have any more information about him?"

"Monks? You think Monks did this?" Fran was horrified.

Moroney held up his hands defensively. "We don't know if anyone *did* anything, as such. But, if Luke has been kidnapped, then, if your wife's information is correct, Monks might be a suspect. Or he might have information regarding his whereabouts."

Fran felt his anger mounting. "So have you arrested him?"

"We have his office and his house under surveillance at the moment. He hasn't shown up at either location yet. His wife's at home, but we don't want her to know we're waiting for him. If he is responsible for Luke's disappearance, she might warn him off."

"What is this, some kind of TV cop programme? Why

can't you find this man and arrest him? He could be killing my son now, for all we know!" Fran knew he sounded hysterical, but he couldn't stop the pitch of his voice from rising.

"Mr Laverty, please, we're doing all we can. There's no firm evidence that anything like that has happened to your son. We're just taking what precautions we feel are necessary. The best way you can help us is if you can think of anywhere Luke might go, or of anybody else who might know where he is."

Fran calmed down finally, but he could not concentrate on Inspector Moroney's words. He buried his face in his hands, and moaned, "Oh Jesus, I should have known something like this would happen. We should never have let Luke's story out. We were practically inviting his kidnappers in the door. It's all my fault."

There was a knock at the door. A few moments later, Jimmy McGinnity was in the room, his hand on Fran's shoulder in sympathy. "I've just heard what happened, Fran. Anything I can do to find young Luke, I'm at your service."

Fran looked up at him in dazed confusion. When his eyes focused and he saw who it was, he suddenly had somewhere to direct his anger. He launched himself from the chair, grabbing McGinnity by the collar and forcing him back against the wall. "If it wasn't for you," he snarled, "we'd still be living happily in our old house, shut away from the world, instead of hoping and praying that our child isn't lying dead in some alleyway!"

McGinnity's arms flailed pathetically. He was trying to speak, but Fran was blocking his windpipe. Inspector Moroney and one of his gardaí finally wrestled Fran off him. McGinnity composed himself, trying to regain some dignity. He shrugged. "As I say, anything you need, I'm at your service."

It had been a hard day on the road for Peadar Monks. By the time he pulled into his leafy driveway, waves of fatigue were sweeping over him. He couldn't wait to get stuck into his dinner, then he would have a good soak in the bath, and he might even persuade his wife to give him a massage. However, as he closed the car door, he realised that something was up.

There were three men in his driveway, all dressed in sober suits.

One of them spoke to him. "Peadar Monks?"

"Yes. Can I help you gentlemen with something?"

The man who had spoken produced an ID card. "Special Branch, Mr Monks. I'm Sergeant McCullough. We'd like to ask you a few questions. Could we go inside, please? We'd hate to put on a show for your neighbours."

Paula Monks had been watching from the side window. As her husband came in the front door, followed by two of the men, her bewildered expression changed into one of fear. *The bastard,* she thought, *he's brought it down on our heads now.* They made their way into the living-room and sat down.

She launched straight into him, "Christ, Peadar, they haven't . . ." Her husband's withering expression cut her off in midsentence. The two policemen stared from one to another.

"Mr Monks, a young boy named Luke Laverty went missing today," McCullough told him. "We have reason to believe he may have been kidnapped. Do you know anything about this?"

Monks was indignant. "I beg your pardon? What does this have to do with me?"

"So you aren't from the Revenue?" asked Mrs Monks. Her husband shot her a warning glance, but the two Special Branch men ignored her.

Sergeant McCullough continued. "I understand you've been in touch with the Laverty family, that you were harassing them?"

"Certainly not! I mean, yes, I have been in touch with them, but I wasn't harassing them. I made them a business offer. How dare you suggest that I might be involved in kidnapping their son!"

"I'm sorry, did I say that?" McCullough asked him innocently. "Nothing was further from my mind. I was just curious to know if you had heard about it. For instance, did you know that there was a previous attempt to kidnap Luke, about seven or eight years ago?"

Monks looked at him cautiously. McCullough had a boyish face with a wry, mischievous smile, but the effect was spoiled by the intensity of his stare.

Peadar Monks was unnerved. "Yes," he said slowly, "I seem to remember something about it on the news."

"Coincidentally, that was about the time that you first contacted the Lavertys, I believe?"

Peadar Monks thought about his options for a moment. There wasn't much point in playing dumb if they knew everything already. "Well, there was nothing coincidental about it, really. As I say, I saw him on the news, and I thought to myself, *there's a good way of making money*."

"Making money?"

"Yes," replied Monks. "I'm sure Mr Laverty has told you the story already. I approached him with a business proposal. I wanted to take Luke on the road – as an inspirational healer, I suppose you could say." He watched the two men for a response, but their faces gave nothing away. "I suppose you probably think I'm just cynical. But I'm a businessman, and this was just a business idea. Nobody would have got hurt. Anyway, as you know, the Lavertys weren't interested."

McCullough looked up at his assistant, but he was speaking to Monks. "Some people might consider kidnapping to be a profitable business."

Monks smiled, refusing to rise to the bait. "Luckily, I'm not one of those people, Sergeant McCullough. You see, I'm a cautious man, and I would see kidnap as a high-risk venture. I only take risks if I believe they will pay off."

"Why did you contact the Lavertys again? Another proposal?"

"Yes, as a matter of fact. Something along the same lines as before. Only I didn't want to pretend that Luke was a faith healer this time. Maybe I'm getting soft in my old age, but I realise that some people take such things very seriously. So my proposal was to bring Luke on a tour of the country as a storyteller. A sort of travelling *seanchaí*, taking his imagination to the people of Ireland and beyond."

"Very generous of you. And, apart from a glowing feeling inside, what exactly would you have got out of this deal?" McCullough asked sardonically.

"Well, of course, as the child's manager, I would expect a modest fee, a small percentage of the takings. By the way, the Lavertys were quite happy to listen to my proposal. I set up one session for them a couple of weeks ago, which went very well. Last time I talked to them, they were considering accepting my proposal."

194

"I see." McCullough chewed his pencil for a moment. "Mr Monks, where were you this morning at around eleven?"

The shift in the questions threw Monks off balance for a moment. "I was with a client. In Portlaoise," he answered frostily.

"Can your client verify this?"

"Of course he can. Look, Detective, or Sergeant, or whoever you are. I've already told you. I know nothing about this kidnapping, if that's what you say it is. I have every sympathy for the Lavertys, but I really don't see what any of this has to do with me." He raised his voice to what he knew was its most authoritative level. "And frankly, I don't like the tone of your questions. As you can see, you're upsetting my wife."

Mrs Monks, who was thoroughly lost at this stage, suddenly perked up on hearing herself mentioned. She tried to look upset, but in fact she was seething at her husband.

McCullough grinned. "Oh, I've plenty more questions, Mr Monks. Maybe you could come down to the station and we could continue this there? Then we wouldn't have to disturb your wife's sensibilities any more."

Monks stood up and opened the door of the living-room. "I will do no such thing. In fact, as far as I'm concerned, this interview is finished. I'm tired of your allegations. I might even consider suing for slander. Now, I would appreciate if you would leave us in peace. I've had a long day."

Sergeant McCullough nodded to Mrs Monks and slowly stood up, followed by his assistant. As he reached Monks, he handed him a card. "Questions, Mr Monks, not allegations. As far as we're aware, no crime has been committed. So how could we allege that you were involved in anything? Anyway, if you think of anything else you'd like to tell us, give me a call. Otherwise, I'm sure we'll see you again soon."

Once they were outside, McCullough turned to his silent assistant. "I want two unmarked cars to stay on this house. If either of them leave, I want them followed. Anybody else calling to the house, follow them when they leave."

Inside, Peadar Monks mopped his sweating head and thought about what to do next. The name Oliver Fuller came to him, and he wondered if he should call the police again and tell them about him. He reached for the telephone, but paused. No – he'd had enough of the police for one day. Instead, something made him take a piece of paper from his back pocket and dial the number written on it.

It rang for a while before it was picked up.

"Hello?"

The deep voice chilled him now. He regretted having got involved in all of this.

"I need to talk to you. There's been a change of plan," said Monks, trying to keep the trembling out of his voice.

"What are you talking about? Have the Lavertys made up their minds?"

"No. It's Luke. He's disappeared."

There was silence at the other end of the line.

"Do you have any idea where he might be?" Monks asked tentatively.

"Should I?"

Monks found the sweat rolling again. "No, no. I just thought . . ."

"I'll meet you in an hour at the warehouse." The phone went dead.

* * *

Avril was finding it hard to adjust to her surroundings. She had never been in a police car before, and the squeaky feel and worn smell of the leather seat made her uncomfortable. This couldn't be real. This was not happening.

They had been driving around for the best part of three hours, slowing down as they passed laneways, peering through shop windows. Avril felt as though they were actors in some movie being filmed in slow motion. The car seemed to drift, swimming through honey, and with it drifted her mind. It was as though some other reality had taken hold of her life from the moment Luke was born. She imagined another version of herself in another dimension, with a child whose only magic was the life in him. She thought of this woman moving through her life as an ordinary mother, with an ordinary child doing ordinary things. What could possibly threaten them?

Instead, she found herself cruising the streets of Dublin in a police car, searching for her extraordinary, magical child. And all she wanted to do was to fall asleep and wake up as that other woman, as though it had all been a dream and Luke lay sleeping in his room. Before she knew she was doing it, she was cursing the God that touched her child's life with light.

"What was that?" The young garda driving the car braked beside a lane and tried to focus on a point in the shadows. A flash of colour, fleeting movement. "There! Did you see it?"

His partner squinted. "I don't see anything. A cat, maybe?"

Avril moved her head slowly. She found it hard to shake

herself free, to disconnect from the other dimension. She peered down the shaded lane where the others were looking, but could see nothing. How could he be in such a place?

"Let's check it out," said the driver, opening his door.

His partner looked back at her. "Could you wait here, Mrs Laverty? It's probably nothing. But we'd better just check it out."

Avril shivered, but said nothing. She watched the two gardaí walking down the lane, still moving as though underwater. Even in the afternoon, it was dark down the lane. One of them had a torch, which he flashed about, lighting up the detritus of the city. It was damp in the lane, and the rows of bins gave it the appearance of a metal and plastic graveyard. Another brief movement, and the torch swung. The two men moved towards the spot, looking around them as they went. A cat darted out from behind a bin and ran past them. They gave the rest of the lane a cursory search before turning back.

As they drove off, one of the gardaí turned again to Avril and spoke to her softly. "I'm sorry, Mrs Laverty. False alarm."

Avril, staring out the window, spoke without looking at him, her voice defeated. "Could you take me home now, please?"

Chapter Thirteen

At the darkest, furthest end of the lane, Luke crouched with the Lost Boy, shielded by the latter's dark cloak. The torch shone this way and that, but seemed to pass over their hiding-place. Instead of showing up their cowering figures, the light seemed to disappear in the cloak before it moved on. Despite the warmth of the cloak, Luke felt a chill deep in his bones.

He watched the two gardaí turning and walking away from his hiding-place, and he looked beyond them at the small huddled figure of his mother in the car. She, like him, appeared to be cloaked in darkness, but it was a different sort, a kind of resigned despair. She was staring straight at him, and for a moment Luke thought that she must be able to see him. Why didn't she do something, why didn't she call to him? Then it would be so easy to stand up out of this darkness and go to her, and life could go on. But she sat unmoving in the car, her eyes fixed on him but seeing something else. Luke knew that he was invisible to her.

Again, as the two men got into the car and started the engine, Luke felt a great urge to run after them, to tell them to wait, that he was tired of playing hide-and-seek. But a strong force held him back – not the arms of the Lost Boy, because Luke knew that he would never be hurt or forced to do something against his will by this boy. What held him back was a deep instinct that warned him that the danger ahead would have to be faced alone, and to turn back now would risk not only his own life but also those of his parents. So he lay still under the cloak and watched the car drive away. A single tear escaped and ran down his face. If the car had still been there, the glint of light refracted in this tear would have dissolved all the darkness around.

They stayed that way for a couple of minutes. Slowly, the Lost Boy stretched his limbs and began to stand up, pulling the cloak off Luke, wrapping it around his own shivering body. He looked at his young companion, and spoke to him. "Did you want to go to her?"

Luke nodded.

"It's not too late. You can still go back."

But Luke shook his head.

The Lost Boy gathered his belongings into the small bag which he put on his back. "Come on," he said, "Let's find somewhere warmer. I don't think we should stay anywhere around here. It's too dangerous. We'll have to get out of the city centre before it gets dark. When we get there, I'll find us some food. We can eat, then we can talk, then sleep."

He windmilled his arms, each in turn, starting the blood circulating again. Then he turned and walked back down the lane towards the street. Luke scrambled to his feet stiffly, shook himself and ran after the boy. To anyone who gave them a passing glance, they would have looked like two brothers, the older one looking after the younger. A closer examination would have revealed two stray souls, dirty and cold, their faces clouded in uncertainty and fear. The Lost Boy did his best to show that he knew what he was doing, so that Luke would take comfort from him. But he was sure that Luke could read the signs of his discomfort.

As they walked, they looked around, ready to hide again at the first sign of a police car. They walked a long way, and as they got further and further from the city centre, their shadows began to lengthen. Luke gazed at the world around him, the colours and smells of the city. He saw a poster, bright and brash, and tried to make out the words: *The Greatest Show in the Universe – Circus Oculus – Where Human Feats of Daring meet Technology to create the Most Elaborate Feast the Eye has Ever Seen!* Luke wondered what a circus was.

They passed the canal, and still they kept moving. The Lost Boy was absorbed in his own dark thoughts, and it was a while before he looked around at Luke again. When he did, he felt a rush of guilt. Luke was grimacing with pain, limping weakly. The Lost Boy stopped, and, without a word, shifted his bag so that it rested against his chest. Then he lifted Luke's small body gently onto his back. Luke didn't protest; he buried his head in his friend's shoulder, and dozed.

The Lost Boy had great reserves of strength, but he eventually had to rest. Besides, it was twilight now, and time to find food and shelter for the night. He could feel the grumbles in Luke's stomach against his back, and realised how hungry he was himself. He soon found what he was looking for. A Chinese restaurant. He carried Luke around to the back. The restaurant's ventilation system blasted hot air straight out through a wire frame. Before the air rose into the evening sky, it had time to heat a large section of the alleyway.

The Lost Boy stooped, and Luke climbed wearily off his back. He took off his cloak and wrapped it around Luke. He told him to sit down against the wall of the restaurant while he went to see about getting some food. Luke found himself alone for a few minutes. The warm rushing air brought with it a great variety of cooking smells, and Luke's mouth began to water. He was weak with hunger, and his eyes fluttered in exhaustion. He was too weak, too tired, to cry now. His dreaming mind drifted, and he wondered again why he was here.

He thought of his mother's face, the shock of realising what he had done, the great desire to undo it, but the overwhelming feeling that he would have to go through with whatever choice he had made, even though he had no idea where he was headed. He knew that Sandy had something to do with it, that her death had changed everything for him, and that he had to find some part of himself that she had taken with her when she died, before he could come back. He knew the great pain he was causing his mother and father, but something – instinct, his subconscious, his Guardian Angel – told him that it was necessary, that he would otherwise be subjecting them to even greater suffering, an irredeemable pain. He knew all this with his heart, but in his mind it was all a mess of confused words and pictures and feelings, which he could not tell apart.

The Lost Boy came back, carrying two small foil containers. "Careful," he said, "it's hot." Luke pulled his sleeves down over his fingers and took the proffered container. He breathed in the fragrance, like a wild perfume, and his mouth watered again. He looked at the food in the container: bits and pieces of chicken, beef, even a couple of prawns, peppers and onions and carrots, all drowned in a steaming sauce. He looked up at his friend quizzically. The Lost Boy had already started eating. He grinned, a stringy piece of chicken stuck in his teeth.

"Don't worry, it won't bite you. It's all leftovers, but it's safe to eat. The man was very nice. He must be used to people like me begging. He gave me a lot of good bits of meat. You'll have to use your fingers, though. Go on, eat up."

Luke grabbed a piece of beef, scalding his fingers. He dropped the meat and stuck his fingers in his mouth, sucking them.

The Lost Boy sniggered. "All the trouble I went to, and you end up eating your own fingers!"

Despite himself, Luke laughed silently. He tried again, blowing on the food, and handling it more gingerly. It tasted like heaven. The warm sauce flowed down his throat, and he felt a glow deep inside. He wolfed half of it down, and began to hiccup, setting the two of them off again in a fit of giggles. Luke ate the rest more slowly, savouring it now. He had never eaten Chinese food before, and he wondered what else he was missing.

While he was eating, he had no thoughts for his situation. However, as soon as he finished, the Lost Boy quietly took the container from him, laid it on the ground and produced a plastic bottle of water from his bag. They took it in turns to drink. The Lost Boy watched Luke constantly. Luke avoided his eyes.

"You tired?" he finally asked him. Luke nodded. "OK," said the Lost Boy. "We'll sleep soon. But first, we talk." He paused. "You didn't have to follow me, you know."

The words came into Luke's head. As he thought them, he knew that the Lost Boy understood them. *I had to.* He looked up at his friend, willing him to understand why.

"But what about your parents? They'll be worried sick about you."

Luke hooded his eyes. *I know.*

203

"You can still go back. It's not too late."

I'm afraid to go back. Something is wrong.

"And that's why you ran away?"

Luke shrugged.

"Are you going to try to contact them?"

I don't know.

"Is this because of Sandy?"

Maybe. If it wasn't for me, she wouldn't have died. Now I'm afraid they'll all die.

"That's crazy. If it wasn't for you, Sandy would have died a long time ago. You gave her life."

Luke shook his head and stared at the ground. *I can't go back until I work it all out. It's up to me now.*

The Lost Boy laughed. "And what can you do, a scrawny little kid? You're not even twelve yet!"

Luke looked up at him furiously. The Lost Boy was surprised at the depth of feeling he read in his eyes. *I can look after myself.*

"If you say so. But, at the moment, you need me. So let me look after you for now, then we'll see."

Suddenly, Luke beamed at him, and all the worry seemed to melt from his face. *So what do we do now?*

"Right now? We sleep." And he detached his sleeping bag from the end of his rucksack. He sat down on the ground, took his shoes off, and climbed in. He looked at Luke. "Come on." Luke hesitated a moment before removing his own shoes and climbing into the large sleeping bag with his friend. They clung to each other until their combined body heat wrapped them in a cocoon of comfort against the cold night air and the hard ground, and they slept.

* * *

The hollow echo of the warehouse door closing behind him startled Peadar Monks. He froze in his tracks, waiting for an earthquake to happen. After a few seconds, his shoulders slumped when he realised with relief that he was alone. His nerves were frayed to snapping point. He did not want to be here. He thought of his soft bed and wished he was there.

He regretted having agreed to meet at this god-forsaken hour, in these sinister surroundings. He regretted having called the Dark Man at all. Scratch that: he regretted ever having met him, ever getting involved in all of this, ever having heard of the Lavertys. He was in deep now, and he was panicking, looking around wildly for an escape. He thought of the police, of the phone number which he had in his pocket. He could just turn around and go home, and call that Sergeant – what was his name? McCullough? That's it, he'd call him and tell him all about Fuller and the suspicions he had about him.

He turned on his heel, and all his paranoia came flooding back. Standing between him and the door, as though he had always been there, was the Dark Man. Monks took in a sharp breath. They watched each other. The Dark Man spoke first.

"You weren't followed, I hope?"

"Followed? No." Monks was puzzled.

The Dark Man nodded. "So, the child has disappeared?"

"Yes. This morning. They've been looking all over for him."

"And the police came to you?"

"Yes, but . . ." Monks trailed off. The Dark Man was silent, forcing Monks to ask him, "Do you know anything about it?"

The Dark Man looked irritated. "You asked me that on the phone. How could I know anything about it?"

"Well, it's just . . . they mentioned kidnapping. I thought – "

"You think I'm capable of kidnap?" The question held a distinct edge of menace.

"No, no, of course not. I just thought since you were so interested in young Luke – "

The Dark Man interrupted him again. "Tell me what the police asked you."

Monks recounted the events of the evening in a babble of words. The Dark Man listened in silence, nodding. When Monks had finished, the Dark Man stood in thought, chewing a knuckle.

"You didn't mention me at all?"

"No, not at all. I don't think they know anything about you."

"Good." The Dark Man thought in silence.

Monks waited for him to say something else. The seconds stretched out interminably. He could feel a trickle of sweat running down his neck. Finally, he had to break the silence himself. "So, I suppose we'll have to abandon our little venture, then?" He laughed nervously.

The Dark Man sighed. The smile which he turned on Monks made him flinch involuntarily. "If only it were that simple, Mr Monks." Suddenly there was a gun in his hand, and Peadar Monks stepped back further into the shadows of the warehouse, whimpering. "You see, you know more about me than you should. I was careless, I let you get too close. And I realise now that I can't trust you. You were going to call them again, weren't you?"

"No, no, I wasn't, I swear to you!" His voice had risen to a squeak. "I know nothing about you!"

"You know my name, don't you? Or at least, one of my aliases. For that, I'm afraid I'll have to shoot you." He raised the gun, pointing it to Monks's head.

"Please don't kill me," Monks squealed as his bowels gave way. "Listen, I can help you. I don't know what you've done with him, but I can help you."

The Dark Man laughed a deep throaty laugh. "That's what's so ironic about all this! I didn't kidnap the bloody kid, I have no idea where the little shit is!"

At that moment, there was the distinct sound of a car door being closed outside. Immediately, Monks began to scream, *"Help, somebody, please help me, he's going to shoot me, he's a madman!"*

"Shut the fuck up!"

Suddenly, there was a loud pounding on the door, and a megaphone voice called in to them, "This is the police. We have the building surrounded. There's no way out. Surrender your weapons and come out of the warehouse with your hands in the air."

"You bastard!" shouted the man who had called himself Oliver Fuller. *"You fucking brought them here!"*

"No, I swear to you, they must have followed me! Oh Jesus, *help!*"

"Ahh, fuck!" The Dark Man took aim and fired two shots into Peadar Monks' head.

As the sound of the shots reverberated around the warehouse, the police battering-ram burst through the door, followed by two armed gardaí. They quickly took in the scene: one man lay dead, a pool of blood beginning to spread thickly around his head. There was no sign of his killer.

* * *

That night, Fran and Avril lay awake in Mary's house, each with their separate thoughts. They were both exhausted, but could not think of sleep. They lay side by side, but they could not bring themselves to touch, to hold each other for comfort, to draw solace from the other's arms. It was as though Luke had become their bond, the knot that kept them close, focused on their internal world. Now he had disappeared, they were forced to look up and, seeing each other, were afraid to search for an intimacy which might have disappeared with their son.

Avril was still as numb as she had been earlier in the day. She clung to the idea that she was walking through a dream landscape from which she would wake up to find the world making sense again. By contrast, Fran's mind was in overdrive. He was frantically turning over all the possibilities in his mind, hoping that he would think of something that would lead to Luke's whereabouts. When they did eventually sleep, they were united by their nightmares, in which Luke was drifting slowly away from them, constantly being jerked just beyond their reach by some dark, twisted form. They both awoke, feverish, their heads pounding, to the realisation that the phone was ringing.

It was Inspector Moroney, with the news of Peadar Monks's murder. It took Fran a few moments to comprehend what he was being told. "So you think this has something to do with my son being kidnapped?"

"Firstly, Fran, we don't know that Luke has actually been kidnapped," said Moroney. For some reason, Fran resented this man calling to give them this news, and he resented him using his first name. Moroney went on, "However, if that is the case, then the man who murdered Monks may well have been his accomplice. Maybe they fell out. Maybe Monks had no idea this man was going to kidnap Luke, which is why he went to confront him in the warehouse last night. If this is the case, then we can be sure that this man is holding Luke somewhere in Dublin. We're hopeful we can find him."

"So, I take it you have no idea who he is?"

There was a long pause at the other end of the line. "That's the strangest thing about last night's murder, Fran. The killer completely disappeared. We searched everywhere, but it was as if he had crawled through a crack in the floor. In fact, he vanished in much the same way as Luke did."

"Do you think he's going to kill my son?"

"God, no! If he does have him, he may simply be looking for a ransom, in which case he may try to make contact soon."

"But we aren't rich! Surely he'd be better off kidnapping a politician's child, or a businessman's?"

"That's what makes me think it isn't money he's after. There must be some ulterior motive for wanting to abduct your son, some connection with Luke himself, maybe even something he knows about Luke that we don't."

"In which case, he may not contact us at all."

Another long pause. "That's a possibility. But, listen, Fran, at the moment, we have no idea if Luke has really been kidnapped. This thing with Monks may be pure coincidence. It could well be that he just ran away, for whatever reason kids run away. Was everything OK between you and your wife, for instance?"

"Yes . . . well, I suppose we might have had the odd

209

argument . . . do you think that's what made him run away? Oh God!" Fran groaned, the weight of his guilt bending his back.

"I don't know. It could have been anything," said Moroney, quickly backtracking. "In the meantime, we've got a murder investigation on our hands, which may or may not link with Luke's disappearance. We'll have to wait and see what forensics turn up at the warehouse, and we'll talk to Monks's wife and people who know him, to see if they have any idea who might have killed him. There's a garda calling around to you later, to see if there's anything you need, and I will try to come over at some stage in the afternoon."

After he had hung up, Fran went back to the bedroom and told Avril the news. She stared blankly into space while he was talking, and didn't appear to notice when he had finished. He watched her for a moment, and then stood up, sighing.

"I'll go and get you a cup of tea." As he reached the door, he heard Avril's voice, smaller, more vulnerable than he had ever heard it before.

"Fran?"

He turned back to her.

"Will you hold me, Fran?"

He came back to the bed, and suddenly the floodgates opened, and she wept uncontrollably. She could not stop, all her pain and fear and despair poured out of her in a river of tears. Fran held her tightly, stroking her hair, muttering, "It's going to be all right, it's going to be all right," over and over.

Luke woke suddenly in a strange place, feeling trapped and cramped. He started to panic, looking around wildly for his parents, for some familiar mark of his life. He felt somebody stirring beside him, and fear gripped his heart, until a voice spoke to him, "What is it, Luke? What's wrong?" and then the Lost Boy was there, holding him, reassuring him, and everything that had happened came back to him. He was stuck here in a sleeping bag on the hard ground, miles away from his mother and father, lost and lonely. He sank back and began to cry.

"That's it," said the Lost Boy, shuffling out of the sleeping bag. "We're going to get some food, and then I'm taking you home."

But Luke looked up in fear, and shook his head vigorously, brushing away his tears roughly. *No! He'll kill them.*

The Lost Boy was exasperated. "OK, but we have to do something, we can't keep wandering the streets until you work out what to do next. You'd never last." He pondered for a moment. "Listen, why don't I go and tell your parents that you're safe? I won't even say where you are. I'll just tell them you have to work this thing out yourself, and when it's over, you'll come back to them. How's that sound?"

Luke avoided his eyes. He wanted so much to say, yes, go back, but take me with you. I want to go home. Instead, he hardened his heart, and shrugged. The Lost Boy shook his head slowly.

"OK," he said, "you wait here while I get us some food, then we'll find somewhere quiet for you to hide while I go and find your parents."

The Chinese restaurant was closed, so the Lost Boy had further to go to find them some breakfast. While he was gone, Luke sat and breathed in the morning air. He tried to avoid thinking about what was going to happen, but it was impossible not to be aware of his situation. He really had no idea what he was going to do. He knew that the Lost Boy was right. He would not survive long living like this. Something would have to happen, and soon. He tried to call on the old Druid, to come to him and give him guidance, but he couldn't think straight, and he was sure the old man couldn't hear him. Maybe he was dead too.

The Lost Boy returned with some bread and cheese, and a flask of hot tea for their breakfast. "We have to give the flask back, of course."

Luke accepted the food with gratitude. The improvised sandwiches filled a gap, and with the hot tea coursing through his veins, he felt his energy returning rapidly, and with it, things began to look a little brighter.

After they had eaten, the Lost Boy stood up again. "Come on," he announced. "I've found somewhere you can stay for a few hours while I go and talk to your parents."

A few minutes away, they reached a small house with its windows boarded up. The Lost Boy led him straight around the back of the house. "I've found a way in," he said, pointing to a gap in one of the windows. He squeezed through, and, leaning out, pulled Luke in after him. Luke looked around. It was dark with all the windows blocked, but once his eyes had adjusted, he could see that it was not as derelict as he had suspected. There was still some furniture – an armchair and a small table, and an old bed in another room.

"I think whoever owned this place must have died a couple of years ago," said the Lost Boy. "They must have been very old, and there was nobody to deal with the house, so it's just been left here until somebody decides to do something about it." He sniffed the air. "It isn't too damp, anyway. A bit musty, but it's better than staying in the street. And look what I found!" He opened a cupboard door in the kitchen, and proudly took out a couple of cans of baked beans. Luke was impressed. "I don't know why these were left here, but there are some other tins here too. Corned beef, tuna . . . and look, there's even an opener." He pulled open one of the drawers, and produced the essential tool. He was obviously quite pleased with his find. "Nothing to cook with, I'm afraid, but I'm sure you won't mind cold beans."

Luke patted the seat of the armchair, and watched the dust rise. When it had settled, he sat up in it, his feet dangling. The Lost Boy became serious again. "I'd better go, then. Listen, Luke, are you sure you don't want to come back with me?" Luke shook his head firmly. The Lost Boy took his cloak off and laid it across Luke's legs. Then he walked back to the gap in the window. "OK, you're the boss. So I'll tell them that you're safe, that they aren't to worry, that you just need to sort something out, and then you'll come home. Anything else?"

Luke looked at him, and his eyes misted over. *Tell them I love them. But please don't tell them where I am.* The Lost Boy watched him a moment longer, then nodded and left.

Once he was gone, Luke felt a sudden need to urinate. He found the bathroom upstairs. The toilet, he discovered, was in a worse state than the rest of the house, and he had to hold his nose until he had finished and was able to go downstairs again. He sat back in the armchair and pulled the cloak back over his knees. He felt in his pocket, and realised that Lenny was still there. He took out the small dog, placing him on top of the cloak. He thought of the Old Druid again, and called for his help, but he found himself blocked again, as though somebody had boarded up the windows of his mind.

He thought of Sandy, and he tried to sense her spirit out there, but again, he could only feel an empty space. He tried to conjure up the Cowboy, and this time he could certainly see him at the back of his mind, riding across the plains, but he was only a vague shape, a mirage, never coming closer. Eventually, he too faded.

He thought of the Lost Boy, and he felt sad for him. Luke had trusted him, had believed that he would be able to help him to find the right path. That was what had prompted him to go to him in the park. But now, Luke realised, the Lost Boy seemed as bewildered as he himself was. *How could he be anything else?* thought Luke. He is a part of me, after all.

He thought of his parents, and he hoped that they would understand his reasons for leaving, even if he didn't understand them well himself. He knew that they had been trying to help him, and they had made some progress in working out who he was. But instinct told Luke that he would have to face the last few steps alone. For the last while, a shadow had been tracing his steps, and it was getting closer, matching him footfall for footfall.

A rat poked its nose out from under a floorboard a few feet from the armchair. Luke was not afraid of it. They watched each other curiously for a few minutes, before the rat decided not to venture further afield. It disappeared again. Luke dozed.

His belly let him know that a couple of hours had passed since the Lost Boy had left. He went back to the kitchen, took a tin of beans and a tin of tuna and armed himself with the opener. After a struggle, he managed to open a jagged hole in each tin. He found a spoon, and dug in. The cold beans and the smell of the tuna made his stomach tighten, but he gulped them down. When he had finished, he felt his belly curdling with wind, and he let a few loud, satisfying farts. Their echo in the empty house made him giggle in his own silent way.

Suddenly, he had the strangest feeling that he was not alone. He glanced around. It wasn't the rat. He looked at the window where they had got in, but there was no sign of anybody. It wasn't the Lost Boy, he was sure of that. He moved around the house silently, looking out of all the windows. Nothing. Yet he felt sure that there was somebody . . . yes! There it was again, like a double heartbeat overlaying his own. He was close, Luke was sure of it. If he jumped backwards, he would jump on the shadow. The house suddenly felt smaller, more closed in. *I have to get out,* Luke thought. *He'll trap me here.*

Grabbing the cloak, he went straight back to the window, and struggled to squeeze his body out, jumping the last few feet to the ground. Without looking back, he ran to the back wall and climbed over. As he ran down the lane, his heart fluttering, a thought struck him, and he stopped. Lenny! He had left the little dog sitting on the armchair. He hesitated a moment, but fear crept up on him again, and he could not go back. He broke into a run again, convinced that the Dark Man was on his heels, that he would be lifted from his feet at any moment and swallowed into the shadows.

He ran for many minutes, and then he had to stop. He fell on the ground, panting for breath. When he was able to breathe again, he was on his feet immediately, and ran again. Now, he was no longer thinking of the Dark Man. All he could think was *Run!* So he ran, not knowing why. He watched his feet as they moved, as though they were independent of his will, *thud-thud-thud.*

Eventually, he was aware that there were no more houses around him, that his feet were on grass. His legs seemed to gain weight, until they were heavy as lead, and he sank to his knees. He looked up, and the sky swirled above him. He could see a huge white space in front of his blurring eyes. It was shot through with lights, coming from inside, twisting, turning colours. He could hear music, too, a strange, dancing, tune, eerily familiar. The lights moved in time with the tune. Luke felt drawn to it. He struggled to his feet, his head spinning, and he tried to focus on the white space in front of him. He walked, half-blind, towards it. The music got louder. Before he realised how close he was, he had reached the edge, and he tripped over something. Pain shot up from his ankle as he fell over. Instead of hitting the ground, though, his body was caught by the whiteness in front of him, breaking his fall. He realised it was some sort of cloth. He felt around with his hands to where the cloth met the grass, and he lifted a corner of it. The music got louder yet, almost deafening him. He crawled under, and collapsed. A voice came to him, a gentle voice, but he didn't understand the words. It was some strange language. He saw an old man bending over him, a look of surprise on his face. Was it his Druid? Luke sighed and then passed out.

Back in the abandoned house, a solitary figure stood beside the armchair, holding Lenny in his frail hands. He cursed himself aloud. "Damn, damn! Am I too late, then? Oh Luke, I have failed you. I am getting too old for this. I could not hear you call, and when I did, you must already have gone. How can I find you now?" The Druid looked at the small puppy, then turned to go.

Chapter Fourteen

Inspector Moroney settled himself comfortably in Mary's living-room, accepting her cup of tea gratefully. He sipped the tea and grunted with satisfaction, before beginning, "Well, we have established that the gun that was used to kill Peadar Monks was the same *type* that was used at the attempted kidnap of your son. Not the same gun, mind you. The same type of gun." He paused to sip again. "This doesn't prove anything, but it *might* indicate that the same man was behind both crimes."

Avril and Fran sat opposite him, red-eyed and pale. "Were there any witnesses?" asked Fran.

Moroney shook his head. "Apart from the garda car that followed him, one or two people saw Monks arrive at the warehouse. But nobody has come forward so far to say they saw the other man arrive or leave. The gardaí on the scene are convinced that there's no way he could have got in or out without being spotted."

Avril, awake now and totally focused on the search for her son, leaned in close to Moroney. "So, what hope is there of finding this man now?"

Before the Inspector could answer, there was a soft knock at the front door. They all waited, tense with anticipation, while Mary went to answer it. On the threshold stood a young dishevelled boy, fifteen or sixteen years old, a sad solemn expression on his face. He stood there so long, saying nothing, that Mary began to close the door on him.

Then he spoke. "Is Mrs Laverty in?"

In the living-room, Avril heard the question and rushed to the hallway. She stared at the Lost Boy and he stared back. There was something so familiar about him, but she couldn't pin it down. "Yes?" she asked, unable to keep the tremor from her voice.

"Mrs Laverty, I just came to tell you that Luke is all right. He has a few things that he needs to do by himself. He says to say that he's safe, and that he loves you both."

Waves of relief washed over Avril. She grasped the Lost Boy by both hands and sobbed, "Oh, thank you, thank you. Where is he? Take me to him."

The Lost Boy avoided her eyes. "I'm sorry, but I can't tell you. He made me promise . . ."

Avril was confused. "What do you mean? Please, if you know where he is, take us there."

"I'm sorry," the Lost Boy repeated. "I have to go now." But Avril, panicking, gripped him harder. He begged her, "Please, let me go. You're hurting me."

The others were in the hall now. "What's going on?" Inspector Moroney demanded. Seeing Avril struggling to hold the Lost Boy, who was desperately trying to squirm away, Moroney grabbed his arm and roughly pulled him into the house, closing the door. Immediately, the boy's eyes filled with tears and he tried to shrink into a corner.

They all stood around, the adults staring at the Lost Boy, he staring back in fear.

It was Mary who spoke eventually, addressing the boy: "It's OK, nobody's going to hurt you. Let's just sit down and talk. Come on, we'll go in here." And she walked back into the room. Hesitantly, watching Avril, the Lost Boy followed her, and soon they were all sitting down, waiting for him to speak again.

When he eventually did speak, his voice was very small. "I'm sorry, Mrs Laverty, I didn't mean to frighten you. I just came to tell you that Luke is fine, he told me to say he loves you – both of you," he added, glancing at Fran.

"Please tell us where he is," Avril beseeched him again.

The Lost Boy hesitated before answering, "I can't tell you that. He wouldn't let me tell you that."

"Who wouldn't?" Inspector Moroney leaned in, but a look of confusion crossed the Lost Boy's face. Moroney asked another question: "Who's your boss?"

"I . . . don't know what you mean. I don't have a boss." The Lost Boy was becoming increasingly bewildered. Maybe it was a mistake coming here after all.

Moroney drove the point home. "Come on, you don't expect us to believe you kidnapped Luke all by yourself, do you?"

The Lost Boy's eyes flew wide in panic. "Kidnapped? I didn't kidnap Luke!"

Avril was as surprised by Moroney's question as the boy himself. "I don't think . . ." she began, but Moroney wasn't listening.

"So why won't you tell us where he is?" he demanded.

"I can't. He asked me not to."

"What's your name?"

The Lost Boy was silent. How could he tell them he had no name? He wished this man wasn't here. He had given his message to the Lavertys and now he just wanted to go.

Inspector Moroney stood up. "Right – well, if you won't tell us here, maybe you'll tell us down at the station. Come on." He grabbed the Lost Boy by the arm. The boy looked around him, pleading. Fran and Avril were unsure what to think or do. Inspector Moroney must surely know what he's doing.

"Will you two follow me down to the station?" Moroney asked Fran and Avril as he dragged the boy out of the room. "You should probably be around if he tells us where he's hidden him. Could you wait here with Mrs Cullen, Sergeant?"

As they reached their cars, the Lost Boy turned around in Moroney's grip. His voice was close to tears. "I didn't kidnap him. He came with me. He just wants to sort everything out, then he'll come home. He asked me to tell you." Fran and Avril glanced at each other as Moroney pushed the boy into the back seat of his car.

Five minutes later, Inspector Moroney glanced at the Lost Boy in the rear-view mirror. He was cowering in the back seat, a look of abject terror on his face. Moroney was sorry he had handled him roughly. "Look, I'm sorry for scaring you. It's just that there's a nice mother and father back there who are very concerned about their son. So the sooner we get this over with, the better." He looked back at the road, then glanced back in the mirror. "Shit!" he cursed, and slammed on his brakes.

In the second car, Fran had to hit his brakes too, narrowly avoiding a collision. "What's he playing at now?" he muttered as they both pulled in to the kerb. Moroney got out of the car and opened the back door. He stared in for a moment, and this time Fran and Avril both heard him cursing. Fran rolled down his window and asked, "What's the matter?"

Moroney glanced up at him. "Come and see for yourself." Fran got out of the car, puzzled. He went to stand beside

Moroney and peer into the empty back seat. He frowned. "Where's he gone?"

Moroney, between gritted teeth, said, "You tell me."

Fran walked back to the car and told Avril the latest twist. Avril stared blankly ahead as she spoke: "That boy . . . he was so familiar, so strangely familiar." She looked at Fran. "I think he was telling the truth. I don't think Luke has been kidnapped at all. And now we've lost a chance to find him. What are we going to do?"

Back in the abandoned house, the Lost Boy stood in the same spot where the Old Druid had stood a couple of hours earlier, looking more forlorn and disconsolate than ever. He had no idea where Luke could have gone. He might not have got far, but then again . . . *I should never have left him, or I should have brought him home*, he thought. *In fact, I should never have taken him away in the first place. What am I going to do?*

To Luke, it felt as though a lifetime had passed since he had last seen light. In fact, it was only a matter of a few seconds. He awoke with the feel of somebody holding the back of his head. A cold smooth surface touched his lips, and he tasted water. He opened his lips and welcomed the drink, cool and soothing. He drank a long measure, gradually feeling the life begin to flow again. As it did so, memory came to him in patches, and a question struck him. Who was holding him, supporting his head while he drank? Was he home again, and was this his mother's touch? No, he would have been able to smell her perfume, but his nose was filled instead with strange, exotic fragrances. Was it the Druid? Yes, that seemed more likely. He was sure he had seen him just before he passed out. Or . . . maybe it was the Dark

Man, who had chased him here? The possibility filled him with an icy dread.

Slowly, fearfully, he began to open his eyes. When he saw it was not the Dark Man, he breathed a sigh of relief, but he was puzzled. He didn't recognise the face of the old man who was smiling at him, singing strange words. He felt no fear towards this man, however. Maybe it was the gentle sound of the song he sang – a lullaby, just like his mother used to sing to him. The language was different, but the meaning was the same. *Sleep now, rest now, feel no more fear.* Luke let the music wash over him, and he felt at peace. Then he realised that, behind the old man's lullaby, he could hear another sound. It was the music he had heard, the swirling, dancing music, and he remembered the lights that accompanied it.

He opened his eyes again and tried to sit up. The old man broke off his song and spoke in English, his accent thick and guttural, "Slowly, child, slowly. Rest. You tired. Much sweat. Run a long way." He made a running motion with his fingers, and wiped his brow in mock exhaustion. He grinned at Luke.

Luke finally managed to sit up, his back supported by the old man. He looked around, seeking the source of the music. The room he was in was small and cluttered, filled with buckets, mops, stacks of chairs, and many strange objects that Luke didn't recognise. He noticed the dancing lights on one of the cloth walls. The music was coming from behind the wall.

The old man noticed the direction of his gaze. "Your mother and father in there?" he asked, pointing to the wall with a thumb. Luke frowned and shook his head. The old man raised his eyebrows. "You alone?" Luke nodded. "You have ticket?" Luke was puzzled. "You know, for circus?" Luke's frown deepened. The old man was surprised. "This Circus Oculus, no?" Luke remembered the poster he had seen, but it still meant nothing to him.

The old man seemed to understand. "You not know what is circus, is true?" Luke shook his head. "Come, I show you." He stood up and held out his hand. Luke took it tentatively. The old man led him over to the wall of light. He chose a chair from one of the piles and set it before the wall, lifting Luke on to it. Then he took a flap of the canvas wall at Luke's new eye-level and peeled it back, revealing a gap of a mere two inches, through which a stream of colour spilled immediately. He gestured to Luke, inviting him to look through. "Welcome," he said. "Welcome to the Circus Oculus."

Luke pressed his right eye to the cold canvas and peered in. The sight that greeted him was unlike anything he had ever experienced before.

The vast dome of the tent was awash with colour. Images formed and dispersed, colliding with each other. A blue sky suddenly darkening as clouds rushed by. Rushing water, rapids crashing over rocks. A flower bloomed, its petals spiralling out, revealing its delicate heart. Then it burst into flame, and an explosion of fire appeared to engulf the tent, causing the unseen audience to gasp, before they realised that the fire itself was just another projected image. Gradually, the fire died down, and the music softened with it, as the dome turned into the night sky, an astrodome of twisting constellations.

It was then that Luke became aware of the woman. At first, she was just a darker shape against the dark dome, blocking out and revealing the stars as she passed them. Gradually, the light grew around her, and Luke caught his breath. The trapeze on which she sat was almost invisible against the blackness, and she appeared to be flying in slow motion, her body moving in graceful time to the shifting astral spectacle. As the light around her increased, Luke noticed the texture of her skin, so soft and supple, and how her long black hair streamed out behind her. Her body flowing through the stars was the most beautiful thing Luke had ever seen. He fell in love immediately. Just for now, he felt as though all twelve years of his life had been leading up to this moment.

She shifted her weight on the trapeze and, in one swift movement, swung out and down, appearing to slip through the air, so that the audience gasped again in anticipation of her imminent plunge to the hard earth below. But just at the last possible moment, she twisted her legs outward, and her ankles caught the edges of the trapeze, and she swung, never breaking the rhythm. A thousand hearts had skipped a beat, and now throbbed again in relief as the audience applauded. The woman threw her arms out to the sides and arched her torso upwards. She looked more like a bird than a human being. She hung there as though the air was her element. She continued to arch her back, until she was able to raise her hands to the trapeze. Now her body formed a perfect circle. She held the pose for a moment, and then slowly released her legs, swinging them out and down beneath her. Finally, she flicked her arms, and swung back into the seat. The look of intense concentration vanished, replaced by a broad smile of satisfaction.

At that moment, Luke felt she was looking directly at him. Her dark eyes bored into him, and he involuntarily stepped back from the gap in the canvas. The chair wobbled and he would have fallen, but the old man caught and steadied him. He was a little shaky, and had to sit down.

The old man grinned at him. "You like her, yes?" Luke

blushed. "Ha! I knew you like Katrina. Katrina, she is star." The old man's face became wistful for a moment. How often had he stood in this spot and watched Katrina's act?

He shook his head and looked back at Luke. "So, you have name?" Luke nodded. "Yes? You want tell me?" Luke pointed to his mouth. The man frowned, before realisation dawned. "Ah! You no able speak!" Luke smiled. Despite his lack of language, and the old man's limited English, he felt that they understood each other well.

The old man patted his pockets and took out a pen and a slip of paper. "You write?"

Luke took the paper and slowly spelt out L-U-K-E.

"Luke! Nice name. I please meet you. I name Anisim." He shook hands with Luke, laughing.

"So, Luke, you like Circus Oculus?" Luke nodded vigorously. "That is good. But this last show in Dublin. Next time, maybe, you see whole show, yes? Now, you must go. I have work." He waited for Luke to climb down, but the child hung his head and showed no sign of moving.

Anisim sighed. "You want me take you home? To parents?"

Luke shook his head, and suddenly a tear escaped.

"Oh, why you cry?" The old man used a corner of his sleeve to wipe Luke's face. He stepped back, pensive, rubbing his chin. "You have parents?" Luke gave no sign. "Oh, no, you no have parents? They die?"

Before he knew what he was doing, Luke was nodding assent. His parents' faces flashed before his eyes for a moment, but he felt that he had reached a turning point, and he could not go back now. Though it hurt him deep inside, he denied them.

Anisim was deeply touched. He placed his hand softly on Luke's head, muttering, "Poor child, poor Luka . . ." He bent down and looked into Luke's tearful eyes. "So, little Luka, where you live? Aunt? Uncle?" Luke shook his head. "You not have home?" Luke shrugged. Anisim was horrified. "My God, so young! So, maybe I take you police, hmm? They look after you."

Luke's eyes flew wide and he shook his head firmly. Anisim grinned. "Ahh, I see now. You in trouble. Police chase. Maybe why you run, yes?" Luke nodded. That sounded like a good story. "So what you do? Steal sweets?" Luke looked gravely at him and shook his head. "More serious, yes?" Anisim thought for a moment. "Ah, I think I know. You in prison, home for bad children? You run away." Luke nodded. At least, this time, it was a half-truth.

"So, you want hide here a while?" Luke grinned. Anisim sighed again. "OK. I not much like police. I live in same place when I your age, Luka. Run away to circus, just like you. They catch me, put me away, I run away again. So I soft. I like you." He listened to the sounds of the circus for a moment, then declared. "Is finish. I work. You stay here, quiet." He laughed when he remembered that there was no need to say the final word. Luke was not likely to make much noise.

It became obvious to Luke that Anisim was some sort of janitor to the circus. He chose a large brush from the corner of the room and waited until all the people had left the main tent, then he went out to clean up. Luke hid in a corner, but nobody else came into this little room. Luke realised that this was Anisim's domain. Here, he was king and ringmaster.

Luke could hear the hustle and bustle as the circus crew moved about. He felt a great sense of excitement. Who are all these people? Is this what they do all the time? Are they all like Katrina? The thought of Katrina brought him back to the image of her floating through the air. He closed his eyes and imagined her floating above him. He pictured himself as her sole audience, gazing up in hushed awe. She twisted and turned her body for him alone. She looked down and smiled, her wide generous mouth thrilling him.

Luke must have dozed off then, because he awoke to Anisim gently shaking him by the shoulder. "Come Luka, I take you my home. They take tent down now. My work done. Need big strong men take tent down. I too old."

Anisim's home was one of a couple of dozen caravans scattered around the tent. It was small and cramped, and it was obvious that the old man lived alone. It smelt of old clothes. He offered Luke the only chair in the caravan, and busied himself at the tiny kitchen section. "You hungry?" Luke nodded, suddenly feeling his stomach growl. The old man turned back, concentrating on his cooking. He said nothing more to Luke until he triumphantly produced two huge steaming bowls of soupy stew. The smell of it made Luke feel dizzy, and he spooned it voraciously. The warmth of it sank deep into him, and he felt content.

When the meal was over, the old man spoke again. "So, Luka, you not have place to go?" Luke shook his head. "You sure?" Luke nodded. "OK," Anisim sighed, "tonight, you stay here. In the morning, circus leave Ireland, travel around Europe, Belgium, France, Italy, Germany, Hungary . . . all around. You, my friend, stay here, Dublin."

Luke was downcast. He had half-expected Anisim to ask him to come with them. The old man stood up and stretched expansively. "So, now, we sleep, yes?" Luke glanced over uncertainly at the dishevelled single bed at the far end of the caravan. But Anisim chuckled. "That where I sleep. You, here." He pulled out a small bed which was folded against the wall, and covered it with fresh sheets and a blanket. Luke stood up and bowed to him in gratitude. The old man laughed again, "You just like acrobat, full of, how to say? Theatre!"

Despite his exhaustion, Luke lay awake for much of the night. The bed was more comfortable than he had expected, but his mind was alive and would not rest. In the other bed, Anisim snored loudly. Luke was thrilled by the experiences of the day, and yet fearful of what they might mean. The old man had been so good to him, and he was fascinated by the whole circus idea. But the spectre of the Dark Man hung over him. Luke thought he had been chased from the abandoned house, but now he was no longer so sure. He had certainly felt his presence, searching for him, but, he now realised, he might not have been *physically* there. Just as Luke had tried to reach out mentally to Sandy, to contact her, so the Dark Man was trying to reach Luke. The further he got from him, the safer he would feel. So maybe that was why he was running.

He thought of his parents again, and he wondered if the Lost Boy had told them he was safe. He hoped so, because he knew they would be worried sick about him. He missed them, but he knew there was no turning back now. Besides, that was one of his reasons for running away in the first place: to keep the danger away from them. As for the Lost Boy, Luke considered the possibility of somehow letting him know where he was. But the only way of doing that was to return to the abandoned house in the hope that he was there. The thought of going back there made Luke shiver, so he abandoned the idea.

He was on his own. Even the Old Druid appeared to have abandoned him. The only course of action that was open to him was to try to persuade Anisim to take him with the circus. After that, he had no idea where the path led, but he had to follow it to the end. And he felt, increasingly, that various paths were converging, and that the end was almost in sight.

Luke finally drifted into a log-heavy sleep in the early hours of the morning. When he awoke, it was almost midday already. He looked around him. The other bed was empty, and Anisim was nowhere to be seen. Luke lay back and waited. He was sure the old man would return soon.

A few minutes later, there was a sudden knock on the door, and Luke quailed when he heard a female voice call out, "Anisim?" The woman opened the door and looked in. Luke lay still in the bed, and she didn't see his small form. She climbed into the caravan, and Luke realised with dismay that it was Katrina. She walked straight to the kitchen and seemed to be looking for something. She found it: a tin-opener. She turned to go, and then she noticed him.

Katrina gasped, and Luke tried to hide under the bedclothes. He was as much embarrassed by his thoughts as he was afraid that she would betray his presence to the rest of the circus. She spoke to him in the strange language which Anisim used. All Luke knew was that she sounded angry. He peeked out from the bedclothes. She spoke to him again, then switched to English. Her accent was as strong as the old man's, but she was much more fluent. "Who are you? What are you doing in Ani's caravan?"

Luke shook his head and was trying to indicate that he could not speak, when Anisim walked in. "Katrina!" he said in surprise, glancing down guiltily at Luke. "You meet my friend Luka?" He smiled nervously at her. When Katrina spoke to him in their own language, Luke sensed the great affection that existed between them. They talked for a couple of minutes. Luke heard his name mentioned a number of times. They seemed to be debating something. Finally,

229

Katrina turned her warmest smile on Luke and sat down at the end of his small bed. Luke's heart did another backflip.

"So, little Luka, Ani tells me you are an orphan, and that you run away from the police. This is true?"

Luke nodded. He regretted his lies, but he couldn't take them back now.

"And you have nowhere else to go?"

A shake of the head, a melancholy expression. Luke was settling into his role.

Katrina glanced up at Anisim, who looked like he was about to protest. Instead, he raised his hands in a gesture of surrender. Katrina turned back to Luke with a satisfied smile. "So, little man, how would you like to join the Circus Oculus?"

Luke couldn't believe his luck. He nodded enthusiastically, and had to stop himself from throwing his arms around Katrina's neck.

She held up a hand to indicate that she wasn't finished. "Wait, there are conditions. You will have to work for Anisim here. He is an old man now, and there are some tasks he should not be doing. You are small, but you can hold a brush, I bet." Luke grinned up at the old man, who shrugged theatrically. "The second condition is: you stay out of the way of the others, especially Nikolai. We will tell you about Nikolai later. Third condition: if police, or anybody else, come looking for you, we know nothing about your trouble. We hand you straight over, if we are in Dublin, Ostend, Prague . . . wherever. Finally, if you lie, or if you do anything you shouldn't, I will take you home myself, and hand you to the police. OK?"

Luke was bewildered with this sudden turn of events, but he wasn't about to argue with her. He just nodded again, and Katrina was satisfied. She spoke with Anisim for a few minutes, then left. The old man and his new apprentice looked at each other, and started laughing.

And so it was that, a few hours later, Luke found himself standing on the deck of a ship beside old Anisim. He wore the Lost Boy's cloak, which hid his face, and appeared to make him all but invisible to the other members of the circus except Katrina, as invisible as he had been to the customs officers at the port. He watched the lights of Dublin twinkle and fade in the distance, knowing there was definitely no turning back now. He knew what he was leaving behind, but he had no idea what he was facing into, and he was suddenly very afraid. He thought of his mother and father, and all he wanted was to feel their welcoming arms, to smell their smells and hear their voices, and to see the light of love in their eyes. *Why did I do it?* he thought, *Who will love me now?* He felt more lost and alone then he had ever been. He looked up at the tall old man standing beside him. He was all Luke had in the world, and he had scarcely known him a day. How could he find love out here on this wild ocean? Anisim looked down at the boy, and put his hand gently on his shoulder. Luke leaned in against him, sheltering from the wind which drew tears to his eyes.

If Luke had looked at a newspaper that day, he would have seen his own photograph, beside a story about his disappearance, appealing for anybody who might know of his whereabouts. Indeed, if Anisim and Katrina had any interest in Irish newspapers, they would surely have seen his picture and realised that Luke was not an orphan, that he had a grieving mother and father who were devastated at his loss, who would have given up everything just to know he was safe and well. But neither Anisim nor Katrina had seen the newspapers.

Chapter Fifteen

During the journey south, Anisim and Katrina told Luke all about the circus. In truth, Anisim was reluctant to tell the story. But when Katrina insisted on talking to Luke about it, Anisim's pride forced him to interrupt her. It was, after all, his story. The story of how he had run away to join the circus himself when he was "small, like you, Luka. Many, many years ago. When circus meant something to people. Now, just a joke. A . . . how you say? Old thing?"

"Antique," prompted Katrina, "like yourself, dear Ani." Her words held no cruelty or mocking, just a deep affection.

Anisim smiled at her. "Antique, yes. That is word. No more mean anything real." He paused, frowning in remembrance. When he spoke, his voice was soft, as though dragged from a great distance. "One time, circus come through village. Very poor village, near Kiev. My father dead – like yours, Luka." Luke avoided his eyes. "My mother, she work very hard, but she not able look after us. Six brothers. Me, youngest. My brothers, they work. I too small. Decide to join circus. Never see mother again. I learn to be clown." The old man stood up in the cabin and performed a quick Charlie Chaplin walk. Luke and Katrina giggled. But Anisim's old bones made it seem like hard labour, so he gave up with a shrug.

He continued the story: "Then, I learn . . ." Not having the word, he mimed a juggler. "Then, acrobat. I learn quick.

Fifteen years, I become ringmaster. After many years, I save much money, I marry beautiful wife, Irena." He paused again to bless himself and to smile a wistful smile. "Thirty, forty years ago, old man Ivan, he retire, give circus to me. Give new name, same as now, eh? Circus Oculus. You know this, Luka? Oculus? Eyes." The old man pointed at his two eyes, rolling them in mock wonder. He was getting very excited. "I create feast for eyes. Spec-ta-cu-lar, yes? We travel all over Europe. Famous, famous. Then my son born. Nikolai."

Suddenly, Anisim had finished the story, as though his son's name was all the ending necessary. Luke remembered Katrina mentioning the name the previous evening, and the sense of tension it created. He looked at Anisim, waiting for the story to continue. Instead, Katrina laid a comforting hand on the old man's shoulder, and whispered something to him in their language. Anisim nodded and, smiling at Luke, left the cabin to go up on the deck of the ship. Luke, left alone with Katrina, became intensely aware of her perfume, and acutely embarrassed at his own trembling. She was oblivious to the strength of his feelings as she picked up the thread of the story.

"I joined the circus when I was twelve years old. I was a great trapeze artist, and I soon became the star of the show." She said this without any hint of boastfulness or pride. It was just a fact. "At the time, Nikolai was eighteen, nineteen, very handsome, big man. I fell in love with him, but he would not look at me, of course. Anyway, his father hoped he would take over the circus from him, but Nikolai had no interest. A couple of years later, he left the circus to become a businessman. Anisim's heart was broken. So was mine, but I had to hide it. The circus continued, but the old man began to lose interest. He missed his son. Seven, eight years passed, and suddenly Nikolai was back, a rich man, handsome as ever. Anisim was overjoyed. He easily accepted Nikolai's offer to buy the circus. It was, I think, a very small amount, but Anisim would have given it to him for nothing.

"All my feelings for Nikolai came back when he did, and, now that I was a woman, he finally noticed me. I went after him, and soon we were married. Oh, he was a brilliant man then. He said he was going to transform the Circus Oculus, that it was time for a new vision. He had so many ambitions for it. He wanted to make it the Greatest Show on Earth. And he did. He was so full of energy. He bought a lot of equipment – computers, projectors, screens, all very high-tech. He wanted to . . . what was the word? Fuse! He wanted to fuse the human body with the new technology, to make Anisim's 'feast for the eye' a reality. And he was very successful. Oh Luke, you should see it, it is beautiful to watch, the most beautiful thing in the world. The way the lights . . . but what am I saying! You will see this in our next show, when we reach France."

Katrina's face had grown dreamy as she spoke, and Luke took secret pleasure watching her dream. But now her expression shifted, became more sorrowful, and when she spoke next, her voice was filled with regret.

"I didn't see it until it was too late. Nikolai began to change. He had made this circus into a wonderful thing, but he found no beauty in it himself. He wanted more, he wanted fame and fortune. Of course, the circus was making more money, but Nikolai wasn't happy. He became more and more obsessed with making the circus perfect, so that at times he forgot that it was made up of people, human beings. He fired a lot of my friends, just threw them out, not even paying some of them what they were owed.

"He even forced his own father, poor Ani, to retire. The

old man wouldn't leave, so Nikolai let him stay on as caretaker. He actually thought he was being kind to him."

Luke watched Katrina's face cloud with emotion. He reached over and touched her softly on the arm. She looked down at him and smiled.

"As for myself, I was still in love with him – still am. But he has no interest in me as a wife. To him, I am just a part of the circus. Not that he's cruel to me. I suppose I have thought of leaving him, but I always stay. Mostly because of Anisim. I am afraid what Nikolai would do to his father if I left. While I am around, I can protect the old man, who I call my spirit-father. I have threatened to leave, many times, but only to keep Nikolai calm, when he is unkind to Ani. Anisim is my comfort, and I am his. And he will never leave. He loves the circus too much, and he has nowhere to go. So he will be here until he dies. After that, I don't know. Perhaps I will leave. Or perhaps not. Because I do still love Nikolai. Maybe I think that I will be the one to save him."

There was a soft knock on the cabin door, and Anisim poked his head in. He pointed up, towards the deck. "France," he said.

They followed him up to the deck, where a small group of their fellow travellers were gazing out at the misty land in the distance. Luke joined them at the rail. *It looks just like Ireland from here*, he thought. *I wonder what it will be like to live with these strange people, in this strange land?*

As another day passed without word of Luke, Fran and Avril felt the crushing sense of reality pressing on them like a vice. They decided to go home to "Exiles". Mary reassured them that she could cope. She just needed a little more time, and she promised to join them as soon as she could.

But for Avril, at least, the guest-house became a place of limbo, where the full horror of the waiting game that they were forced to play could be seen.

Inspector Moroney rang them regularly with an update on their investigations. The most significant lead came when a Chinese restaurateur contacted the police on seeing Luke's picture in the paper. Apparently, two boys, one matching Luke's description, had slept rough outside his restaurant the night of the disappearance. The older of the two boys – they realised he must have been the boy who had come to them the following day – had come begging for food. When the owner came back to his restaurant the following day, they had disappeared. The gardaí made house-to-house enquiries, and searched the area, but there was no further sign of the two boys.

"At least it tells us one thing," Moroney told the Lavertys. "He's alive, and we can almost certainly rule out kidnapping."

As for the other strand of the garda investigation, the murderer of Peadar Monks had left no clues: no fingerprints, no sign of an escape route or vehicle, nothing but the two bullets he had left in Monks's head.

"So what you're saying," fumed an increasingly frustrated Fran, "is that Luke, this boy, and Monks's murderer have all vanished without trace?"

"Apparently so." Moroney tried to sound as reassuring as possible, but the strain in his voice was showing. "You must understand, Mr Laverty, that this is one of the most unusual cases we've ever had to deal with. It may take time to follow up on all our leads. I know it's a lot to ask, given everything you've both gone through, but, please, be patient."

They made an appeal for information on the *Crimeline* TV programme, including a reconstruction of Luke's known movements. It was bizarre, watching a Luke lookalike acting these scenes, as if their son had run away to become an actor in some new cop series. There was a small response to the programme, but no solid leads.

When a week went by with no further word, the relief and the hope that they had clung to after hearing of Luke's brief sighting abated, and the despair returned to them, multiplied tenfold. Avril sank deeper into an enraged depression, hitting out at whoever provided the nearest target. "Why the hell didn't we believe that boy? If only we'd listened to him, he could have led us to Luke."

"If only . . ." Fran replied testily. "If only we'd done things differently. But we didn't, so now we just have to do all we can to find Luke, and to move on."

Without telling Avril, Fran decided to pick up a trail that had been dropped when Luke disappeared: to follow up on everything that he and Joshua Pitford had been told by James Abbott. When was that? Less than two weeks before? My God, already it felt like a lifetime away.

He called Jimmy McGinnity, who had been conducting his own investigation into Luke's disappearance. "I want you to try and trace a man who lived in Clifden in the thirties. Find out if he has any living relatives, or if any of the older people remember him. His name was Thomas McAndrew."

McGinnity was confused. "What? You want me to give up looking for Luke, and to find some old man who lives in the west instead?"

"Well, I think the police are doing all they can to find Luke. And this man, McAndrew, doesn't really 'live' in the west any more. If he did, he'd be about a hundred and thirty years old now. The thing is, you might find something that will lead us to Luke, because McAndrew had the same abilities as Luke." Fran went on to tell McGinnity everything that they had learned from Abbott, including the fact that McAndrew had become a part of local legend, dating back a century. McGinnity was doubtful, but he agreed to see what he could find out.

Fran didn't know why, but as he hung up the telephone, he felt his hopes rekindled. Why this route would bring them any closer to finding Luke, he had no idea. But he had a hunch. For once, he decided to follow his instincts.

Luke settled into his ringside seat, surrounded by a large crowd of boisterous French children. He peered into the darkness at the back of the ring, and was relieved when he made out Anisim waving to him. Katrina had arranged this seat for him, and he tingled with the anticipation of watching his first full show.

The tents had been set up on the outskirts of Lille. Luke had watched the circus coming to life from the shelter of Anisim's caravan. He had never seen so many people working together so intensely for a single purpose, and he was amazed at the speed with which they made it all grow from the ground. At one point, Anisim and Katrina had come to the caravan and announced that it was time to introduce Luke to the rest of the troupe. They brought him around in proud procession, introducing him as Anisim's new assistant to the various acts who were rehearsing for the evening's performance. Nobody asked any questions about where this young boy had come from. They all greeted him warmly, and Luke felt accepted. His two protectors steered him away from Nikolai's caravan, however. The owner would be busy with his accounts, Katrina explained. "Now is not a good time," she added.

Luke glanced at the window of Nikolai's caravan. He could see a figure in silhouette, hunched over a table.

Luke was thrilled when they told him they had arranged a ringside seat for him. He was now immersed in that atmosphere which he had sensed through the peephole that first day. The excitement of the other children was infectious, although, to Luke's mind, many of the adult faces looked terminally bored. The music – the same swirling music that Luke had heard before – gradually rose in volume, and the hum of the young audience rose with it.

Suddenly, the music ceased, and the tent was plunged into total darkness. The hush of the crowd was punctuated by a few isolated screams from some of its younger, more timid members. A few of the others giggled nervously. Then a spotlight pierced the darkness, and was quickly followed by another, and another, until the blackened roof of the tent was punched by holes of pure white light, one-eyed stars staring down at the children below. Slowly, the spotlights began to move, turning in opposite directions, some in wide swallowing circles, others in tiny staccato jerks. As the lights swirled, a faint drumbeat began, slow, languorous, but gradually increasing in frequency and pitch as the movement of the lights accelerated. As the rhythm increased, flashes of colour began to appear in the midst of the lights, and soon the white light had been displaced by fabulous spirals of colour, twisting and turning in the air like acrobats.

Luke glanced around. All of the children, and most of the adults, were staring at the spectacle with a mixture of awe and fear. Luke looked back at the lights.

It was a while before he became aware of the acrobats. At first, it was a brief flash from a sequinned torso, or a slice of bare limb, quickly swallowed by the dark. Then a couple of the spotlights picked up and followed a few of the acrobats as they swung in their own circles at the top of the tent. They emerged from the darkness suddenly, and were just as quickly engulfed by it. Soon, there were hordes of them, twisting, turning, layer upon layer of humanity moving in opposite directions, clinging to dozens of trapezes.

Luke recognised Katrina among the faces, and one or two of the people he had met earlier. They all looked intent, concentrating on their own choreography.

Luke looked down at the ring itself then, and realised that there were more of them there, dancing in the rain of light: jugglers, clowns, more back-flipping acrobats, fire-eaters.

Gradually, the spotlights slowed and the main lights came back up, as those suspended in the air were lowered to the ground, where they were greeted by their comrades. The relentless drumbeat was joined by other instruments now, in a variation of the music that was already becoming familiar to Luke, and the entire circus troupe, now grounded, danced around the ring to its rhythms. As they did so, the atmosphere lightened considerably. A huge bag of sweets and other goodies appeared in the centre of the ring, and the troupe began to throw them to the eager, clapping children. Luke joined in, scrabbling for his share. Katrina passed him, blowing him a kiss and throwing him a bag of jelly-babies. Luke's heart melted again.

Suddenly, the music ceased, and there was another shift in mood. All of the performers fell to the ground, facing the centre of the ring, and prostrated themselves there. A few seconds ticked by, and then the darkness returned, deeper than ever. Hundreds of small hearts thundered silently around the tent. And then, a light flared at the very apex of the tent. It was like a Hallowe'en sparkler, and it began to grow and circle. Soon, there were hundreds of sparkling lights at the top of the tent, and they gradually began to move down. At the very centre, a man hung, suspended by the light. Luke could see no strings. The main lights came up once again. The man stood there calmly, as though there was not a hundred-foot drop beneath him. He wore a bright red suit, and an enormous top hat. His arms were folded, and his face glowered at the crowd. Nikolai, thought Luke, and he felt both afraid and fascinated.

Nikolai descended slowly towards the centre of the ring, the sparkling fire still circling him. Just before he reached the level of his prostrated troupe – three feet above the ground – he came to a sudden halt, and the fires vanished. He hung there, glaring around. Then he threw his arms wide and a broad grin lit his face, so that he no longer looked like a demon to Luke. In a strong voice, he proclaimed: "*Mesdames et Messieurs, petits et petites, j'ai le plaisir de vous présenter . . . Le Circus Oculus!*" And with that, he tipped his hat, blowing kisses to all around, as whatever invisible force held him aloft whisked him back to the roof of the tent. The music recommenced, and the troupe jumped to their feet, cheering and dancing around the ring. One by one, they danced out into the darkness backstage, until only the empty ring and a relieved, wildly cheering crowd remained.

Luke was dizzy with the experience, and was sure there could be no more, but when the cheering had died down, Nikolai walked out into the centre of the ring, looking like an ordinary human being, and introduced the first act. Luke sat back in his seat to savour the rest of the evening.

The first performers were a group of male acrobats, stripped to the waist, their bodies criss-crossed with fearsome paint. The rhythm of the music was a jungle beat, with a screeching something backing it up. Each of the eight acrobats carried a totem pole, which they fixed into an invisible track that ran around the ring. They shimmied to the top of the poles. They clapped their hands, encouraging the audience to take up the rhythm. The poles began to move clockwise around the ring, slowly. In unison, the acrobats stood up, paced themselves, and at a signal began to jump from pole to pole, anti-clockwise. They would each leave their pole at the exact same moment, so that no two acrobats ever came close enough to touch and break the movement. The rhythm picked up, and they jumped faster and faster, until they gave the illusion of hopping lightly across stepping stones, or climbing an ever-rising staircase, like in an Escher drawing. Then, all at once, they broke into somersaults, still moving from pole to pole in perfect synchronisation. The totem poles began to spin on their own axes then, and the eyes lit up, sending out an eerie light into the crowd. The acrobats became human juggling skittles, seemingly under the control of the poles. If one of them should fall, the pattern would be destroyed, and disaster strike. They kept up their frantic somersaults just long enough for it to seem impossible that they could stop, and then they stopped. They simply froze on their poles, throwing their arms in the air triumphantly, before sliding to the ground and carrying their totem poles out of the ring.

And so it went on. There were tightrope-walkers walking where Luke could see only a laser beam; jugglers who juggled everything from telephones to blowtorches; and a contortionist belly-dancer whose body was covered with tiny electrodes. As she gyrated, a computer picked up her movements and translated them into light patterns which it then projected onto the roof of the tent, until she became a streak of light herself. There were even clowns who performed pratfalls alongside computer-generated hologram clowns. They would throw custard pies at the holograms, hitting each other instead, or lean against what looked like another clown, only to find it vanished, reappearing at the other side of the ring.

Then there was Micha, the human lightning-rod, whose body absorbed and spat out electricity as if it was air. He looked like a science experiment, a current of fire running between his outstretched arms. Many of the children were frightened of his act, but Micha reminded Luke of his own abilities.

However, Luke's favourite – apart from Katrina – was probably the simplest act of all. Her name was Lillian, and she was twelve years old. Most of the lights in the tent were darkened as she performed a delicate ballet around the ring. Her dance was a floating, ethereal orbit of the few remaining spotlights, which shone upwards from the floor. As she moved between them, she flicked her wrists in and out of the lights. In one hand, she held a mirror; in the other, a prism. With these basic – almost primitive – instruments, she created a parallel ballet of colour, which danced its way just as delicately around the tent, alighting on the heads of the delighted children, creating spilling rainbows which they felt they could almost grasp. Of all the acts, she wove the deepest spell over the crowd.

As Luke watched her, a terrible sense of isolation crept into his soul. She looked just like . . . for the first time in days, he thought of Sandy, and the loss of her came back to him now in full force.

Katrina's trapeze act was last. Some of the pain of Sandy's memory eased as Luke watched her, his breath caught by the grace of her as she floated above him, the projected images the perfect backdrop to her body's song. As she came out of her final circle, she detached something from her belt, and threw it directly to Luke. A small red rose. Luke held it to his nose, and thought, *Nothing could ever smell so sweet.*

Anisim whistled a lonely tune at the far side of the tent. As he wielded his brush awkwardly, Luke thought again of Micha's act, and he wished that his own powers were with him again. But, ever since Sandy's death, it had all been blocked out. The thought of Sandy made him sad again, and he thought of his parents and home.

But his thoughts were interrupted by a booming voice from behind. He turned around to see Nikolai, dressed now in a regular pair of jeans and woollen jumper, striding towards him. Luke cowered, attempting to hide behind the sweeping brush, but Nikolai was still shouting at him in the strange language that Luke had learned was Russian, with an occasional French verb – "*Allez! Partez!*" – thrown in for good measure. He pointed towards the door of the tent, and asked Luke a question. Luke stared at him blankly. He asked the question again, in French, with the same lack of reaction.

Finally, he grabbed Luke roughly by the shoulder, at which point Anisim finally intervened. He calmly explained the situation to Nikolai, his voice pleading. There followed a heated argument in Russian, and Anisim stood his ground. In the end, Nikolai let out an exasperated curse, and let Luke go. Luke stood there rubbing his shoulder, tears starting to his eyes.

Nikolai bent down, smiling at Luke as though nothing had happened. He took the boy's chin in his hand and turned his head from side to side, rubbing his own stubbled cheek in contemplation. He reached a decision, nodding sagely to himself. He spoke in English for the first time: "So, the old pig has found himself a new piglet to suckle. Very well. Luke, is it?" Luke nodded. "OK, Luke, my father says you will work hard for him, I will take his word. But one move out of place, if once you get under my feet, I will leave you at the next town." He stood up to go. As an afterthought, he turned a finger on Anisim, and said to Luke, "And if you go, you take him with you!" He turned on his heel then and strode out of the tent. Anisim and Luke looked at each other and smiled in nervous relief. "OK, Luka," said the old man gently, "back to work."

That night, listening to Anisim's snores, Luke's mind again drifted home. He could just leave now, hand himself in at some police station, and in a few hours he would be safely in his mother's arms. But he knew that he couldn't do it, at least not yet. His whole heart ached to see them again, but stronger still was the sense that he was nearing the end of his search, that soon he could turn back on the road without feeling that danger was waiting to ambush him and destroy his whole family. The image of the Dark Man floated through his head, and he trembled.

He thought of the Cowboy, and of the world of light he had created, which seemed so far away now. He saw him riding across the plain again, and he called out to him, but the Cowboy couldn't hear. *Why can't I have a real voice?* He tried to concentrate, to bring the Cowboy to the surface, but all he could see was the Dark Man, snapping at his heels.

He thought of Sandy then, and he had an idea. *What if I can imagine her as though she was light? Can I bring her back to life? Could she survive outside of me, as the Lost Boy lives?*

He focused on Sandy's face, and put all his energy into it. He tried to call her to him from across the widest gulf. He felt her stirring, smiling at him, and he concentrated harder. Yes, he was sure of it now. She was there, just beneath the surface. He strained and strained, until . . . suddenly, her face was there, floating above his head, surrounded by light. But it was only a brief flicker, and she was gone again almost immediately.

He looked over at Anisim in the other bed, but the old man was still snoring heavily, oblivious to all but his dreams of past glory. Luke decided to try again, and he pushed again, until he felt he was almost at bursting point himself. And this time it worked. He looked down, and there she lay, at the end of his bed.

Luke stared at Sandy in awe. In the fragile silence, he could hear her breathing, and he knew she was real. But his immediate elation quickly disappeared when he realised there was something terribly wrong. She breathed, yes, but she stared at him with empty eyes which did not recognise. She lay unmoving, her cheek pressed against the bed. A shudder passed through her frail body. Quickly, Luke went to her, pulling a blanket around her. He held her to him. Already her breathing was becoming more ragged. Luke put a hand to her heart, and it was faltering. Even as he held her, it slowed to a tiny flutter, and then it ceased. Her lungs released their last rasping breath, and as it did so, her body lost its solidity, became insubstantial, a wraith, which faded and faded. Within a minute, Sandy's life had been recalled and dissipated, so that Luke clutched an empty blanket close to his chest. All that remained of Sandy was an after-image floating in his tears.

Over the following days, Luke made a number of attempts to revive Sandy. But he was doomed to failure. Each time he brought her back, she teetered on the edge of death. Nothing he could do could prevent her from taking the final step and disappearing into oblivion again. After watching her die over and over, he finally gave up. He had lost her forever. The fact that he had found his powers again was little comfort to him in his despair.

246

Chapter Sixteen

Jimmy McGinnity's least favourite thing about detective work was trawling through an ocean of documents, which is what he found himself doing in a bed-and-breakfast in Clifden about a week later. Outside, summer was blazing, and Connemara was calling his name. He had some relatives out this way whom he had intended looking up. But, as he gazed around at all the paperwork that lay ahead of him, he wondered if he'd have any time left for social calling.

If it weren't this particular case, Jimmy would have dismissed it as a non-starter, a needle in a haystack if he'd ever known one. He had earned a lot more, and a lot more easily, from the occasional rich businessman who suspected his wife of not being true to her vows, than he could ever hope to get from the Lavertys. Of course, they had their guest-house, and he knew that they would gladly sell up and take to the streets if it would help to find their son. But, for Jimmy, money wasn't an important part of the equation in this case.

Something had struck a chord with him, ever since he first heard about Luke, and the resonance was still there. Whatever it was – and Jimmy fought shy of philosophising about it – it had made him re-evaluate his life, and had, to an extent, led him down the path he was on now. So he felt he owed something to Fran and Avril, and particularly to Luke. If Fran instinctively felt that searching for records of this Thomas McAndrew character would somehow lead them to Luke, then so be it. Instinct was good. Jimmy could work with instinct.

The last time he had seen Fran and Avril, they were miserable. They definitely had not been sleeping. They were both thin and pale, with puffy red eyes and ragged voices. They blamed themselves for Luke's disappearance. They now believed he had run away because, in their haste to try to make sense of his life, they had forgotten the little boy in him. They believed that Luke felt that he was the cause of all their troubles, and running would take those troubles away.

Despite their appearance, Fran and Avril had tremendous reserves of energy, all of which they now channelled into the search for Luke. They were constantly in touch with the police, or making appeals, or organising meetings of relatives of missing people. Outwardly, both of them, but especially Avril, used this energy to the limit, earning the admiration of anybody who came in contact with them. But inwardly, Avril was always close to breaking down. She came to lean more heavily on Fran than she ever had, and Fran himself was not far behind her in despair.

Not that Jimmy saw all of this. Much of it he sensed from glances and gestures. Some of it he gleaned from Mary, with whom he had formed an unlikely alliance. Mary was really the support who kept both of the Lavertys from sinking in the quicksand, as Avril had helped her through her grief, just a few short weeks earlier. In fact, Mary had taken it on herself to put Avril's suggestion into action. She gave up her own job, sold her house, and moved into the guest-house with them. If it wasn't for Mary, "Exiles" would never have survived those days. She effectively took over the running of the guest-house while Fran and Avril looked for Luke. It was therapy for her as much as a helping hand. She recovered much more quickly from the trauma of Sandy's death than she would have if she had been alone.

Now, surrounded by photocopies of parish records, local histories, genealogies and other assorted delights, Jimmy was lost, uncertain what the next step should be. The poorhouse where, according to Abbott, McAndrew had been born in the 1860s, had burnt down sometime in the 1870s, all records destroyed. He had found no records of any McAndrew in almost 150 years of the parish, apart from a Scottish writer who had visited Clifden in the 1960s. (Jimmy managed to contact him at his Edinburgh home, but the trail turned out to be a cold one.) Jimmy hadn't been hopeful from the start. The local historian had apologetically explained that any records dating back to the 1860s would have been scant and unreliable, particularly with the amount of poverty and emigration at the time. And so it had proved.

Jimmy had little more luck in talking with the locals. A few of the very oldest villagers did recall tales of strange lights and visions from their childhood, but they could not remember any details. None of them had ever heard of McAndrew. The most vivid description came from a ninety-year-old called Maisie, who claimed she saw coloured lights in the 1920s, when she was a young woman. She was bright and sprightly, and surprisingly mobile for her age. Her description of the strange happenings was so clear it sounded as though it had been yesterday. To Jimmy, she might have been describing Luke's "clouds".

However, all of this was ancient history, and Jimmy found it hard to listen patiently to the old stories. He wanted something that would say to him, *This is why you came here, this will bring you close to Luke*. But looking at the mass of paper around him, he felt instead that he was drifting further away.

There was a knock on the door. It was *bean a' tí*, the "woman of the house", with the news, "You have a visitor, Mr McGinnity". Jimmy's curiosity grew as he followed her out to the old-fashioned parlour, which was crammed full of tiny ceramic figurines. In the middle of them sat Maisie, looking like a figurine herself, if a little more wizened. For a 90-year-old woman, she looked like a bundle of energy, all edgy excitement.

"Hello, Mrs O'Doherty. I wasn't expecting to see you again so soon."

Maisie O'Doherty waved her hand impatiently. "Please, call me Maisie, so I can call you Jimmy. Well now, Jimmy, I have some news for you." Perched on the edge of the armchair, she could barely control her excitement.

It was infectious. Jimmy found himself sitting in the other armchair, leaning towards her expectantly. "Yes?"

"They're back!" Having delivered her news, Maisie sat back in the armchair proudly.

Jimmy was confused. "Who is back?"

"It isn't a who, it's a what! The lights! The lights are back!"

Suddenly it dawned on Jimmy. "Where? Where did you see them?"

"Near the old place. Where I lived when I was a wee child. After I talked to you yesterday, I went back there. All those memories. It was like travelling back to my childhood."

My God, thought Jimmy, *Is it really possible? Could Luke be here?* He had no idea how or why he was here, but surely there could be no other explanation? Should he ring the Lavertys? No. Better to wait until he had some definite news for them. Think how they would feel if he was to call them and say, *Would you like to speak to Luke? He's here beside me.*

Jimmy hadn't heard what Maisie was saying. "Sorry, what was that?" he asked, mustering an apologetic smile.

"I said, would you like to come and see?" Maisie repeated.

"Is he . . . is it still going on?"

"Oh no, but I'm sure he'll be back again this evening, at the same time. About ten o'clock, I think it was." She nodded, remembering.

Jimmy was confused. "How do you know he'll be back? Have you talked to him?"

"Of course not. But that's how it happened when I was a babby. He always came back at the same time each night, sometimes for a few weeks, sometimes just a few days."

Jimmy, trepidatious, knocked on Maisie's door in the centre of the town at twilight that evening. All afternoon, he had been fighting down the urge to make his own way to the spot that Maisie had described, to see if Luke was there. But she had insisted that he would never have been able to find it by himself, and that there was no point in going too early. It might scare him off, she said.

She answered the door wrapped in a bulky tweed coat and a headscarf. She also wore a pair of wellies. She looked Jimmy up and down, and shook her head, tutting.

"What?" asked Jimmy, feeling like a petulant child with dirty hands.

"You'll catch your death, Jimmy, dressed like that," Maisie informed him. Jimmy wore his leather jacket over a shirt, a pair of jeans and what he considered to be his country shoes. The night was balmy, and he felt quite warm.

Maisie shrugged, and pulled the door behind her. Then she looked around at Jimmy again and frowned. "Where's your torch?"

Jimmy noticed that she had one poking out of the pocket of her overcoat. "I . . . didn't bring one," he admitted, flushing uncontrollably. It was a long time since anybody had made Jimmy McGinnity feel so small.

"Never mind," said Maisie. "Just stick close to me, and watch where you're walking." She turned to walk down the street.

Jimmy called after her, "Eh, Mrs O'Doherty . . . Maisie? My car is just here."

She didn't break the rhythm of her walk, nor did she look back. "Don't be silly, a stór," she called over her shoulder, "the engine would scare him off."

Jimmy could see the logic in that. "Well, could we not drive part of the way, and walk the rest?"

Maisie finally stopped and turned to him. "Oh, come on. It's not that far. We'd be halfway there already if you hurried up." And she was off again.

Jimmy sighed and resigned himself. He activated the alarm on his car, and found he had to run to catch up with her. She walked like a woman half her age, and Jimmy himself felt youthful energy surging through him. The air was electric, dancing with anticipation, but it wasn't thunder. This was a new force that Jimmy had never felt before.

Three-quarters of an hour later, they were still walking. They had left the streetlights of Clifden far behind, and were relying on Maisie's torch, which she swept across the road, over and back. Jimmy was sure the torch was more for his sake than hers, as she stepped sure-footed, as though she knew every inch of the road. Jimmy, on the other hand, had stumbled three or four times over a rough patch of road, and had stepped in enough cowdung to fertilise a small kitchen garden.

The night had an edge now, and a chill had crept into the air. Jimmy pulled his jacket tighter around him, his hands deep in the pockets. A rat ran across his path, and he pulled up sharp, stifling a scream. There goes another nightmare, he thought, shivering. He took a couple of deep breaths, and looked back. The absolute blackness behind him sent a shudder up his spine. He felt the night closing in around him, and he turned to catch up with Maisie and the light. But she was gone. The same blackness lay in front of him. She was a ghost, and now she had abandoned him to deal with his demons. Panic set in. He felt it grip him around the chest, and the adrenaline rush almost knocked his feet from under him.

With huge relief, he heard Maisie's voice, calling to him. Swivelling to his left, he saw the torchlight through a hedge. Behind it, he could just define the vague shape of the old woman, and her voice again: "What are you doing, son? It's this way. Come on, or you'll get lost." She shone the torch at a gap in the hedge, and Jimmy squeezed through.

After that, he didn't look back, although he could feel the darkness dogging his heels. He walked faster to keep right up with her, ignoring the cow-shit and clumps of grass which threatened at every step to twist his ankles. He felt the energy in the air again, urging him on. They walked for a further ten minutes, crossing a few more hedges, before Maisie suddenly drew up sharply. Jimmy stumbled into her, and she shushed him.

"We're here," she whispered, and played the light on an old stone cottage. Jimmy saw that it was derelict. No windows or door, though the roof was, for the most part, still intact. They went inside, and Jimmy realised the house was being used by a local farmer for storage. One of the two rooms was filled with mechanical equipment, old ploughs, scythes, a roll of fencing. The other room was stacked high with straw bales, and it was into this room that they went.

"You used to live here?" Jimmy asked Maisie.

She nodded, smiling wistfully. She pointed to a couple of bales on the floor, not far from the open window. "We'll sit here. The straw will keep us warm." She settled down on one, and Jimmy awkwardly sat on the other. She was right. He could feel the heat emanating from the stacked bales.

"So what do we do now?" he asked her.

"We wait," she said calmly, and switched off the torch.

Jimmy froze at the sudden invasion of black. "Why did you do that?" he squealed, unable to keep his voice to a whisper.

"Shhh . . . we don't want the batteries to run out. We still have to get home, you know." She reached out and patted his hand. He gripped it, like a small boy grips his mother's hand when he is afraid. She withdrew it slowly, speaking to him softly: "Don't worry, your eyes will adjust in a couple of minutes."

They did. Five minutes later, he could make out most of his surroundings: the piles of straw, Maisie, and, through the window, a few trees, the deeper blackness of the mountain against the sky, the stars. A strange sense of calm descended on him, and he found he wasn't afraid any more.

He heard a rustling in the straw behind, and realised there must be rats there. But he found he wasn't afraid. If I don't disturb them, he thought, they won't bother me.

Soon, the heat of the straw began to make him feel drowsy. His eyelids drooped. The rustling rats became a soft shuffle behind his deepening breath. Just as he was about to go the final distance, and fall off the bale completely, Maisie grabbed his arm again, startling him awake.

"He's out there," she whispered urgently.

Jimmy peered into the darkness beyond the window, but could see nothing. Maisie moved quietly to the window and scanned the fields. Jimmy slid over beside her, but couldn't see what she was looking at. "I can't see – "

"*Shhh!* Listen!"

It came to him faintly on the breeze then, a faint humming, a drone almost. It could have been the wind, but that had a sound of its own, and had been lightly whispering to Jimmy all night. This sound was more musical, and yet not music. It took Jimmy a few moments to realise it was a human voice, humming softly, a tune that sounded strange, but eerily familiar. Electric tingles played around the tips of his fingers. He strained to hear the direction from which it was coming, but the closer he listened, the more ethereal, other-worldly it sounded. Then it faded into silence. They waited a few minutes, and the time stretched out. Jimmy opened his mouth to speak, but Maisie sensed it and raised a thin bony finger to her lips. And then the light tumbled in on top of them.

It began in one corner of the field, about a hundred yards from the house where the watchers crouched. It rapidly spiralled upwards, giving the appearance of a tornado of light, twisting faster than any wind imaginable.

The watchers were almost blinded. The tower of light turned the night sky into day, illuminating the field below. A few startled night animals dashed for shelter. It hung there for a moment, and then it began to spread out, breaking into colour as it did so. A symphony of colour, dancing in perfect choreography. Instead of the patterns and figures and images that Luke could produce, this harked back to his earlier, formless, chaotic clouds. But this was ten times more spectacular. The strength and energy that pulsated through this flow of light was stronger than anything Jimmy had ever seen. He found himself falling to his knees, vaguely aware that Maisie had done the same, as he felt a throbbing prayer rush through his veins.

They remained that way for a few minutes, before Jimmy shook himself, and, despite Maisie's restraining hands, ran out the door of the old cottage and down towards the corner of the field, the source of the light. The one thought that raced through his mind was, *I've got to get to Luke*. He reached the spot. There was a hollow, surmounted by a number of large lichen-covered boulders. Jimmy climbed on top of one and looked in.

There was no sign of Luke. Instead, a very old man sat squat-legged on another boulder in the centre of the hollow, his hands raised, his eyes closed. He was the light-source. It came directly from a point at the centre of his snow-white head. Jimmy stared, uncomprehending, and then the old man opened his eyes and saw him. Immediately, the light faded, leaving just enough for the two figures to make each other out. Then it dawned on Jimmy.

He stood up, expecting the old man to flee. Instead, he continued to sit, and he smiled up at Jimmy. Jimmy greeted him: "Hello there! Are you Thomas McAndrew?"

The old man inclined his head in what might have been a nod, but was more a contemplative pose. "Well, it's a long time since I heard that name, but, yes, that's what I used to call myself." His voice was old, and it spoke of grace and regret.

My God, thought Jimmy, *could this really be?* He scrambled over the boulder and down into the hollow. The man who used to call himself Thomas McAndrew stood up to greet him. They shook hands, Jimmy looking uncertainly into his eyes.

"You're the same Thomas McAndrew who visited a Dr James Abbott in the thirties?" Jimmy was still trying to get his head around it.

"Well, yes, I suppose I am," said Thomas, his smile playful now.

"So that makes you . . . how old?"

Thomas frowned. "I'm not sure. A hundred and thirty? It could be more."

Jimmy sat down heavily on the boulder. For once, words, though they flooded his head, meant nothing.

Thomas broke the silence. "It's usual, my friend, to return the compliment of giving your own name." Jimmy stood up, muttering apologies, but Thomas held up his hand and went on: "However, I know who you are. James McGinnity. And I know why you're here."

Jimmy had almost forgotten his mission. "Really?" he asked excitedly. "Do you know where Luke is, then?"

The old man's face darkened. "Unfortunately, no," he sighed. "I have been looking for him, same as you, though my methods are a little different. In fact, that's what I was doing when you interrupted me."

"Oh, I'm sorry, I didn't mean—"

"Not at all, not at all. I haven't had any success. I am

growing old, you see, finally growing old. My magic is not what it once used to be." He dug in his pocket and took out a small fluffy dog.

Jimmy recognised it as Luke's. "Where did you find that?"

"In an abandoned house. I was too late, you see. This little toy was my link with Luke. But he lost it, and now I can't find him. He's all alone, somewhere."

"But he's alive?" Jimmy felt his hopes soar.

"Oh yes, absolutely."

Jimmy thought for a while. "Listen, Mr McAndrew, I would like you to come to Dublin, to meet Luke's parents. I think you need to tell them everything you know." The old man sighed heavily, but nodded.

They climbed to the top of the hollow. Maisie was coming down the hill towards them.

"Maisie, I'd like you to meet Thomas McAndrew. Thomas, this is Maisie O'Doherty."

Thomas was the height of politeness. He took Maisie's bony hand in his own frail fingers, and kissed it delicately. "I am honoured to meet you, young lady," he said.

Maisie stared at him as if he had two heads.

Avril and Fran both had similar reactions when Jimmy – a broad grin lighting his face, the cat who'd got the cream – introduced Thomas to them at "Exiles" the following day. It wasn't just the fact that this was *the* Thomas McAndrew, and that yes, he was a hundred and thirty years old. Somehow, they had been expecting him to be alive, though they never would have admitted it to themselves. What stunned them was the realisation that they had met him before.

"You . . . it was you, wasn't it? The puppy?" Avril blurted out.

Thomas produced Lenny from his pocket, handing it to Avril sheepishly. "You may as well have him back. He's no use to me now."

Avril tentatively accepted the toy dog, holding it like some ancient relic which could turn to dust at any moment. She looked between the dog and Thomas. Tears of bewildered incomprehension stung the backs of her eyes.

Fran asked for her, "Where did you get this? Do you know where Luke is?"

Thomas sighed heavily. "Alas, no. When I got there, he was already gone. He left the puppy behind, so I have lost him. I've failed him, and I've failed you." Suddenly, his eyes flooded with tears, and he tottered forward, almost falling. Fran steadied him, and led him to the couch. They all sat down, watching while he gathered himself.

Avril spoke first, gently urging him to talk. "So this little puppy – Lenny – was some sort of . . . link between Luke and you?"

"It was how I knew where he was. It was how he called to me when he was afraid, or in danger. But I haven't been vigilant, and now I can't find him anymore."

Avril handed the toy dog back to him. "I want you to keep him. I don't know how, but I feel that you can help us find Luke. Maybe Lenny can help."

Thomas said nothing, but accepted the puppy back solemnly. He stared at the toy, sunk in a silent reverie.

Finally, Fran could wait no more. "Please, tell us what you know about all this."

The old man was silent, as though he hadn't heard her. Then he sighed again, and, lifting his head, looked Avril right in the eyes. All his frailty vanished, as she stared back into those ancient depths. When he spoke, his voice came from far down, as though he had to drag it from history. "I am an old man. I have lived far too long. Better for the world, better for your Luke, if I had died a long time ago. But I'm a coward, and I have run away from death each time it came knocking. So I thought the best I could do with my life was to protect Luke. Now, I realise, I couldn't even do this thing."

He paused for so long that they thought he was finished. Avril and Fran wanted to ask him more about Luke, but when he started to talk again, it was his own childhood that he painted in words. "Thomas McAndrew isn't a real name, you know. After my mother died, the women of the poorhouse took care of me between them. They named me Tomás, but I had no other name until I started talking to them in pictures. Then they thought I was a demon of some sort, and would probably have drowned me in the river if it wasn't for one kind soul, who told them that my father was a druid, a *draoi*, who was my mother's lover before he was taken up by his ancestors. I suppose the story could be true, but it saved my life, at least. From then on I was *mac an draoi*, and when the English Quakers wrote down my name, it became Thomas McAndrew. When I learned to speak myself – which wasn't for another fifteen years – it was English I learned, so the name stayed with me."

He went on to tell them how he had left the poorhouse and had lived as a wanderer. People were afraid of him, he said, so he had never belonged in any society. He had spent his time honing his powers, but then, many years later, he did something that had turned his world on its head – something he was to regret all his life – and made him seek help to reverse what he had done. That was when he had met Dr Abbott, whom he hoped might be able to help him find out why he was the way he was, and if there was some way of destroying his powers. When this failed, he took to his wanderings again. That was how it had been for over sixty years, until he heard about Luke, and his life had a purpose again.

As Thomas finished his story, Fran was frowning. "But I don't understand. What was this thing you did? What could have been so bad that you would want to destroy everything you had?"

When Thomas looked up, the loneliness of a hundred and thirty years of wandering could be read in his eyes. "That's the hardest part. I'm not even sure how to tell you." He paused, summoning strength. "I've never told this to another living soul. Not even Dr Abbott." He looked at each of them, seeking understanding, sympathy. Then he told them.

When he had finished, Fran spoke at last. "I still don't understand. Why didn't you come to us before? Why did you never tell us this?"

"Fear," answered Thomas immediately. "Fear that I would bring him to your doorstep. Fear that telling you the truth would somehow put Luke and yourselves in danger."

Hundreds of miles away, in a circus tent in Seville, events were unfolding which would provide them with the news they had been waiting for.

Chapter Seventeen

Luke had reached a low point. His failure to recreate Sandy had hit him hard. He knew now that she was gone from him, and he would never find her again. Why was it only after he had lost her that he realised how much he loved her?

He had been with the circus for almost two months now, and he still had no idea why he was here. Nothing sang of destiny to him. Nothing brought him closer to finding the truth. He wanted to go home, but could not think of any way out. How could he tell Katrina and Anisim that he had lied to them, that his parents were still alive? That they were probably frantic with worry, looking for him? Or were they? Maybe they had forgotten him already. Maybe they had decided to put him behind them, to get on with their lives. Who knows, maybe they had started a new baby to replace him?

So for now, it was inertia that held Luke in place. Each day, when they were not travelling, he would be busy for a few hours at a time, helping Anisim clear up, or running errands for some of the other performers. Nikolai, in particular, was determined to make full use of his cheap labour. Anisim had tried to persuade his son to add Luke to the payroll. Nikolai sarcastically told him that Luke was not his employee, but Anisim's, and that he would have to pay him out of his own wages. So, apart from sharing Anisim's living quarters and food, the old man gave Luke half his wages every week. Luke would have refused, but Anisim insisted. Every day, Nikolai made the boy clean his living quarters, which turned out to be surprisingly spacious and luxurious for a caravan.

Luke didn't mind these extra tasks. They kept him occupied, distracted his mind from thoughts of home and the life he had abandoned. They were also an opportunity to be close to the presence, physical or otherwise, of Katrina. These were, after all, her living quarters as well. When she was alone with him in the caravan, he was intensely aware of the mix of emotions that threatened to swamp him. He was sure she would notice his embarrassment. Surely she would laugh at him, and throw him out, like the pathetic little puppy he was? But no, she was always kind to him. When Nikolai wasn't around, she would talk to him, telling him stories about the places she had travelled with the circus, fascinating him with the people she had met. All the while she talked, she would be helping him with whatever task he had to perform. And even while Nikolai was there, she would still pay attention to Luke, winking slyly at him, slipping him a packet of sweets or a bar of chocolate, a conspiratorial finger raised to her lips.

When Katrina was out rehearsing or performing, Luke could still feel her presence in the caravan. Her delicate perfume scented the air he breathed, sending goose pimples up his arms. He could sense the last place she had been, whether it was sitting at the table, lying on the bed, working in the kitchen, because he could feel a residual warmth lingering. Even as he took in these signs of her recent presence, Luke was constantly watching over his shoulder, for fear he would be caught in his dreaming.

When he had no work to do, Luke distracted himself by walking from tent to tent, watching the various performers in rehearsal. He was still fascinated with how they used their bodies to create something beautiful. Everybody got to know him, and soon everybody treated him like the circus mascot.

The one person who he couldn't get close to, however, was Micha, the human lightning-rod. He would never let anyone watch him rehearse, and the others warned Luke to stay away from him, if he didn't want to be burned to a cinder, which, they told him, could happen if Micha was in a bad mood. Luke believed them, and was disappointed. He had hoped to meet Micha at some stage, to show him that he had similar powers, except that he spoke in light, not electricity. But it was not to be.

As for Lillian, the ballerina of light, Luke found her snobbish and spoiled. Any resemblance she bore to Sandy quickly dissipated once he met her. She treated him like a small boy (which he was), where the others, to Luke's mind, treated him like an equal – even though Lillian was closest to him in age. She would stop her rehearsals as soon as he came near, and would watch him, nose held high, until he left again. Despite his feelings, however, Luke still had a sneaking admiration for her when she began to dance. He would watch her from a distance, hidden behind a box or a flap of tent, as she moved delicately among the rainbows she was creating. It was as though she became a different person when she danced.

In these ways, Luke kept his mind active during those weeks. It was when he was alone, left to his own devices, that his loneliness set in with full force, and he thought of the life he had abandoned. It was during one of his reveries that he felt the stirring of something that had been absent for a while, since before Sandy's death. It was a rumble of energy from deep within, gradually building in force, until it became a thunderous roar in his head. He closed his eyes, and all he could see was dust: a huge cloud of it, a storm of it, billowing towards him. And behind it, the sound of a thousand hooves, the volume rising and rising. Luke found himself pushing back into the pillows where he lay, trying to get away from the stampede. He could see their shapes now, looming towards him through the dust. He covered his head as the first of them reached him and leapt over him. He felt the slipstream of him, and he smelt the rank life of his thick hide. Buffalo. Hundreds of them, stampeding over the plains of his mind, which were suddenly clear to him again.

Luke opened his eyes, and he realised that the thundering shapes were spilling out of his mind, out of his head. Incredibly, the great herd of wild animals seemed to fill the tiny caravan, rocking it treacherously, before receding in some imaginative distance. Luke could vaguely discern, miles away across the plain, the horizon, and his great ball of red fire boiling there, beckoning him to follow where the buffalo raced. They continued to storm through the space, and then the last of them was gone, and the dust gradually settled. The plain began to recede, but before it disappeared completely, the Cowboy was there, galloping after the herd, his lasso arcing wildly around his hat. He reared his horse suddenly, turning half-circle until he faced Luke. He smiled and waved, and then turned again and was gone. The horizon moved in until it was the caravan's wall again, and the light darkened to the twilight outside.

Suddenly, the door of the caravan burst open, and Anisim fell over the doorstep. He picked himself up and looked about frantically, panting hard, but all was normal, everything in its place. His eyes lit on Luke, and he rushed to the boy, searching for signs of some terrible catastrophe that he could not name. "Luka! What happen? I see light, and caravan move, just so." He jogged his hands in a rocking motion. "Are you OK? What happen?"

Luke smiled back at him, his expression blank, pretending he did not understand what the old man was talking about.

Anisim frowned at him, and gave the caravan one last, careful sweep with his eyes. He shook his head, looking back at Luke. "I don' know. Maybe I see things. But I not think I crazy. I think you a . . . how you say? Strange fish." He watched Luke for another minute, then shook his head and, bending over, kissed the child on the forehead. That seemed to be the end of it.

Over the following days, Luke gradually rediscovered his powers. His desire to communicate was stronger than the sense of despair and loneliness which had threatened to engulf him. He found he was able again to control the visions. He began to anticipate his journey of light as soon as he woke up in the morning. He would rush to finish his day's work and, instead of wandering through the circus watching the performers, he would sneak back to Anisim's caravan, and begin.

Luke was careful not to let the buffalo return, as he didn't want to attract attention to his secret. Instead, he played a silent symphony of light. Everything he had absorbed, all the spectacle of the circus, came out in his new visions. The people who populated them spun through space and light, their bodies merging with the air as they floated, imagined acrobats. They were all clothed in light, and as they twisted, they transformed into rainbows. A thousand trapeze artists turned into a huge, dipping flock of birds, which became a river of colour, which eddied and swirled into a cloak of silk. Astride the whole scene, the Cowboy bent in his saddle and retrieved the silken cloak before it touched the ground, wrapping it around his shoulders where it became a magnificent constellation, glimmering like his belt.

Luke was so relieved to be able to release his pent-up imaginings that, after careful consideration, he decided to let Anisim in on the secret. He didn't want to frighten him, however, so he decided to prepare him for it. One evening over dinner, he laid his plate aside and, tugging the old man by his sleeve, he wrote on the slate that Anisim had provided him with, *I want to show you something*. The old man smiled at him, expectant. Luke wrote, *Please don't be afraid. I have a magical gift. You must not tell anyone*. Anisim stared at the words, puzzled. He looked back at Luke and shrugged. Luke sighed. He would just have to show him.

Slowly, as Anisim watched, a worm of light spiralled upwards from Luke's head. It spread out and up, dispersing over the ceiling of the caravan, forming a thin film of stars. The stars hung there for a minute, before starting to fall like a cooling rain of light, tiny drops of glittering colour. Anisim seemed quite unsurprised by the vision. His face lit up with joy, and he lifted it to the rain. Anisim realised that there was an area growing inside the rain of light where no light was falling, as though there was an invisible umbrella holding it off.

Indeed, as he watched, an umbrella did appear and,

gradually, a shape could be discerned holding it. It moved towards Anisim, and the figure of the Cowboy materialised. He smiled at the old man, and held out his hand. Tentatively, Anisim shook it, and was surprised at the solidity of the grip. The Cowboy held the umbrella out to him, gesturing for him to take it. "For me?" asked the old man. The Cowboy nodded. Anisim accepted the umbrella graciously. He looked up through it at the rainfall of light, which bounced off it, sending shimmering patterns of colour through it. As he twirled it above his head, the patterns changed: a kaleidoscope umbrella.

Anisim was so enthralled with his kaleidoscope that he didn't notice the light fading and the Cowboy disappear. When he looked down again, there was just himself and Luke in the caravan. The umbrella had not vanished, however. It looked like an ordinary umbrella, but when it was held up to the light, the same patterns could be seen playing on its under-surface.

Luke had never seen the old man look so happy. Anisim beamed at him, and, laying down the umbrella with exaggerated care, embraced the boy. "Luka, Luka, you are miracle. I knew it. I knew something special with you. Now I see, I was right. Child, you make an old man very young."

For the next few days, Anisim proudly carried the umbrella with him everywhere, to Luke's dismay. Most of the performers, seeing him strutting about under its shelter, when there was not a cloud in the sky, thought he had finally cracked up. Anisim did not care. They couldn't see what he could see when he looked up, seeing the sun, as though for the first time, through this window of wonder.

They let Katrina in on the secret, and soon, all three of them spent their evenings cramped in the tiny caravan, while Luke opened the vast world of his imagination to them. Katrina seemed as unsurprised as Anisim, merely shaking her head and looking at Luke with fresh respect.

For the first time in months, Luke found he was truly happy again. The evenings he spent with Anisim and Katrina became the centre of his life here, and he felt that he belonged. He was comfortable with his own powers now. He felt sure he was moving on the right path now, although he had no idea where it would lead him. Of course, he desperately missed his home and his parents, but he felt he had found something new here in the circus, and his appetite had been whetted for more.

However, the cosy intimacy of feeling part of a family again would soon be shattered, and the path he was on would become a little clearer. Nikolai was the catalyst.

After Lille, they had moved slowly south, winding their way through Paris, Lyon, Nice, and on into Spain, through Bilbao, Barcelona and Madrid. The circus would set up in each location for a week, two weeks, sometimes three, before dismantling itself again and moving on. The journeys broke the pattern of life, and Luke was fascinated by the changing landscape and people as the journey progressed. The people got darker, burnt by the ever-hotter sun, and their clothes got brighter, more varied. It all felt strangely like home to Luke, to whom light and colour were the vibrant core of life.

He had lost track of time, and was almost surprised to find them setting up the tent in Seville in the height of the Andalucian summer. The scorched ground was piping hot under his feet as he skipped across ropes and layers of folded canvas. It was three months since he had seen his family.

There was always more to do on the first and last days at a particular stop. Seville was no different. Luke found the sun gruelling. Anisim watched him carefully as he helped out at the main tent. At one point, Luke felt dizzy, and had to sit on the ground. Anisim used the opportunity to persuade him to go back to the caravan and rest. "Is too hot for small boy." Luke gratefully took his advice.

Alone and exhausted in the caravan, Luke fell into a fitful sleep. He was disturbed by dreams in which the Dark Man loomed closer to him, his face liquid, unformed. The melting face became Anisim, then Katrina, Nikolai, Jimmy, Sandy, the Druid . . . and finally, his father's and mother's faces seemed to merge on that terrible head. Luke woke with a start, his body soaked in sweat. He poured himself a large glass of water and sought comfort from the darkness in his visions of light. The Cowboy came to him again and showered him with glittering stars.

Nikolai, grumbling, strode broadly through the camp. It was past five o'clock, and Luke had not yet arrived to clean his caravan. He decided that this was the opportunity he needed. Once he had done the work, Nikolai would throw the child out on his ear. He had enough of him. The young brat had taken in both his father and his wife, and the three of them, for some reason, were spending a lot of time together. Plotting against him – Nikolai – no doubt. The child could have his father, as far as Nikolai was concerned, but to have cast his spell on Katrina . . . that was another matter. A man had a right to spend time with his wife. He was, after all, only a man. He had urges.

Nikolai burst into Anisim's caravan. By the time Luke saw him, by the time the Cowboy had vanished and the shimmering stars had sunk into the darkness, it was too late.

270

Nikolai stared at the boy, his face cascading with expressions. In two quick strides, he was at the bed. Luke cringed, prepared to ward off the blow. Instead, Nikolai swept him in his arms, and, holding him at arms' length, let out a huge bellow of laughter.

Anisim, having seen Nikolai approach the caravan, had feared the worst. When he stepped in and saw the expression on his son's face, he was bewildered. Nikolai, seeing him, set Luke down on the bed. With another great bellow, he grabbed Anisim's shoulders and hugged him to him. Anisim felt his old bones wilt under the force of his son's embrace.

"Ah, my father," said Nikolai, "you have been very bad. You have kept young Luke's secret from me. But you should know me better than that! I would have found out, sooner or later."

Anisim extracted himself from Nikolai's arms and stared at him uncomprehendingly. "Don't you see?" asked Nikolai. He pointed at Luke. "This could be the making of the circus. This is what I've been searching for all these years. Remember? Circus Oculus? A feast for the eye? This is the perfect freak! And we don't even need to use any tricks, any mirrors or projectors or computers!"

Anisim, finally understanding, shook his head. He sat on the bed beside Luke and put his arm around his shoulder protectively.

Nikolai sighed, seeing he had a battle. "Oh, come on, father. It's the perfect opportunity. Anyway, it isn't up to you." He switched his attention to Luke, shutting out his father. "Luke, what do you think? Would you like to be in the circus? A performer, I mean? You wouldn't have to do any more hard work. No more cleaning toilets. Just stand in the middle of the ring and show everybody what you can do. What do you think, hmm?"

Luke hesitated. Was this what was supposed to happen? He looked at Anisim, but the old man was staring ahead. Luke was surprised to see his eyes glistening with tears. He turned back to Nikolai and shook his head.

Nikolai chose to ignore the gesture. "Tell you what, don't answer yet. Come to my caravan in one hour. Then you can tell me." He turned to go, but turned back at the door. With a sly smile, he dealt his trump card: "Of course, if you don't do this thing, I will throw you out on the street." He laughed, and was gone.

Luke sat silently beside Anisim. The old man said nothing. He stood up without looking at Luke and went to lie on his own bed, a tired old man.

Is this it, then? thought Luke. *Is this what I came here for?* He thought of the time of his first "performance", a few months earlier, back home in Dublin. He remembered the strange, thrilling mix of feelings.

An hour later, he knocked softly at Nikolai's door and entered at the gruff command. He peered around, but Katrina, his hope of support, was nowhere to be seen. Nikolai sat at his desk, watching the boy. "Well?" he demanded.

Luke hesitated another minute. He found himself nodding, a small, almost imperceptible gesture of resigned assent.

Nikolai grunted approvingly. "Good. So, we will start you tomorrow, at the end of the show. You will be paid the same as the others. If you want, you can stay with my father. Otherwise, I'll find you somewhere better. Now, show me some more of your magic."

So Luke did.

* * *

The following day, Luke stood trembling behind the curtain in the main tent. He could hear the murmur of the crowd, and their *oohs* and *aahs* as Katrina swooped through the air high above them. He looked down at his small body, barely recognising himself. Nikolai had commandeered an outfit for him from Grigor, the circus dwarf. It was the right length, but the wrong shape. Luke felt he was swimming in a sea of purple spangles. "It doesn't matter," Nikolai had reassured him. "They won't be looking at your costume."

Luke waited, his heart thumping.

Thunderous applause; Katrina had just finished. She swept through the curtain, breathing heavily from her exertions. Her face was still in deep concentration, but it broke into a smile as soon as she saw Luke. She went straight to him and, bending down, kissed his head. Her lips were hot and soft. Luke could smell the sweet sweat from her. "Don't worry, Luke. I'll be here all the time. You'll do fine." She held and squeezed his hand while Nikolai went out to announce him. Luke heard the booming voice.

"*Señores y Señoras, niños y niñas* . . ."

And, with a soft push from Katrina, he was out.

The cheering of the crowd gradually died down. They waited in hushed expectation. Luke stared around at the children, many of whom were the same age as himself. Fear froze him to the spot in the centre of the ring. Time stretched out, and many of the children became restless, shifting in their seats. Who was this boy, who stood there doing nothing? Where were the acrobats and the clowns?

Somebody whistled, and a slowhand-clapping began, gradually picked up by the whole crowd. A few hisses, the

273

odd boo. As the noise of the clapping built up, Luke glanced around at the curtain. He could see Katrina there, gesturing to him to go on, and Nikolai behind, his face turning red. He turned back to the crowd and closed his eyes.

Suddenly, the crowd let out a gasp as a column of fire shot from the top of Luke's head, reaching up to the apex of the tent. There, it spread out and down, so that it appeared as though licks of flame were consuming the tent. A few of the children and a number of adults screamed, believing the fire to be real. But then the scene was transformed as the fire turned into the rain of light that had fallen on Anisim. The crowd looked up in silent awe as the drops fell softly on their heads like glistening jewels, shot through with unimaginable colours.

Through the rain, above the ring, shadowy figures appeared as darker patches in the light. It was a group of trapeze artists. As the rain dispersed, they became visible as streaks of light trailing across the tent, leaving comet-tails behind. There were dozens of them, more, it seemed, than would fit in the space they occupied. Their costumes changed colour constantly, and their blurred bodies grouped and regrouped as they flew above the crowd. As they criss-crossed, they gradually merged, until there was only one left, suspended in mid-air. She stood on the trapeze, and gradually her body toppled forward. As she fell, the audience held its breath. Before she hit the ground, however, she was transformed into an eagle, which swooped over the heads of the enthralled crowd, finally coming to rest on Luke's upheld arm.

The eagle vanished, to be replaced by a bunch of flowers which Luke presented to a woman in the audience. An old trick, known to every magician, surely? Except that the flowers began to reproduce themselves spontaneously, appearing to grow out of every available space in the tent. The ring soon became a carpet of coloured petals, and the walls of the tent, right up to the roof, sprouted wonderful splashes of tulips, chrysanthemums, carnations, daffodils, pansies, buttercups and daisies. The scent of them was overwhelming, driving the audience into a frenzy of sniffing.

Luke turned slowly around, and a breeze picked up, gradually building in strength until it began to pluck the petals from the flowers. Soon, the entire tent became a swirling, impenetrable mass of petals, which, as they ascended, transformed themselves back into light.

The audience were, by now, on their feet. Luke stood at the centre of the petal storm, absorbing their wild applause. His mind was in turmoil. All his fears had vanished, to be replaced by thoughts which came at him from nowhere. He felt as though he had been building to this moment all his life. Not for fame; for acceptance. He had come into his own at last. He was a storyteller at heart, and now he had a chance to bring his imagination as far and wide as he could travel. To the world. This was why he had to leave his parents' protection. This was why he had to come to this strange land with a group of people he didn't know. Nikolai was right. The perfect freak.

The petals of light were spinning still, gathering in the ring around Luke. The storm died down, and soon the lights hung there like jewels. Luke left them there, while inside his cocoon of light, he began to tell a story, painting his characters with light drawn from the jewels around him.

He told them about the knight who, having rescued the maiden from the dragon, turned out to be a dragon in disguise. He told them about the pirate who went in search of treasure, only to find his own demons buried at the bottom of the ocean. He told them stories about places he had never been, and places that didn't exist (as far as anybody knew). Eventually, after two hours of storytelling, Nikolai had to call a halt. To rapturous applause, Luke ended his first show.

Luke was an unqualified success. Nikolai was delighted, and Katrina was pleased that it had worked out so well, and particularly that Luke himself was happy. The only one who didn't share in the celebrations was Anisim. He felt he had lost his friend Luke to Nikolai. Indeed, Nikolai refused to let Luke help Anisim any more. "You are a star now," he told him. "Stars do not sweep up other people's rubbish." Luke tried his best to draw the old man out of himself, but nothing would lift the air of melancholy that surrounded Anisim.

Word spread quickly around Seville and the surrounding areas about the circus boy who could summon a field of flowers out of thin air, who could tell stories with light, creating the most fabulous, exotic characters – princesses, knights, pirates – from his own head. The circus was packed the next day, and the next, and the next. Eventually, Nikolai had to put on four shows a day, and at each one, Luke put on a different display, told a different story.

The local newspapers picked up on the electric atmosphere at the circus. One of them dispatched a photographer, and the next day, a proud Nikolai appeared in the paper, his hands proprietarily on a nervous Luke's shoulders. The story underneath detailed how Luke, a young Irish orphan, had joined the circus a few months previously, and went on to describe his extraordinary abilities.

Two Irishmen looked at the photograph and the article with particular interest.

One of them, Henry Coyle from Balbriggan, was on a

two-week holiday in Seville with his wife and three children. A few weeks before their holiday, Henry had read in the *Herald* about the disappearance of Luke Laverty. There had been a photograph then as well. That article had referred to Luke's magical powers.

Henry recalled all the ruckus a few years earlier, when the same boy was all over the telly – because of his magical powers. Henry stared at the picture of Luke now. His Spanish wasn't great, but he was able to pick out the words for "Irish", "magic" and "circus". He was convinced it was the same boy. "I'm sure it's him," he said to Angela, his wife. "I think we should call the police – or the embassy! Maybe we should contact the embassy?"

Angela was less convinced. "I don't think it's him," she said, studying the photo over her husband's shoulder. "Anyway, it's none of our business." Mostly, though, she didn't want to spoil the holiday by getting involved in some hunt for somebody else's child. She had enough on her plate with her own children. They were already whining about going home, and they hadn't been there a week yet.

Henry was aghast. "Angie, this is our business. This is an Irish boy who . . . who, for all we know, might have been kidnapped by these . . . these gypsies." He looked at the expression on his wife's face, and realised that compromise was in order. "Tell you what, why don't I take the kids to this circus tomorrow, and you can get some shopping done. I'll get a proper look at the kid. If it's him, I'll call the police."

Angela shrugged, but was inwardly ecstatic. A whole day without Henry or the kids. Bliss.

The other Irishman was retired gangster, Alan "Alfie" McCabe, aged thirty, late of Dublin, currently resident in Malaga. He had absolutely no doubt who the boy was.

Chapter Eighteen

Inspector Moroney phoned the Lavertys, the excitement tripping his words. "I think we've found him. Spain. Seville. He's with some circus, apparently. The Spanish police are waiting for confirmation. They'll probably swoop the place this afternoon. I'm flying out there in a few hours." It sounded too much like some *Boys' Own* rescue story to Avril. Surely they couldn't be talking about Luke? But the news galvanised her.

"We're coming with you," she replied without any hesitation.

Moroney smiled to himself. "I thought you'd say that. The next flight is at half past eleven. I'll arrange for a couple of extra seats. I'll meet you at the airport, and I'll explain everything on the flight."

They had no time to talk, or even to think, as they rushed around "Exiles", grabbing passports and essentials. They quickly explained to Mary what had happened, and she promised to take care of the guest-house while they were away. They said a hurried goodbye to her, still unable to think straight. It was only when they were in the car and on the road that Fran and Avril allowed themselves to breathe. Avril looked at Fran behind the wheel of the car. He looked so much older and thinner than he had a few months earlier. The fevered look in his eyes as he stared at the road ahead disturbed her. She dared not look in the mirror. In the cold light of this day that they had begged would come, she was afraid of what she had become.

"How long has it been?" she asked him. Before this, they had never once mentioned the time that had passed to each other, but both of them had silently notched the days in their minds.

"Fourteen weeks and three days," answered Fran immediately, his voice that of an automaton.

Avril nodded, but said nothing. She closed her eyes, and let the riot of feelings wash over her, without really feeling any of them: relief, anger, pain, fear, apprehension, disbelief . . . all tripped over the surface of her soul and passed on, leaving its one occupant in peace: an empty exhaustion that she had no wish to evict. Forgiveness, she knew, would come later with its companion, understanding. Forgiveness for herself, for Fran, for God, but mostly for Luke. But for now, she could find no place for it. All she wanted to do now was to curl up on the floor and sleep forever.

An hour and a half later, they met Inspector Moroney at Dublin Airport. He quickly shook hands with them, and ushered them through the departure gate.

"We don't have much time. They've been holding the plane." As they jogged through the tunnel, Moroney dug in his pocket and handed Avril a crumpled piece of paper, explaining, "Just after I talked to you on the phone earlier, I got a fax from the police in Seville."

Avril found herself looking at a photograph of her son, slightly distorted by the fax machine, but unmistakably her son. Luke, standing under the protective, smiling figure of a stranger, was so familiar to her, and yet so unfamiliar. His shy smile bore an added knowingness, a maturity that Avril didn't recognise. His eyes also, staring back at her, held new depths.

279

Suddenly, the emptiness inside filled with such force that she had to stop and grasp Fran's hand to steady herself. She realised that she had all but resigned herself to never seeing her son's face again, and the photograph had thrown wide all her expectations and fears. As the tears came without cease, Fran held her to him and cried silently into her hair.

Moroney indulged them for a minute, and then hurried them on again.

Five minutes later, the three of them were sitting among a couple of hundred happy holiday-makers. As the airplane taxied towards the runway, Moroney began to tell them what had happened. Before he had uttered a sentence, however, Avril noticed a number of passengers staring out of windows, muttering and pointing. A moment later, the airplane ground to a halt, and the pilot emerged from the cabin and peered out one of the side windows.

Inspector Moroney frowned and went to join them. "What's the trouble?" The pilot pointed at two figures who were racing across the runway, heading directly for their plane, waving frantically. Moroney squinted, but could not make out their faces. "What are they doing? And what's the one on the right wearing? He looks like a high priest or something."

On hearing this, Fran came forward and peered over Moroney's shoulder. "It's Thomas. And Jimmy is with him," he told them. "I think they want to tell us something."

The pilot looked at Moroney, then at Fran. Moroney had earlier introduced himself and the Lavertys as being on "official police business". He hadn't mentioned extra passengers, but the pilot didn't want to get into an argument now. With a shrug, he ordered the doors to be opened.

At this stage, Thomas and Jimmy had come to a halt about ten metres from the plane. A number of uniformed airport security staff were racing across the tarmac. Jimmy was bent double with exhaustion, his breaths coming in ragged gasps. Thomas, on the other hand, was unaffected by their dash. The old man greeted his friends and, with an apologetic grin shouted up, "Would you have room to squeeze in two more?"

When Jimmy had caught his breath, he told the Lavertys, "Mary . . . Mary called and told us. He insisted on coming. Couldn't stop him."

A few minutes later, after some shouted explanations to the security staff, and apologies to the pilot and other passengers, they were airborne.

Inspector Moroney was finally able to tell the full story of how they had located Luke. How a holidaymaker had recognised him in a local newspaper and, after seeing him perform in the circus, had called the Spanish police.

Avril interrupted at this point: "What did you say? Luke was *performing* in the circus?"

Moroney smiled apologetically at her. "So it seems. His, you know, tricks. From what this man said, he appears unharmed, and it doesn't sound like he was being forced into anything."

"So why haven't the police done anything yet?" demanded Fran.

"You must understand, Mr Laverty, while Luke appears to be in no danger, it's possible that he was kidnapped by this circus crowd. We've discovered that they were here in Dublin about the time your son disappeared. If he was taken against his will, then the Spanish police might meet some resistance. That's why they have to act with caution."

"But he is safe?"

"Oh yes, according to Mr Coyle, the man who saw him. And I think it's unlikely these people are kidnappers, given that they allowed Luke to appear in the newspaper."

Avril looked again at the newspaper article she clutched. "We're coming, Luke," she whispered, stroking his face in the picture. "Not long now."

A few seats back, Jimmy McGinnity was fast asleep, snoring noisily. Thomas McAndrew sat beside him, staring out the window. In 130 years, he had never been on a plane. The beauty of the clouds, dense as snowdrifts, brought tears to his eyes. He had never been this close to the sun, and, without fear of blindness, he stared directly into its light. Such light! He felt very, very old. With half an ear, he had been trying to catch the conversation of the others over the sound of Jimmy's rumblings. He had heard Moroney's confident reassurances that Luke was safe. But Thomas was uneasy. "I hope so, I hope so," he muttered under his breath, quietly so that nobody else could hear. An ancient fear was stirring in his heart again.

The Spanish police sergeant who met them at Seville Airport looked embarrassed.

As soon as introductions had been made, Inspector Moroney took him aside. "Have they got him?" he asked in a low voice. "Is he safe?"

"We have the . . . eh, suspects in custody. We arrested them just one hour ago." There was an edge to the man's voice which made Moroney uneasy.

"But the boy? Luke? Did you find him?"

The sergeant looked at his fingers. "I'm afraid I don't know all the details. There were some . . . complications."

"My God!" exclaimed Moroney, struggling to keep his voice down. "He isn't – "

The sergeant quickly interrupted. "No, no! He is fine. We think . . ."

"You didn't find him? Is that what you're telling me?"

The sergeant gathered himself, became more officious.

"You better talk to the *capitano*. I don't know the details. I'm just here to drive you."

Nothing more could be got from him. Fran and Avril were, by this time, looking anxiously at Moroney. He couldn't meet their gaze. "They've arrested the circus people, it seems," he told them. "But I'm not sure what's happened with Luke. We have a short drive to Seville, half an hour. Then we'll find out the full story."

Avril and Fran both felt their hearts sink. They had dared to hope again, and now uncertainty threatened to knock them to the floor again.

Thomas was in pain, but he hid it well. A low moan, which nobody else could hear, escaped his throat.

Nikolai, Katrina and Anisim sat in separate holding cells in a police station in Seville. The police had released the rest of the circus performers. These three, it appeared, were the main conspirators. They had been arguing animatedly for an hour, and the police had a hard enough time trying to get any sense, never mind the truth, out of them. Nikolai seemed to be the only one who possessed even a minimal amount of Spanish, and he was being the least co-operative. He refused to translate what Anisim and Katrina were trying to say, choosing instead to shout what sounded like abuse at them. Between them, the police officers in the station spoke barely enough English to glean the facts of the case. Certainly, none of them spoke Russian, which was the language currently being hurled from cell to cell.

"Don't accuse me, old man," shouted Nikolai. "If it wasn't for your bleeding heart, encouraging the brat, he'd never have left Dublin in the first place. We would have handed him over to the police, and that would have been the end of it. Instead, you had to take him under your wing, poor lost soul."

Anisim was hurt. "He was lost. An orphan with nowhere to go. OK, so he'd been in some trouble with the police. So what?"

Katrina rushed to Anisim's defence. "How dare you, Nikolai? Attacking your own father like this! You are the one who insisted on putting Luke on display. Not because he wanted to, but because you thought he might draw a big crowd. Well, he did draw a crowd. And look where it's got us!"

Nikolai, furious, rattled the bars. "Don't you dare talk to me like that! You are my wife. You and that pig," he pointed at his father, "have been plotting against me for years!"

"Stop it! Why don't you tell the police what you did? Trying to sell a child like that. You're just a criminal!"

"I did not! This is all your fault. The boy was besotted with you, and you led him on!"

The guards stared at them, bewildered. One of them looked around, asking, "Where is that interpreter? Somebody, please, make sense of all this!"

The interpreter just happened to arrive at the same moment as the Irish party, accompanied by the evasive Sergeant Gomez. While Jimmy went to find a coffee machine, and Thomas hovered miserably in the background, Inspector Moroney and the Lavertys were introduced to the Captain, who, through the interpreter, explained that they were still trying to establish the facts of the case.

"Where is Luke?" Avril demanded. She had felt rested during their trip, and much of her old strength had returned.

"I'm afraid your son has disappeared, Mrs . . . eh, Laverty," explained the Captain through the interpreter, his voice mournful with regret. "When we raided the circus, he was not there. All of my men have been alerted, and we are searching for your son. We arrested a number of suspects from the circus, but most of them claim they do not know where he is. We still have three of them in custody, and we are hoping to find out the truth – "

He broke off, as Avril was no longer listening. She had spotted what she guessed to be the holding area for suspects, behind a guarded door, and now she turned and strode towards it, demanding to be let through. The guard shook his head firmly.

Moroney looked at Fran. Fran shrugged wearily. Moroney turned to the Captain. "Maybe you could let her talk to them. She's the mother, after all. They might be more willing to talk to her than to police."

So Avril was let into the holding area, followed meekly by her entourage. Unsure what to expect, she was surprised to see an old man in the first cell, and, further down, the stranger from the newspaper photograph of Luke. Instinctively, however, she went straight to Katrina in the middle cell. The two women stared at each other through the bars. A moment passed.

Katrina was puzzled. "Who are you? Are you the interpreter?"

"You speak English?" Avril demanded in return.

"Yes."

"Where's my son?"

Katrina frowned, uncomprehending at first. Then her eyes flew wide. "You are Luke's mother?"

"Yes, and this is his father. Now, do you know where he is?"

"But he told us – " Katrina caught herself in time, and doubled back on her words. "No, he has disappeared. We were just beginning to search for him when the police arrived."

A moan came from Anisim's cell. To the surprise of Avril and all of the watchers, the old man began to cry softly, rocking back and forth on his heels. "Luka, Luka, Luka," was his mantra.

Katrina spoke to him in Russian, offering words of comfort. She turned back to Avril, apologising, "He was – is – very fond of the boy. We're very sorry. We feel responsible for him, and now he has disappeared, and you are here . . . he was like a part of our family."

Avril was confused. She should, she told herself, have been angry with these people. They had, if not kidnapped, at least sheltered her son for three months, without making any attempt to find his parents. And yet, she was touched. She thought again of the photograph, of Luke's apparent happiness, and the word "family" floated through her head. Despite the urgency of trying to find Luke, she knew she first had to find out something about the last three, missing, months.

"Tell me what happened," she asked Katrina softly.

So Katrina told her, carefully skirting the parts where Luke implied that he was an orphan. When she reached the end, she could not hold back her bitterness towards Nikolai. "Now he is gone," she spat out, "and it is all his fault. He is the one who sold your son to the devil!"

The words were out before she realised how they would sound. A shiver chilled Avril's spine. Fran, Moroney and the others were silent. Thomas, somewhere in the background, was mouthing silent words. Jimmy had found his coffee and was happy.

Avril turned to Nikolai in the third cell at last. He was gesticulating frantically in denial. "No, no, you are wrong, Katya. I would never do such a thing . . ." His voice trailed off.

Inspector Moroney stepped forward. "You know something about where Luke is?"

Nikolai sighed. He could hedge no longer. "I don't know where he is now, but yes, something did happen. There were two men . . ."

Chapter Nineteen

Twenty-four hours earlier, the Dark Man had received a phone call.

"Why are you calling me? I told you never to call me here."

Alfie, at the other end of the line, gulped twice. "He's here."

The Dark Man knew what he was talking about immediately. "Where is here?" Alfie told him. The Dark Man thought quickly. "OK, I'll find a flight, and I'll ring you back in an hour. Don't do anything until I get there. Keep an eye on them, but don't do anything."

The Dark Man took his number, hung up, and chewed his thumb pensively. Opportunity had wound its way in and out of his sights now for twelve years, ever since Luke's birth. He had tried to reach his goal a number of times, though he was never sure if the boy was strong enough, mature enough for the task. Now, the gods were tempting him again, and this time, the chance seemed too good to be true. This time, the boy was older. More importantly, he was separated from his parents, and therefore more open to other influences. What was it Alfie had said? Performing in a circus? Too much. Surely there was a catch somewhere?

The Dark Man came to a decision and reached for the phone again.

* * *

Alfie waited anxiously at Seville Airport the following morning. He had debated which course of action to take. Years earlier, after he had left Ireland, he had decided to make a fresh start. He had been looking for some excuse to leave his wife, anyway, so he looked on it as a fortunate opportunity. He had settled in quite happily here among the beaches and women, and lived for a couple of years off the money he had got from the Dark Man.

Banjo, it seemed, had been less fortunate. Alfie had heard it on the grapevine. Banjo loved his wife, and was not so happy to "start fresh". He had grown homesick after a couple of months, and had sneaked back to Dublin. The next thing Alfie heard was that an unidentified, decapitated body had been found washed up on some beach. The Irish media had described it as a "vicious gangland killing" but Alfie knew exactly who it was and what had happened to him.

So Alfie decided to stay put, to do what he'd been told. This life suited him, and when his money ran out, there was plenty of work on the beaches.

Now, the thought of abandoning it all again for the criminal life didn't appeal to him. In the end, however, his skinny wallet drove him to call the Dark Man, despite his fears.

The boss arrived on the scheduled flight, and they set off for the city in Alfie's car. The Dark Man explained his plan as they drove.

Luke sat in Anisim's caravan, preparing himself for the day's first performance. Anisim sat watching listlessly as Luke created another masterpiece. The old man was unhappy. He had discovered Luke, after all, and now he felt that he was losing him. The boy reminded him so much of himself at the same age, and that made him homesick.

Luke was homesick too. The initial thrill of showing off to an audience had worn off, and suddenly he felt like a stranger again. These people had been good to him, certainly. He regretted the impulse that had driven him away from home in the first place. A different impulse was urging him homewards now. He thought of the word "home" and he knew again where to find it. He didn't know if he had achieved what he set out to achieve, but he felt that, in the last three months, he had grown more than he ever had before. Where previously, he was a small boy overwhelmed by his own wide imagination, now he felt as though the imagination fitted. He had grown into it, and it was as much a part of him as his hands or feet.

He looked at Anisim. The old man was studying him curiously, rubbing his chin. On an impulse, Luke decided to tell him the truth. About his parents. About how he had run away, not from them or from the police, but because he thought there was something out in the world for him to find. He didn't want to hurt Anisim, but he couldn't lie to him any longer. He would tell him now, and maybe the old man would be able to help him get home.

Luke gestured to Anisim, indicating that there was something important he wanted to tell him. And then, all of a sudden, he froze as a chill ran down his spine. Anisim felt it too, and a dark cloud passed over the caravan. *He's here*, thought Luke, *he's found me*.

Nikolai stared across the table at the Dark Man. He tried to feign a defiant, superior air, but the fact was, he was totally unnerved by the man's stillness and sense of purpose. It didn't help that Nikolai could hear his skinny companion behind him, roaming freely about his caravan. Nikolai wanted to turn around, to ask him what he thought he was doing, but he found it impossible to break eye contact with the Dark Man. So he just gulped nervously, waiting for the man to say something. Time stretched out, and the stand-off continued. Finally, Nikolai broke.

"OK, he is here. But I didn't know he was in trouble with the police, I swear it to you. If I had, I'd never have taken him in. I'd have handed him straight to the police."

"But you didn't, did you? You don't think they'd believe you now? Even if he wasn't in trouble, they'd still get you for . . . well, kidnapping for a start."

"But he wasn't forced to join us!"

"The police aren't going to see it that way, are they? I'm surprised they haven't caught up with you before this. But they will soon. In fact, they could be on the way here already, for all we know!"

Nikolai felt his grip on reason slipping. He finally broke the magnetic gaze, and cupped his head in his hands. "Just when I thought everything was going right," he moaned. He turned his head quickly at the sound of the caravan door opening. The skinny man was on his way out. "Where are you going?" demanded Nikolai.

"Fresh air," said Alfie, closing the door behind him. He didn't see Katrina walking towards the caravan, but she saw him as he walked away. Katrina was puzzled. She approached the caravan. Hearing voices inside, she sneaked around to the back. The open window was too high to see in, but she could at least hear the conversation.

Inside, the Dark Man stood up. It had been almost too easy, frightening this man. Now, it was time to go for the throat. "I have a proposition to make," he announced generously. "I would like to buy the boy off you."

Nikolai thought he had misheard. "I'm sorry?"

The Dark Man sat down again and spoke to Nikolai as though he was explaining something very simple to an idiot. "If I give you money, the boy will be gone, it will be as though he never existed. The police can't charge you with hiding something that you never had, can they?"

"But . . . the photograph . . . the show! Everybody knows that is Luke. How can I say otherwise?"

"OK then, tell them he begged you to take him in. Tell them he ran away again when he heard they were coming. If he's gone, who's to contradict you?"

Nikolai couldn't think straight. It didn't sound right. Besides, who was this man who could persuade with his eyes? Nikolai's arguments were getting weaker: "But what about the performance? Luke is my star now!"

"Oh come on! You can't think of putting the boy on show again with the police breathing down your neck. This is my offer: fifty thousand pounds."

Nikolai held his breath. The figures danced before his eyes, and a sense of reckless bravado took hold. "Well, I could have made a lot more from Luke, you know. I've made huge profits already this week. He's worth a lot more than fifty thousand pounds."

The Dark Man smiled humourlessly. "I can see you are a businessman. But you know your profits will sink once the police arrive. I'm a generous man, though. Sixty thousand."

"One hundred thousand," countered Nikolai, licking his lips.

At that moment, Katrina stormed in, her face red with rage. She quickly took in the scene, and, ignoring the Dark Man, strode straight to Nikolai.

"Do you mind, Katrina, this is bus–" Nikolai was cut off by a sharp smack across the cheek.

"How dare you!" screamed Katrina in Russian. "You would sell Luke? Over my dead body!"

The Dark Man watched the scene with amusement. He stepped to the door. Turning, he spoke quietly to Nikolai: "I'll leave you two alone to discuss this. Seventy thousand is my final offer. Take it or leave it. I'll come back in an hour to hear your decision."

He closed the door softly on the screaming couple. Once outside, his demeanour changed. Looking around, he quickly spotted Alfie. They met behind the main tent, and spoke in quick, urgent whispers.

"Well, have you found him? Can we grab him and run?" demanded the Dark Man.

Alfie flushed. "No, chief. I can't find him. He could be hiding in one of the caravans. Maybe if we sit and watch from the car. He might come out."

The Dark Man thought a moment, and sniffed the air. "No, he isn't here. He's running. I'll find him. You get the car, bring it around to the far side of the wood." He set off at a trot across the parkland, in the direction of a small wooded area. Alfie sighed and, after a short pause, turned and walked to his car.

Back in the caravan, Katrina was still shouting at an increasingly wilting Nikolai. They were so intensely involved in their argument that they didn't hear Anisim come into the caravan, panting and shaking as he leaned on the doorjamb. They didn't hear his hoarse, ragged voice, until he raised it to a level that surprised even himself.

"Stop it! He's gone!"

They finally froze at his words. Katrina looked at him, a frown creasing her brow. "What are you talking about?"

"Luka! He has run away. We were sitting in my caravan, and he was trying to tell me something. Suddenly, I had this ominous feeling. I think Luka felt it too. Next minute, he had run to the door, and was gone. I tried to run after him, but I am too slow, an old man. I saw him disappearing into the woods. Come, come, we must try to find him." He turned to go, but Katrina took his arm and shook it urgently.

"Those two men!" she said. "Where did they go?"

"I didn't see two men." Anisim thought for a moment. "I did see a car, though. A man driving away in a car."

"Maybe they've gone, then?" suggested Nikolai meekly. Katrina glared at him fiercely.

Luke was running. He didn't know how he knew, but he was sure of it. The Dark Man was here. The Dark Man was after him. This time, Luke was sure, he would not give up until he had him in his grasp. He reached the small wood. Through the thin layer of trees, he could see light, and the noise of traffic came to him. He would find safety there. There would be police and protection. The circus could no longer offer him shelter. He was running from it, and he told himself he would not look back.

He plunged into the wood, and the trees closed in around his small frame. He ran on towards the light that beckoned him at the far side. The tall shapes of the trees loomed over him. He quailed, imagining them as menacing killers, sweeping their branches at his head. He paused for breath and looked up. The sunlight above was completely hidden from view by the thick, yellow-green summer leaves. He set off again towards the light directly ahead. Now that he was in the midst of the trees, it was harder to make out the traffic ahead.

A few minutes later, Luke realised that there was something wrong. He should easily have reached the other side of the woods by now. Instead, the sound of the traffic had disappeared, as had the clear sky ahead. The trees, if anything, were denser, taller. He had lost his sense of direction. He felt very tired, sluggish, as though his legs were being pulled down by quicksand. He paused again and leaned against a tree. Then, for the first time since he had started running, he looked back.

The circus had disappeared. He was completely surrounded by the wood, which was more like a forest now. As he looked back, a shadow flitted between two trees. Absolute terror seized Luke and he began to stumble blindly forward, dodging among the trunks. He felt the shadow move closer, and he raced as fast as he could. An outstretched root caught his foot and he was flying. The pain didn't reach him, because he had blacked out before he hit the ground.

The Dark Man was suddenly anxious. He had seen the fall, and he was afraid Luke had cracked his skull. But a cursory examination showed only a few cuts and bruises. Satisfied, he removed his dark coat, spread it over the boy and, grunting, picked him up. He found his way out of the small wood to the car waiting outside.

Chapter Twenty

Thomas stumbled out of the police station, his breath coming in heaving, ragged gusts. He hobbled down the street, attracting curious glances. He searched frantically for an open space. A park loomed before him. Moments later he was standing on a green hillock, trying to concentrate.

Jimmy was the only one who had seen the distraught look on Thomas's face, and had followed him outside, leaving the others listening to Nikolai's story. Now, he saw the old man halfway across the street, unaware of the blaring horns of cars swerving to avoid him. Jimmy called to him, but Thomas didn't hear. Jimmy, reluctantly throwing the rest of his coffee away, braced himself, and raced after him. By the time he reached him, Thomas was already slipping into a trance. Jimmy shook him gently by the shoulder.

Thomas opened his eyes, surprised to find Jimmy standing beside him. "Please," he begged him, "I need to concentrate."

"But what are you doing? Why did you run out like that?"

"I can find him," said Thomas. "He is near, I can sense him."

Jimmy's hopes rose. "You know where Luke is?"

Thomas didn't contradict Jimmy, didn't say that the "him" he spoke of was not Luke. That connection had been severed. Instead, what he had sensed was an older connection, one that he had desperately shut out for decades. Now, he knew it was the only way to save Luke.

He closed his eyes again, and pushed his fears deep down where they could not emerge again. Then he set his mind to searching.

Jimmy stood on the hillock and watched.

Luke awoke in the back of the car. Everything was black, and he thought at first that he was blind. He could feel the bump of the road under the car, and he gradually realised that he was covered in some sort of cloth which completely blocked out the light. His nose was filled with the suffocating smell of old smoke which permeated the cloth. He lay still in fear, listening. He caught occasional sentences, spoken in curt tones by two men.

A dull pain in his right temple brought it back to him gradually. The fear, the running, the fall . . . he knew the Dark Man had come for him at last, and had found him, and he felt himself gulping for air as he tried to calm his rising panic. He forced himself to think of home, and his heartbeat slowed to a quiet listening.

The time passed, and Luke's stiffness grew. They must have been driving for almost an hour when he sensed that the car was slowing to a halt. He heard one of the men questioning in a puzzled voice, "Why are we stopping here?"

"It's quiet. Nobody ever comes here." The Dark Man's voice was calm, unfazed.

"But why aren't we heading straight for the airport, getting out of the country? I thought that was the plan."

"They'll be watching for us at the airport." There was silence for a moment before the Dark Man spoke again. "I need some time alone with the boy. I want you to leave us here."

There was a pause while the other man considered this. Then there seemed to be some unspoken agreement, because Luke heard a car door opening. A moment later, he froze, as he felt hands and arms slip under his body and lift him, still covered in the coat. He remained unmoving, afraid to reveal himself as conscious, for fear of what they would do to him.

Through the cloth, he felt a faint stirring of fresh air, and he surreptitiously gulped as many mouthfuls as he was able, glad to be out of the stuffiness of the car. He felt himself lifted over a shoulder, and he heard the voice of the Dark Man again. "Don't worry, Alfie. I'll be finished here in a few hours. I'll get us out of here. Come back and pick me up about midnight." The slamming of the car door, the firing of the engine, the sound of the car pulling off. A faint whiff of petrol fumes. And they were alone in the silence.

Grunting, the Dark Man began to walk with his burden still slung across his shoulder. Despite his position, Luke somehow, paradoxically, sensed that he was being treated with gentle care. The big hands held him firmly but safely. He could hear the Dark Man breathing heavily, panting. There was the sound of a door, old and creaking on rusted hinges, and a strong smell of old straw and long-departed animals. Then they were climbing steps, two flights, more creaking of worn timbers. The Dark Man didn't lay his burden down until Luke heard them entering a room of some sort. Luke heard the fluttering of wings, and felt a breath of air. Glass crunched under the Dark Man's feet. He stopped for a moment, then turned and carefully lifted Luke off his shoulder, and laid him down on a soft, damp surface.

Jimmy saw the others leaving the police station. Glancing back at Thomas, he ran towards them, shouting and waving his hands. The small party bunched outside the station watched him coming with curiosity, and followed his pointing hands to the still figure, rooted like a standing stone to the hillock.

Avril waited, a coiled spring of energy, bursting for somewhere to direct it. She watched Jimmy intensely, dying for his news.

Jimmy had to stop for breath before he could speak. When it came out, the words were garbled, but Avril, at least, knew what he meant. "Thomas, he . . . Luke . . . he's trying to find . . . I think he can find him."

Luke lay still, scarcely daring to breathe, dreading what might happen next. He strained his senses to gain some idea of where he was. The occasional fluttering of wings and the sound of wind through broken glass told him that the building was abandoned, probably derelict. The smells and sounds spoke of the countryside. A barn, he guessed. But he could still see nothing. The black coat was darker than anything he had ever seen, blacker than night, and he could only smell and taste its staleness. He thought about touch, feeling his way around, but that would require movement.

He listened again. Silence. Nothing stirred. Was he alone? Had the Dark Man brought him to this place and left him? Or perhaps he had just gone for a few minutes, and would be back soon. Thoughts of escape suddenly leaped to

Luke's mind, but he restrained himself from jumping up and running blindly, wildly. He had already tried that once today.

Instead, tentatively, he spread the fingers of one hand against the rough texture he could feel under his body. Straw. Somehow, it reassured him, despite its dampness and the promise of creepie-crawlies. He moved his arm a little, stretching further, and then he froze. The Dark Man spoke, disconcertingly close.

"So we're awake, then?"

Luke held his breath, but he knew it was useless to pretend further. A small whimper escaped his parched throat. He wanted to sink into the deep straw and disappear. He heard the Dark Man shifting about, and then suddenly the coat was removed and light flooded in.

Luke was blinded. He threw his hands to his eyes to ward off the attack of light. The dull pain in his head became sharp momentarily, and he touched his temple tenderly. For the first time, he realised that there was dried blood caked in his hair. As his eyes adjusted to the brightness, he peered through his fingers.

The Dark Man was watching him with, Luke was surprised to see, something close to concern. He bent over him and took his head carefully in his hands. His touch was cool against Luke's pained temple. He examined the wound for a moment, before announcing, "It's only a scratch. Nothing broken. I'd better find something for it, though. Wait here, don't move." And then he *was* gone.

Luke peered around at his surroundings. A pair of pigeons stared back at him from a large, empty window frame. The remains of the windowpane were scattered on the floor, along with the well-aimed stones that had put them there. The roof slanted down on both sides, and it was obvious that he was in some sort of loft. There was a large, gaping hole in one corner of the roof, through which most of the light flooded. The beams around the hole were cracked, and the roof in general sagged with the weight of age. More pigeons watched him cautiously from the rafters.

He sat up and shook his head to test the pain, which was thankfully abating. Immediately, he went into action, determined to find some means of escape. There was only one door to the loft. Luke tried it, but the Dark Man must have locked it from the other side. He went to the empty window and peered out. In the distance, he could see a river, trees, fields. The barn itself was in a large, unkempt field. He looked down. The thought of escape that way was quickly dispelled when he saw how far down the ground was. The wooden walls offered no grip, no comfort.

He looked around the loft again, and for the first time noticed a large scythe in one corner. He ran to it, and gripped the handle. The blade was badly rusted, but he reckoned it would be enough to hack through the door. He tried to lift it, but the weight of it threatened his balance. He tried again, attempting to concentrate all his strength in his arms. But it was useless. He made a few more attempts, but gave up after a few minutes, flopping down in the straw. Staring at the scythe, a thought suddenly struck him, filling him with horror. What if the Dark Man decided to make some use of it? Luke's fear froze in his belly, and he quickly looked away from the tool.

A sound caught his ear, a dull mechanical rumble. He ran to the window again. In a field about a hundred metres from the barn, a farmer was driving a tractor. Luke's immediate thought was to shout to him, but he quickly rejected that idea as an impossibility. Apart from the fact that the man was too far away, and would hear nothing over the sound of the tractor's engine, Luke remembered that he had no voice. Then he remembered: of course, there's one sure way of attracting his attention.

He concentrated his mind, willing the light to shoot in the farmer's direction. But just at that moment, the door behind him opened and the Dark Man strode in. Luke quickly released a bolt of lightning, but the Dark Man was on him already, and the coat descended over his head again. All the light suddenly went again. Luke found it sucked into the dark fabric of the coat. No way through. He was lifted bodily and placed back on the pile of straw.

The Dark Man sneaked a look out the window. The tractor continued its circuit, its occupant blissfully unaware. The Dark Man grunted with satisfaction, and turned back to Luke. As he did so, a faint pain in his head caused him to frown. He had felt it earlier, a ringing sensation. It was vaguely familiar, but he couldn't place when he had felt it before. Anyway, it was gone again now. He shrugged, and turned his attention to his captive.

The police captain was sceptical, but he let two officers drive them wherever Thomas wanted to go.

Thomas, sitting up front, concentrated again. He felt his mind reaching out, and he sensed its general direction. Waves of images floated before his mind. He felt the Dark Man's confused rage, and he saw snatches of light and shadow. Vague shapes, a window, sunshine, fields. A figure. Human, small. Luke. Then it was gone. Darkness again. The connection broken.

Thomas sat in silence, breathing heavily from his

exertions. His brow was creased with uncertainty and reluctance. Avril watched him anxiously. The occupants of the car behind were waiting for some signal to begin.

Finally, Thomas shook himself, reaching a decision. "He's there. He has him. He's safe, I think."

"Oh God," said Avril, desperately trying to keep her panic in check. "Where are they?"

"South, I think. Yes, south. In the country."

The cars pulled out.

The Dark Man looked at the bundle lying trembling in a heap. He stood thinking for a while, and then came to a decision. He crossed the room and knelt down in the straw beside Luke. He removed the coat again. Luke shied away, cringing into the straw.

The Dark Man was carrying a plastic bag, from which he now produced a bottle of disinfectant and a pile of bandages. His voice was chatty, familiar, friendly. Luke eyed him with suspicion.

"It's amazing that there are still people in this part of the world who don't lock their back doors." He gestured towards the window. "Our friend out there, he keeps his house well stocked. I don't think he'll notice a few missing bandages. Oh, and look what else I've got!" He beamed at Luke and, like a magician, pulled a bunch of grapes from the bag, following it with apples, bread and a carton of orange juice. "Are you hungry?"

Luke was ravenous, his mouth watering, but he held back, watching his captor carefully. The Dark Man held the grapes out to him.

"Go on! I'm not trying to poison you. Look." He plucked a handful of the grapes and shoved them into his own mouth. He chewed and swallowed with exaggerated pleasure, spitting the pips in a machine-gun, staccato rhythm at the wooden floor. He looked up and grinned at Luke. The boy looked uncertain, hesitant. The Dark Man leaned over and dropped the bunch of grapes into his lap. "Here, eat as much as you like," he said, "then I'll have a look at that head." Then he picked up an apple and started eating.

Luke hesitated a moment longer, then plucked a grape and bit into the soft skin. His mouth flooded with the glorious juice, and everything else melted into the background as he devoured the food with intense concentration.

The traffic thinned, and the two cars were soon in open countryside. Fran and Avril watched anxiously out the windows for some sign of their son's whereabouts. The Andalucians stared back at the police cars and their occupants with curiosity. The land was scorched dry, the hills peppered with uniform rows of olive trees. They drove for twenty, thirty miles, the scenery constant, unchanging.

Thomas ignored the landscape around them, however. He was guided by a sense stronger than sight. His eyes were closed in deep concentration.

"Which way?" asked the driver.

"Left," replied Thomas without opening his eyes. "Not far now."

The Dark Man watched Luke pensively, letting him eat his fill. When he had finally finished – his face and hands a mess of juice – the Dark Man moved closer to him. Luke flinched, but didn't pull away. The Dark Man poured some of the disinfectant onto one of the bandages and held Luke's head steady. "I'm sorry, but this will hurt." He cleaned the wound thoroughly while Luke bit his lip and the tears started in his eyes. As he began to wrap a fresh bandage around Luke's head, the Dark Man spoke to him, his voice quiet, reassuring, calling on Luke's trust. But there was still an edge of menace to it.

"Luke, I need you to listen to me. First, I need you to promise that you won't try to use your powers again. At least, not to escape. If you do, I'll have to use my coat again." He picked up the coat and made a show of examining it with curiosity, before holding it up to Luke. "You see, it's a very special coat. No light can get through it, in or out. It just absorbs it. So there's no point in trying to throw out your smoke signals. So promise me you won't try?"

Luke nodded. He didn't move, however, unwilling to succumb to the Dark Man's persuasive tones.

"Good," said the Dark Man, satisfied that they had overcome that hurdle. "Now, I'm going to tell you why I brought you here. You see, ever since you were born, I have been trying to find you, to get you alone. You're a clever boy. You know this. You know it was me who tried to kidnap you.

"Let me tell you a bit about myself, Luke, and why I need your help. I was born seventy years ago, and I had the same face then as I do now. It never changes. I was never young, and I can never grow old. I was born without a name, and have had to borrow names as I borrowed lives. I was born without a mother. The closest I had to a father was . . . well, he's the reason we're here today.

"You see, Luke, you've met my father. He's an old man,

now, and he grows older every day, and closer to death. He came to you at your most difficult times, and he comforted you. Do you know who I'm talking about?"

Luke nodded. The face of the Druid stood before his mind's eye, smiling at him now.

"The thing is, he came to you because you're the same as him. You have the same powers. He can create pictures and fabulous creatures with light, just like you. And I was his greatest creation. He created me out of his loneliness, his self-loathing. He wanted to create a companion, somebody he could talk to, a mirror image of himself. But when he saw me, all twisted, a demon, he ran away from me. Do you understand? He made me, and he abandoned me, left me to fend for myself. Do you understand?"

Luke nodded again. The Dark Man's voice had risen a notch, and was beginning to crack.

"He never acknowledged me. He never came to see me, unless it was to kill me, to destroy what he had created. But he didn't have the courage. Because he knew that he could only kill me if he destroyed himself. Our paths have crossed a few times in the last seventy years, but he always backed down. That's why he's been running all these years. And now, he is dying himself. Even his own magic can't keep him alive much longer. And when he dies, I die. But," he said with a sly smile, "the thing is, I don't want to die."

He paused for effect, looking to see if Luke could anticipate what was coming next. "Whereas you, Luke, you are going to live for a long time. You have a lifetime of experience ahead of you. And you can help me. You see, there's a link now between my father and me, but it is getting weaker as he does. When he dies, that link will be broken, and I will cease to be. Unless I can form a new link with you. Do you understand what I'm saying?"

Luke shook his head, his fear creeping back to him. The Dark Man reached his hand towards the boy, encouraging him to take it. Luke held his arms firmly by his sides, stubbornly refusing to move.

All of a sudden, the Dark Man folded into himself, clutching his head as though in pain. His arms wrapped around his skull, trying to block out some demon that was invading his mind. He fell on the floor and began to scream. Luke stared in horrified fascination as he writhed about the room, struggling with his invisible enemy.

Thomas had been silent for some time now, nodding occasionally when the Spanish police driver looked at him for directions. Suddenly, he moaned loudly and clutched at his head. His back arched as though he'd been struck deep in the spine, and he began to writhe uncontrollably.

The driver had to pull over to the side of the road. The others could only watch helplessly as Thomas thrashed from side to side in apparent agony. His eyes bulged, pure white, rolled back in their sockets, and a white froth formed at his mouth. His body was as taut as a bow, every muscle ready to snap.

Then, just as suddenly as it had begun, the convulsion ended. The old man's body went limp, sagging in the seat. The others stared at him, unable to move, held back by the horror of what had just occurred.

Finally, Fran whispered, "Is . . . is he dead?"

For answer, Thomas moved his head to the side and slowly opened his eyes. Immediately, his relieved companions went to his aid, opening the car door, helping him to sit up and breathe. The strength returned very quickly to his body. He shrugged off their hands, stepped out of the car and began to walk with a sense of purpose across the road and into a field.

Fran and Avril looked at each other. Fran ran to catch up with him. "Wait, Thomas, where are you going? You're not well, you've just had a fit."

Thomas paused and looked at him. The cold look of determined rage frightened Fran, before Thomas masked it with a smile. "I'm fine," he said, "Never felt better." He turned and started to walk off again.

Inspector Moroney and Jimmy McGinnity in the second car watched with increasing bewilderment, finally getting out and following them.

"But where are you going?" Fran repeated.

Without looking back, the old Druid pointed ahead. "Over that hill. He's there. We must hurry."

Gradually, the Dark Man's screaming subsided and his movements slowed, until his body became still again. He lay there, sweat soaked through his clothes, for so long that Luke thought he was dead. He leaned over him, looking in the face that had haunted him throughout his childhood, and that now looked like a deathmask.

But the Dark Man was not dead. He opened first one rheumy eye, fixing it on Luke, then the other. Luke thought of running, but he knew he wouldn't. Not when he felt so near the end of his journey. Besides, he didn't think his legs could carry him.

The Dark Man rolled over on his side and pushed himself to his knees, took a beat, breathed, and slowly raised himself back onto his feet. Luke made no effort to cringe away from him this time. He waited while the Dark Man regained his composure. He studied his greyed face. He looked old now; not a physical ageing, but a withering of the soul.

The Dark Man finally turned to him, and the pain was visible in his face. "He's here," he said. "He's out there somewhere, and he's coming to destroy me. There's no more time to lose, Luke. You have to help me out. Please, Luke."

Luke made no move of assent or denial. He just continued to stare at the Dark Man. He felt no sense of compassion, or pity, or disgust, or fear any more. He was simply filled with curiosity.

"Luke, I need you to concentrate. I need to form a link with you in your mind. The way you did with Sandy. I need you to tune in to my thoughts and my spirit. Can you do that, can you do that for me?"

Still Luke made no move to answer. He looked away from the Dark Man's eyes, which still held some hint of his great power, his persuasive spirit. The mention of Sandy angered him. He had loved Sandy, and her loss had convinced him he could love no one else. How could this monster think he could trust him?

"It could all be over in a few minutes," went on the Dark Man. "If you have a picture of me, complete, in your mind, then I can live on in your imagination. Otherwise, I will die when he does. And things will be so different in the future. You and me, we could reach great heights. There's nothing we can't achieve. Please, Luke, look at me. Help me, and I will help you."

Luke stared at his hands, telling himself, over and over, *Don't look at him. Don't look at his eyes.* But instead of listening to his own voice, another voice spoke in his head, a stronger voice than any he had heard before. It didn't come from the Dark Man, nor did it come from the Druid who Luke was willing nearer with every beat of his heart. It came from deep within him, and he turned now and, holding the Dark Man's sharp gaze, spoke the words aloud, to his own amazement.

"I don't need you."

His voice was clear and strong, not the voice of his childhood dreams, but a voice that, for the first time, he could truly call his own. He was suddenly so thrilled that he beamed from ear to ear. The Dark Man chose that moment to lunge for him.

Luke could see the whites of his eyes, filled with menace now, all trace of false friendship vanished. The Dark Man's hands were around his throat, and he felt himself lifted, struggling, choking. Panic rose like acid in his throat, and as the Dark Man relaxed his grip, Luke vomited grapes and apples.

Disgusted, the Dark Man pushed him away. His voice filled with hate now, he spat out, "OK, you little shit, if that's how you want to play it." He pulled a gun from somewhere and, holding Luke by the collar, placed it against the boy's cheek. "Now, I'll give you a choice. Either you do as I say, or I shoot you now . . ." he paused, staring into Luke's eyes, enunciating every word, making sure Luke understood what he was saying, ". . . and then I will go back to Ireland, and I will shoot your mother and your father!"

Luke's face collapsed in defeat, all defiance drained from him. The cold steel pressing at his cheek left him in no doubt about how real the threat was. All Luke's running had come to nothing. This man had the power of life and death over his parents.

Seeing the resigned look on his young captive's face, the Dark Man grunted with satisfaction. "Good. Now I want you to concentrate. I want you to look at me."

Miserable, Luke did as he was told. The Dark Man's eyes were empty pits. As he looked at them, they seemed to grow and grow until they filled his whole field of vision. The black depths of them pulled Luke in, and he felt himself losing control, unable to resist, slipping into a trance.

Luke felt all the light in his head being sucked into the darkness, feeding it, nurturing it. At the same time, faces appeared before him, dozens of faces, and Luke knew they were the faces of those whose lives the Dark Man had taken or destroyed. They were the agonised, despair-filled faces of hell. Luke recoiled, trying desperately to pull back from the brink, but the Dark Man was stronger. Luke felt himself tumbling.

And then suddenly, the Druid was there, halting his fall, holding hard to his wrists, lifting him, pulling him back.

Luke was afraid, but he heard the Druid's voice, fighting against the Dark Man's pull, urging him to understand. "You are not me, Luke. Don't make the mistakes I made. You have a family who love you. I had nobody, no family, to guide me to what was right or wrong."

Luke struggled against the sucking emptiness, dragging himself back from the edge. He fought off the desire to let the darkness take him.

The Dark Man felt the connection snap, and he turned around in fury. Thomas McAndrew, the Druid, the closest he had to a father, stood in the doorway.

Luke hung limp, still caught in the trance, still dizzily on the edge of the abyss. The Dark Man growled and swung the boy around, pressing the gun against his temple. "Come on then," he screamed at the Druid. "What are you waiting for, old man? You came here to destroy me, didn't you? This is your chance! You're dying, and if I pull this trigger, I lose my shot at immortality. Ironic, isn't it?"

The Druid smiled, unmoved, calm. Time slowed down in that smile, enough for the Druid's searching mind to find Luke's again, and to beckon. *Remember the light, Luke. Remember the light.*

Aloud, he asked the Dark Man, stalling him, "Why are you doing this? So you can live a hundred years more? For what? To build your empire of hate and fear? To ruin the lives of thousands more?"

At that moment, Avril came stumbling, breathless, up the stairs behind Thomas. The pistol swung in her direction. Seeing her son in the clutches of the Dark Man, she screamed his name.

"LUKE!"

Remember the light.

And Luke, hearing his name, remembering, pushed the darkness away, and suddenly shot a bolt of purest white light like a laser through the soft spot at the back of his skull. Blinded, the Dark Man clutched at his eyes. Luke and the gun clattered to the floor in an untidy heap.

Thomas sprang into action, his age abandoned in the rushing of his spirit. He was on top of the Dark Man before the light cleared from his eyes. Instinctively, the Dark Man fought him, kicking and punching blindly. The old man, despite his fierceness, was no match for the hulking strength of the younger man, and he tried to make the most of his advantage before the other's sight cleared. He grabbed him around the chest and, with all his strength, squeezed.

Luke, dazed, watched the struggle. He picked up the gun beside him, but its weight and ice-cold metal scared him, and he dropped it again. Avril ran to him and wrapped her arms around him, shielding him, scarcely believing how real his skin felt against hers. Fran, Jimmy, Moroney and the others arrived, quickly taking in the scene.

Gradually, the Dark Man's eyesight cleared, and with it his strength became focused. He grabbed Thomas around the neck, trying to pull him off his chest. They stood that way for a moment, caught in a final embrace. Then, without warning, Thomas sagged, seemingly in defeat. But Luke saw his plan immediately.

Suddenly finding no resistance, the Dark Man was caught off balance. The force of his own grip on Thomas sent him toppling forward. Thomas obligingly stepped backwards, anticipating the Dark Man's teetering steps as he tried to avoid falling over completely. Then the Dark Man saw the window. Thomas let out a last triumphant bellow and, tightening his grip again, pulled the Dark Man the last step. Like a pair of lovers caught in a dance of death, the two men fell through the empty window frame and plunged thirty feet in silence.

A moment before the two figures disappeared from view, Luke thought he saw them merge into one. And he thought he understood at last.

For a moment, those left in the room froze in a stunned tableau. Then, Fran ran to his wife, and the two of them held Luke. Luke was still dazed, but the abyss had receded, and he craved sleep. He looked up, thinking he was dreaming, and his mother's and father's faces floated above him. He could feel their warm, comforting arms around him, and he spoke to them, his voice soft and weary. "Remember the light," he said. "Remember the light."

Fran and Avril, hearing their son's voice for the first time, wept in grateful relief.

And Luke slept.

Chapter Twenty-One

They took Luke to hospital, but he was suffering from no more than exhaustion. The doctors assured Fran and Avril that the wound in his head was only minor and would heal quickly. They watched their son sleeping. He looked so different, so much older, and yet his face held the calm of his earliest life. He was their son, and he had come back to them.

Luke slept heavily, and his dreams were deep and strange. He dreamed that he was home, that he had never been away. Sandy was there. They were playing a game, chasing each other around the garden in Wicklow. They dodged, each trying to touch the other without being touched. Suddenly, Sandy slipped in under his outstretched arm and placed her hand, warm and soft, over Luke's heart, and she whispered to him, *I love you*. And he spoke it aloud, "I love you", and his voice was familiar, natural. He wanted to cry with happiness, because he realised he would never lose her as long as he felt this love, and he knew he would feel it always. His magic had failed, but here was his love, felt truly for the first time, keeping her alive.

In his dream, Luke heard a noise and looked up. The Lost Boy stood in the long grass. He waved at him, and the Lost Boy waved back. Shadows danced around him, but the light held them off his face. And then the Cowboy was there too, all brilliant gleaming and phosphorescence. And between them stood the figure of the Druid, old and bent, but happy, and he was made of light himself. They waved again, and turned around. As they faded into the long grass, so did the dream.

The morning came. Slowly, Luke came out of his deep sleep. He opened his eyes, and for a moment he thought he was back home. Unfocused, he could have sworn he saw his parents' faces, looking at him with smiles. He blinked and realised it was true. He found his voice again, relieved that it had not fled him again while he slept.

"Mam? Dad? Am I home?"

A thrill ran through his parents as they realised they had not imagined his voice, and they hugged him tightly.

Luke spoke into his mother's shoulder, the words that had tripped on his tongue for three months, "I'm sorry."

"Don't be sorry, Luke," said Fran, stroking his son's head softly, still amazed at how real it felt. "We've all made mistakes. It's time to go home now."

When the police, accompanied by Jimmy McGinnity, went to look, there was only one body lying broken on the concrete path under the barn. The Druid's face was turned up towards the sun, and a smile lit up his face. His ancient, frail bones had simply disintegrated as soon as he hit the ground. Despite this, the police were amazed at how peaceful and serene he looked.

Jimmy bent down to the pathetic, crushed body, and a mood of melancholy tugged at his normally cynical spirit. He barely knew this man, but he touched him now tenderly on the cheek and muttered, "Goodbye, my friend."

Just as he braced himself to stand up, Jimmy noticed something peeking out of the top pocket of Thomas's coat. A piece of brown fur. He pulled it out. Lenny. The toy puppy, the worse for wear but still recognisable. Attached to Lenny's tail was a piece of paper, with a scrawled note. *For Luke*, it said. *Take care of him.*

* * *

The Dark Man was nowhere to be seen. They never found a second body, and his file was never officially closed. An international manhunt was mounted, but it was soon abandoned. It was impossible to trace a man who had no name, no identity and a face that nobody could really remember accurately enough to describe.

It was as though he had never existed.

Thomas McAndrew had no relatives, but Jimmy insisted on arranging for his body to be brought home. They buried him a week later at the bottom of the hollow in the field in Connemara where Jimmy first found him.

They picked up Alan "Alfie" McCabe when he turned up at the barn as arranged. As soon as he saw the police cars, he tried to reverse away, but they caught him easily.

The Lavertys stayed on another day in Spain. But none of them could sleep that night. Luke was wide awake and fresh now, and Fran and Avril had never felt so alive. Luke talked all through the night, telling them everything that had happened since he had run away. They listened, but they scarcely heard what he had to say. They were held in thrall by the sound of his voice. He was talking about something that already felt a part of the past. All they could hear in his voice was the future.

By the time they caught the flight home the following morning, Luke was all talked out. They were all silent, sunk into themselves, filled with their own thoughts, as the plane lifted into the clouds. Luke had never been in a plane before, and the strange feeling of being airborne silenced him.

Luke had said goodbye to the circus. Katrina, Anisim, even a much-abashed Nikolai had bade a tearful farewell to him at the airport. Now, he imagined them below him, getting smaller and smaller, fading from sight. But, at the back of his mind, the swirling melody of the circus tunes played now, and would never fade. *Someday*, he promised himself, *I will go back to the circus*.

Sandy and the Druid were above him somewhere, he was sure of it. He remembered his dreams, and he smiled to himself. He was getting closer to them every minute. *I will watch for them and wave*, he thought, peering out the window at the swirling mists around.

He looked down at Lenny the puppy. For the first time, he noticed an expression on the cloth-and-fur face. It was a slightly sad-eyed hound-dog look, and Luke picked him up and hugged him for comfort. Lenny was just a toy now, he knew that. The magic was gone. But there was a new magic now, and Luke knew its name. And some day, the old magic might join with this new language, and he'd find somebody else who could play with him in the light. He knew what was possible, that there was more to life than he could ever describe in words. In the meantime, he was happy to play in the shadows.

Luke looked out the window again. As he watched, the clouds thinned out around the plane, and then they were through and still climbing. Luke looked down in awe. The clouds stretched out on all sides like an endless plain of snow. The sunlight silvered their undulations. There were hills and troughs, and the occasional swirl of storm cloud, but they were above it all. Here and there, brief glimpses of land, then sea, then land again, the world turning beneath his feet. For the most part, though, it was just the clouds. Luke imagined himself running light-footed, skimming the surface of the clouds, running towards the promise of light.

Later, he dozed. Avril pulled a blanket over him and held him in the crook of her arm, keeping him warm.